Jacob's Bend · Book 1

BROKEN ACRES

A NOVEL

ANNE WATSON

Broken Acres
© 2017 Anne Watson
This edition published in 2019.
Published by Fitting Words
www.fittingwords.net
watsononline1711@gmail.com
www.annewatsonauthor.com

Library of Congress Cataloging-in-Publication Data

ISBN 978-1-7322391-7-3

Cover photos by Janis Rubus
Cover design by Sarah O'Neal/Eve Custom Artwork

ALWAYS FOR THE KING

"There's something delicious about writing the first words of a story. You can never quite tell where they will take you. Mine took me here."

— Beatrix Potter

ONE

Terror whispers loud.

The pain from the cut of the blade severed her grip on the pie tin as Madison turned her ear to an odd sound. *Pay attention, girl. Your wandering thoughts are forever causing trouble.*

Sucking the blood from her thumb, she rummaged through the junk drawer for a Band-Aid.

Madison shook her head and brushed an unruly curl from her eye, tucking it behind her ear where it belonged. Jeff was right, she should never be allowed to handle sharp objects.

Another strange noise. Had Jeff let some injured animal in the house? No, he was way too cautious for that.

So why was her heart pounding?

Dessert tray in hand, Madison gave a shove with her backside and the kitchen door swung open. A couple of quick steps helped her avoid the swinging door.

"Ready for some coffee and apple pie, hon?" She eyed her husband's leather recliner in the corner. Empty. A glance to the left found his office unoccupied. Canvassing the living room, her search ended abruptly.

"Jeff!" she screamed.

Crashing glass and cymbals of clattering metal resonated from the floor.

Maddie knelt in the debris scattered around her feet, rolled her husband onto his back, and placed her ear to his mouth. "What did you say? Jeff, I can't hear you."

Jeff's strained whisper begged for help. "Maddie, I-I can't."

"Oh, God, help me."

Grabbing a pillow from the couch, Maddie gently placed it beneath her husband's head. She crossed the distance to the telephone in four giant steps, eyes glued to Jeff's ashen face. She pounded 911.

"This is Madison Crane. Please, I need help. My husband . . ." Maddie's fear-soaked eyes watched Jeff struggle to take a breath.

"My address?" Her brain froze. She looked at the front door, then down at the desk. The electric bill showed 1624 Brookhurst Lane. "Yes, that's right, Brookhurst. Hurry. Please." The groaning from across the room suddenly went silent.

The handset plummeted onto the desk and tumbled to the floor while the emergency dispatcher shouted orders to no one. Maddie hugged Jeff's body to her breast.

"Jeff, don't leave me. Not now." She buried her face in his thick blond hair.

Within minutes paramedics propelled through the unlocked door, running to where she sat on the floor, sobbing, rocking a limp body.

"Miss, we need you to move aside so we can work on the patient. Miss?"

Maddie tightened her grip on Jeff's unresponsive body as slim fingers pried her arms loose. With gentle determination, a female firefighter helped Maddie to her feet.

"Don't make me leave him. They might need my help," Maddie heard herself pleading. "He doesn't know them."

Her arms reached for Jeff, but the other woman gently moved Maddie away from the lifesaving efforts, offering calm words of encouragement and a firm arm around Maddie's slender shoulder.

"Please, you have to help him." Tears blurred Maddie's vision. She looked over, her hands pleading, "Why don't they help him?"

A man's voice called out, "Clear."

Maddie blinked with sudden horror. The scene shook her from the confusion that ricocheted in the confines of her mind. Jeff's strong, healthy body convulsed as a powerful electric shock coursed through his heart.

"Continue CPR." The man holding the shock paddles released a long-held breath.

Another paramedic thumped fast and heavy on Jeff's chest, taking short breaths as he counted, "One, two, three . . ."

Maddie ran trembling hands through defiant auburn curls, pushing them back from her face. She turned again to the woman beside her. "What are they doing? Why don't they take him to the hospital?"

"Clear." Another electric shock jerked Maddie's gaze back to the floor. Her questions hung in the air, stretched as taut as her husband's body.

Maddie felt the air leave the room. Her mind paralyzed, she tried desperately to catch her breath. "Is-is he—"

"They're doing everything they can for your husband, Mrs. Crane." The woman's tone was anything but comforting.

Maddie's horror-filled eyes questioned the paramedic kneeling over her husband. Perspiration heavy on his forehead, breaths coming fast, he hesitated, then glanced in Maddie's direction to make eye contact with the female firefighter and ever so slightly shook his head.

Reality slammed through Maddie's brain.

"No-o-o-o," she wailed.

Panic shrouded Maddie's pounding heart. Gasping for breath, she battled to subdue her body's violent shaking. Terror pulsed through her. A raspy scream tore from her throat, "This can't be happening. This *is not* happening. Jeff . . ."

What seemed like hours later, the wheels of Jeff's deathbed edged toward the front door of their home. Maddie anguished over her son, David's tears, though she was thankful for his strong arm around her shoulder.

"Please, can I say goodbye to him?" Maddie asked the men pushing the gurney to the door.

The paramedics stepped aside. Maddie bent over Jeff's lifeless body, caressing his strong arms, gentle hands, unresponsive fingers. She imagined his slender frame and long legs beneath the sterile sheet. Pressing a clenched fist to her head, she squeezed tight and breathed deep.

Smoothing wavy blond wisps from Jeff's forehead, she ran her finger along his tanned face, across his chiseled chin and perfectly shaped mouth. Kissing his lips, hot tears fell onto cold cheeks.

Maddie hugged Jeff's neck tight and whispered in his ear, "I-I love you."

The attendant covered Jeff's face with the white sheet and rolled the gurney out to the waiting transport vehicle.

Shallow breaths were all that kept Maddie's heart pumping.

TWO

F ragments of a nightmare turned reality.

That was how Maddie remembered the days that followed. Thank goodness David still lived in Chicago. Arriving minutes after he received the news about his father, David had taken control, handling the countless details that came with an unexpected death.

In her fog-laden mental state, Maddie knew she was no help to anyone. Her mind moved in slow motion. Cocooned in Jeff's black leather recliner, she caught a distant glimpse of the long line of mourners gathered in their home to share her grief. They passed on both sides of the chrome and glass dining table, filled their plates with sandwiches, casseroles, and desserts, and entered into a cacophony of awkward background chatter and mindless babble.

Maddie's only conscious recollection of the memorial service was of Isaac Birnbaum's distinct baritone sharing nostalgic memories of Jeff's prestigious career. Why that moment stood out, she didn't know. "Jeff was one of a kind in the investment field, much wiser than his forty-seven years. We will greatly miss his contribution to the corporation."

Is that all he was to you, a contributing body to increase corporate assets?

"Jeff was a nice guy, smart too, but hard to get to know," Maddie heard Isaac say now. A slender, attractive woman listened attentively to Jeff's boss.

Who is that woman Isaac is talking to?

"Yeah. Ah"—the woman cleared her throat—"he was all business whenever I worked on projects with him." Glancing over her shoulder at Maddie, the woman quickly turned her attention back to the older man.

Do you suppose she—did it really matter now?

Maddie smoothed the simple black Armani dress down to her crossed knees and glimpsed her Alexander Wang sandal-clad foot bouncing ever so slightly. She fiddled with the Mikimoto pearl necklace Jeff had given her last Christmas as she watched Isaac and the woman walk out to the patio.

She breathed deeply and glanced down at her dress. *Jeff would approve of this outfit.* She could feel the heat move up her chest to her face. Of course he would have approved. He'd bought every single designer thing she was wearing.

A clenched jaw defended her against the unsettling queasiness taking command of her stomach until riotous laughter from a group of men across the room awoke a familiar loathing within. John was telling another stupid joke. At his brother's funeral, no less. Maddie felt her hands tighten around the arms of the recliner.

Look at them. Eating, drinking, laughing. Life went on as if nothing had happened. What was wrong with these people? *Don't they get it? Jeff is gone. Forever.*

Maddie closed her eyes, locked her hands together, and took several deep breaths. Why didn't Jeff's parents say something to their self-obsessed son?

She scanned the crowded room and found William, stiff and solemn, sitting on the leather couch in Jeff's office, his arm around tiny Deborah, both staring at nothing, no one. Tears streamed down Deborah's cheeks.

Maddie's outrage broke as her heart ached for the grieving couple. The two, who lived very close to poverty level, seemed out of place sitting in their son's sterile, affluent office. William, a coal miner, wore the same suit he had worn to their wedding, old even then. Maddie knew Deborah saved the black cotton dress for special occasions.

We're practically strangers, she realized. *If only—*

Chaotic car horns entered the cacophony.

"David, can you *please* go outside and monitor traffic? It's out of control."

Her daughter Ruth's ranting brought a brief smile to Maddie's lips.

David was such a blend of Jeff and Maddie. Her red hair, green eyes. Tall and handsome like his dad. More muscular than Jeff. Of course he was, working three physically demanding jobs instead of sitting behind a desk all day at an investment firm.

"David, please. Traffic control," his sister pleaded with a smile, hands on her hips.

Ruth. My dear Ruth. Maddie watched David disappear out the front door as Ruth's slim frame moved on to the next task, her mass of strawberry blonde curls begging to be gathered with one of her Brighton hairbands. Definitely her father's daughter. Maddie wished she had Ruth's confidence.

Instead, the two women shared a different trait—their tempers. When emotions flared, both sets of sea-green eyes glared black as coal.

Maddie ran her fingers through thick, rebellious waves, setting them comfortably on her shoulder. Bringing her hand to her forehead, she rubbed hard to relieve the rhythmic pounding that needed a strong cup of coffee. She squeezed the bridge of her nose. A smile lightened her grief when she remembered something Jeff had said on one of their first dates. *"That light touch of freckles on your nose will always be unmistakably Maddie."*

Shattered glass and metal echoed from the kitchen. Maddie opened her eyes to glimpse Ruth standing stiff, eyes closed, breathing deep.

"Are you all right, Mom?" Bracy had come to sit at Maddie's feet, placing her head on her mother's lap, face tipped up.

Maddie looked into her youngest daughter's mournful brown eyes and stroked her short hair. Bracy looked so much like her father, her wild blonde curls loose around her face. A college freshman, Bracy was still more legs than anything. Like Jeff.

"I'm okay. How are you doing?"

"I keep expecting him to walk through the door, pick me up, and twirl me around like he did when I was a little girl. It hurts so much, Mom." Tears ran down her freckled cheeks.

"I know, honey. I know." *Oh, Bracy, we'll both have to grow up now.*

Bracy wiped her cheeks. "Are you sure you're all right, Mom? We've been worried about you. You won't do anything crazy after we all leave, will you?"

"What? Of course not." Maddie smoothed her daughter's hair. "You guys don't need to worry about me. We will all make it through this."

I hope.

*   *   *

"Madison, I think Jeff's parents are ready to leave."

Maddie searched the room for the familiar voice. Dressed in her signature black fishnet nylons, three-inch heels, thigh-length skirt, and low-cut blouse, her mother motioned toward the door.

"William, Deborah." Maddie rose and walked to where her in-laws stood. "Are you leaving so soon?"

"It's a long drive to Pittsburgh." William looked past his daughter-in-law, nervously turning the key ring in his hand, rattling the keys.

"Let me find the kids so they can say goodbye."

"No need."

Deborah frowned at her husband.

"Bracy, find David and Ruth. Your grandparents are leaving."

Maddie's mom waved from across the room. "It was good to see you, William, Deborah."

Deborah acknowledged the greeting with a painful smile. "Good to see you too, Genny."

When the kids offered to walk their grandparents to the car, Maddie headed for the kitchen, but turned when she felt a hand on her back.

"How are you doing? Can we talk?" Genny asked.

Maddie took a deep breath. "I need some coffee. Let's talk in the kitchen."

"Madison, I know you're hurting. Even though it's been more than twenty years since your father's death, the pain is still there." Genny squinted, clearly testing her daughter's mood.

Maddie leaned against the counter and wrapped her arms around her torso. How ironic. They finally had something in common. "I know." Her eyes moved around the sterile kitchen. "How many husbands ago was that?"

Genny walked over to her daughter and looked her square in the eyes. Only the slight flare around her nostrils betrayed her reaction. "Madison, I know you disapprove of the way I've lived my life since your father's death. I'm sorry if I've hurt you."

Maddie tapped her fingers against her crossed arms.

"But you're very young, not even forty-three. You're going to be surprised how loneliness creeps into every part of your life. It can cause you to do things." Her mother paused. "Things you never thought yourself capable of doing."

I'll never live my life the way you have. Never.

Lips pursed, Genny gave her daughter an awkward hug. "Madison, I just want you to know I'm here if you need a listening ear. I understand what you are going through."

Do you really? I wonder. Maddie followed her mother into the living room. Genny hugged her grandchildren, took her fifth husband's arm, and left the gathering.

THREE

The silence was haunting.

With Carolyn, her best friend, visiting her mother-in-law for a few days and the other mourners and guests finally gone, Maddie roamed the empty house listening for Jeff. Each step recalled his voice, his face, his touch. His absence was palpable.

Opening the louvered doors to their bedroom closet, Jeff's shirts, trousers, and ties hung color coordinated, ready for another day at the office. Shoes polished, set in order: tan, brown, black.

Maddie caressed a crisp white shirt. Her hand swept across a handsome brown sports coat and her favorite pinstriped shirt. When she touched Jeff's black leather jacket, she felt her knees buckle. Yanking the jacket off its hanger, she collapsed to the floor. "This can't be real. You can't be gone forever."

Maddie buried her face in the supple leather, and the dam that had held through the day crumbled as she sobbed brokenly. "I can't do this. I don't want to live without you. If only I could just go to sleep and not wake up."

Bracy's words of concern echoed in her mind. *"You won't do anything crazy after we all leave, will you?"*

Maddie squeezed the jacket tight with both hands. Paper crinkled inside a pocket. Wiping her eyes, she pulled out a slip of blue paper. She had known Jeff would wear her favorite jacket on their date six months ago, so she had put a love note inside. *"Let's make this the best date we've ever had. I love you."*

Maddie brought the note to her face and inhaled the scent of Jeff's aftershave. Tears distorted the words on the paper.

FOUR

Rage does not speak love's language.

"Maddie? When was the last time you had a shower?" Carolyn sat on the edge of Maddie's unmade bed.

"What do I care? No one is going to see me, least of all Jeff."

Maddie pushed oily hair back from her face and bowed her head to check out the clothes she had worn for days. Coffee stains and lasagna sauce were splattered across Jeff's pinstriped shirt. She snickered.

"Ironic, isn't it? Jeff would never approve." Maddie's slim fingers brushed a stain that refused to fall in defeat. "Shower? I don't know. Why does it matter?"

"Maddie, Ruth called me. You're scaring your kids." Carolyn's blue eyes hadn't dimmed a bit since they'd first met in grade school. "How are you sleeping?"

"I don't know. Not more than a couple hours at a time."

"Have you considered taking something to help you sleep?"

"No. Not really." Yes, she had. She'd considered taking the whole bottle.

"Maddie, you're still a horrible liar."

"And you're still a horrible best friend." Carolyn gave a small grin as the old joke slipped out before Maddie could stop it.

"What's got you so stuck?"

"I'm sick of remembering all the bad times."

Carolyn's eyes flashed. "That's not a surprise, is it? You had enough of them."

"So why didn't I stand up to Jeff? Each time his rage grew worse than the time before. Why did I always believe him when he promised things would be different?" Maddie flung the blankets back and stomped to the bathroom.

9

She looked terrible. Her hair was a tangled mess. It looked more like a greasy pan of spaghetti sauce than the lovely auburn people raved about. And those sea-green eyes everyone said they admired were bloodshot and elusive. The mirror didn't lie.

A deep sigh interrupted her thoughts.

Carolyn walked over to comfort her friend slumped against the vanity.

"Why does that stuff with Jeff make you angry now?"

"Because last year was a new beginning for our marriage. At least I thought it was. Wasn't it?"

Carolyn gave a noncommittal shrug. "You were headed in the right direction."

"And then Jeff deserted me, right when things were turning around." Maddie stepped back into the disheveled room. "Of course I'm angry. He left me to wonder how wonderful it could have been and what made it so miserable in the first place."

"It was a good year," Carolyn agreed. "Jeff made major strides in managing his temper. It was probably because he knew I was watching him. I came so close to calling the cops, Maddie." Carolyn closed her eyes tight. "I still remember that horrible night. Bracy's frantic voice on the other end of the phone, the sounds of all hell breaking loose in the background."

"So then why?" Maddie walked past Carolyn and fell silent.

"Stop it, Maddie. You're going to drive yourself crazy."

Maddie picked up a book on the bedside table and flung it across the room, shattering a glass of water in its path, soaking the open pages. "I hate this. All those wasted years."

Carolyn stood quiet for some time. Maddie lay down on the bed, pulled her knees up in a fetal position, and cried herself to sleep.

FIVE

After finding out from David that Maddie had been having a recurring dream about Jeff's death, Ruth had quickly gotten on the phone to arrange a counseling session for her mother. Maddie had reluctantly agreed.

"A caterpillar makes its own prison."

Maddie looked at Eleanor in surprise.

Eleanor, a licensed grief therapist, leaned back and asked a question: "What do you suppose happens if it doesn't break out?"

Maddie looked around the office as if the answer might be on the natural-fiber throw cushions. Eleanor waited quietly.

"It gets trapped. Like I was." Memories of the lost years flooded Maddie's mind. Years she could never get back. Wasted years. Wasted trying to please and appease a man who'd lifted the bar with her every successful attempt. Bars that became the prison she'd struggled to survive in.

"And what happens when it does break free?"

Break free. Freedom.

Jeff, can't you understand? I want my freedom, but I want it with you.

"It has crumpled wings." Maddie smiled briefly at the memory of finding a chrysalis under her grandparents' porch one summer.

"Did you feel like your wings were crumpled?"

"I didn't want them to be."

"What did you want?"

"I wanted the good things. Jeff could be so tender, so romantic. But if I said or did something he didn't agree with, he could be just as controlling, just as angry. He could be volatile." Maddie closed her eyes against the memories.

"You think that was your fault?"

Why was she telling Eleanor all this stuff? She'd only agreed to see a counselor because of Ruth's pressure to talk to this woman who was supposed to be so great with grieving. This has nothing to do with grief.

"Maddie, do you think you caused Jeff's tirades?"

Maddie opened her eyes and took a deep breath. "If only I had tried a little harder to be the wife Jeff needed me to be, he never would have lost his temper like he did."

"What happened when he lost his temper?"

Maddie sat back on the couch. A cold shudder ran through her body. "I remember him screaming at me one time, 'Just what is it you want?' So I told him that I was a prisoner under his control, held captive by the fears and insecurities he'd instilled in me. I told him he'd badgered me into this dark pit of hopelessness until I couldn't think for myself anymore. He made me feel like I was completely incapable of doing anything on my own."

Maddie took a deep breath, the memories of that night sharp and painful.

"I told him I wanted my freedom, but I wanted it with him. I wanted to find out who I was and to stop masquerading as the perfect little wife he was trying to mold me into. I said I was miserable and that I knew he was frustrated. Then I told him he was even more insecure than I was.

"That set him off."

SIX

December.

Puffy eyes stared into another grim morning. Snow lay heavy on lifeless plants. Maddie's heart felt as desolate and cold as the fallow ground of the dreary garden. Her soul shivered with the chill of loneliness.

Walking through the empty house, Maddie's eyes took in the stark beige walls adorned with costly original art pieces. Cold chrome and glass shimmered from the glare of the sun that broke briefly through the cloud-shrouded sky. Neat, orderly, functional. No frills. A touch of blue and green in the paintings, a speck of red. The rest of the room, black, white, shiny, and sterile. All part of Jeff's idea of a prosperous lifestyle. An image he'd enjoyed.

I hate modern art.

Buying a house in the upscale Bridgeport neighborhood had been part of Jeff's master plan. As with the rest of the homes in the neighborhood, master gardeners and landscapers maintained the grounds. Professional painters took care of the mandatory exterior painting every three years. Interior designers sparred to transform the vintage homes, employing new trends yet keeping the old-world charm.

Maddie was never consulted.

The backyard garden, however, was all hers. Every year Maddie looked forward to spring. She planted seeds that sprouted into peppers and beans, cauliflower and tomatoes. Basil, parsley, and garlic thrived in small pots. She loved to change it up each spring with something new to add flavor and variety to the mix, something she remembered from her grandmother's garden.

Eyes closed, Maddie slipped easily into childhood memories.

"Mads, what are you doing to that poor creature?"

A young girl, no more than seven years of age, smiled up at her Gram. "This little bird fell out of his nest from way up there." Maddie pointed to the tall maple. "I'm covering him with leaves so he won't get cold."

"That's very nice, Mads. Come on in now for lunch while he sleeps."

Maddie smiled, remembering how some years later Gram confessed that Gramps had taken the rigid bird and buried it before she realized it was dead. Time and again while on her grandparents' farm, Maddie rescued lost cats, injured birds, and stray chicks. She'd loved comforting other children with scraped knees and bloody elbows and bringing them to Gram to receive her tender loving care.

She had told Gramps that someday she was gonna be a doctor.

Thinking about his tender smile and gentle hug took her back to his encouraging words. *"You will be a very good doctor, Maddie."*

Mug in hand, Maddie walked to the sink.

The farm. She'd believed anything was possible there. She was never afraid to dream big.

Big dreams. What dreams? She knew the dreams Jeff or the kids had, but hers? Maddie wrapped her arms around herself like a comforting quilt, drinking in the dreary day and its cold dampness.

SEVEN

"When are you coming, Mom?"

"Oh, Ruth, I don't think that's a good idea."

After Jeff's death, Ruth expected Maddie to move to Texas and live with her and her husband, Matt. Matthew Oldfield was an investment manager for Isaac Birnbaum Investments in Austin. Unlike Jeff, Matt kept his priorities straight. Family, then job.

Maddie sighed. Living with Ruth and Matt would never work. Only married a year and a half, they had just begun to settle into their life together. The last thing they needed was a depressed, confused widow hanging around.

"Mom, we talked about this."

"No, Ruth, *you* talked about this. I appreciate it, but I need to learn how to take care of myself. I love you and Matt and I'm grateful for the invitation, but I have to say no. Again."

"But, Mom."

"Trust me, Ruth. This is best."

Wasn't it?

* * *

The three most influential men in Maddie's life—her son, her banker, and Isaac Birnbaum, her investment counselor—all advised her not to consider any drastic changes, like selling the house, for at least a year, maybe two. She was having second thoughts as to the wisdom of that advice. Here she sat, day after day, doing nothing meaningful. Life was passing her by.

Maddie stirred ingredients together for lemon muffins while watching the Food Network. She spoke to the woman on the screen. "I hate rambling around in this big house all alone. Too many memories. Maybe I should rent the house out?" She tucked a loose strand of hair behind her ear as if expecting to hear an answer from the overly zealous cook.

"Or maybe I should sell it. But where would I go? An apartment? What would I do in an apartment? Why not get a job?" She shook her head at the TV. "A job? I'm not trained to do a doggone thing."

The effervescent woman in the spotless TV kitchen bounced over to the oven and popped her muffins inside. Maddie plunked hers in the oven too. A quick glance over her new reading glasses brought a sassy remark to the TV personality. "These better turn out. I did everything exactly as you did, except for the bounce." Maddie rolled her eyes.

She picked up a magazine that sat on a tall stack of unopened junk mail. Skimming an article about people who overcame incredible obstacles to climb Mount Everest, she tossed the magazine in the trash. Mount Everest. Good grief, she wasn't even sure she could make muffins.

Her eyes moved around the room. She'd never had to consider the future before. Jeff had their life mapped out from the day they were married on into retirement. They'd had plans. Now there was no *they*. She hung her head, shaking it as if that might magically change everything. She needed to figure out what was next.

What she needed—Maddie took a deep breath—was an adventure. Maybe a cruise? A cruise. Alone. Yeah, right.

She slumped onto the chrome and black leather barstool. "I hate this."

EIGHT

Maddie shot up out of a deep sleep. Panting, her attempts to catch her breath failed. She put her hand to her chest. Thumping heart palpitations. *Am I having a heart attack?*

Terror once again threatened to close her airway. Several deep breaths and her pulse slowed. She raked her hands through her hair and rested her head against the headboard. She moved her hand gently over Jeff's side of the bed. Empty. He would never lie next to her again. She'd never feel his warm body against hers, his strong arms wrapped around her.

Tears traveled the contours of Maddie's face.

The telephone's sharp peal set her heart pounding again.

"H-h-hello," she whispered, wiping her wet face with Jeff's crumpled T-shirt she slept with every night.

"Maddie, what's wrong?"

"Carolyn, you d-don't know how g-good it is to hear your voice."

"Maddie, are you all right?"

"No. I can't stop crying. It feels like m-my throat is c-closing up. It's hard to breath."

"Take deep breaths. Breathe in, breathe out. Breathe in, breathe out. Is that helping?"

"Maybe."

"What happened?"

"Carolyn, I can't take this excruciating pain anymore. I miss Jeff so much. Everything here reminds me of him."

"Did you sleep at all?"

"Not much. Just long enough to have that horrible nightmare again." Maddie had told Carolyn about her recurring dream, sobbing her way through the telling. Always the same, Jeff and Maddie started out on a hike in the mountains, but it ended with him plunging to his death.

"I don't want to be in this house without him, but I don't want to be anywhere else either." Maddie picked up a family photo from the nightstand. A fresh tear fell on the glass.

"Maddie, you are going to make yourself sick if you don't stop this. It's gonna take time to get past the loneliness. You just need to take it one day at a time."

Maddie placed the picture back on the nightstand. "I'm trying. The thing is, I don't have any idea what to do without Jeff. I never thought I'd have to deal with this. A job doesn't make much sense. Who would hire me?"

"Madison Crane, you've lost sight of what a terrific woman you are."

"Spoken like a true friend."

"Maddie, there is a lot more to you than you give yourself credit for."

"Uh-huh, right."

"I know you don't believe this, but someday you will see the beauty God created inside and you'll be excited about living out your dreams."

She sounded like Gram.

"Why don't you sell that big ole house and come live in Jacob's Bend?"

Maddie's mind flashed through memories that had taken place in each room of their home.

"You've always adored quiet, sleepy little towns. Jacob's Bend is definitely that. Alex and I would love to have you here. An elderly friend of ours died a few months ago. His cottage is for sale. It would be perfect for you."

Maddie sat up straighter. "Ah, well, I don't know."

"What's to know? Sell the house, have a huge yard sale, store what's left, and drive on out here."

"Drive all that way by myself? What if I got lost or the car broke down or—"

"So get on a plane and buy a new car when you get here."

"I couldn't to that."

Carolyn sighed. "Madison Crane, you can do anything you put your mind to. Why are you so doggone afraid of everything? You've always had a tendency toward insecurity. What's holding you there? You *can* do this."

Insecure? *Am I?*

An unsettling frown lodged between Maddie's eyes. "Besides, I'm not so sure this upscale neighborhood would like my having a yard sale. Never seen one here before."

"Oh, I forgot about that. Your CC&Rs probably don't allow it."

"My CC and what?"

"You know, covenant, conditions, and restrictions. Most high-end housing developments have them."

"Ah, okay, yeah."

"You don't have a clue what I'm talking about, do you?"

"Carolyn, there is so much I don't have a clue about. It's been an exhausting, uphill learning curve since Jeff died. I'm not sure I'll ever get it all."

"You're doing great, Maddie. Really you are. Why don't you come to Jacob's Bend and let Alex and me help you navigate some of those curves?"

Maddie shook her head. "I don't know, Carolyn. There's a lot to consider."

"Oh really? Like what?"

Maddie fidgeted with the torn binding on her blanket. "Like . . . like the master gardener program. I've only got a few more months to complete it. And the quilting guild. I *am* the president, you know. Not to mention my volunteer commitment at Southside Manor. I help the residents balance their checkbooks, read to them. I visit with them and—"

"Oh, well, I didn't realize you had so many *important* things going on in your life." Carolyn's annoyance rang loud over the phone line. "Maddie, there are lots of people who could take over those things. Are they really enough to keep you there?"

Silence.

"Maddie?"

"It hasn't been long enough."

"What?"

"It hasn't been long enough. I've been told I shouldn't do anything drastic for at least a year. Did you know the death of a spouse ranks number one on the list of life's most stressful events?"

"Okay, I can see the wisdom in that. But what about after the year is up? It's been six months since Jeff—"

"Actually, day after tomorrow it will be seven months."

Carolyn's voice softened. "I'm sorry. I know this is difficult. I won't push you. But please think about it. Your kids are spread out all over the place. I know this is selfish on my part, but I miss you. I miss your wisdom."

Maddie stared at the phone in her hand. "What wisdom? I feel like a baby just learning to walk for the first time. Three steps forward and *plop*, I fall on my backside."

"I never saw it like that. Besides, you know my church is always looking for wise, mature women to encourage others."

Maddie rolled her eyes. "You sound like Gram."

Carolyn let out a long sigh. "Will you at least give it some thought? Think what an adventure it would be."

"What did you say?"

"I said you could use an adventure. Your life has been planned for you since you were a little girl. Wouldn't it be fun to start a whole new life, make your own choices for a change?"

"Carolyn, you won't believe this, but that's exactly what I told myself yesterday, that I need an adventure."

Maddie stepped into her slippers and walked around the room while she talked. "Even so, Carolyn, I don't think I'm ready to traipse clear across the country in my car all by myself."

"That's ridiculous. Of course you're ready. You know darn well if you don't do it now, you never will. Besides, it's high time you grew up."

Maddie halted her steps. Flashing heat raced from her neck to her face. She glared at the phone in her hand. "You don't think I act like a grown-up?"

"You have been sheltered all your life, Madison Crane. First your dad, even your Gram and Gramps, then Jeff. They made every single decision that had to be made for you. Growing up means you make your own decisions. Reap the benefits. *And* suffer the consequences."

Maddie pulled the curtain back, searching for some kind of answer.

"You are so afraid of everything and everyone. Sometimes you put on such a tough outer shell. I know you had to protect your emotions because of Jeff. But doggone it, Maddie, why are you so darn determined to do whatever it takes to cover up the caring woman inside?"

Maddie sat down on the edge of the bed. Did she really do that?

Carolyn was tenacious. "You know I'm right, Maddie."

"Small town, huh?"

"You would love it. Will you at least think about it?"

"Oh, Carolyn, how I wish Jeff were here to share it with me."

"Come on. You know that never would have happened."

Maddie sighed. "Yeah, I know. It's funny, you wouldn't think I'd be so lonely when I fought so hard for my freedom."

"Jeff was a good guy. He really loved you. He just didn't know how to show it sometimes, and besides, you loved him to pieces."

Swallowing hard, tears blurred Maddie's vision. "I think about him every day, almost every hour. When will my mind get on to something else?"

"Maybe this is the key to start that process. But one thing is certain. Whether you move here or not, and I hope you do, you need to come into the twenty-first century and invest in a cell phone. Hardly anybody has a landline these days."

"I know, my kids tell me the same thing. But there is a sense of security knowing my home is actually connected to a place. To the phone company."

Maddie could hear her friend's heavy sigh.

"Maddie—"

"I can't imagine what all that might look like. It really would be an adventure. Wouldn't it?"

NINE

" C arolyn, where is my raincoat? I need to pack it for my Seattle trip," Alex yelled over the top of the suitcase.

Carolyn leaned against the doorjamb to their bedroom, arms crossed over her chest. "It was in the coat closet, where it always is." She held the coat out to her husband. "Alex, do you have to make this trip to Washington?"

Alex stopped packing, walked over, and pulled Carolyn into a tight embrace. "I wish I didn't have to go, but it's part of the job."

"I know, but—"

Alex bent Carolyn backward over his knee, smiled the smile he saved especially for her, and kissed her on the lips. "I love you. You know that, right?"

Carolyn giggled. "Yes, I know." Alex gently pulled her up so they were eye to eye.

She brushed a mass of curls out of her eyes. "I talked to Maddie today."

"Oh yeah, how is she?"

"Doing as well as can be expected. I asked her to move here. Actually, I challenged her to move here."

Alex grabbed three pairs of socks out of a drawer and threw them in the suitcase as if shooting the winning shot through a hoop. "Yes." He pumped his fist. "Really? That's a great idea."

Why did he think that was great? Just because Maddie was more coordinated than she was and could hit the hoop three out of four times? Maybe he missed shooting hoops with her. Or maybe he was sorry he had stopped dating Maddie and started dating her.

Alex cocked his head. Carolyn could tell he was sensing her insecurity. "Carolyn, we've had this conversation a hundred times."

"What conversation?"

"You don't think I can read your thoughts and your body language after all these years? You are the love of my life. No one else. Besides, Maddie and I only had one date, and it ended when she met Jeff that night. I was yesterday's news on the same day."

Carolyn's crimson cheeks showed her embarrassment. "I'm sorry. I don't know what is wrong with me."

Alex pulled her into a tender hug. "Wanna come along with me on this trip?"

Smiling, she kissed his nose. "I wish I could, but I've got my exercise classes, and the ladies were not very happy the last time I left them hanging for a week."

"Carolyn, you have never left those ladies hanging. They all seem to think they need someone to hold their hands, even after they've been in your class for over a year."

"I know, I know. Some of them just lack confidence."

Alex looked deep into her eyes. "Hmm, unlike their very confident instructor."

Carolyn chuckled. "Okay, okay, I get it."

"I love you, Carolyn."

Her lopsided grin said, "I love you too."

TEN

The blinking light on the answering machine caught Maddie's attention as soon as she stepped into the kitchen. The brisk walk had cleared her head after Carolyn's call.

She punched the blinking button. "Hello, Mrs. Crane. My name is Adele Smith. I work for Harrison Phillips Realty. I found your number in the telephone book along with several other residents on Brookhurst Lane. I am looking for a home for one of my clients. I've toured other homes similar to yours on Penny Circle and Diamond Lane, and I've checked the specs on your house. It sounds exactly like what my buyers are looking for. Could you please give me a call as soon as possible?"

Maddie sank into a chair. *What?*

A quick glance at the clock broke her thoughts. It was already after ten. She'd have to hurry to be at Southside Manor on time for her volunteer shift. It was the one commitment she'd faithfully kept since Jeff's death.

*   *   *

Maddie studied Jonathan Richards's peaceful countenance as he slept. The eighty-five-year-old, who had macular degeneration, enjoyed her renditions of swashbuckling adventures and thought-provoking detective thrillers.

What a dear man. His mind was as sharp as a twenty-year-old's.

Maddie glanced at Jonathan's left arm and on down to where his left ankle hid beneath the covers, both set in heavy plaster casts from a fall he had taken two weeks prior. His failing health, including two strokes that left him partially paralyzed on the right side, tugged at her heart.

Intelligent, creative, sympathetic. Handsome to boot. A real charmer. Jonathan had outlived two wives with some pretty interesting stories to tell. Maddie smiled and gently touched the elder's hand. He blinked his eyes open.

"Anybody in here?" A tall young woman poked her head around the corner and winked; her long blonde hair swished over her shoulder.

Jonathan beamed. "Hi, sweetie. Wish I could stand and give you a proper hug."

Heather smiled and hurried to her father's side. She held him tight around the neck and kissed him on the cheek. "Soon, Dad. Soon."

Jonathan glanced over at Maddie.

Heather followed his gaze. "Hi, Maddie. Is he giving you any trouble today?"

"Well, if you don't count the two times he chased me around the room, he's been a perfect gentleman."

The three laughed at the thought.

Maddie set the book she had been reading to Jonathan the day before on the bedside table. "I'll leave you two alone."

No sooner had she left the room than, Heather rushed to catch up with her.

"Maddie, can I talk to you? Do you have time for a cup of tea?"

Maddie glanced at the clock.

"It's okay. Dad dropped off to sleep again. I think we need to cut back on his pain meds."

"Sure, I'd love a cup of tea. Is everything all right?"

"Yes, I'd just like to ask you something."

As the two women walked through the cafeteria line, Maddie hollered over the clattering pots and clashing dishes, "Hi, Charlotte."

The sixty-two-year-old helper had just shoved a tray of dirty dishes into the supersize industrial dishwasher. Charlotte turned around, smiled, and shouted back, "Hi, Maddie. Can I get you something?"

Maddie reached for a tea bag and an empty cup. She yelled above the chaos, "Yeah, could I have one of George's *delicious* orange scones?"

George, Southside Manor's chef, bantered from behind the counter, "I heard that, Madison Crane. You tryin' to get a free handout with those compliments?"

"You bet. Did it work?"

"Not on your life."

"They really are wonderful, George. Someday I'm gonna steal you away from this place to cook for me."

The cook held up his hand to ward off the thought. "No way. It's tough enough cookin' for a hundred and fifty after servin' three squares a day to fifteen hundred sailors. If I had to cook for just one person I'd go nuts."

"Okay, okay. I guess I'll just have to be happy with whatever I can confiscate here."

George smiled and tipped his ball cap.

The two women grabbed a seat in the corner. Heather looked down at the table, then back at the woman sitting across from her. "Maddie, can I ask you something?"

"Sure."

"How long have you lived in the city? And how long have you been a volunteer at Southside Manor?"

"Well, let's see, I started coming over here about eight years ago. Someone brought a flyer to my quilt guild saying volunteers were needed. I showed up the next day. Been coming here every week ever since. That's how I met your father. He's a wonderful man."

"He is my favorite person in the whole world."

"As far as living in the city, well, I was raised in the country, on my grandparents' farm, until I was about eight. One day my mom and dad decided they wanted a change, so we moved lock, stock, and barrel to the city. We had very few locks, stocks, or barrels at the time." The two women giggled. "My parents were young and foolish, or so they told us kids years later. I've lived in the city ever since."

Heather shook her head. "My mom died when I was eighteen. Poor Dad has lost two wonderful women to cancer."

Maddie nodded. Jonathan's story, like many love stories, was bittersweet. His first love, Doris, succumbed to cancer at age fifty-five, and his second love, Julia, died just as their daughter was starting out on her own. Maddie recalled one blustery winter day not long ago when Jonathan confessed there *was* life after Doris's death. A happy, fulfilling life.

Maddie had set down the paperback she was reading aloud and asked him to share his own legend. "Tell me your story, Jonathan."

"Four years after I became a widower, at the age of fifty-nine, mind you, I met the second love of my life, Julia. Seventeen years her senior, we both fell hopelessly in love the first time we literally bumped into each other at a Memorial Day rummage sale." Jonathan's eyes sparkled with the memory.

"We were both trying to buy the same piece of art. An unbelievably exquisite watercolor." Jonathan closed his eyes. "You could almost hear the wildflowers, dotted among the tall willowy grass in the spring meadow, singing. The more I admired the painting, the more I could swear I felt the slightest breeze compelling the flowers to sway gently to a light tune." Jonathan swayed slightly, as if the breeze he described was wafting through his room.

Maddie sat back in the chair, one leg folded up under her. "It sounds lovely, Jonathan."

Jonathan's eyes blinked open and he laughed. "Sorry, Maddie. Sometimes I get carried away when I think about that painting.

"Anyway, I had that beautiful treasure in my hands, ready to make the purchase, when this young woman backed into me, saw the painting, and brazenly asked how much I wanted for it. I laughed and said, 'Fifty dollars,' thinking no one would pay such an extravagant price for a painting at a rummage sale.

"In the next breath Julia countered with, 'Sold.' Her reply startled me and I shrank back, a little embarrassed. I confessed the painting didn't belong to me, that I was just about to buy it. She gave me the most radiant smile. Took my breath away. The devilish look in her eyes suggested a compromise. 'What would you think of splitting the cost of the painting? You could take it to your house, hang it in a prominent place of honor, with the stipulation that I have visitation rights?'

"That sly little fox was trying to pick me up. Can you imagine an old guy like me having a beautiful young woman putting the make on him?"

Maddie giggled and clapped her hands together like a child hearing the story of Peter Rabbit for the first time. Her eyes gleamed with anticipation. "What happened next?"

"Of course I agreed wholeheartedly to her plan . . . with one exception. I offered to cook dinner.

"We both laughed till our sides ached when we found out the lady who owned the painting was furious with her husband who had painted it. She wanted it sold and wouldn't take any more than five dollars for it. Two months later Julia and I were married. Our joy became complete with the birth of our daughter, Heather, named after the meadow scene."

Coincidence or not, Heather had become a highly acclaimed artist, her paintings sought throughout the world. When this beautiful young woman visited her father, she always brought along her painting supplies. The two often strolled arm in arm in the garden. Heather would sit on a little stool in front of an easel next to her father's cushioned lawn chair and paint for hours, asking his advice while he watched and occasionally napped. Maddie couldn't help but admire the pair, who were truly devoted to each other.

The sharp clatter of metal pans caused Maddie to look over her shoulder and grin at George, who gave her a shrug. She smiled at the young woman sitting across from her. "I'm sorry about your mother, Heather. She sounds like a wonderful woman."

Heather pulled herself closer, resting her elbows on the table. "Thank you. She was an incredible woman." Heather took a deep breath. "Maddie, can I ask you something else? How long have you owned your home?"

"Gosh, Jeff and I had been married a little over a year when we bought it. That would make it around—twenty-three years." She looked past Heather into the distance. "Twenty-three years in the same house. Can you believe it?"

"You must think it odd, even presumptuous, for me to ask all these personal questions."

"I *was* wondering where all this was leading."

Heather fidgeted with her napkin. "Ah, I was just wondering . . . have you ever considered selling your house?"

Fierce heart pounding. Maddie looked away. "No. I mean, yes. Well, I'm not sure."

Heather's face shaded red. "Maybe it's too soon after your husband's death to think about selling the home you shared for so many years. I'm sorry for even bringing it up."

"No, no, don't be sorry. It's okay. I presume you're asking for yourself?"

Heather nodded. "I want a home closer to my dad. I'm actually hoping to have him come live with me with the help of a nurse until he is up and around." Love for her father radiated from Heather's brilliant blue eyes. "I understand you don't live too far from here."

"Brookhurst Lane. Just a few blocks that way." Maddie pointed over Heather's right shoulder. "I often walk here. You can actually see the roofline of Southside Manor from one of my windows."

"That's perfect. If it's not possible to have Dad live with me, at least I would only be a few blocks away."

"Heather, you don't even know what my house looks like. How do you know you would like it?"

"Oh, if you live there, it has to be great."

This was ridiculous. She didn't even know how much she'd sell the house for. Besides, it had only been nine months since Jeff's death. She needed to wait at least a year.

*   *   *

That afternoon, moving about Jeff's office, Maddie opened the top drawer of the file cabinet. She had never gone through Jeff's files before.

"This is absurd," she told herself, her voice echoing in the stark room. These were her files too. She needed to see what their investments looked like. What if the money ran out? What then? She pulled out a file that said "Retirement" and shook her head in frustration. She hesitated a moment and picked up the phone.

"Isaac? It's Maddie. I've been looking at Jeff's retirement file. I can't make any sense of these figures. Can you help me?"

"Of course. I was going to call you this morning anyway," came Isaac's professional voice. "Remember you asked me to look into Jeff's life insurance policy?"

"Yes. I know the policy was only a year old, but it was supposed to be for five hundred thousand dollars and the insurance company doesn't seem to know why it's not being processed."

Isaac was quiet for a moment. "Maddie, there isn't any life insurance money."

"What do you mean, there isn't any life insurance money?" Maddie's insides trembled.

"I'm still trying to figure out why, but for some reason Jeff stopped paying the premiums a few months before his death."

"Isaac, I don't understand."

Isaac's voice was apologetic, "Maddie, I don't know what happened. Obviously Jeff wasn't planning on dying—"

"Isaac, I need that money for my future. I'm thinking of moving to Jacob's Bend where my best friend lives. What am I going to live on?"

Did she just say that?

"You're thinking of moving?" Isaac's voice held a hint of surprise.

Maddie turned the pens in the square holder on the desk upside down. "There is really nothing holding me here. David has a life of his own; we don't see that much of each other. Ruth is in Texas. Bracy's at Wheaton College. I might have a buyer for the house, but without the insurance money—"

Isaac's laughter caught her by surprise. "Maddie, you have more than enough money with your investments and the sale of the house. Go ahead with your plans. Start a new life. I'm glad to hear you are moving forward."

*   *   *

The next day Maddie called Heather to ask if she wanted to see the house.

Heather didn't hide her excitement. "Oh, could I? How about today?"

"Ah, sure. Just let me straighten the place up a little. Give me an hour." Maddie gave her the address. "Do you need directions?"

"No, I'll find it. I have to confess, after our conversation I drove around your neighborhood checking out the houses."

Maddie smiled. "Okay, I'll see you in an hour."

Heather arrived exactly one hour later. A grin spread clear across her face when Maddie led her into the foyer. As the two women walked from room to room, Heather was strangely quiet.

Maddie shook her head. Maybe she was wrong about these things being signs to move forward. It was pretty obvious Heather didn't like the house.

The tour ended in the living room. Maddie motioned to the tray sitting on the coffee table. "Would you like some coffee?"

"Yes, thank you." Heather smiled, accepting the cup with both hands. Tears shone in her eyes.

Maddie sat down beside the young woman. "Are you all right?"

"I just knew this would be the house for Dad and me. It's perfect. The sunroom off the back is ideal for a studio. This house is more than perfect. This is home. Maddie, please say you'll sell it to me."

"But you haven't even asked about the price."

"I don't care what you want. I'll pay it."

Maddie looked down at her coffee cup. "I don't even know what it's worth. It's been paid off for the last five years, so there's no mortgage."

"You know, Maddie, houses in this area are selling for as much as four hundred fifty thousand dollars. I've checked in a ten-mile radius of Southside Manor. That is certainly not too much to pay for your home. It's in excellent condition. You and your husband have kept it up beautifully."

"You can't be serious."

"I'm dead serious. Please say you'll sell me the house. I've accumulated quite a bit of money from my paintings. I'll pay whatever you ask."

Maddie walked to the window. Heather's anxious eyes followed.

Maddie turned to face her visitor. "Heather, I need to think about this. Would it be okay if I called you in a few days?"

Heather's eyes shone disappointment. "Sure, that's fine."

"By the way, if I do sell you the house, when would you want to move in?"

"I wish I could say tomorrow, but I have an art show in New York in two weeks. I won't be back for at least two weeks after that. How does ninety days sound?"

Maddie took a deep breath. "I'll let you know."

*   *   *

Outside the kitchen window, barren oaks, stark rose bushes, and an awning-covered swing unearthed long-forgotten memories. Jeff, shirtsleeves rolled up, relaxing on the cushioned swing. *"We are staying right where we are. One day we'll collect the equity from this house and retire in style."*

Maddie lifted a bottle of wine from Jeff's abstract Anthony Caro wine rack. She turned the bottle in her hands, closed her eyes, and pulled it against her chest. Maybe just one glass and the memories would stop.

Unwanted memories lead to the aftermath of Jeff's drinking binges.

Maddie, you don't need an escape. You need a purpose.

A lonely sigh slipped past her lips as she placed the unopened wine bottle back in the rack.

Eleven

Nathan snatched the wine bottle from the floor where it lay after his father's drunken tirade. A red blotch had seeped into the carpet. Mom would have to move the furniture. Again.

A bitter sneer and flaring nostrils gave witness to the ten-year-old's disgust and anger, while burning cobalt-blue eyes glared at the man snoring on the couch, his arm outstretched, a limp hand open where the empty bottle had been.

The boy wanted nothing more than to run from the nightly tongue-lashings, which usually included a slap or two across the face and the slamming of his body against the nearest wall. But he refused to leave his mother with this self-pitying drunk, who had once turned on her until Nathan jumped between them, taking the full force of the dizzying punch meant for his mother.

Nathan bolted up, breathing hard; his eyes carefully scanned the room. Why did these nightmares haunt him? The digital clock read 2:16 a.m.

Sitting on the edge of the bed, he ran shaky hands through shaggy brown hair. Sweat beaded on his forehead. He glanced around the dark room and grabbed the gun from the bedside table drawer.

Nathan's gun hand hung taut at his side, finger on the trigger. He took a deep breath and slowly walked into the kitchen, carefully checking every dark corner along the route. Satisfied he was alone in the house, he took a glass from the cupboard and ran the cold water. Nathan reflected on the gun in his hand. He wished he'd had this when he was a kid. He shook his head and set the gun on the counter.

Most nights Nathan ended up catching a few hours of sleep on the couch where he tried desperately to forget the man who ruined the lives of his entire family. You'd think after thirty years, he would have been able to forget. Nathan rubbed the bristles on his chin. He needed to let this go.

TWELVE

Maddie picked up the phone on the second ring. "Hello."
She set down the paperwork she'd been going over and grinned at the exuberant greeting on the other end of the line. "Good morning."

"Hi, Heather."

"I called to talk business."

"What kind of business?"

"The house?"

"Oh yeah, the house. What about it?"

"Are you going to sell it to me?"

"Actually, I think I just might."

Heather squealed. "Really? I can't believe it. I'm so happy. Dad is going to love it. I'll get the money together and have my lawyer draw up the papers." Heather slowed her speech. "That is, if that's okay with you?"

Maddie cleared her throat. "Heather, what exactly did we decide with regard to price?"

"Four hundred fifty thousand dollars."

"Good grief, no. I told you there is no way this house is worth four hundred fifty thousand dollars. I will *not* sell it to you for that much. How about three hundred fifty thousand?"

"It's worth every bit of four hundred fifty."

"No way. No sale."

"Okay, okay. How about four hundred twenty-five thousand, then?"

"No. That's still too much."

Heather let out a rip-roaring, from-the-gut laugh. It sounded like she might be rolling on the floor.

A deep frown creased Maddie's forehead. "What's so funny?"

"If anyone heard this conversation they would never believe it. The buyer trying to pay more and the seller asking for less."

"It is kind of funny."

"All right," Heather said, "how about a compromise, four hundred thousand?"

Maddie glanced down at the last piece of paper Isaac had sent over. Surely she would have enough for a fresh start.

"Sold." It came out with the finality of a gavel pronouncing the sale at auction.

*   *   *

"Mom, you awake?" David hollered from the front door. Maddie could see him standing at the foot of the stairs looking up. "I don't smell coffee brewing."

"I'm in here." Maddie cleared her throat, suddenly tense with anticipation.

David turned and walked into the kitchen.

"Thanks for coming over, son."

"Mom, you okay?"

"Yes, of course." She busied herself with coffee cups while the espresso machine brewed shots of megadose caffeine. "Muffin?"

David squinted and gave his mother a curious gaze. "Mom, why did you ask me over?"

Maddie cocked her head, watching the young man who looked so much like his father, with the exception of his wavy red hair. "Well, I have some news to tell you." She looked into her son's eyes to see if he was listening. "And I need you to help me tell your sisters. Well, Ruth at least."

David pulled the chrome-rimmed, black-and-white checkered chair up to the table. "Okay, what is it?"

"David, I—" Maddie broke off.

"It's okay, Mom." David reached for her hand. "Take your time. I don't have to be at work until eight. What's this big news?"

Gram's encouraging voice echoed through Maddie's head. It had been her first job interview and Maddie was too scared to go.

"You can do this, Mads. You are stronger than you think."

"No, I can't. I don't know how to do any of this stuff."

"Mads, my sweet girl, you have tucked away all the beautiful things that were placed in you."

Maddie inhaled deep. What was wrong with her? She glanced at her son. "Tell me how your job is going."

"Oh no you don't. You're not going to pull your change-the-subject thing. Tell me your news. You're starting to worry me."

Maddie gave a heavy sigh. "I'm sorry, David."

"Mom, I am an adult. Whatever it is, I can take it."

Maddie stared into her mug, then looked up. "I sold the house."

David's blank look caught her off guard. "The house? What house?"

"This house."

"*Our* house?" David sat poker straight in his chair.

Maddie looked at him in surprise. "My house, David." She gave him a moment to let it sink in.

"Why?"

Maddie took a sip of coffee to collect her thoughts. "You know, your dad vowed when we were in college that he would never be poor like his parents. He said he would do whatever it took to have a better life." Maddie paused. "Actually, I liked his determination. It gave me a sense of security I hadn't felt since before my dad died. Living in poverty didn't much appeal to me either."

"I never knew that, Mom."

"Your dad said coming home to me from his business trips always made him feel safe." Maddie stared into another realm as if Jeff stood in the room. "This house was the symbol of his own success. But the cost was high, David. Maybe too high." Maddie shook her thoughts free from the past.

"It wasn't an easy decision. This house has a lot of memories. But you're busy with work, Bracy's established at college, Ruth has Matt, and I am on my own."

Maddie watched the thoughts turn over in her son's mind. Then he looked directly at her.

"They wouldn't all be good memories you'd be leaving behind, would they?"

Stunned for a moment, Maddie could only stare. But David had more patience than she'd ever had and sat quietly waiting for her. She cleared her throat, tracing the ring from her coffee cup on the glass tabletop.

"Well, your father and I had a few tough times."

"More than a few, Mom." David looked into her eyes. "You don't think I know all about that?"

"You do?" Maddie frowned at the thought of one of her children knowing the dark secrets she'd done her best to keep from them. "How? We were so careful not to discuss any of this stuff in front of you kids. We even waited until we were sure you were asleep before we, ah, talked."

"You mean battled, don't you?"

"What are you talking about?"

"Mom, Ruth, Bracy, and I heard a lot more than you think. I heard him yelling at you, calling you those horrible names." The veins in his neck were strained, his shoulders tight.

"David, I had no idea. I tried so hard to shield you kids from your dad's explosive temper, his drinking, and his aff—"

"Affair?"

"You know about that too?" Maddie was dumbfounded.

David looked down at the mug in his hand. "Yes. But how I know is not important right now." He smiled at his mother. "Tell me about your plans."

"Oh, so *you* can change the subject, but I can't?"

"Yes." He grinned his little boy grin he saved for his mother. "Mom, I hate that you had to go through all that. I wish I would have stood up to Dad."

Maddie reached over and took her son's hand. "I'm sorry you had to hear it. It wasn't just your dad who lost his temper. I did some ranting and yelling myself."

"Yeah, but you never got physical with him."

"I'm *really* sorry you know about that."

David took a sip of coffee, starring into the black mug.

Maddie looked around the room. "You know, honey, your dad always handled everything. I'm sure he probably thought since I didn't finish college I wasn't smart enough to take care of the budget, the bills, house repairs. David, I think it's time for me to learn, don't you?"

"But is selling the house the only—"

"What are my other options? Move in with Ruth?"

David grinned, then sighed. "No, not a good choice. So tell me about your plans."

THIRTEEN

"**S**o what are your plans?"

Nathan shook his head at his business partner and best friend, leaning cross-armed against the windowsill of the conference room. "To get outta Dodge."

"Come on, Nathan. What are you going to do? Where are you going?"

"I just want to disappear for a while. Think things over." Nathan looked Tim O'Leary, square in the eyes. "You know what's-his-name threatened to sick the sheriff on me for flattening his nose."

"Yeah, well, that was a really dumb thing to do. What did it prove?"

"It didn't prove anything, but it sure felt good. I don't get how Chelsea can think she's in love with that jerk."

Tim shook his head and turned toward the window. "Chelsea is a woman who wants a lot out of life, including a guy who appreciates her *talent*. A guy who has clout and a lot of money."

Nathan's nostrils flared. "I appreciate her talent. She's a knockout. Her face, not to mention the rest of her body in the swimsuit edition"—Nathan paced—"has been on more magazine covers than I can count. I gave her an engagement ring the size of Houston."

Tim grinned. "I know, buddy, but—"

"It doesn't really matter. I'm taking some time off. You can handle things here. I'm just gonna get in my truck and drive. Wherever I end up, I end up."

"You *are* going to keep in touch, right?"

"Yes, Tim, I'll keep in touch." When? Now that was another question.

FOURTEEN

inety days passed quickly. Heather had deposited a large portion
of money for the house in an escrow account before leaving for
New York. Her lawyer saw to all the legalities. The paperwork
went through with no problems.

* * *

"Mom, this just isn't like you," Ruth argued. "You've never done anything
so crazy in your entire life. Maybe you need to see a doctor."

"Ruth, I don't need to see a doctor. I need a new life. You told me I
should live life to the fullest."

"I did. But I never thought you would take it to this extreme."

When Maddie mentioned her plan to drive across the country to Jacob's
Bend by herself, Bracy applauded the adventure.

Ruth, on the other hand, put her foot down. "Mom, what are you
thinking? You can't do this. Have you lost your mind? You've never driven
alone more than fifty miles from home. The farthest you've ever gone is to
Grandma's house. And you've never even been to Jacob's Bend."

Maddie took a deep breath. Maybe Ruth was right. But she'd already
sold the house. What if she'd made a huge mistake?

In the back of her mind, Bracy's encouraging words eased her fears.
*"Remember what your Gram always said, Mom. 'You can do more than you think you
can.'"* Her grandmother's long-forgotten words made her smile.

Maddie let out an audible sigh she was sure Ruth could hear all the
way in Texas. "Ruth, I think it's time I stretched outside the confines of
this city."

Ruth's voice was incredulous. "Clear across the country? Mom, at least let Matt or David drive you. Or take one of your friends."

"No. The boys are both too busy to take off work. I'll be fine. This whole thing is an adventure, Ruth."

"But, Mom—"

"No buts, young lady." Maddie smiled to herself. "I'm doing this and I'm doing it by myself. I know you're not used to me taking control of my life, but I have to now that . . . Dad is gone."

"Dad always said you were a woman of extremes. Now I understand what he meant."

"Maddie, you always get ahead of yourself. Why do you do that?"

Maddie had watched Jeff's pacing increase, each rotation around the room bringing him closer to where she sat, uncertain what had triggered his outrage.

"You're always so sure you know best. Well, you don't."

Maddie exhaled loudly. "Ruth, I really believe this move to Jacob's Bend is the best thing for me."

"I don't understand why you would say that."

"I'm just saying I don't know who I am without your dad or you kids here. I've always just been Jeff's wife or your mom. There must be some kind of purpose for my life now that I'm all alone. I need to take the first step and go."

Ruth let out a long sigh. "Mom, sometimes . . ." Ruth took a deep breath. "Will you at least call me and check in every night when you're safe in your motel room? You *are* planning on traveling only during the day, right?"

"That sounds like something your dad would have said." Maddie let out a sigh of her own. "Of course I'll travel only during the day."

"But you've never done anything like this before."

"It never occurred to me that I could. And your dad wouldn't have liked it."

No, he wouldn't. He'd sit, thumping his fingers on his chair arm, seething with anger, eventually stalking toward her.

"Mom, are you there?"

Her daughter's apprehensive response reined in her thoughts. "You don't need to get so upset, Ruth. This is an adventure, not a suicide mission. Yes, I will call every night until I reach Carolyn's house, if you think it's necessary."

"It is *definitely* necessary unless you want me to wind up with an ulcer worrying about whether you're dead or alive."

"Okay, okay. I'll be sure to call when I stop for the night."

"And, Mom, promise me you won't pick up any strangers along the way."

Maddie rolled her eyes. "Ruth, I would never do anything that stupid."

"I'm not saying you're stupid, Mom. Just too trusting. Remember the time you picked up that man, his little boy, and their dog?"

Maddie paced. "That was different. The poor man was stranded. His car died right there in the middle of the expressway. They were miles from the next phone." She'd never admitted out loud how good it had felt to help someone. Not after seeing Jeff's reaction. "Your dad was livid. I still can't understand—"

"Dad was just concerned for your safety, that's all. You have to admit that was a pretty dumb thing to do. You should have been more careful."

"You know, Ruth, sometimes you say some pretty hurtful things."

"I'm sorry, Mom. I know it must be hard for you with Dad gone, living in that big house all alone."

"That will change. Soon. I *promise* to call every night along the route. Does that make you feel better?"

"Yes, it does. Thank you." Ruth's voice calmed. "It sounds like you really have thought through all the details of this move."

"I do have to admit I'm a little nervous about the move after living in the same house all these years. But I'm also excited."

"I'm trying to understand, Mom. But I'll sure miss the old place."

"Me too. But just think how much fun it will be when you come visit me in my new home."

"Yeah, that will be different."

Maddie shook her head imagining Ruth's sour expression. "I love you, Ruth. We'll talk next week."

"I love you too, Mom."

*   *   *

In her quiet moments alone, those conversations echoed in Maddie's mind.

She had thought this through, hadn't she?

Maddie shook her head. She was not a child who needed permission from her kids. And how could Ruth think she would drive alone at night. She wasn't that naïve. And she would never pick up strange people.

"Good grief," Maddie told her jacket as she pulled it out of the closet. "There are a lot of nice people out there. They aren't all deviants and rapists."

It was an adventure. Wasn't it? Maddie's thoughts once again drifted to Jeff. *If he were still alive he would never let me drive from Chicago to the northwest all alone.*

Her heart rate increased. Her face grew hot. She did not need permission from *anyone* to do this. She was going and she was going alone. That was all there was to it.

The most trying part left for Maddie was sorting through twenty-three-plus years of accumulated stuff. Each room flooded her with memories. Some ran wild with laughter; others were set on a secluded shelf in her mind with the hope they might be forgotten.

Cleaning out the attic one day, she voiced her uncertainty into an old mirror. "Madison Crane, you need to look to the future. That's where you'll find who you really are." But what exactly did that mean? What did that look like?

I don't know; you're asking the wrong person.

She rolled her eyes and pointed a finger at her reflection. "Move forward, Maddie. Let go of the past, that's what it looks like."

Only the barest of necessities for her trip to Jacob's Bend were set aside. Sales and donations cleared out the rest.

Looking at the boxes sitting ready for the movers, a chill of excitement tingled down her arms. Jacob's Bend, her home.

FIFTEEN

Walking down Main Street, Ben Farrington slowed his pace to watch the people coming and going from various businesses. Ben smiled and waved at Granny Harper when she stepped out of Harper's Hardware across the street. He loved this little town. Jacob's Bend had become home.

Still, he couldn't help reminiscing about his teen years on his uncle's ranch . . .

* * *

The older cowboys' shouting, jeering, whooping, hollering, and hat throwing outside the corral had egged Ben on. He was determined not to fall off this bronco as he had the last six. From the time he was twelve, Ben knew busting broncs was in his blood. As a young boy, his short stay in Africa with missionary parents was exciting, but living on a horse ranch, herding cattle, sleeping under the stars on the open range during a roundup, that's what he called adventure.

"Ride him, Ben," hollered one of the hired hands.

"Don't let him get the better of you. Show him who's boss. Woo-hoo. Ride him, boy." Uncle Terry waved his cowboy hat in the air.

"Hang on, don't let go now. He's gettin' tired, slowin' down a bit. Hang on tight." Ben knew his aunt Linda still had reservations about her young nephew breaking bullheaded horses.

Ben pulled the reigns back when the horse stopped bucking and took off in a gallop across the dirt pen. He broke into a trot and sauntered over to where Aunt Linda held half an apple in the palm of her hand. The horse gobbled up the apple, snorted, and looked back at Ben as if to say, "You did okay."

"Ben, you did it." Uncle Terry jumped down from the corral fence and walked toward him.

"I told you I would."

"Ah, yeah, you've been saying that for the past six months."

"Well, this time I did it."

Uncle Terry looked up at the boy he now called son. Ben could feel his pride. "That's just the beginning. You keep it up and we'll enter you in the saddle bronc riding competition at the county fair this summer."

"Ah, actually, Uncle Terry, I'd really rather just ride here on the ranch. This is a dream come true for me."

Squinting, Uncle Terry smiled at him. "Okay, son, whatever you want. Your cousins and you will own this ranch one day, you know."

After wiping the sweat from his forehead, Ben settled his hat back on his head and smiled even bigger. "As long as they'll let me work on the ranch and live here, that's all I want."

Terry looked over at his son and daughter. They both loved Ben like he was their true blood brother.

"Well, y'all, it's time to get cleaned up to head back to church for Sunday night service," Aunt Linda said as she walked toward the ranch house.

"On our way."

Linda sent a wave back at the group over her head.

On his way from the barn, Ben looked out over the cattle grazing on acres of green Idaho farmland. He nodded in agreement with an unseen companion. This was the life he was meant to live.

*   *   *

It seems I was wrong. The memories quickly settled back into his past. Ben tipped his hat and opened the door for two longtime residents of Jacob's Bend to enter Lettie's Café.

SIXTEEN

July eighteenth.

The telephone's blaring ring echoed off the walls of the empty house.

"Hi, Mom. You doing okay?" Bracy asked.

"Yeah. Just getting the last few things in place before I hit the road. How about you?"

"Does it sound crazy that there are days when I still think Dad is just away somewhere, like on a business trip or golfing? I know he isn't, but sometimes it feels like it."

"I think it would be sad if you *didn't* have those feelings. I do the same thing. Sometimes I look out the front window and think he'll be driving into the garage any minute or coming through the door, one of his brilliant smiles lighting up the room. Sometimes my heart aches to see him." Maddie took a deep breath. "I know it will get better. It has to."

"Thanks, Mom. I know it will. Just takes time."

"It's a new day, a new beginning."

"You're right." Bracy hesitated. "How in the world did it work out for you to leave on the first anniversary of Dad's death?"

"Like I told your brother and sister, I did not plan for it to happen this way, it just did." Maddie sighed. "Bracy, I'm sad too. But this might be a good thing. I'm looking to the future. Moving forward. Why not turn a sad day into a celebration?"

Was it really going to be that easy to turn off the past?

*   *   *

Maddie remembered a similar conversation with Ruth.

"Celebration? What exactly are you celebrating? Dad's death or your freedom?"

"Ruth. That is a cruel thing to say. Even though we struggled, I loved your dad. I have always loved your dad."

"I know. I'm sorry. I don't mean to say cruel things—they just seem to pop out. There are too many changes."

"I understand. You've never been comfortable with change, just like your—" Maddie stopped short.

"Why do you always say that?"

Maddie shook her head.

"Mom, I'm me. Yes, I have some of Dad's traits, but I also have some of yours."

"You're right. I'm sorry. Let's not fight, okay?"

"What's so wrong with being like Dad anyway?"

"Nothing. Your dad was a wonderful man." Maddie bit away the *if only*.

"I wish you'd get a cell phone." Frustration again. "That way I could keep track of you along the route. What if you have car trouble or something terrible happens?"

"Ruth, we've had this conversation."

"I know, but why on earth did you ship your computer to Carolyn? You could have mapped out the entire trip and even emailed me."

"I like doing things the old-fashion way. I don't like being connected to technology every minute. I want to see sights, stop in out-of-the-way towns, meet people. I'm taking good ole paper maps with me. And if I get lost, what's the big deal? I'll just stop and ask for directions."

"Mom, don't kid about getting lost. It's not funny."

Maddie shook her head. "Ruth, don't be such a worrywart."

"Aren't you in the least bit intimidated about taking this trip?"

"Intimidated? No, I'm excited." Well, mostly excited.

"Well, don't forget to call me tonight, okay?"

Maddie rolled her eyes. "I promise to call every night from my motel room."

"Please promise to be careful. I love you very much."

"I'll be fine. What's the worst thing that could happen?"

"Don't *even* get me started on that list." Maddie could imagine Ruth's green eyes snapping in frustration.

"I promise to be careful and to call. I love you too."

*   *   *

Bracy's gentle voice broke into Maddie's thoughts. "What time are you leaving, Mom?"

"In just a few minutes. I'm putting the last of my things in the car and then I'm off."

"Okay. Be safe. Talk soon. I love you."

"I love you too."

In spite of the excitement, it was still hard when Maddie stepped out the front door of her family home for the last time. Tears welled up and her heart ached as she locked the past on the other side of the door.

Maddie swiped the tears with her arm and shrugged as she stowed the last item in the back seat of her car.

One last tear. One last sniff.

This *was* an adventure.

SEVENTEEN

Mom's tears.

Nathan's memory spun with unforgettable scenes. Drunken anger. Verbal abuse. Hunger. He hung his head. *I don't want to think about anything. I just want to forget.*

After a hot shower, shave, and clean change of clothes, Nathan strolled to the motel office to ask about a place to eat.

"Good afternoon, Mr. Carter. Did you sleep well?"

She seemed friendly enough. "Yeah, thanks. Hey, can you tell me where I can grab something to eat?"

"Well, there's Lettie's Café. That's me, Lettie." She smiled big. "It's right down the street." The woman pointed over his left shoulder. "You can't miss it. It's the cutest building on Main Street." Lettie boasted of her husband's delicious liver and onions. The sound of that dish caused Nathan's stomach to churn.

Lettie beamed with pride. "Now, you be sure and tell Ken I sent you over for a late lunch. He'll take real good care of you. He doesn't usually do the cooking, but the cook is home sick. It's one of Ken's favorite things to do. Cooking, I mean."

For some reason Nathan felt like he had come home when he entered the little restaurant. Ken made him feel like a long-lost friend. This guy was even nicer than his wife. Ken chatted over his shoulder as he prepared food for the early dinner crowd while Nathan savored his hamburger and fries, choosing to forgo the liver and onions.

Nathan hung around Jacob's Bend a few days. The more people he met, the more he liked the friendly little burg. A drive in the country, taking in the peaceful surroundings, helped him decide to stay awhile. Maybe here the haunting nightmares from his past, and the pain that always accompanied them, would stop.

With no houses available to rent in Jacob's Bend, Nathan found one twelve miles out on Highway 47. The old Thompson place.

Happy doing nothing but sitting on the porch of the Thompson house, Nathan relived every detail of his recent painful experience in the city. The ache in his heart was surpassed only by the guilt he felt for how he had handled the situation. After three days of doing nothing but remembering, he got antsy.

Nathan sat in Feinberg's barber chair getting a trim when he spied the calendar on the wall. Big red marks crossed out previous days. July eighteenth jumped off the wall. Nathan closed his eyes. *"Oh, Nathan, honey, it's the perfect day for a wedding. Not too hot, not too cold. We'll have a quiet little ceremony at a justice of the peace and a gigantic reception afterwards at the country club. Won't it be fabulous?"*

Yeah, fabulous. Was Chelsea on what's-his-name's yacht today? Man, was he ever glad they didn't tie the knot. Really, Nathan?

EIGHTEEN

Maddie drove through the city in bumper-to-bumper traffic, cruising past familiar haunts she and Jeff had frequented. A lifetime of memories swept through her mind. *It's time to move on, look to the future. The future.*

Just outside the city limits, Maddie shouted out the window, "Goodbye, big city." To the road ahead she said confidently, "Hello, world."

The freeway soon became a two-lane highway. Breathtaking scenery rose on all sides, stretching for miles. Countless weathered oaks spread across lush rolling hills, their heavy branches content to soak in the sun's warmth. Meadows came alive with vibrant white, yellow, and purple wildflowers.

Ruth was right, she couldn't ever remember driving this far outside the city. She had no idea there was country like this only a few miles from home. What a ridiculously isolated life she'd lived.

Adventure. Excitement. Challenges.

Maybe she'd just strike up a conversation with every person she met. There had to be some interesting characters out there. She was going to live this new life to the fullest, starting right this minute. This was the beginning of the new Madison Crane. Off with the old, on with the new. No more wimpy, isolated housewife. "Look out, Jacob's Bend, here I come." She glanced in the rearview mirror and smiled.

For hours the lush countryside spread before her. When her stomach made rumbling noises, she spotted a flashing red neon sign and pulled into the crowded parking lot. The busy counter at Lu Lu's Diner stretched from one end of the small building to the other, with black vinyl stools inviting patrons to take a seat. Several booths covered with worn, fire-engine red vinyl sat on either side of large, hazy plateglass windows. Deafening chaos came with the lunch crowd.

Maddie took a seat in the first booth that came available. The cook behind a tall counter dividing the kitchen from the serving area looked up and smiled in her direction. She watched him move methodically and quickly to fill orders for the slew of truck drivers and travelers packed into the tiny diner while whistling along with a song that played on the old jukebox. An oldie she recognized, "Why Do Fools Fall in Love." *Yeah, why do they?*

The forty-something waitress, a kickback from the fifties, was a real piece of work. Anabelle hailed from Tennessee, the talkative hostess who worked the register informed Maddie while she waited for a seat. It seemed Anabelle moved north ten years ago after an ugly divorce. Maddie got the impression the hostess wasn't too fond of Anabelle, giving sordid details Maddie would rather have not known.

A twang in her talk, a friendly smile, and a suggestive walk that caused truckers to whistle, whoop, and holler when she sashayed by defined Anabelle's southern heritage.

"Can I get y'all some iced tea, honey?" Anabelle asked with a wink.

Maddie looked up at the waitress, who smiled with her eyes, and nodded. "What's the best thing on the menu, Anabelle?"

The southern belle chomped and popped her gum while giving the question some thought. "Well now, the soup's pretty good, but y'all probably don't want no soup with this here hot spell we're havin'. How 'bout the tuna salad? Ole Jim back there makes it look real pretty on a bed o' fluffy lettuce. Don't taste too bad neither."

"Sounds great." Maddie hoped it wouldn't take ole Jim too long to make it pretty. She was starving.

Mumbling to herself, it seemed impossible to decipher the large chart spread out on the table before her. Reading and following maps had always been Jeff's job. Still, Maddie was determined to conquer the tiny numbers, colored landmarks, and various shaped lines and dots, even if she got lost a dozen times doing it. Sipping her tea, she spotted a sixtyish-looking couple walk into the diner holding hands, laughing. A heavy melancholy fell over her.

All those wasted years battling for control. She always thought retirement would heal past hurts.

The older man pulled out a map and pointed to a northern destination. The woman's eyes lit up.

Look at them, excited about what's ahead. What did she have to look forward to? Glancing around the diner, animated couples occupied most of the spaces. Tears burned, aching to flow. No. She did have a future. Even if it was alone.

Loud voices from two booths in front of her redeemed Maddie's lonely thoughts.

A couple sat with their backs to Maddie. The man sounded furious. "I am leaving, and nothing you can say will change my mind."

"But, honey," the woman pleaded, "I said I was sorry, even though I didn't do anything wrong. There has been a total misunderstanding. I love you."

The man's voice responded heavy with disgust. "You sure have a funny way of showing it."

The woman's shaky response told Maddie she was crying. "I told you, it was not me Calvin saw at the motel on Saturday. I was helping Mary Jane with her baby."

"Why would Calvin make up a story like that?"

"I have no idea. You know he's been jealous of you ever since we started dating. He probably thinks if we break up I'll go back to him. Fat chance. I can't stand that liar."

Anabelle set Maddie's tuna salad down in front of her. "Anything else I can get ya, honey?"

Maddie motioned with her finger for Anabelle to come closer. "Anabelle, do you know the couple in the booth up there?" she whispered.

Anabelle looked up, chomped her gum, and whispered back, "Oh sure. That there's Kenny and Sally Elders. Them youngins are newlyweds. Only been married 'bout six months."

"They seem to be having a disagreement of some kind. Something about a Calvin seeing Sally at a motel."

"That Calvin Sanders, he's nothin' but a troublemaker. He's been fumin' ever since Sally threw him over for Kenny a couple of years back.

There ain't no way that sweet girl did nothin' like that. When did that slitherin' snake say he saw her?"

"Sally said something about Saturday."

Anabelle stood to her full height, hands on her hips. "Well, Lawd have mercy."

Maddie put her finger to her lips.

Annabelle bent over and whispered. "I was right here workin' on Saturday, and I saw Sally clear as day havin' lunch with Mary Jane Anderson. The reason I 'member is 'cause that there baby of hers was quiet. First time he wasn't screamin' at the top of his lungs."

Maddie smiled at Anabelle. "Do you think, I mean, maybe there's some way you could let Kenny know Sally was here with Mary Jane on Saturday?"

Gram's voice. *"Dear Mads, always concerned for the hurting and the underdog."*

Anabelle nodded. "You betcha, and I mean right now."

Maddie watched Anabelle make a deliberate strut over to the Elderses' booth, grabbing a fresh pot of coffee along the way.

She was a slick one.

Anabelle jumped right into the middle of the argument.

"Well, Lawd Almighty, if'n it ain't Sally and Kenny Elders. How all y'all doin'? How was the honeymoon? That Niagara Falls still a'fallin'?"

Maddie took a bite of salad while listening shamelessly.

"Well now, Sally honey, you must be mighty partial to ole Jim's cookin', seein's how you been here twice in three days. I woulda thought Saturday woulda been enough to cure you of Jim's vittles." Anabelle cackled. "It's good to see you again, honey. You too, Kenny. Can I warm up your coffee?"

Anabelle moved past Maddie's booth with a wink and a smile. She sashayed toward the counter, stopping to fill empty cups, sparring with the customers along the way.

Kenny's voice again, humble, quiet. "Wait till I get my hands on that Calvin Sanders. I'll wring his neck."

"No, Kenny, please. Let's just let it go and show everyone he's a liar and a gossip. If we're together, everyone will see he's wrong."

"I guess you're right. What good would it do anyhow? He'd just deny it and find something else to lie about. Thank God Anabelle saw us sitting here. Sally, I'm sorry. Can you ever forgive me?"

"You know I do, sweetheart. We'll forget it ever happened. I love you."
Maddie grinned.

*   *   *

In the short distance she had traveled, Maddie saw sights she had no idea
existed outside the city. And the people made life interesting, spicy. She
couldn't wait to see what the rest of the states she'd travel through were like.

The scenery changed little as she drove the long stretch of highway.
Once on the interstate she would head northwest on route to her new home.

She wondered why she hadn't done this a long time ago. There were
millions of people out there, people with interesting stories, problems, and
solutions to those problems. She wanted to meet them all.

"Maddie, you are a foolish woman." Jeff's voice. *"You are such a woman of
extremes. You can't possibly meet them all."*

Well, maybe not, but she was going to give it her best shot. "What do
you think of that?" She looked over at the passenger seat, imagining Jeff
sitting there shaking his head.

Maddie, you are *a fool. What are you doing talking to an empty seat? Get a grip.*
Glancing once again at the passenger seat, she spoke with confidence.

"I am going to be my own person." She looked to the road ahead. "I am."

NINETEEN

Determination leads you home. Or so the wise sage propounds. Driving west, the sun took its time to rest behind lazy clouds, rays spread wide. On the horizon, red blended with blue in a stunning purple palette.

An old motel with three of its four lights fighting to stay lit became Maddie's rest stop for the night. Dinner at a rundown old truck stop next to the motel brought with it no busy hubbub or couple arguing. One lone waitress stood behind the register filing her fingernails. No smiles. No friendly, "How are you?" Simply, "What can I get you?"

The cook, wearing a long white apron with bulging arms beneath a black T-shirt, sat on a barstool thumbing through a muscleman magazine.

They looked so sad. Hopeless. Empty. Maddie sighed. She'd been there. When you're stuck, with no hope, you just . . . exist.

After her obligatory call to Ruth, Maddie fell into a deep sleep.

*   *   *

Panic shook her awake. Feet tangled in sheets, blankets looped over her head, she was suffocating. Eyes wide. Darkness surrounded her. Maddie yanked the covers from her head and kicked at something on the bed. She searched the room, her breaths quick and short.

Where was she? Breathing hard, she caught sight of her lone suitcase on the floor. A neon sign flashed outside the window of her motel room.

Oh, yeah.

Sitting up against the bed's headboard, she pulled the blanket up to her chin, peeked over the top, and scanned the floor near the bed. Nothing.

Why did this paralyzing fear come at the most senseless times? The nightmare reminded her the realities and fears of life had engulfed her subconscious.

She was seven years old again, her family traveling west on an adventure. Her dad found a three-week construction job along the way to earn some money to help reach their destination. They had rented an old two-room cabin. Maddie remembered it as a shack. The living room and kitchen were all one big space with a door that separated the bedroom in the back of the shack. Mom and Dad slept in the bedroom, along with her older sister, Patricia, who slept on a small rollaway bed. Maddie and her little brother, Dennell, slept in the living room, Maddie on another rollaway, Dennell on the other side of the room in a crib that was too big to fit in her parents' bedroom.

Each night, in the still darkness, while everyone else slept, Maddie kept the vigil, listening for the *click, click, click* of tiny feet. Scratching and gnawing in the kitchen cupboards sent Maddie over the edge of fear into the realm of terror. Quick shadows skittered across the floor. One. Two. Three. She stopped counting at three. She could see them darting toward her bed. There was no way to keep them from crawling up the covers.

She knew if she yelled her mom would just tell her to go to sleep. Her dad could sleep through anything. But why didn't he come and rescue her? She was all alone out here.

Night after night, feeling abandoned by everyone, Maddie tucked the covers in tight around her body, pulled the blanket over her head, and cried herself to sleep.

*   *   *

Maddie reminded herself that had happened years ago. She was a grown woman now.

Yeah, a grown woman terrified of mice.

After sprinting to the shower, Maddie made her way to the motel office to check out. She grabbed a cup of coffee and a Danish. Excitement pulsed through her veins. Or maybe it was the megadose of caffeine from the country brew. Slipping into her car, she looked back at her motel room. It was time to leave that one behind. The nightmares could stay with it.

By midmorning the sun-soaked sky that had been scattered with cotton-puff clouds drifting lazily overhead had morphed into an ominous dark gray. At first only a few drops hit the windshield, but within minutes Maddie found herself in a hammering downpour.

Lightning ignited all around her with the thunder's piercing crack close after each flash. Maddie felt her car sway under the sonic backlash of each roll of thunder. Mesmerized, she pulled to the side of the road to watch the magnificent light show.

Dark, angry clouds vied for dominant positions. One section of the sky resembled a gorge between two ferocious cloud clusters. Lightning bolts ignited from both sides of the gorge, colliding with fierce power. It looked like a major skirmish in the middle of a battlefield. Maddie thought back to a night when she was a child. A particularly violent storm moved through the farm where Gram and Gramps lived.

"Mads, did you know there is a war going on in the heavenlies? The devil's spiritual forces are fighting against God's angels for souls here on earth."

Safe inside the old farmhouse, Maddie had clung to her Gram, terrified at the display of power above the downpour around them.

"Gram, are the good angels or bad forces winning?"

A shiver moved down her back. That was exactly what the surreal display of ferocious darkness and intense light above her conjured up. Maddie envisioned shimmering swords clashing as the lightning bolts violently collided.

A massive surge of water from a passing eighteen-wheeler roused Maddie from her reverie. With no idea how long she had been there, the torrent around her caused her to rethink her situation. She realized she'd better find a safe haven. And fast.

The map showed the next town ten miles away. Pulling carefully onto the highway, Maddie drove at a cautious speed. Rain fell in sheets so thick she could barely make out the lines in the middle of the road. She searched for a road sign for the turnoff to town.

Nothing.

What if the road flooded? She could be washed away. No one would be the wiser. *Why didn't I listen to Ruth and buy a cell phone?* "Madison Crane, sometimes you are too stubborn for your own good," she mumbled.

Then she saw a sign. She could barely make out the words. "Thornton Road Turnoff One-Quarter Mile." That was it. If she could navigate her way through this downpour to that little town, she could find a nice cozy room for the night.

Difficult to see through the heavy rain and driving wind, Maddie slowed to a snail's crawl. Her lights flashed on a sign that read "Thornton Road." Pulling off, she squinted to make out what lay ahead.

A few yards up the road, a bridge sat precariously above the surging water of a river that looked like it could be deep and hazardous. On the other side of the bridge, the only corridor to town, lights shone from friendly windows.

Maddie weighed her options. Stay put and risk being washed away in the flood that would surely come, or take her chances and cross the dilapidated bridge to safety on the other side.

She panicked. *What am I doing out here? I was crazy to think I could do this.* Tears threatened to blur her vision even more. Choosing to gamble, she moved toward the bridge. "I can't believe I'm doing this."

As she crept forward, her car began to slide sideways down the right embankment. All she could do was hold on until her car came to a stop in a small ravine.

Maddie pounded the steering wheel with the palms of her hands. "This is just great. Stuck in a ditch, in the middle of a torrential thunderstorm, threatened by a flood."

Struggling to push the car door open against the heavy wind, Maddie stepped into ankle-deep mud. The door slammed hard behind her. Fighting her way to the rear of the car, she held tight to the door handles, fearful the wind would carry her away. Her two right wheels were stuck in mud to the middle of the rims. Her frustrated kick at the closest tire nearly knocked her off her feet.

Maddie climbed back into the stalled car. Nearly soaked to the skin and shivering from the cold wind and the fear that threatened to seize her, she screamed hysterically, "What am I doing out here in the middle of who knows where? All alone, soaking wet, stuck in the mud?" Her head collapsed on the steering wheel, her tears mingling with water that dripped from her hair.

Jeff never would have gotten himself into a mess like this. She looked into the rearview mirror and wiped her tears.

"Madison Crane, you are a complete fool. You should have stayed right where you were." She shook her head. What was she supposed to do now? She needed help.

Her cry for help had barely left her lips when a pair of headlights flashed in the mirror. A pickup truck sat on the road above. A man got out and hurried toward the driver's side of the car.

Oh please let him be friendly.

The man pointed a flashlight directly into Maddie's face. Shading her eyes with her hand, she rolled the window down about an inch.

He hollered through the slit, "Are you all right?"

Maddie shouted over the howling wind, "I'm fine. But my car is stuck."

No kidding. That was a genius remark.

The man yelled back, "I can see that. Let me pull you out with the winch on my truck. You just put the car in neutral and let me do all the work, okay?"

Maddie vigorously nodded.

The man hooked his truck's winch cable to the car. In a matter of minutes she was out of the mucky ravine, up on the road again.

When he returned to her window, she made hand signals to thank him, but he held up his own hand and motioned for her to follow. Not sure she wanted to do that, she looked over at the truck. A woman and two others were crammed in the front seat, eagerly motioning her to follow.

A man and his family. That should be safe, right?

She could hear Ruth scolding her, "*Mom, what are you thinking?*"

She waved off the admonishment. That little town was unreachable.

Following the truck onto the sodden highway, they traveled cautiously for about five miles, turned onto a dirt road, and drove several more miles pulling into a long, wide gravel driveway. At the end of the driveway sat a lovely ranch-style house. The truck stopped adjacent to the front door. Maddie followed.

Rain pelted the ground. Everyone in the truck, except the man, jumped out and ran for the house. The man ran over to Maddie's car and hollered above the gale-force wind for her to follow his wife. She gladly obeyed.

The entire entourage moved into the entry of the house, shaking the rain from their bodies.

The woman gave Maddie a gracious smile while shaking the water from the coat she had just removed. "I'm Nancy Walters. These are my twins, Grant and Georgia. Oh, and this rain-soaked hero over here"—she gestured to her right—"is my husband, Phillip."

Maddie wrapped her arms around her body. "M-my name is Mad-Madison Crane. Most people c-c-call me Maddie."

Phillip grinned. "Are you all right? When we saw the bridge give way, we thought for sure you were sliding into the river with it."

Maddie looked dumbfounded. "The bridge washed out?"

Grant joined in, "Yeah, we thought you were a goner for sure."

Maddie closed her eyes and took a deep breath.

Nancy broke the silence. "You must be freezing. You're soaking wet. Follow me to the guestroom. You can take a warm shower and change your wet clothes. After you've freshened up, come into the living room and sit next to the fire to get warm. Is there anything Grant can get for you from your car?"

Shivering, Maddie smiled. "Yes, m-my suitcase. Thank you. And thank you, Mr. Walters, for re-re-rescuing me from that ravine."

Phillip Walters's face burned red. He lowered his head. "I'm just glad I was able to help."

Nancy led the way to the guestroom. Grant followed a few minutes later with Maddie's suitcase. It was a charming room, with a queen bed covered by a soft yellow comforter with tiny purple flowers that matched the curtains. Along the right wall sat an antique dressing table and ladder-back chair. Purple and lavender pansy wallpaper covered the back wall, and the remaining walls were painted the same pale yellow as the comforter. The whole effect made her want to grab the quilt at the foot of the bed and bury herself in a good book in the overstuffed chair near the window in the corner. It was one of those cozy rooms that immediately made you feel at home. Maddie spotted a full bath through the open door near the dressing table.

"I love this," Maddie heard herself say.

Where did that come from? This was nothing like their home in Chicago. Glass, chrome, sterile. Who would have thought she would have been drawn to something so cozy?

Her eyes came back to the quilt. One of her favorite patterns. She had made the log cabin pattern many times. Even so, most of her quilts were given away. Too traditional and old-fashioned for Jeff's steel, glass, and stiff taste.

"It's fine the way it is," he'd always answer when she asked to make a change. *"I like the look we have."*

Of course he had liked it. He furnished the house with things handpicked by him to impress his colleagues and clients. Her face heated as she pursed her lips.

Why was she so angry?

Maybe because not a single one of her quilts had graced their home. Her quilts had been banned from the sterile modern environment Jeff created, although her friends and her children all had one of her cozy quilts, custom-made for them.

She had kept one quilt that traveled with her. Tucked away in her fabric closet and pulled out on cold nights when Jeff was away on business trips, she would snuggle up in its warmth and read for hours. Maddie gasped. That quilt was purple, yellow, and lavender.

Nancy gently touched Maddie's arm. "I'll see you in a little while, Maddie."

"Oh, sure. Thank you, Nancy."

Behind a lacey yellow shower curtain, Maddie soothed her body beneath the flow of warm water in the old-fashioned claw-foot tub shower. She would love to soak in a tub full of bubbles. Maybe in the morning. She grinned with anticipation.

Less than thirty minutes later, Maddie, hair tossed and not quite dry, made her way down the long cedar-lined hall toward the living room, stopping to watch the flurry of activity taking place in the Walters' home. While Nancy and Georgia prepared dinner, Grant set the sturdy oak dining room table. Light from an antique chandelier above the table illumined a large round ceramic lazy Susan, complete with salt, pepper, butter, hot sauce, and other accoutrements.

Phillip sat, pipe in hand, at a small table near the living room talking with someone on his ham radio, gathering information about the storm. The person on the other end of the radio reported three bridges washed out and power lines down due to lightning strikes. Several hundred people were without electricity.

Phillip spoke into the radio mike, "I'm sorry to hear that."

"Those poor people."

Phillip spun around at the sound of Maddie's voice.

He smiled. "Oh, don't worry about them. We're used to the electricity failing. They're stocked with firewood, lanterns, propane cook stoves. They'll be fine until the power lines are repaired."

Nancy placed two serving bowls on the dining room table. "We all stock our freezers and pantries and have gas-powered backup generators for these kinds of emergencies. Dinner's ready."

Phillip signed off, laid his pipe in a glass tray next to the radio, and led the way to the table.

The scent of pot roast, potatoes, and carrots made Maddie's mouth water. Her stomach had been making "feed me" noises for the past hour. She couldn't wait to taste the mouthwatering dishes sitting before her.

Phillip took a bite of pot roast and smiled at his wife. "One of the guys on the radio said the storm is slated to diminish somewhat, but continue strong through tomorrow."

Nancy looked over at Maddie. "Why don't you stay with us until the storm lets up, Maddie? We would love to have you. I hate to think of you out in this storm."

It took all of five seconds for Maddie to gratefully accept Nancy's offer.

"Phillip, I can't tell you how thankful I am you came along and pulled me out of that ditch."

"I'm just glad we happened to see your headlights. It was kind of surreal. Your car started sliding into the ravine at the exact same time the bridge washed down the river. That's why we thought you were on the bridge and definitely a goner, like Grant said. We watched for your headlights to move downriver. Your lights stopped, but the bridge kept going. I told Nancy that maybe you weren't on the bridge when it washed out after all. When I got out of the truck and looked over the side, there you were, stuck in the mud. Funny how that happened. By the way, what stopped you from crossing the bridge?"

"Well, I'm not quite sure. I was really scared out there all alone. I had just realized I needed help. It never occurred to me the bridge had washed out. I was on my way to the other side. To town and safety, or so I thought."

Phillip shook his head. "You know, that bridge has been on the county's replace or repair list of old bridges for years. It's been threatening to give way for I can't tell you how long, and with this unexpected heavy rainfall I'm really not surprised it finally broke loose. I'm just glad you weren't on it when it did."

"Me too." Maddie handed Nancy her plate to add to the stack she was taking to the kitchen. "Delicious meal, Nancy. You are a fantastic cook."

Phillip smiled at his wife. "Yes, she is. Sometimes I think we take her loving gifts for granted." Patting his wife's hand, Phillip glanced at the twins.

Nancy's face reddened. "We have homemade apple cobbler. Would you like some, Maddie? With ice cream?"

Maddie smiled at the loving interaction. "You bet. I would never pass up homemade apple cobbler."

Georgia stood, pushing her chair from the table so hard Maddie thought it might crash to the floor. She stomped into the kitchen, dirty dishes in hand.

Nancy shook her head and sighed.

After dinner, everyone turned in early. It had been a grueling day. Maddie read for a while, and then fell into a deep sleep, dreaming of quilts, blue skies, pansies, and cottages with porch swings.

TWENTY

I t's a matter of opinion, isn't it?

Bracy had a hard time keeping her mind on her English teacher's lecture. *I already know all this stuff. I should have tested out of this class and taken something else. That way I could get this semester over with. I thought college would be a lot more challenging.*

"Bracy, your grades throughout your adolescent years are excellent," Mrs. Broughton, her guidance counselor, had told her the summer before she was to attend Wheaton College.

"Thank you Mrs. Broughton. I've always loved school."

"What extracurricular activities were you involved in?"

"Oh, I love to have fun too. I was on the debate team, the school newspaper and yearbook, I was a member of the chess club—"

"All highly academic, mindful endeavors. Were you part of anything that wasn't academic? Were you athletic as well?"

"I was in my friend's church youth group. That's how I discovered Wheaton College. We did quite a bit of community service projects and we went to summer camp."

Mrs. Broughton looked at Bracy as if to say, *And?*

"And I like to swim."

"Competitively?"

"Well, no." For the first time in her life Bracy felt inadequate.

"Did you ever have a job?"

"No, not a paying job. My dad was an investment consultant. He made lots of money. I did volunteer at the local newspaper, though. That's where I decided to become a journalist."

"Did your mother work outside the home?"

"Oh, no. Like I said, my dad made really good money. He liked having Mom at home."

Mrs. Broughton frowned over the top of her glasses. "Your father insisted your mother stay home?"

Bracy could see disgust in her counselor's eyes. "Well, I don't think he forced her to stay home, he just preferred it."

"I cannot understand that logic. Surely your mother wanted to receive training for some kind of career?"

Bracy cocked her head and squinted, trying to think of anything her mom ever wanted to do outside of being a mom and a wife. "Gosh, Mrs. Broughton, I've never really thought about it. All she's ever done is take care of the three of us."

"Humph."

"Maybe I'll ask her the next time I'm home."

"Well, I should hope so. Now, let's get back to your class choices."

Bracy had taken all the classes Mrs. Broughton suggested without questioning whether they would be too easy for her. After all, weren't college classes supposed to be hard? She realized she either needed to get another guidance counselor or sit in on the classes she wanted to take next semester. Every one of her classes right now was so doggone easy—and boring—with the exception of PE.

Heavy sigh.

TWENTY-ONE

Howling winds shook the bedroom windows.

One eye closed, Maddie squinted to look around the room. She pulled the blankets over her shoulders and burrowed deep into a mass of comfort. This was much better than yesterday morning's wake-up call. She shivered at the thought and glanced over the top of her covers to scan the floor.

After a lengthy, soothing bubble bath, Maddie made the bed, placed her things neatly in her suitcase, and headed down the hall. Angry voices drew her to within a few feet of the kitchen.

"You don't even know him, Mom. Why can't you at least give him a chance?"

"He's trouble, Georgia. He causes trouble wherever he goes. It's like he's begging to be locked up."

"Oh, Mom, come on. You're not being fair. Has he ever done anything to you?"

"No, but that's not the point. I don't want him doing anything to you, or should I say, I don't want you with him the next time he loses it. Besides, he's a lot older than you."

"Only two years. He's a senior. Just a year ahead of me in school. Mom, can't you at least meet him?"

Nancy's voice rose an octave. "I've been around him, Georgia. He's cocky and arrogant, always drawing attention to himself. I don't really care to be around people like that, and I definitely do not want to meet him."

Georgia sparred back, "He is cocky sometimes, but that's just because he's so insecure. He needs people to accept him for who he is. You've always taught us to be kind to everyone, especially the underdog."

"This is different. Rumor has it he's been in jail more than he's been out in the last six months. Why?"

"I don't know, Mom. Maybe he's got family problems or school problems or—"

"From what I've heard, he's never in school long enough."

"How can I find out what's bugging him if you won't let me see him?"

Nancy threw up her hands. "What is it about this guy, anyway?"

"It's . . . it's his heart. Under all that tough-guy stuff he's got a big, tender heart. I've seen it. Remember the day we went into town after school to shop for my leather jacket?

"I was sitting on the grass up against that big old oak tree in front of the library, reading my English lit book. Jaime and Scotty Nelson came barreling unsteady, down the sidewalk on their bikes." Georgia gestured with her hands. "They were out of control all the way down the block, traveling way too fast.

"Scotty hit a rock, lost his balance, and went down. Right behind him, Jaime swerved. She went down over the curb and sprawled out in the street. It wasn't a minute later, a car full of kids—they must have been from Henderson High, I didn't recognize them—came speeding down the street at about fifty miles an hour and the driver was looking over his shoulder toward the back seat.

"I jumped up and ran as fast as I could to grab Jaime. Out of the corner of my eye, I saw a flash of blue, headed straight for Jaime. It was Billy. He saved her life, Mom. By the time I got there, she was crying hysterically because of the twisted mess the car made of her new bike and Billy had her cuddled in his arms, telling her it would be okay.

"The driver of the car was in tears, shaking, probably in shock. He thanked Billy over and over and said he would pay for the bike. When Billy saw me run up, he put on the tough-guy act.

"I told him he was a hero."

Her mother's face showed alarm, but Georgia pressed on.

"He was, Mom. But he just shrugged it off. He told Jaime and Scotty's mom she had no business having kids if she couldn't take care of them.

When Billy left I told Mrs. Nelson what really happened. She didn't seem to believe me, but it was true.

"Don't you see, Mom? That's the point. People are going by what they hear, not by who Billy is."

"And just who is he?"

Georgia blew out a blast of frustrated air. "Mom."

Maddie stepped into the kitchen.

Georgia shook her head and stomped out the back door.

"Good morning."

"Good morning, Maddie."

"I gather you and Georgia were having a difficult conversation."

"To say the least." Nancy gave a deep sigh. "She wants to date this boy who is an insufferable troublemaker. Trouble always seems to find him."

"Doesn't it kind of make you wonder?"

"Wonder what?"

"Oh, nothing."

"No, what? I'd really like to know what you think. I could use some wisdom right about now."

Maddie grinned at Nancy's choice of words. "Well, when someone behaves in a way that is, say, less than acceptable, it always makes me wonder why. I mean, they weren't born troublemakers. Something must have happened in this boy's life to cause his rebellious behavior."

Nancy looked Maddie in the eyes, one eyebrow raised. "Hmm. I haven't given him much of a chance, have I?"

"I don't know, have you? Have you ever met him?"

"Well, no. But I've heard so many bad things about him that I really don't want Georgia mixed up with him. We've been having this battle for two months."

Maddie gave the woman a knowing smile.

Nancy glanced out the kitchen window to the barn where Georgia sat sidesaddle on a bale of hay chewing on a piece of hay. She hesitated, obviously thinking something over. "Maybe I'll have Georgia invite Billy over for dinner. That's safe."

"That's a great idea."

Nancy gave Maddie an *I'm not so sure* grin.

A few minutes later, Maddie ducked into the barn, shaking the rain off her jacket, squinting into the warm dimness.

"Georgia? Breakfast is just about ready. Your mom asked me to come out and fetch you."

Just outside the first stall, Georgia sat, elbows resting on her knees, head in her hands. She wiped fresh tears from her cheeks. "My parents don't care about anybody but themselves."

"Maybe they care more than you realize."

Georgia looked up. Tears continued to fall from red-rimmed eyes. "Even Grant is against Billy. He doesn't want me to go out with him either. He says he's the kind of guy who only has one thing on his mind."

"But you don't think that's what Billy has on his mind?"

"How do I know? My parents won't let me get close enough to find out."

"Your parents love you, Georgia. They don't want you to get hurt."

Georgia looked down and picked at the hay. "I might not get hurt. I might be able to help him."

"That's true."

"How can I make them understand?"

Looking into the teen's tearstained eyes, Maddie was about to speak when the clang of a dinner bell rang from the front porch.

"I guess we'd better join your family for breakfast."

Board games, a thousand-piece puzzle of a French farmhouse and barnyard, and listening for some kind of change in the weather on Phillip's ham radio occupied the rest of the morning.

Georgia chose to bake. Maddie watched with some satisfaction as Nancy excused herself to join her daughter. Nancy's soft voice was as sweet as the scent of warm cookies on such a wet afternoon.

"I'm sorry about our argument this morning," Maddie heard Nancy say and saw Georgia's head come up, a look of amazement on her face. "I haven't really given Billy a chance and we can't go by gossip, now, can we?" Nancy smiled, put an arm around her daughter's shoulder, and gave her a squeeze. "If you would like to invite Billy over for dinner sometime, Dad and I would like to meet him."

Georgia's wide eyes sparkled. "Really? How about tonight?"

"Tonight? With this storm—"

"The weatherman predicted it would clear up by midafternoon. Please, Mom. Can I ask him to come over tonight?"

Maddie almost laughed out loud at the dismay on her host's face. "I guess tonight is okay."

Georgia rushed to find her cell phone, searching frantically for Billy's number. Maddie heard Billy pick up after the second ring, his brusque voice carrying across the room. "Yeah?"

"Billy, this is Georgia Walters. You know, from school?"

"Oh yeah, hi, Georgia. What's goin' on?"

"I was . . ." Georgia cleared her throat of the squeak. "I was wondering if you had plans tonight? I'd like to invite you to my house for dinner." Maddie could see Georgia holding her breath.

Long pause. "Ah, really? Sure, I'd like that. I mean, yeah, I guess I could come over, since I don't have anything else goin' on."

The tough guy act again. She doesn't care. He's coming for dinner. Maddie carefully hid her smile from the radiant girl.

"Great. Six o'clock? Oh, do you need directions to my house?"

"I'll find it. What's your address?"

*   *   *

Nancy walked into the dining room and flopped down in a chair. Her announcement sounded more than apprehensive. "Well, it looks like we are having another guest for dinner. Billy Chambers."

Phillip looked at Nancy from across the room, eyebrow raised. Grant shot his mom a disgusted look but didn't say a word.

"Maddie, how about this piece?" Grant asked.

"I think it goes, right—about—there."

TWENTY-TWO

"That's the missing piece I've been looking for." Ben squinted at his Bible and reference books spread over the kitchen table. Sunday's sermon was coming along pretty good. Stretching his arms over his head, he smiled, remembering his studies at seminary.

*　　*　　*

Youth is wasted on the young. So says George Bernard Shaw.

Ben started awake when his roommate came into the dorm room. Ben sat up and rubbed his stiff neck to stimulate the muscles that ached. He had fallen asleep on the desk cluttered with textbooks and his laptop computer, where a picture of the famous playwright, novelist, and political activist, flashed on the screen.

"What time is it?"

"Four in the morning."

"You just getting in?"

"Yeah, we pulled an all-night study hall that turned into a party around twelve thirty. You should have been there, Ben. It was great. Todd's sister invited six of her friends over to spend the night."

Ben groaned and rubbed his back. "How do you guys party all night and pass tests the next day?"

"It's our youth."

Ben smirked at the young guy who was more than ten years his junior. "Very funny. I know I'm slow in starting, but I'm gonna put you young pups to shame. Not to mention you better watch your back. They catch you sneaking in at this hour with anything but pizza on your breath and you're history at this school."

"Believe me, I'm very careful, and I never drink. I'm always the designated driver."

"Well, that's one for your side."

The two flopped into their beds and slept soundly until the six o'clock alarm broke the snoring rhythm.

"Most of you gentlemen are here because you didn't know what to do with what you say is your *calling*." The professor scanned the chamber, studying the young faces. He stopped abruptly when he made eye contact with Ben, who was watching him intently. "You, sir. What is your name?"

"Ben Farrington, sir."

"Well, Ben Farrington, do you believe you were *called* by God into full-time ministry?"

"I do, sir. I kinda wish He would have called me a few years earlier, I'm getting a late start."

Laughter around the room.

"It is never too late to hear God's call, young man. It's hearing and doing nothing about it or taking it lightly"—the professor once again scanned the chamber—"that saddens God."

The students buried their heads in their theology textbooks.

Ben turned to the page the professor quoted. Oh yes, this was definitely what he was *called* to do. No question in his mind.

Ben grinned, taking notes as fast as his hand could write.

*   *   *

He was really glad they'd had tough profs. He had learned how to find the answers to the tough questions the people in his congregation asked. Of course, the best answers always come from heartfelt prayer. Ben smiled and closed his eyes.

TWENTY-THREE

By five thirty the Walterses' house smelled of fresh-baked bread and hearty vegetable beef soup. Nancy made another cobbler. Boysenberry. Maddie set six places at the dining room table.

The rain had stopped around four o'clock encouraging the sun's rays to frame what was sure to be a magnificent sunset.

Billy Chambers arrived at precisely six o'clock. Georgia checked her reflection in the mirror and hurried to answer the door. Maddie could see why Georgia was so taken with the young man.

Billy stood over six feet tall, jet-black shaggy hair cut just below the collar, the deepest sapphire blue eyes Maddie had ever seen and a smile that could win the heart of any skeptic. His black jeans, tan chambray shirt, and black leather jacket did tend to give him a bad boy look.

"Hi, Billy." Georgia encouraged him into the foyer.

Red-faced, Billy looked at the floor. "Hey, Georgia."

"Come in, come in. You know Grant."

Billy offered his hand. "Yeah, hi."

"This is my dad and my mom."

Phillip shook Billy's hand. "Hello, Mr. Walters, Mrs. Walters."

Nancy appraised the young man from head to toe. "Welcome to our home."

Billy pulled his left hand from behind his back and presented Nancy with a large bouquet of yellow daisies. Nancy accepted the flowers, a gentle smile in her eyes.

Billy smiled awkwardly. "My mom always loved fresh flowers. I hope you do too."

"Why, yes. Yes, I do love fresh flowers. Thank you for the thoughtful gesture, Billy. They will make a beautiful centerpiece for the table." Nancy glanced over at Phillip with, a questioning frown between her eyes that said she was not quite sure what to make of this young man.

"Oh, and this"—Georgia steered Billy in the opposite direction—"is Madison Crane."

Grant chimed in. "We fished her out of a ditch last night."

Maddie glanced over at Grant, laughing at his introduction. She extended her hand. "Hello, Billy."

"It's nice to meet you, Mrs. Crane."

"Thank you. It's very nice to meet you too. Please, call me Maddie."

Nancy retired to the kitchen to find a vase for her centerpiece. "Dinner will be ready in a few minutes. Everyone take a seat at the table."

Georgia hung Billy's coat in the hall closet and Grant led their guest to the table.

Maddie sat next to Grant on one side while Georgia relished her seat next to Billy on the other. All eyes were fixed on Billy, who refused to look up from his plate. The silence in the room was stifling.

It wasn't long before Grant had everyone in stitches when he described the scene of Maddie's car stuck in the mud. "After the bridge washed away, Dad saw Maddie standing outside in the pouring rain, waving her arms and screaming at her car. Drenched and treading heavy to the front of her car, he said she looked like a frustrated puppy that paddled fast and struggled hard to rise up out of the river."

Phillip looked in Maddie's direction. "What in the heck were you doing out there all alone anyway?"

Maddie swallowed, and it felt like the bread in her mouth went down whole.

"Well, I'm on what you might call an adventure. I'm on my way to Jacob's Bend, where my best friend and her husband live. Have you heard of it?"

"No, can't say I have."

Nancy tilted her head. "But, Maddie, why are you traveling all alone? Where is your husband? Is he meeting you there?"

"I . . . ah. How did you know I was married?"

Nancy lifted Maddie's left hand. "You can hardly miss that gorgeous diamond on your finger."

Maddie looked down at the table, tears forming. She took a few minutes to collect her thoughts. Clearing her throat, she moved into the explanation for her upside-down life.

"I'm a widow. Jeff died of a heart attack a year ago."

Nancy gasped. "Oh, Maddie, I'm so sorry. We should never have asked so many personal questions."

"No, no." Maddie gathered her composure. "Really, it's all right. I'm beginning to adjust to this new way of life." She smiled and took a deep breath.

"I've learned a lot about myself in the last year. Things I probably never would have realized if . . . Jeff were still alive."

Maddie looked around the table at the gloomy faces and tried to lighten the mood. "It's really been quite an eye-opener. I recently sold the house my husband and I lived in for over twenty-three years. We raised our children in that house. It was silly, actually, one woman living in that big place." She looked down at her ring finger.

"Are you okay, Maddie?"

Nodding at Nancy's gentle touch on her arm, she continued, "I sold most of our possessions. What's left is in storage until I reach the Pacific Northwest." Maddie smiled at the prospect of finally reaching her destination.

Billy joined in, "Is that where Jacob's Bend is?"

"Yes. Alex and Carolyn have lived there for three years. I really miss them. You'd think I would have gone to visit my best friend at least once during that time, wouldn't you?"

Georgia's curiosity seemed to get the best of her. "Didn't you leave family in the city? Don't your kids live there?"

"Yes, my son lives in Chicago, but he's so busy working three jobs, we don't see much of each other. My daughter and her husband are in Texas, and my youngest daughter is at Wheaton College."

"Why wouldn't you live near one of your children?"

Maddie shrugged. "Ruth and her husband asked, but they are practically newlyweds. I can't do that to them; it wouldn't be fair. They don't need Mom hanging around, cramping their style. Not to mention they would be so overprotective they'd track my every move. I *definitely* don't need that.

"No, I need to find my own way. I've never done anything like this before. So far it has been quite the adventure, making this trip across the country—alone. As evidenced by your pulling me out of that ditch." Everyone laughed at Maddie's wide-eyed gesture.

"This trip has brought me in contact with some very special people." Maddie looked around the table.

Billy spoke up, "You are one brave lady. I don't know if I'd be strong enough to do what you're doing."

Maddie bit her bottom lip. "Really? I guess I never really thought of it as taking strength. Stupidity, maybe."

Everyone laughed.

"No, really, Mrs. Crane—"

"Maddie, please. You make me feel like an old lady when you call me Mrs. Crane."

"All right, Maddie. It takes a lot of courage to start a totally new life and make it count for something." Billy looked down at the table. "You've given me a lot to think about."

Maddie smiled knowingly at Billy, having pieced together from the dinner conversation that his mother had died recently. She understood his pain, sensing a sharp stab to her heart, even this long after Jeff's death.

Nancy's suggestion of dessert carried Maddie's thoughts back to those around her. Served in the Walterses' cozy living room, the after-dinner treats of hot boysenberry cobbler smothered with vanilla ice cream, fresh brewed coffee, or ice-cold milk encouraged a warm, comfortable atmosphere.

Once again, Grant started with the jokes. Everyone laughed so hard they were all in tears. When the clock chimed nine Billy stood to leave.

"Thank you, Mr. and Mrs. Walters, for your hospitality and the delicious dinner. It was really great meeting all of you."

He turned to face Maddie. "Especially you, Mrs.—Maddie."

Maddie offered her hand, then pulled Billy into a hug. "It was nice meeting you too, Billy. I have a strange feeling we'll be seeing each other again. You'll have to come out for a visit when I get settled."

The young man smiled and unexpectedly asked, "Would you mind if I wrote to you when you get to your new place?"

"Of course, Billy." Maddie smiled. "I'll send my address to Georgia once I have one. It's a little strange being homeless."

Billy just nodded. "Yeah, it can be." Then he turned to Georgia. "Thanks for inviting me. I guess I'll be seeing you at school. You too, Grant. Good night."

Maddie smiled as the teens walked Billy to the door and closed it behind him. "Well, it's time for me to say good night too. I need to get up early and hit the road."

Georgia scrunched her nose. "Do you have to go so soon? I have so many things I want to ask you."

"I'm afraid so. My friend, Carolyn, is expecting—"

Maddie's face turned grim. "Oh no."

Nancy sat up abruptly at the look on Maddie's face. "What's wrong?"

"I completely forgot to call and check in with my daughter last night *and* tonight. She is such a worrier. She's probably got the highway patrol in six states searching the countryside for me."

"Why don't you call her right now?" Phillip handed her his cell phone.

"Thank you, Phillip."

He smiled and walked toward the kitchen.

"I really need to get a cell phone. My daughter has suggested it more than once," she mumbled to herself since everyone else had cleared the room.

Maddie could only imagine the severe reprimand she would receive. *Might as well get this over with.* The phone rang once.

TWENTY-FOUR

"Nathan, buddy, how ya doin'?"

"I'm good, Tim. What's up?"

"Just checking in to see if my partner is ever gonna come back to work? It's kinda lonely around here without you."

Nathan grinned. "Yeah, right. So, why are you really calling?"

"No, really."

"Tim?"

"Well, Chelsea did call to see if she could get your new phone number."

The hair on the back of Nathan's neck bristled. He frowned at the phone in his hand. "Do not, under any circumstances, give her my number or tell her where I am. You got that, Tim?"

"I hear you. But aren't you just a little curious to know what she wants?"

"No. I don't want to have anything to do with that wit— woman."

"Okay, okay. I'll tell her to disappear."

Nathan took a deep breath and let it out slowly. "Thanks, Tim."

"Seriously, Nathan, when are you coming home?"

"I don't know. I'm just not ready yet. I'm doing odd construction jobs around town. It keeps my mind busy." *When I'm not sitting up all night remembering the mess I left behind.*

"Okay, I get it. Do you need anything? Money? A visit from a friend?"

"No, Tim, I'm good. Really. You just keep our company alive. I appreciate you taking over like you've done. Although you were practically running the business by yourself anyway. You are the brains, you know."

Tim chuckled on the other end of the line. "Yeah, and you're the brawn."

Nathan shook his head and laughed along with his longtime friend. "Call any time. I might not answer." Nathan could imagine Tim shaking his head. "Just leave a message and I'll call you back."

"Very funny. Why don't you use your cell? Why the landline and answering machine?"

"For that very reason. I don't have to talk if I don't want to. Besides, I don't want the locals to know what I do for a living. They know I've done some construction, but that's all they know."

"Oh yeah, your cell phone message. Well, gotta run. Stay in touch, buddy."

Nathan walked to the front window. *What could Chelsea possibly want?*

TWENTY-FIVE

The Walters family walked Maddie out to her car. Hugs and goodbyes followed. When she took to the road, headed once again for her new home, Gram's encouraging words came to her. *"You can do a lot more than you think you can."*

"Maybe I can."

Three hours into the drive she noticed the needle on her gas tank pointed to empty. A passing billboard caught her eye: Gas – Car Wash – Best Soup in the State.

She needed all three, so how could she pass that up? Maddie took the exit onto a narrow road. Her car was filthy from all the rain and mud. And she was starving.

After filling her gas tank and sending her car through the car wash, Maddie went inside the café to feed her growling stomach. An empty seat at the end of the counter gave her an opportunity to peruse the diner. Tough, haggard, good-ole-boy trucker types shared the counter with her. A few looked her way and smiled. She smiled back, a bit self-conscious, and glanced out the window. Half a dozen big rigs sat in the parking lot.

Distracted by the rumbling in her stomach, all Maddie could focus on was the sandwich and fries sitting in front of the man beside her. *This place must have good food if the truckers eat here.* At least that's what her dad had always said.

A waitress broke into her thoughts. "Hi, can I get you something to drink?"

Corrie, according to her name tag, probably no more than eighteen, a tiny thing, all of about five feet tall, showed a dimple in each cheek when she smiled.

"Iced tea, please."

"Comin' right up."

Maddie watched her move behind the counter from customer to customer like a bee buzzing from flower to flower.

"What's the soup of the day?"

"Homemade chicken noodle with carrots and celery."

"Sounds delicious. I'll have a bowl of soup and a roll."

"Comes with a small loaf of sourdough."

"Even better."

Halfway through her soup, Maddie heard a commotion in the kitchen.

"You can't leave, it's time for the lunch crowd. You know all the truckers and military people we get in here."

"I have to go. It's my first baby and I'm gonna be there when he comes into this world. My face is gonna be the first one he sees, with the exception of his mama's."

"He? How do you know it's gonna be a boy?"

"I just know, that's all. Besides, we ain't got no girls' names picked out, so it's gotta be a boy."

Corrie came out of the kitchen, a look of panic on her face.

Maddie's curiosity got the best of her. "I couldn't help but overhear. Is someone back there having a baby?"

"Well, not someone back there." Corrie's dimples flashed. "Our cook's wife. It leaves us in a world of hurt. Tom, the owner, doesn't cook and out of the three waitresses on duty, Velma's the only one who has ever done any fry cooking. I could cover her tables, but then who would cover the counter? We'll just have to close the counter for today. That'll really back us up."

Maddie's mind reeled with crazy thoughts. Should she offer to help? *No, I can't. Oh, why not?*

Her wild heartbeat made her think twice, but she heard her own voice say, "Ah, I could cover the counter."

Madison Crane, what are you doing? Are you crazy?

"You can do a lot more than you think you can, Mads."

Oh Gram.

Corrie eyed her hopefully. "Have you ever worked a counter before?"

"No. But I helped in the snack shack when my son played football." Maddie hoped that would suffice.

"Good enough. Here's an apron and a tablet. Thanks. By the way, what's your name?"

"Maddie."

Corrie stared past her to the front door.

"Okay, Maddie, get ready, because here they come."

Maddie turned to see a line of cars and big rigs pull into the parking lot. *Here goes nothin'.*

With only sixteen stools at the counter, they filled up fast. When one became empty, another body quickly occupied the space. The first two customers Maddie served were easy. Hamburgers, french fries, and soda. She was surprised to discover the rhythm of the diner's service came easy to her.

Maddie hardly noticed the time pass during the two-hour lunch rush. She met some pretty colorful characters and even learned a little diner lingo.

"Order up," Velma called from behind the counter.

"On it," Maddie hollered back.

When she served a thirty-something man dressed in greasy overalls soup and a sourdough loaf, he gave her a chew-toothed grin and spit into his soda can. "You new round here? What time you get off work?"

Maddie's face flushed red. She looked around to see if anyone was watching.

"Here, let me freshen your coffee," she said to a man at the far end of the counter, filling cups along the way.

A handsome man who looked to be in his fifties, dressed in Dockers, a blue shirt, and tie, patted Maddie's hand. "You have to watch out for that guy." He nodded toward the other end of the counter.

Maddie smiled and patted his hand in appreciation for the warning.

His eyes made a cursory journey over Maddie's body.

Velma called out Maddie's order.

"On it."

Velma closed in on Maddie. "Watch your back, sweetie. That one," she said, casting her eyes on the well-dressed man, "is a weasel. You be careful with that hand-pattin' stuff."

"I didn't mean—"

"I know that, and you know that, but these guys take that as an invitation. Get my drift?"

Maddie sucked in air. "Really?"

Velma lifted an eyebrow and nodded.

By the time two thirty rolled around only a couple of stragglers sipped coffee. A shrill ring came from the wall behind the cash register. Tom grabbed the phone. "It's Jerry. His wife is still in labor and he doesn't know how long it's gonna take."

Corrie shouted back, laughing, "I could've told him that. My sister's first baby took eighteen hours."

"Do you think you'll make it back for the dinner crowd?" Tom scanned the diner. "That's okay, Jerry, we know what it's like. Besides, we have a new employee. Ms. Madison Crane is helping us out. Doing a darn good job too."

All the employees cheered and clapped. Maddie stared at the floor, hoping no one saw her blush.

Tom turned his attention to the woman behind the grill. "Velma, you okay back there?"

"Yeah, I'm fine. Tell Jerry not to worry, I've got it under control. But I definitely *do not* want his job."

"You hear that, Jerry?"

"Jerry says thanks, everybody."

The waitresses returned to filling salt and pepper shakers, catsup bottles, and coffee creamer dishes.

Tom walked to where Maddie wiped the counter. "I really appreciate you helping us out, Maddie. I guess you heard the conversation with Jerry."

"Yeah, he sounds a little flustered."

"Aren't we all with our first baby?" Tom rubbed the gray stubble on his chin. "Maddie, would it be possible, could you—"

"I would love to stay and help with the dinner crowd. Is that what you were going to ask?"

Tom smiled. "You saw how crazy it gets in here." His large meaty paws shook her hand vigorously. "Thanks, Maddie. I really appreciate this."

"Is there a motel nearby where I can get a room for the night?"

"Sure, the Cottonwood. It's clean." He laughed. "And the only one in town. Let me pay for your room. And of course I'll pay you for all the hours you work."

"Oh, no. That would spoil everything. You have no idea what this is doing for my self-confidence. Never in a million years would I have thought I could waitress a counter. My kids won't believe it."

"I couldn't possibly let you do this for nothing."

"Oh, yes, you could and you must or I won't help with the dinner crowd." Maddie folded her arms in defiance.

Tom threw up both hands in front of his face. "Okay, okay, you win. Thanks."

"It is truly my pleasure. It's been fun. I think I could learn to like this job."

They fed even more during dinner. Though hectic, Maddie loved the activity and interaction with the people. By the time she checked into the motel her feet were swollen, her back muscles ached and her neck was stiff. Man, was she ever out of shape. She could use a massage.

Instead, she settled for a warm water massage in the shower. Before dozing off, she checked in with Ruth.

"Hi, hon. You will never believe what your mother did today."

"What did you do now—go up in a hot-air balloon?"

Maddie rolled her eyes. "I was a waitress for a day."

"You what? Mom, why on earth would you do something like that?"

"It was fun. I stopped at this little diner for lunch. The cook had to go to the hospital. His wife was having a baby. They were shorthanded, so I volunteered to work the counter."

"And they let you? Didn't you tell them that you've never been a wait-ress before?"

"Yes, I told them. It didn't matter. They even taught me how to work the cash register."

"Oh, Mom, really."

"Oh, Mom, what? I told you I am going to try new things."

"What does that mean? You aren't going to try anything dangerous, are you?"

"Ruth, I'm not trying to kill myself, just take a stab at life. Do things I've never done before."

"Why?"

"Because I can. Your dad was so overprotective. He hovered over me."

"Dad just wanted to make sure you were safe. Just like I do. Mom, this trip—"

"Ruth, let's not argue. I'm really tired from working today."

Heavy sigh on the other end of the line. "Okay, Mom, I'll let you go. But, Mom, don't do anything stu— Please be careful. I love you."

Maddie shook her head. "I love you, too, sweetheart."

Within seconds she fell into a sound sleep, until a knocking startled her awake. Dragging herself out of bed, Maddie wiped the sleep from her eyes and looked through the peephole in the door. No one there. Wary, she slowly opened the door, making sure the chain latch held secure. Squinting, she raised her hand to block the sun's glare. A tray sat on her doorstep with a note: *It's a girl. Madison Joy. Jerry's way of saying thank-you. Thanks for all your help. The crew at the diner.*

The tray held coffee, a fresh-baked cinnamon roll, eggs, bacon, toast, and a paper sack. Inside the sack, a ham and cheese sandwich, chips, 7UP, and a piece of apple pie sat under another note: *One for the road. Thanks, Maddie. Be safe.*

Maddie sat at the tiny table in her room, a bite of cinnamon roll in her mouth, a big grin on her face. This was a beautiful world with some wonderful people. Here she was, trying to help them out and they helped her see she could do more than she thought she could. *I think I'm beginning to like this new Madison Crane.*

At that exact instant an overwhelming sense of loneliness swept over her.

Jeff, why couldn't we have done this? We could have traveled, had so much fun together. How could you go and leave me all alone?

Furious with Jeff, Maddie held her face in her hands, tears seeping through her fingers. Once again he had left her. This time forever.

By the time she ate, showered, and dressed, the clock showed nine. Resting her lunch in a small ice chest, she hit the road. Today she would connect with the highway that would take her to Jacob's Bend.

TWENTY-SIX

Ben couldn't thank his aunt and uncle enough for all they'd done for him throughout his life, especially after his parents died. They helped him make major decisions and encouraged him to take counsel with others when they just didn't have the answers. Like how to get a job.

*   *   *

Fresh out of seminary, Ben sat at his aunt Linda's dining room table staring at a computer screen, scanning the classified ads across the country. "They never told me it would be so hard to find a job as a pastor."

"Don't they have a site especially for ministry jobs?" Aunt Linda asked as she chopped carrots for beef stew.

Ben's dazed eyes found his aunt in the kitchen. "That's where I've been for the past two hours."

"Oh."

"I'm not too sure what I'm looking for exactly."

"Well, God will show you what, where, and when. Isn't there a church here in Idaho, preferably near the ranch, that might be hiring?" She smiled, her eyes bright with anticipation.

"I wish. That would be perfect. But I don't see a thing. Maybe I should start as a youth pastor or even a janitor, just to get my foot in the door?"

"Hmm, somehow I don't think that's how it works," Uncle Terry spoke from his office.

"Yeah, you're probably right. Any ideas or suggestions?" Ben glanced from the office to the kitchen.

Uncle Terry looked up from the ledger spread across his desk. "Why don't you go see Pastor Charley? He knows you, practically raised you along with us. If you weren't here with your cousins, you were at his house riding his horses. He might have some ideas."

"Thanks, Uncle Terry, that's a great idea."

*   *   *

"Pastor Charley." Ben shook the elder man's strong hand.

"I think you're old enough now, Ben, you can call me Charley. Especially since we're not anywhere near the church."

Ben smiled at the man who helped shape his faith in God and encouraged him to follow the call God put on his life. "Okay, Charley. Now that I've finished my schooling and seminary, I don't know what to do next. How do I find a church that needs a pastor?"

Charley looked into Ben's questioning brown eyes. "What say we take a ride?"

"I would love that."

Ben once again rode his favorite horse at the Winston Bar M Ranch. His pastor not only knew the Bible, he knew horses and raised them, same as Ben's uncle, Terry, did.

Spade seemed to know his rider and pawed the dirt, raring to go. Ben gently kicked Spade's side. He took off into the wide-open spaces on a wild gallop. Charley's horse tore out after them and the race was on.

Just before they reached the river, the horses slowed a bit and then stopped for a drink. "Spade hasn't lost his speed," Ben said, breathing hard.

"No, he's determined to win, no matter the challenger." Charley grinned.

The two men took the horses on a slow stroll along the river.

"Ben, God called you to be a pastor; He will surely show you where. And it may not be one of those places you are looking at online. God is very creative in placing us exactly where He wants us."

Ben nodded at his mentor. "You're right. Why am I in such a hurry to make this happen myself?"

"Why not just enjoy some time on the ranch and rest after all the long hours and hard work you've put in. I know you love being there and God will definitely let you know when it's time to move on, and where that might be."

Ben relaxed in his saddle, admiring the beautiful countryside. "You're right, Charley. Thanks."

TWENTY-SEVEN

Back on the highway, the countryside streamed past Maddie's window. She passed an old farmhouse and dilapidated barn on her left. A calf ran crying after its mother in a green pasture. A large blackbird cawed when her car approached his roadkill. It brought back so many memories of Gram's place.

Swerving to miss a jackrabbit preening his long ears, Maddie corrected just in time to miss a truck in the opposite lane. She sucked in air, looked in her rearview mirror, and swerved back onto the highway from the shoulder.

"Good grief. Stop daydreaming and keep your mind on the road, Maddie."

After refueling, she grabbed her sack lunch and spread a blanket on the grass under a shade tree in a small park next to the gas station. A family of five sat on the other side of the park sharing lunch, watching the youngest of three children chase butterflies. He ran so fast that he tripped over his feet when he reached for one of the butterflies. The entire family roared with laughter at the sight of the little guy when he missed his target and ended up facedown in the only mud puddle in the park. Maddie giggled as the scene unfolded. He seemed more upset at not catching the butterfly than being covered with mud.

She missed the days when the kids were little. The funny things they did. They were their entertainment when she and Jeff were first married. They didn't have a lot of money to go out on dates. Those were sweet days.

The confidence that had been so sure that morning suddenly deserted her. Was she crazy to be doing this? How did she let Carolyn talk her into leaving her home? Heavy sigh. Oh, yeah. No Jeff. No kids. No home.

Maddie took another bite of her ham sandwich. What had happened to her determination to stop feeling sorry for herself? *That didn't last very long.* She had to believe this was the right thing to do, even if she didn't know what tomorrow might bring.

Packing up her leftovers, she strolled back to the car and turned to give one last glimpse at the happy family.

Inside the car she spoke to the passenger seat, "I *do* believe, and I'll prove it by not turning around and heading for home."

Glimpsing the road in both directions, she whispered, "Home. Except I have no home now." She breathed deep as her thoughts circled.

What would Jacob's Bend be like? Some small towns could be cliquish. Outsiders didn't always get an open-arm welcome. She tapped the steering wheel with her index fingers. "How would you know?"

Resting her head against the headrest, she finished the debate. "Stop doubting, Maddie. Now. It doesn't do any good to look back; you can't go there. Make up your mind that you will not look back. No. Looking. Back."

She looked out over the stretch of road before her. A soft smile formed on her lips. Even though it was slow in coming, confidence told her to take whatever came her way with excitement, still believing it was an adventure.

That assurance carried her until early afternoon, when a yawning drowsiness threatened to overtake her. She decided to stop at the next town, do a little shopping, grab a snack. Maybe she could find a good book to read in her motel room.

A piquant little village, Cooley River had one gas station, a café, post office, general store, and a few other small businesses. The shop that caught Maddie's eye had a sign that read, "Rare Jewells—Old Tomes and a Few New Treasures."

She loved old bookstores. They had the most intriguing finds.

A tiny bell above the door jingled when she walked in. The scent of weathered leather and musty pages caused her to close her eyes and breathe deep. She looked around. "Hello. Hello, is anyone here?"

An elderly woman stuck her head out from behind a partition near the back of the store. Bowing her head slightly to look over the top of her glasses, she answered in a high-pitched voice, "Hello, there. I'll be right with you. Go ahead and have a look-see."

Maddie soon lost herself among the shelves as title after familiar title caught her eye. Arms overflowing with books, she made her way to the overstuffed chair in an inviting alcove at the front of the store. Three sides of floor-to-ceiling windows allowed the sun to embrace the reading space with warmth and light. So taken with her books, Maddie didn't notice the little woman standing beside the chair smiling down at her.

"You like old books, huh?"

Maddie's head shot up. "Oh, yes. These authors knew how to tell a good story." Smiling, she extended her hand. "Hi, I'm Madison Crane."

"Nice to meet you, Madison Crane. I'm Jewell. This is my store."

"Please, call me Maddie."

Jewell smiled. "Okay, Maddie."

"How do you ever get any work done? I'd be sitting right here reading all day."

"It is a dilemma. Some days that's exactly what I do."

The two women giggled, sympathetic to the temptation.

"Would you like some iced tea, dear? I have some lovely blueberry tea from England."

"I would love some tea if you'll sit and sip with me."

Jewell looked over her shoulder at the antique clock on the wall. "I'm in such a dither this afternoon. The annual art show begins today. I just finished framing my last entry. My friend said she would take them over for me, but she's stuck behind an accident on Highway 86. Traffic is stopped dead. I'm not sure what I can do except close the store and take them over myself." Jewell scratched her head. "What would you think about taking one of these books to your car to read while I run my paintings over to the old firehouse? We can sit and chat when I get back."

The wheels in Maddie's mind spun again. Should she offer to help? No, Jewell would probably think she was pushy. She didn't even know her. Maddie glanced up at the distressed woman. *You'll never know unless you ask.*

"Jewell, I have a thought. I know we've just met and you don't know me, but what would you think if I tended the store for you while you are gone? That is, of course, if you feel you can trust me. I've always wanted to work in a bookstore. Besides, you'll only be gone a short time, right?" Maddie grinned at the frantic woman.

Jewell's gentle smile, small round frame, and bun that topped her gray head reminded Maddie of a loving grandma who would drop everything to sit and listen to the tales her grandchildren had to tell.

Jewell looked into Maddie's green eyes. "Actually, I'm an excellent judge of character. Not to mention I'm rather a rogue risk-taker. Besides, I really hate to miss this show. Art collectors and dealers come from everywhere. Actually, it's quite a large show. Artists from all over the country exhibit their work." The older woman rubbed her chin, eyes searching the ceiling. "I have no doubt whatsoever you are trustworthy. That sounds like an excellent idea. Thursdays are usually pretty slow. But you must agree to let me pay you."

"I don't want money for doing something I love to do. Besides, you just said this would be a slow day. I'll probably sit right here in this comfy chair reading the whole time you're gone."

Jewell frowned beneath her half-glasses. "Well, how about this? For every book you sell, I will split the sale with you. If you say no, I just won't go to the art show." Jewell stood firm, arms crossed over her full bosom.

Maddie had a feeling Jewell would not budge. Well, since Thursdays were usually slow anyway . . . "Okay, if you must."

"Good."

"If it's not too much trouble, could I see your paintings?"

"Of course, dear. I'll just go and collect them."

Jewell walked through a narrow pathway to the back of the store and returned with her arms full of framed canvases. Two were abstracts, another a meadow scene, the fourth a beautiful cobalt blue vase full of vibrant spring flowers. When she began to explain the background of the paintings, Maddie held up her hand, a mischievous look in her eyes. "Let me guess the story behind each painting."

Jewell's smile seemed to say, *I like this woman.*

"These are exquisite, Jewell. You're a very talented artist."

Maddie studied the paintings carefully and felt the abstracts must have been painted at a particularly sorrowful time in Jewell's life. The vase with delicate wildflowers, a gift from a secret admirer. The meadow scene captured her completely. As she studied it, a light went on in Maddie's brain. "Where is this place?"

"I really couldn't say dear. An old friend painted it for me some time ago. It won't go up for sale like the others. I just thought people should have a chance to view its beauty."

"Ah, an old heartthrob, huh?"

Jewell blushed slightly. "I guess you could say that."

Maddie was certain. This was the same meadow in Jonathan's painting, now hanging in his room at Southside Manor. The one Heather was named after. This had to be the same meadow. *Look at the old birch tree in the background with that odd branch that forms a natural seat.*

"I believe I know someone else who has a painting by this artist. I'm sure it's the same meadow. No doubt from another viewpoint and a different time of day. This painting is a bit smaller than my friend's. And the red poppies are more vibrant in your picture."

Jewell gave a questioning glance at the painting, then back at Maddie. "I love red poppies."

"Really? Me too."

Maddie recounted Jonathan and Julia's precious love story for Jewell. The older woman's eyes sparkled.

"This *is* the same artist, isn't it?" Maddie asked.

"Yes, I believe it is. Many years ago we were very much in love. This painting was an engagement gift."

Maddie's eyes twinkled at the telling of a good story. "Oh my goodness, Jewell, tell me what happened."

"Well, his mama and daddy didn't approve of me. They forced him to break off the engagement. They had his whole life planned and it did not include me. The girl they chose for his wife came from a wealthy family with valuable business connections.

"The last time we saw each other he tried to talk me into running away to elope. I couldn't do that to him. His parents had money. They swore to disinherit him if he didn't marry the other girl. He told me he didn't care that his parents would cut him off, he loved me and wanted to spend his life with me, not some spoiled rich girl. But he would have been miserable if we had eloped. I just know it. We had a terrible fight. I told him I didn't love him and to stay out of my life." Tears formed in Jewell's eyes.

"I'm so sorry."

Jewell smiled softly at Maddie. "That was a long time ago. I've toyed with the idea of selling the painting, but just couldn't bear the thought of some stranger hanging it in a back room somewhere, not understanding the painting's special meaning."

Maddie nodded her understanding.

Jewell glanced up at the clock. "I must run, dear. Sell lots of books, now."

"I'll just curl up here in this cozy chair and read until you get back. And, Jewell, if it would make you more comfortable, why not take the money from the register with you?"

Jewell looked over her shoulder as she headed out the door, paintings in tow. "Oh, that's not necessary. I told you, I'm an excellent judge of character."

Maddie gave a contented sigh and turned to the titillating stack of books she had taken from the shelves. *Now, what's it gonna be? Mystery, love story, suspense?*

Before she could open a cover, the bell over the door jingled. She looked up to see a young girl about twelve or thirteen years old, hair disheveled, dress wrinkled and stained. A few of her toes poked through holes in worn tennis shoes.

Maddie welcomed the girl. "Hello. May I help you?"

The girl looked at Maddie and immediately bowed her head, staring at the floor. Fumbling with money in her hand, her voice hesitant, she whispered something Maddie couldn't hear.

"I'm sorry, what did you say?"

"Is Jewell here?" The girl looked beyond Maddie to the back of the store.

"She's gone out. Can I help you with something?"

"Um . . . ah . . . I've been saving my babysitting money to buy a book Jewell is holding for me. *Little Women*."

"That is a wonderful book. Have you read it? No, of course not or you wouldn't be buying it, now would you? Let me look behind the counter. What's your name?"

The girl looked down at her feet. "Sandra Givens."

"Yes, here it is, right here."

Sandra looked up and smiled big.

"This note says it's paid in full."

"Huh?"

"Yep. So I guess the book is yours." Maddie handed Sandra the book.

The bell above the door jingled. An elderly gentleman entered. Maddie gave him a quick nod and a smile.

Sandra's eyes grew big as she clutched the book to her breast. "Thank you, thank you. Please tell Jewell I said thank you. Thank you very much."

Maddie watched the delighted girl twirl and skip down the sidewalk, holding her book tight.

While the man perused some books on the other side of the shop, Maddie pulled a twenty-dollar bill from her wallet and placed it in a little red box she found under the counter to hold the day's sales. She wrote *Little Women* at the top of a list of books sold.

"Excuse me. I said, excuse me."

Maddie looked over at the frowning man. "Yes, how can I help you?"

"Could you get that book on *Little Known Facts* down for me? There, on the top shelf. I can't reach it."

"Of course. Let me get the ladder."

The bell chimed over the door, and continued ringing all afternoon. Maddie didn't have a minute to sit down, let alone dive into any of the books she had chosen. By six o'clock her feet ached and her neck was stiff. When she counted the money in the little red box, it came to a grand total of four hundred fifteen dollars.

If this is a slow day, I wonder what busy looks like. A mischievous grin snuck across her face. *Jewell is going to regret her offer.*

At six fifteen Jewell walked in, all smiles. "The old firehouse is packed with paintings, artists, buyers, and dealers. What a fun time. I'm sorry I was gone so long. I couldn't help myself. I loved seeing all that beautiful art and catching up with friends I only see once a year. How did it go here? How many books did you read while I was gone?"

"Not a single one."

The little woman glanced over at the stack of books that sat on the lace-covered table next to the chair. "What?"

"This place has been filled with customers all afternoon. These people either heard how unique your establishment is or they're bored stiff with the junk on TV."

"You're kidding?"

"Nope. We sold over four hundred dollars worth of books today."

"That's unbelievable. Do you want a permanent job?"

Maddie laughed and handed Jewell the red box.

Jewell pulled out a wad of bills. "A deal is a deal. Here is your share, two hundred twenty-five dollars."

"That's more than half."

"Close enough."

Maddie took the generous woman's hand in hers. "Jewell, I really don't want the money. You will never know how much fun this was for me. How about if you give me a couple of these books here as payment?" Maddie pointed to the stack on the table.

Jewell opened her mouth to object, but stopped. "I can do better than that." Walking over to the door, she picked up the meadow painting. She touched it lovingly and handed it to Maddie.

"I can't possibly take this, Jewell. No way."

"Maddie, I probably won't be around that much longer. I don't want this painting stuffed in someone's attic somewhere. I told you, I want someone to have it who appreciates the story behind it. Someone who will cherish it. I know you will do that."

Maddie stared at Jewell, not knowing what to do.

"Please. It would give me great pleasure if you would accept the painting as a gift."

Thankful for this new friend and the incredible gift she offered, Maddie felt her tears threatening to spill. Maddie caressed the painting with her hand. "Thank you, Jewell. I don't quite know what to say."

Jewell watched Maddie admire the painting. "You've already said it."

Maddie hugged Jewell with her free hand. "I promise this painting will be the first thing to find a place in my new home. A place of honor. I will think of you whenever I look at it."

Jewell grinned. "Maybe I'll have to come for a visit."

Maddie left the painting in the car in the Cooley River Café parking lot and walked down Main Street, stopping at the general store. The place looked to be at least a hundred years old with all the necessities of life, from alfalfa and lanterns to boots and yardage. A clerk wheeled merchandise past her that had been outside, preparing to close the store. Inside, a cold potbelly stove sat in the middle of the store with a table and two chairs filled by two elderly gentlemen, replete with overalls and Coke bottles, playing chess.

It looked like a scene out of a Norman Rockwell painting. She hoped Jacob's Bend was exactly like this. Well, maybe a little bigger. She guessed she would find out in a couple days.

The men looked up and smiled when she walked past to check out the treasures that beckoned from the back of the store.

They readily interrupted their game to answer her question on her way out.

"Is there a motel close by where I might get a room for the night?"

"There's the Jolly R, 'bout six miles north, right off the expressway. Ain't much to look at, but the rooms are clean and the beds comfy, from what folks say."

Maddie smiled. "Jolly R it is."

TWENTY-EIGHT

Hands shaking, Nathan ripped open the envelope.

Sneering at the handwriting, he told himself to calm down. He couldn't believe Tim forwarded this letter to him. He thought he'd made it clear that he was done with her.

Dear Nathan,

First let me say I think your actions the last time we saw each other were reprehensible. Frederick's face is still tender from when you brutally ambushed him. I'm sure he would have been able to defend himself had he known what was coming. Be that as it may, my reason for writing is to say that the prenuptial agreement you and I signed said if for some reason the engagement was called off, you would pay me a substantial amount for damages. I've seen a lawyer and he assures me I have a solid case and that any judge would most certainly rule in my favor. Especially since I'm so well known in society. Oh, yes, that's right, you hate that, don't you?

I would like to keep this as simple as possible and out of court. So if you will just write out a check for the full amount in my name and send it to me through your business partner, Timothy O'Leary, I won't be forced to do something that could potentially hurt us both.

Sincerely,
Chelsea Hodges

Send her a check? She had to be kidding. Nathan tore the letter to shreds, then burned it in the kitchen sink.

He paced throughout the house. Who did she think she was? Fat chance she'd ever get a dime out of him. *We'll just see what my lawyer has to say about this.*

The walls started to close in on him when he recounted Chelsea's threats and arrogance. He needed to hit something. To slam his fist through a wall. Something. Nathan grabbed his keys. The tires on his truck spun and squealed on the dirt road and then onto the highway.

"Especially since I'm so well known in society. Oh, yes, that's right, you hate that, don't you?"

Drive, Nathan. Just drive. That would help him calm down. He needed to find a nice, quiet moonlit grove of trees and walk this off.

"Yeah, that should help."

TWENTY-NINE

Darkness surrounded her.

A thumbnail moon and myriad stars adorned the black sky. Tired of being cooped up in her car, weary of sleeping in a different bed every night, and especially burned out on restaurant food, Maddie was ready for her travels to end. When she called Ruth from the gas station, she conveniently neglected to mention she planned to drive all night if necessary.

After six days on the road, she was anxious to reach Jacob's Bend. She missed having her own things around her. What would it be like to have her own house? One she would live in without Jeff? Lonely.

"Let's face it," Maddie told the dark sky, "I need roots." She was crazy to think she could pick up and move like a gypsy. She shook her head. *Madison Crane, you are a fool.*

Carolyn assured her Jacob's Bend had a friendly group of people living within its borders. But would they welcome a widow from the big city unaccustomed to living on her own? Why was she crying again?

At that moment her stomach let loose a sound that resembled a starving bear cub. Glancing in the rearview mirror, she wiped the tears, patted her stomach, and chuckled. She was *really* hungry. What time was it, anyway?

The clock on the dash read nine forty five. Her hope to make the last leg of her journey without stopping faded. Light-headed, she checked her fuel level. The gas tank was running low, not to mention her blood sugar.

Another growl.

She needed to stop at the next place that served food. Carolyn had said there weren't many restaurants along this stretch of highway.

Ten minutes later she spied a red neon sign that flashed "Sam's Bar & Grill." She didn't have much choice. It was either Sam's Bar or pass out.

With the parking lot full and music blaring out the open door, she scanned the area to see if any unseemly looking characters milled about.

Another growl. Maddie rolled her eyes.

She locked the car and clutched her purse to her chest. Speed walking took her to the door of the bar in a matter of seconds.

Inside, it felt like an underground cave with a few glimpses of dim lights falling across one side of the room. Music screeched from a jukebox. A lonesome cowboy sang about losing his wife or horse or who knows what. This place was definitely more of a bar than a grill. A shiver went up her back.

People talked and laughed; chairs skidded across the floor. Cigarette smoke and the smell of stale alcohol filled the air. At least that was the odor she thought she sensed. She'd never been in a bar before. Another first. Sigh. Was this supposed to be part of the adventure?

Her eyes gradually adjusted to the dimly lit room. At the crowded bar, men hollered and raised their glasses to the TV that hung overhead. Boisterous cheers erupted as a wrestler slammed his opponent to the floor.

A man and woman, cigarettes and drinks in hand, snuggled up close, laughing and whispering in one another's ears. Another man on a barstool against the wall nursed a beer, watching the bartender make drinks.

They looked so sad. *And lonely,* Maddie thought with surprise. *Well, if anyone knows lonely, it's you, girl.* Dizziness threatened, and Maddie realized her need for food was getting serious. She sure didn't want to pass out here. Not that anyone would notice.

She held her hand to her head and blinked to clear her vision. One empty seat. All the way at the far end of the bar. Which meant she had to walk the entire length of the room to get there.

I'm leaving. This is not the place for me. Ruth would have a panic attack if she knew where Maddie was. Her stomach let out a growl so loud she was sure it would stop all activity in the place. No one noticed. Everyone ignored her.

She mumbled under her breath, "I'm going. I'm going."

Eyes glued to the floor, Maddie took one quick step after another to the opposite end of the bar. The bartender smiled a half-hearted greeting. "What'll it be?"

Her pounding heart rose to her throat and she coughed to clear it. "Is there any possibility the grill is still open?"

"Nope, closes at nine."

Maddie sighed.

"You lookin' for somethin' to eat?"

Her eyes pleaded with the man. "Could I get something? Cheese and crackers? Anything?"

"I can get you a ham and cheese sandwich and some chips. That okay?"

"That would be great. Thanks. Is there any possibility I could get a glass of milk?"

The bartender lowered his head and squinted at her. "Are you kiddin', lady?"

Maddie gave a nervous giggle. "Guess not, huh? How about a 7UP?"

"Yeah, 7UP I got."

She thought it best to make a friend of the one person in the place who was not drinking. The bartender's name tag said Samuel. "Samuel, that's a nice name. Are you the owner?"

He looked down at his name tag, then back at Maddie. "Nope, Sam Wiley's the owner. I'm just the hired help." He gave a quick grin, placed her 7UP on the bar in front of her, and walked through a swinging door behind the bar. She hoped he was making her sandwich back there.

Maddie discreetly scanned the bar. A small dance floor sat on the other side of the room where a man and woman danced suggestively to a twangy country western song. Their bodies clung so tightly to each another it would have been difficult to get a quarter between them.

Situated toward the back of the bar sat a pool table with half a dozen people calling out bets over two men who attempted to knock faint-colored balls into the pockets.

No one in the place was smiling. There was laughter and a few coarse words, but no real genuine, from the heart smiles.

Samuel brought her sandwich and chips. Maddie was about to thank him when the man seated near the wall pounded on the counter. Samuel headed to the other end of the bar where the man slurred his demand for another drink. Even though he swayed on his stool, Samuel served him another beer, removing the empty bottle in front of him.

Maddie wolfed down three bites of her sandwich as if she hadn't eaten in two days. The dizziness subsided; her hands and feet warmed; her mind cleared. After another bite she looked up and gave Samuel a friendly smile of satisfaction. Just about that time the man at the other end of the bar looked in her direction. He smiled back, got off his stool, and stumbled toward her end of the bar.

Maddie's eyes grew wider the closer he came to her barstool. Looking straight ahead, she took another bite of her sandwich.

The man walked up behind her, bent over and slurred in her ear, "Wanna dance?"

Maddie swallowed the bite of sandwich. Her hammering heart felt as if it might beat right through her chest. When she turned to face the drunken man, his beer breath caused her to pull back. His bloodshot eyes glared suggestively at her.

"N-no. No, thank you." She quickly turned from him.

"Aw, come on, honey. Just one little dance. I'm all alone. You're all alone. Let's have some fun."

Irritated at his persistence, she turned once again and glared at the obnoxious drunk.

"I only came in here to have something to eat."

"Yeah, right. You came in this dark pit just to eat. Sure. Whatever you say, baby." His body weaved. "You're lonely just like everybody else in this place."

Maddie clenched her jaw and turned to face the counter.

The man set his drink on the bar and rested his hands on either side of her. He clutched the bar, arms locked in place. Drawing close to her ear, he whispered an invitation to follow him home.

Samuel walked over. "Come on, buddy. Why don't you leave the lady alone?"

Maddie held up her hand to Samuel and turned to face the man. Gritting her teeth accentuated the fierce pulse of blood rushing through the veins in her neck. Her eyes black with fury, she glared at the drunk. "How dare you. I didn't ask for your attention. I came in here to eat before I passed out from hunger. That's all."

The man stumbled back at her outburst, tripping over his feet. He righted himself but continued to sway until he managed to grab the bar for support. "Listen, lady, you invited me down here. You smiled at me."

"I smiled at *Samuel* to say thank you for the sandwich."

The man laughed and grabbed the back of Maddie's barstool to keep from falling to the floor. "Sure, like I believe that."

"Listen, you—you. I don't care what you believe," Maddie hissed at him. "Stop bothering me or I'll have Samuel call the police."

Maddie noticed Samuel stood there, watching, not moving away.

The man held his hands up in front of his face. "Whoa, relax, lady. I was just tryin' to be friendly. I'm leavin'. Don't get yourself in an uproar."

The man scooped his beer off the bar and staggered over to the pool table, challenging the winner to a game. He looked over and gave Maddie an obnoxious grin and a hand salute with his beer.

What a jerk. Who did he think he was? Her pulse rate had to be over two hundred.

Maddie asked for the bill and wrapped the rest of her sandwich in a napkin. Seething, her anger rose from her chest, burning her face.

She ought to go over there and teach that guy a thing or two about manners, about how to treat a lady.

She thought better of it when Samuel brought her bill. Slipping off the stool, she held her head high, not the least bit intimidated by walking across the room to the door. She stomped to her car.

Safe inside, however, her body shook all over. Maddie laid her head on the steering wheel, breathing heavy. She couldn't believe she'd just done that. Jeff never would have allowed anyone to treat her like that.

Face it, Maddie. You're on your own. Jeff would never be here to protect her again. *And he'll never hurt me again either.*

Suddenly, without warning, she felt weak, drained. She needed a place to sleep. She couldn't drive in that condition. A sign across the road flashed "Wilderness Motel." It was the wilderness, all right.

After leaving Ruth a message, she fell into bed exhausted. The heavy oppression in the bar and dreams of lonely, drunk people made for a fitful night's sleep.

THIRTY

"A turtle could take this grade faster."

Maddie moved closer to the solid center lines, stretching her neck to glance around an eighteen-wheeler.

Cresting the summit, a colorful sign with a handful of service organization plaques welcomed her to Jacob's Bend. "Population—1,747, Elevation—1,500."

Maddie pulled to the side of the road. Eyes wide, hands clasped on her chest, she breathed deep. For miles, acres of lush green hills flourished with evidence of summer. Vibrant wildflowers. Fields full of mature crops.

Spotted amongst the panoramic hills were ageless oak trees thick with summer growth. In the valley below, cattle and horses grazed lazily. Maddie closed her eyes and inhaled, cataloging every frame into her memory.

Nestled before her, right in the middle of all the splendor, sat the little town of Jacob's Bend. Home.

Maddie pinched herself to make sure she was awake. This was real.

Anxious to see her friends, even more excited to set eyes on her new home, she jumped in her car and picked up speed.

On the outskirts of town, Maddie slowed her driving to breathe in every detail. Victorian homes with manicured lawns and hedges, along with Jacob's Bend Community Church and its tall white steeple, offered a charming welcome to Main Street.

Beauregard Taylor Park took up two blocks. Shaded on all sides by maples and oaks, a large white gazebo bandstand graced the lush green lawn.

Excited to investigate, Maddie parked her car to take a quick stroll through town. The buildings looked very old. Wonderful architectural design, lots of brick and character.

First and Main harbored a Shell gas station. The opposite corner held Lettie's Café with its red-and-white striped awning. A large whiteboard advertised homemade soup and pie. The summer special included a chicken salad sandwich, raspberry iced tea, and homemade ice cream. She would definitely check out Lettie's.

Across from the café, Bev's Beauty Salon, with its white brick, red door, and red trim, boasted ten-dollar haircuts for youngsters as well as a cut and style for adults at the bargain price of twenty-five dollars. Posters of edgy twenty-something men and women modeling the latest hairstyles hung in two large picture windows.

The fourth corner housed the *Jacob's Bend Herald*. The large two-story building had old world charm with its weathered brick exterior. It seemed to tip the tiniest bit. Maddie leaned her head to the right, then left to see if she could stand the building upright. It definitely had a slight slant. Just above the door of the newspaper a flag flapped gently with a design of a scroll, feathered pen, inkwell, and a man blowing a horn.

Lovely.

One of the few buildings exposing more wood than brick, Weatherby's Bookstore displayed black walnut embellishing the windows and the upper part of the building, with a half dozen rows of brick on the lower third down to the sidewalk. Carvings of cattle and farmers working the fields graced the side doorjambs. Placed strategically in the center above the top of the door was a carving of a man with a long beard, blowing some kind of horn. The carving looked to be the same as the man on the *Herald's* flag.

Maddie moved closer. The horn didn't resemble a trumpet or a bugle, but it was definitely a horn of some sort. She needed to find out more about the story of the horn. *At the newspaper I thought it might be someone heralding upcoming news, but obviously there is more to it.*

Peeking in the bookstore's large picture window, two weathered wing-back chairs sat on either side of an aged wooden table. A small Tiffany lamp, cigar box, and crystal ashtray sat on top along with three or four scattered books. Floor-to-ceiling books lined every wall she could see from the window. Definitely one of her first stops when she got settled.

Red brick with white trim, the Pine Needle quilt shop occupied a long narrow building stretching all the way to the alley in the rear. A skinny white door left room for a picture window with one of her favorite quilt patterns on display. The wedding ring.

"You can't put that on our bed, it doesn't go with the rest of the furniture. Maddie, our house is modern, not buckboard country."

Those words had cut deep. When Jeff wouldn't let her display the quilt that took her nearly a year to make, she donated it to the hospital raffle. For the life of her she had never been able to figure out what a modern quilt looked like.

Deep breath. *Let it go, Maddie.*

The enticing aroma of cinnamon and fresh-ground coffee carried her to the open door of Maison la Patisserie. She only went in for a taste of French roast, but came out with a large coffee and a delicious French pastry. *Heaven.*

Maison la Patisserie's white brick, black wood trim, and vintage white metal flower cart overflowing with summer blooms said quaint and very French. Two black metal tables with ornate metal chairs and red and white umbrellas made for a welcome setting to sip, eat, and chat. Oh yeah, this would definitely be a frequent haunt.

The River's Edge Restaurant took up two storefronts with both *enter* and *exit* doors. Elegant tables set with linen tablecloths and napkins, stemmed glassware, and candles were displayed on the other side of the large plate glass window. Maddie edged her eyes up the huge wooden doors to the rippled antique glass etched with the restaurant's name and establishment date of 1856. More intricate carvings graced the wood above the glass as well as the eight-inch-wide white stone doorjambs. And once again, the man blowing the horn.

Maddie sipped her coffee and slowly moved down the sidewalk. O'Donnell's Brier looked to be some kind of gift store. She put this one on the see-first list.

The old brick post office, small and quaint, established along with the town of Jacob's Bend in 1855, or so the plaque at City Hall said, still had mailboxes with combination locks.

Four white columns held the entablature protecting the entrance to the large white building set apart as the Jacob's Bend Library. Ten cement steps spread clear across the expanse of the building. More etchings on the marble pillars of horse-drawn buckboards, hay bales, wheat stalks, and a man with a beard, of course, blowing a horn.

She would have to hear that story.

Very different from the large cathedrals in the city, the small redbrick Catholic Church spoke of simplicity and humility. A building she could imagine a group of monks might have built early in their travels. A simple bronze cross stood atop the single bell tower. Two lancet windows framed the simple wood door. A stained glass fanlight inlay depicting Jesus dragging His cross sat above the door. Resting catty-corner at the north end of Main Street and at the foot of a hill, atop which a beautiful, massive Victorian sat, the church's manicured lawn and carefully trimmed shrubs made for a peaceful setting.

The driveway of the massive Victorian curved its way down to Main Street to a sign that read "Wimbleton House, circa 1855." Encased by a tall black cast iron fence the property looked like it could be sitting on at least a half acre of well-kept landscape. The stately gray-shingled manor sat proud with its two polygon towers and covered porch across the front extending to the right side. The mayor's house?

At the foot of the hill on the west side of the street stood the combined Jacob's Bend City Hall and Police Station. With the exception of the Jacob's Bend police insignia painted on the window, the redbrick building resembled the Jacob's Bend Fire Station at the end of the street. An old horse-drawn fire engine adorned the manicured grass out front.

Feinberg's Barbershop showed off more white brick along with two red-and-white striped barber poles on either side of a black door. With only one barber chair, Carl Feinberg had set chairs around a square table with a backgammon board, no doubt so his waiting customers could enjoy a cup of coffee, talk turkey, and challenge each other to a game or two.

Danby's Drug Store with its red door and white brick had double picture windows, an old-fashioned soda fountain, and a pharmacy in the back. There were more etchings above the door, complete with Horatio Hornblower, or whoever he was.

The largest building on the street, three times the size of most other establishments, Harper's Hardware, boasted massive twelve-foot beams painted white to match the rest of the building. The beams spread across the top of the building with "Harper's Hardware" carved deep into the wood, adorned with red paint. Rakes, hoes, bags of potting soil and compost, seeds of all types were out front to attract curious passersby. The melodic blending of various wind chimes caught Maddie's attention.

I am going to love this town.

THIRTY-ONE

Nathan woke to the melodious singing of birds. Crawling out of bed, he found a flyer on the dresser advertising the Ekhorn Motel. Looking around his surroundings, he wondered where people came up with such off-the-wall names. Shouldn't it be Elkhorn with an *l*?

He must have landed in good-ole-boy country.

Nathan spied himself in the bathroom mirror. *You look just like your dad— the day after.* Head hung low, Nathan rubbed his throbbing forehead.

He dropped his head back against tense shoulders, took a deep breath, and looked back at the bleary reflection in the mirror. "What is wrong with you? Why did you break your promise?" Running his hands through his hair and over the stubble on his face, Nathan wanted to turn back the clock and take back everything that had happened over the last twenty-four hours.

Squinting at the mirror, he asked, "What did happen over the last twenty-four hours?"

Chelsea.

Nathan shook his head. As hard as he tried, the last thing he could remember was jumping in his truck, slamming his foot down on the accelerator, and speeding onto the highway, headed for parts unknown, hoping to find a quiet place to walk off his anger.

He remembered a flashing sign and yanking the steering wheel to the left, crossing over into oncoming traffic, skidding to a stop, dust rising in the parking lot.

He was such an idiot. All it took was one drink to start the all-consuming romance with the bottle. Just like his dad.

Nathan walked to the bedside table, picked up his keys, and hurled them across the room, knocking a mason jar with a handful of dusty, plastic flowers to the floor. He sat on the corner of the bed, his head in his hands. Nostrils flaring. "That is *never* going to happen again. *Never.*"

THIRTY-TWO

arolyn had said Oak Street was a few blocks west of Main. It wasn't long before she spotted the house. Small two-bedroom, yellow exterior, green shutters.

On her knees in the front yard, Carolyn looked up from her work when Maddie's car pulled to a stop. All five feet, eleven inches of her slender, firm body jumped up, flinging weeds in the air.

Maddie leaped out of the car into Carolyn's open arms. Both women squealed with delight, standing on the grass in a tight embrace, joyful tears flowing. They walked arm in arm into the house, talking nonstop.

"It's so good to see you. I can't believe you're actually sitting at my kitchen table drinking iced tea. I've missed you so much."

Maddie grinned, scanning the bright little room. "Not nearly as much as I've missed you." Carolyn hadn't changed a bit. Still as beautiful as ever. She probably had one of her aerobics classes going. Maddie stretched, her muscles tight. She might need to sign up.

Carolyn's unruly brown curls were caught up in a bouncy ponytail. Loose wisps fell around her eyes and temples. Dancing blue eyes sparkled. "So how was the last leg of your trip? Uneventful, I hope."

A flush of red moved up her neck to her face. "Not at all. I actually had a horrible encounter."

Carolyn frowned.

"I'll tell you later. Right now I would love to see this perfect little cottage you have picked out for me. You said it's near your home. Is it in walking distance? I'm so tired of sitting."

"Sure, it's just around the corner. Let's go."

Arm in arm the women headed for the street, giggling like two schoolgirls.

Carolyn stopped, looked to her left, and stretched out her arm. "Here it is."

Maddie's jaw dropped. Her eyes popped wide. There, before her, stood a terrible broken-down shack.

Carolyn quickly responded to Maddie's shocked expression. "It, ah, needs a little work."

Maddie tilted her head to get a different perspective. "Carolyn, you call this a cottage? It's four walls with plaster. Ugly plaster at that. Whoever took it upon themselves to paint it that gaudy gold, of all colors?"

"Oh, that. The owner was a little eccentric."

Maddie squinted at Carolyn. "Ya think?"

Carolyn laughed. "Well, he came out west to find gold. When he realized he missed his mark by several hundred miles, his wife refused to budge. Since he couldn't get to gold country, he painted his house gold to spite his wife. He didn't know she was color blind."

Maddie erupted with laughter. "That story is too funny to be made up."

"It's true, honest. I asked him once. He told me the whole story. Now he's gone on to glory and is surrounded by gold. Do you want to see the inside?"

"Is it safe?"

Carolyn looked at the house and tipped her head. "Well, ah, sure. He lived in it for sixty years. It's still standing."

"Barely. I think I'll pass."

"Come on, Maddie. You can make this into a charming little home."

"I don't think so, Carolyn. It doesn't look very stable." Maddie glanced to the left. "And what about that house next door? It's practically on top of the *cottage*. Why is it so close? There's plenty of room on the lot to put it where there's breathing space."

Carolyn chuckled. "Well, Harold, the owner of the cottage, was a cantankerous kind of guy."

Maddie eyed Carolyn. "No kiddin'."

"His neighbors next door didn't want anyone to build on this lot and swore they would put up a fence ten feet high if anyone did build. In those days they didn't have building codes. Harold didn't leave his neighbor room for a fence. He built his house with about eighteen inches between the two dwellings. After that the two men never did get along."

Maddie raised her eyebrows. "I can't imagine why." She sized up the house again. "Carolyn, this, ah, house is not quite what I had in mind. Maybe we could look at some other houses tomorrow."

"What's the hurry? You can stay with us as long as you want."

"I appreciate the offer, really I do, but the sooner I get settled in my own place, with some of my things around me, the more I'll feel at home. There's no turning back now. Besides, you barely have enough room for you and Alex, let alone a third person."

Carolyn's sheepish look gave Maddie cause for concern. "The thing is, houses don't go up for sale very often in Jacob's Bend. That's why I suggested Harold's place."

"I don't have to live in town. As a matter of fact, when I crested the hill just above Jacob's Bend I stopped to take in the countryside. I could be very happy living out there." Maddie waved her hand toward the farmland she had admired.

Carolyn tapped her lips. "I can't think of any houses for sale in the country."

"There must be a house somewhere."

"I don't know of a single one. We could check with Elias Jones at the county offices in Carterville. Elias knows everything there is to know about the properties around here."

"Why don't we just contact a real estate agent?"

Carolyn laughed. "There aren't any."

"None?"

"Nope. Like I said, houses rarely go up for sale around here. A real estate agent would starve in Jacob's Bend."

"I guess we'd better go have a talk with Elias then. How far is Carterville from here?"

"Sixty miles. About forty-five minutes if we take the interstate."

*   *   *

During dinner Maddie gave Alex and Carolyn an earful about her trip. They laughed so hard their sides ached. They were surprised at some of the things she'd done along the way.

Alex grinned. "You've changed, Maddie. You're a different woman from the one we said goodbye to after Jeff's funeral."

"I am?"

Maddie eyed Jeff's best friend from college. Barely five foot nine, he and Carolyn made an odd-looking but amazing pair. Carolyn's svelte height put her almost a head taller than Alex. Always wanting to blend in, she never wore heals. Alex, muscular and ruggedly handsome, drew Maddie's attention before she'd started dating Jeff. His dark eyes and hair and bronze skin, along with his surname of Moreno, gave clear definition to his heritage.

The phone interrupted her thoughts. "I'm sure that's Ruth. Want me to get it?"

Carolyn grinned. "Knowing your worrywart daughter, you're probably right. Sure, go ahead, grab it."

"Hello."

"Mom, I'm so glad you're not on the road alone anymore. I thought you were *never* going to get there. Now I can relax a little."

"You can relax completely. I'm home."

"It's still a strange place, Mom. You might change your mind."

"Don't hold your breath. It's even more beautiful than I imagined. Carolyn and I are going to look for a house tomorrow. As soon as I find one I'll have my things delivered."

"I thought Carolyn already picked out the perfect house for you. What happened?"

Lowering her voice, Maddie moved into the living room.

"Ruth, you would not believe that place. It is absolutely horrible. I wouldn't step foot in it. I think if you leaned a broom against the front porch the entire house would collapse. It ought to be condemned. Carolyn says there aren't many houses for sale here. That's why she thought, with a little work—I think a bulldozer might do it—ole Harold's place would work." Maddie shook her head. "It's definitely not for me."

Maddie's defenses rose when she heard Ruth's laughter on the other end of the line. "Mom, you're homeless. You don't have a job. You don't know anyone except Alex and Carolyn."

"And that's funny to you?"

"Not really. But why would you stay? Why don't you come and live with Matt and me?"

Maddie blurted out a reality that had been rumbling around in her head for some time, "Because, well, it's time I grew up."

"What are you talking about?"

"It's true. For all my adult life I have relied on your dad for everything from taking care of the finances to helping with the weekly menu. Not to mention my friends were never high on his good list. With the exception of Carolyn. He didn't have a choice when it came to her. We'd been friends too long for that to change.

"Ruth, it's way past time for me to take responsibility for my life. I know there will be obstacles to overcome, but I am determined to stay here and make the best of it."

Maddie looked at the phone in her hand. "Does that make any sense?"

"Honestly, Mom, no, it doesn't. You sound as if you resent Dad taking care of you."

Maddie rolled her eyes. "That's not it, Ruth. I love your dad and I miss the security I felt with him."

"You are an adult, Mom. You're forty-three years old. I don't understand what all this talk is about growing up."

Maddie sighed. *Nothing I say is going to make her understand.*

"Never mind. I'm safe, that's all that matters, right? Besides, you wouldn't be happy with me underfoot all the time and I wouldn't be happy without my own space. Let's change the subject."

"Why do you always do that? When things aren't going the way you want, you either change the subject or shut down completely."

"And why do we always end up in an argument?"

Heavy sigh on the other end of the phone.

"Ruth, I'm really tired after the long drive. I love you. Give Matt my love."

"I love you too, Mom."

*   *   *

That night Maddie dreamt of Harold's gold house. A little girl tried desperately to fix everything wrong with it. Every time she made a repair something else would break. At one point half of the roof caved in. Maddie woke herself up yelling, "I can't do this. I'm not a big girl. I'm too little."

Maddie slid out of bed, knelt beside the window, and looked up at the crescent moon. Maybe Ruth was right. Was this really where she was supposed to be?

In the early morning hours, the sun's rays cast soothing warmth on Maddie's face as she lay in bed. Yawning, she stretched and smiled. *Ruth is wrong. It's a brand-new day to begin a brand-new life. I can do this.*

THIRTY-THREE

T he historic county offices offered dignified charm.

However, Elias Jones, a crotchety old guy, didn't smile or even offer his hand when Carolyn introduced Maddie. For some reason he seemed to wear a perpetual frown. Elias had a lean, lanky frame, graying flattop, and cloudy hazel eyes behind thick black-rimmed glasses.

Carolyn had told Maddie Elias had worked for the county for over forty years and had an insider's take on all the happenings.

Maddie watched him carefully. Elias would make a good gossip columnist with all the information he had accumulated in his brain. However, it seemed for every question Carolyn or Maddie put to Elias, the response came back the same, "Nothin' I can do 'bout it."

Frustrated, Maddie scanned the office. They needed a different plan of attack. Her dad always said people loved to talk about themselves. But what could she possibly ask him that she hadn't already tried?

Then she saw it. On the wall behind his desk hung a picture of Elias, albeit a few years younger, with a huge grin on his face, accepting a blue ribbon for the biggest, homeliest pig she had ever seen.

"Elias, I would really love to find some property. Maybe even a small farm, have a few animals, do a little gardening, raise some pigs. Don't you know of anything like that for sale around Jacob's Bend?"

Elias's face lit up like a boy with his first bicycle. The mention of pigs started him talking nonstop. He may have been backward in everyday conversation, but Elias sure knew his pigs.

Maddie put on her sweetest smile. "I confess I know very little about pigs. I could use someone with your experience to help me pick out the best of the litter. And teach me how to raise them."

Elias's grin spread from ear to ear.

Carolyn scrunched up her nose. "You really want a farm so you can raise pigs?"

Maddie shrugged and winked at her friend.

After fifteen minutes of expounding on the value of pigs, Elias remembered a farm Maddie might be interested in. The old Riley place. It seemed Edgar Riley passed on some years ago, had no heirs. The place would soon go on the county auction block.

Maddie smiled at Carolyn. She felt like dancing. "Now we're getting somewhere. How much land does the farm have?"

"Oh, let's see, I'd say maybe three, four hundred acres."

"Three to four hundred acres. You're kidding, right?"

"Nope. Let's see." Elias pulled a file out of a drawer behind the counter. He licked his fingers and thumbed through some papers. "Ah, yup. Says right here, 427 acres."

"Is that the *only* property available?" Maddie frowned at Carolyn, shaking her head.

"Edgar did a right fine job with that farm. He was the first land owner to rent out plots of land to young farmers who was jus startin' out so's they could bring in a crop and start makin' some money to one day buy their own farms. Edgar was a right friendly, bighearted man. You won't never hear nobody say a bad word agin' Edgar Riley."

Maddie looked at Carolyn. "I'm not saying he didn't. But I think that's a bit more land than I'm looking for."

"Most of them there acres is rented out to others. They either don't have land of their own or don't have enough land to plant what's needed to fill their orders. Some of the land is leased to ranchers with cattle who need extra space to graze. There's really only ten, maybe fifteen acres you'd have to be frettin' about."

Elias glanced from one woman to the other when they burst into laughter. He clearly wondered if the two had gone daft. "What's so funny?"

"Sorry, Elias." Carolyn straightened up. "It's just that Maddie is a wid—single woman and couldn't possibly take care of a farm that big all alone. She might find that a bit much to . . . fret over."

Elias's sour expression turned into a smile when he looked from Carolyn to Maddie. "She don't have to. There's plenty of people round these parts who'd pitch in an' help her. 'Sides, they ain't another piece a property here 'bouts to be had."

"Well, thanks for the vote of confidence, Elias, but I just want a quiet little place where I can tend some flowers, grow some vegetables, and get some rest. I'm sure something will come up."

Elias offered a look of skepticism. "I wouldn't bet my life on it. Ya got some kind a deadly disease or somethin'?"

"Why would you ask that?"

"Well, do you plan to move here to Jacob's Bend, sit in your quiet little place, dry up, and die?"

"No, of course not. Why, I plan to, well, I'm going to . . ." Maddie held her hands out to Carolyn, silently pleading for help.

"He's right, Maddie. A quiet little resting place does sound like you're giving up on life."

Maddie turned her eyes on Elias. "At any rate, I'll need a place to stay while I look for a home. Do you know of any rentals, Elias?"

"You have a little time to think on it. It'll take the county some months to prepare for the land auction. In the meantime I know of three places you can take a look at. Some of these here people just might be wantin' to sell in the future."

Encouraged, Maddie smiled at Elias. "That works for me."

THIRTY-FOUR

"This is not working."

Maddie and Carolyn had driven back to town to review the day's results.

"That first place had lots of room for improvements," Carolyn reminded Maddie with a grin. It had turned out to be nothing more than a small trailer with three or four additions that produced what looked like a camper with three sheds attached.

"Don't be funny, Carolyn. I may not live long enough for that to happen."

Finding the second parcel had proved a little more difficult. They couldn't find 851 Plainsview Lane. The house numbers just stopped. The map showed a big creek smack-dab in the middle of the six and eight hundreds. They found the creek, but couldn't find where the road began again. While Carolyn walked to the other side of the creek through a large grove of trees to search for the road, Maddie scanned the road in the opposite direction for a farmhouse, shack, anything where someone might have an answer to their questions.

About that time a man wearing a black cowboy hat, riding a tall, muscular black horse, galloped up to where Maddie stood with a hand shading her eyes from the sun. The man stopped long enough to offer directions.

"Just take the fork in the road to the left. It'll curve round till you come to the Curry place, big gray house. Keep going until you see the Curry's purple watering trough, turn right down the dirt road. Drive about a half mile, that's where Plainsview Lane picks back up. Flooded out about six years ago. Not much there now but old vandalized buildings."

Maddie smiled up at the rather handsome-looking cowboy. At least from what she could tell with his sunglasses covering his eyes. "Oh, thank you. Thank you very much."

The man smiled, tipped his hat, and rode off into the sunset. *He's riding east. Get a grip, girl.*

Maddie walked toward Carolyn who was squinting at the light as she came from the dense forest. The two considered the directions from the man on the horse.

"Well, what do you think, Maddie? Do you even want to go look at this place?"

"Yeah, sure. At least we'll be able to say we saw every single parcel that *might* go up for sale in Jacob's Bend."

Just as the cowboy had said, the place turned out to be nothing more than overgrown weeds and broken-down buildings. Broken glass in the windows, doors hanging off-kilter from their hinges. Several steps leading up to the porch were missing. The porch had wasted away from years of hard weather and lack of care.

"Do you want to go inside, see what it looks like?"

Maddie smirked at Carolyn. "This place makes ole Harold's place look impeccable. I don't think we need to go inside. I can pretty much tell this place is not for me."

Carolyn breathed a sigh of relief. "Good, I don't even like to think of all the disgusting critters nesting in that empty building."

Critters? Beady eyes, *click-click* of tiny feet, scratching, gnawing. A shiver crawled up Maddie's back. She looked to the ground around her and carefully took several steps back.

Retracing their steps to the front gate, Maddie uncovered a sign that read "Lawson Family Homestead—851 Plainsview Lane."

"Doesn't it make you wonder what happened to this family? Why the farm was abandoned in the first place?"

"Yeah, I wonder if the Lawson family died in the flood."

Maddie looked at the paper in her hand. "There's one more property on the list. I think it might be in town. It's got to be better than what we've seen so far. You want to wait until tomorrow to see it?"

Carolyn rubbed the middle of her back and checked her watch. "That's probably a good idea. Alex will be home soon. Let's go get dinner going. I'm starving."

"Me too."

THIRTY-FIVE

N othing like a growling stomach to let you know you're alive and that the necessities of life are always with us. Ben looked for an open café along the desolate highway that would take him home.

He scanned the heavens, marveling at the host of stars and full moon. They almost felt close enough to touch.

Nothing like death to make you appreciate life.

Charley Winston was one of the greatest men Ben had ever known. A godly man of integrity who instilled in his young protégé an excitement for adventure and a zest for life. Officiating at his funeral brought out emotions Ben had locked away, hoping never to experience again.

Nobody expected a man who had lived eighty-two full years to live forever. And thank God, Charley died the way he always hoped he would, in the saddle. Charley had ridden his favorite horse out to the pasture where Sampson would live out the rest of his days. Charley's foreman was following with a truck to take Charley back to the house when God just graciously stopped Charley's heart.

Death. Never easy to deal with, even when the one who died believed in Jesus Christ and was now in his real home, heaven.

Charley's death brought back the memory of another death Ben had to deal with some time ago. The death of an unborn child. "Why, God? Why?"

He didn't expect an audible answer, but he sure would have liked to hear something. Anything.

Life goes on, and so will I. Alone.

Loneliness was just part of the job, part of life. And thanks to Charley putting him in contact with the pastor in Jacob's Bend, Ben had a new life. He had purpose.

"Still, it would be nice not to go home to an empty house." *Let it go, Ben. You have a full life, busy beyond what you could ever have imagined.* Who would have thought being a pastor would be more than a full-time job? Most thought pastors only worked on Sundays.

Ben laughed. His stomach growled.

"Okay, okay, I'm stopping."

Thirty-Six

"**N**ow this is more like it." Carolyn grinned at Maddie. The tidy little white two-story house looked like it had just been painted. Two front dormers gave the seasoned dwelling added character and charm. Trimmed grass and shrubs framed the property. Best of all, a lovely spacious porch invited visitors to come sit a spell.

The two women walked up the steps, taking in the comfort of a cushioned porch swing. Maddie opened the screen and knocked softly on the solid wood door.

A small face with brown goo smeared from cheek to cheek opened a crack in the door. A little boy, maybe four or five, threw the door open wide.

"Hi. My mommy is talking to my daddy. Want some cake?" He stretched out a chocolate-covered hand, holding what looked like a squashed glob of mud.

Maddie smiled at the little man wearing oversized work boots and a John Deere ball cap.

"No, thank you."

She turned to Carolyn. "Maybe this is a bad time."

"I don't hear any yelling. Maybe we could just ask if they would talk to us."

Maddie bent down to the little guy's height. "Could you tell your mommy and daddy that Madison Crane would like to talk to them?"

The little boy licked his hand. "My daddy's not here."

"But you said your mommy is talking to your daddy."

The boy labored to lick cake and frosting from his fingers. "She is."

Hesitant to proceed, Maddie looked up at Carolyn, who shrugged.

Maddie spoke to the little boy as if playing a game. "Is your daddy in the house?"

He continued licking his fingers. "Nope, he's in heaven." His nonchalant reply sounded like his father had stepped out to the local store.

Maddie caught her breath.

Seeing the little guy through new eyes she said, "Let's start over. My name is Maddie. What's yours?"

The boy stood tall, answering proudly, "Brian W. Metzger."

"Well, Brian W. Metzger, what's your mommy's name?"

"Angela W. Metzger."

"Brian, would it be all right to interrupt Mommy's conversation with Daddy so she could come to the door and speak to me?"

"Oh sure. She talks to him all the time. I'll go get her. Mom. Mom." he shouted into the house, clomping down a hallway in the man's boots.

Carolyn took Maddie's hand. "Are you sure you want to do this?"

"Yes. Maybe I can help somehow since I've been there myself."

A few minutes later a thin young woman, looking to be midthirties, stood behind the screen door wiping her hands on a towel. Dark circles framed her brown eyes.

"Can I help you?"

"My name is Madison Crane. This is my friend Carolyn Moreno. We were told this house might be for sale."

Angela looked from one woman to the other and burst into tears.

Maddie stared wide-eyed at Carolyn. She opened the screen door and encased Angela in her arms.

Sobbing, Brian clinging to her leg, Angela composed herself long enough to invite the two women into the living room.

"Please, please have a seat. I'll be right back."

Somber, Carolyn and Maddie sat across the room from one other.

Angela returned with a tray of iced tea and cookies, her eyes puffy and red, her highlighted brown hair pulled into a ponytail. "I'm sorry for my outburst. I'm Angela Metzger. This is my son, Brian."

Brian peered from behind his mother's skirt.

"You made my mommy cry. You go away."

Angela got down on her knees and hugged her son. "Brian, these ladies didn't make Mommy cry. I was sad because Daddy is gone. That's why I was crying. Do you understand what Mommy is telling you?"

Brian looked from his mother to the women.

"They didn't hurt you?"

"No, Brian."

He ran from his mother's hug and stood in the middle of the room between Maddie and Carolyn. Legs spread wide, hands on his hips, Brian took control. "Okay, you can stay. But if you make my mommy cry, I will make you go."

Maddie smiled at the freshly scrubbed little face. "Fair enough."

Brian skipped off to the back of the house singing, "Old MacDonald Had a Farm." Angela sat on the couch next to Carolyn.

"Brian takes his role as the man of the house very seriously these days."

Maddie fiddled with her hands. "He told us his daddy is in heaven. I'm so sorry."

"I usually do pretty well, but this house is all we have and it looks like we are going to lose it."

"Not to me."

Angela smiled. "How did you know the house might be for sale?"

Carolyn took Angela's hand in hers. "Elias Jones, at the county, told us about it."

"Oh, I see. He would know since we haven't paid this year's taxes yet. My mom and dad have been helping me keep up with the monthly house payment, but the taxes came due all of a sudden and we had no money saved to pay them. I started work last week at the Haystack Motel as the bookkeeper. That will help."

Maddie fidgeted with her keys. "I hope I'm not imposing. How long has your husband—how long have you been a widow?"

"About four months."

Tears seared Maddie's eyes as she studied the pretty young woman. "I understand. My husband died a year ago."

Angela's face registered a look of shock. "Really? What happened?"

"Heart attack."

"Mrs. Crane, I'm so sorry."

Carolyn sniffed into a tissue. "And your husband?"

"He was out working on the parcel we rent. The sheriff figured the tractor stopped running and Keith must have climbed down and forgot to turn it off. Standing in front of the tractor, he would have had to stretch over the engine to check for damage. The sheriff thinks maybe he replaced a loose wire and the tractor started to move, pinning him under the wheels. Keith's helper ran clear across the length of the field when he saw him caught under the tractor. He drove the tractor off Keith, but it was too late. The paramedics said he probably died within minutes."

"How horrible for you."

"It's been a nightmare. I still can't believe he's gone. I talk to him all the time like he's standing right next to me. His presence is everywhere in this house." Angela looked around helplessly. "We were beginning to see a nice profit from our crops. We couldn't afford to buy a farm, but when we heard we could rent a small parcel, we saw that as our big chance. Four years ago we tried our hand at raising sugar beets. Started with fifty acres and worked up to a hundred. Last year we bought this house. It just kept getting better."

Tears rolled down Carolyn's cheeks. "I am so sorry, Angela." Carolyn asked, "Do you and Brian attend church?"

The young widow looked from Carolyn to Maddie, shifting in her seat.

"Brian and I go to North Hills Chapel off and on. The people have been so kind to us since Keith's death. Pastor Farrington performed Keith's service. It's still all such a blur to me."

"I understand." Maddie smiled at the young woman. "I'm brand new to Jacob's Bend." She hesitated, then surprised herself with a suggestion. "Maybe I could go with you and Brian to church sometime?"

"Sure, I'd like that." Angela smiled. "So, you're looking for a house to buy?"

"Yes. But there aren't many homes for sale in Jacob's Bend." At least none she would consider buying, with the exception of this one.

"I know. We were thrilled when this house came available. We waited a long time to buy our first home."

Carolyn nibbled on her fingernail. "Angela, did your husband by any chance have life insurance? I'm sorry, but I guess my mind just naturally goes there since my husband is in the insurance business."

Angela stared at the floor. "No, he didn't. He was only twenty-nine. We didn't think we needed it." She shook her head. "Boy, were we wrong. I'm looking for a second job so I can make some extra money to pay the taxes on the house. If I can do that, Brian and I should be okay. Mr. Sands owns the motel, café, and the movie theatre just outside of town. He's ordered another computer so I can work from home. It will link to the main computer at his office. That way I can keep the records for all his businesses right from here. Brian won't have to go to a sitter. Isn't that wonderful?"

Maddie nodded. "What a thoughtful man."

"He is a very kind man. After Keith died, Ken and Lettie Sands, one of those families I told you were so good to us, suggested Pastor Farrington oversee Keith's service."

Carolyn looked to her friend. "We'd better be going, don't you think, Maddie? We've kept Angela long enough."

"I'm very glad to have met you both. Sorry, the house is not for sale."

Maddie smiled at Angela. "That's okay. The perfect house is out there somewhere."

Carolyn grinned at her friend, and Maddie rolled her eyes in return, knowing Carolyn was thinking of the fact that she had said the very same thing, only adding her forever phrase—God knows.

Maddie handed Angela a piece of paper with Carolyn's phone number on it. "Just in case you want to talk or anything."

"Thank you." Angela gave a half smile.

Brian sauntered into the room with a book in his hand.

"Mommy, read to me."

"In a minute. Say goodbye to our new friends."

"Bye, Sunnie. Bye, Carrie."

"Brian, their names are—"

Maddie interrupted. "No, no, it's okay. Whatever is easiest for him."

"Goodbye, Brian," both said in unison.

The next day Maddie directed Isaac Birnbaum to transfer funds from her account and anonymously pay the taxes on Angela's house.

The distant voice could not be silenced. *I know, Jeff. I know. You don't think this is a good idea. I don't even know the woman. Not yet. But it feels good to have the money to help someone who truly needs help. So stop giving me a hard time.*

She shook her head at the thought of talking this over with Jeff. "Maddie, you have got to get a grip."

THIRTY-SEVEN

Almost two months after arriving in Jacob's Bend, Maddie lay in bed contemplating her homeless state while Alex and Carolyn talked quietly in the kitchen. Carolyn sounded hurt.

"Why does she need to find a place of her own right now?"

"Honey, you know Maddie. She doesn't want to impose on anyone."

"But she isn't imposing. I love having her here."

"You know that and I know that, but she needs to feel like she can take care of herself. Having tasted independence, she likes it. Can't you see the change in her since Jeff's death?"

"Like what?"

"Well, for lack of a better way of putting it, she's growing up, taking responsibility for her life. She looks healthier, too, kind of has a glow about her, don't you think?"

Maddie winced. Why had he said that? Carolyn had always suspected Alex had feelings for her. It had been the one rift in their friendship. But he never did. Did he?

"That's ridiculous, Alex. What on earth are you talking about? She's been a grown-up for a long time."

"I didn't say she wasn't a grown-up, I said she is growing up. All the years we've known her and Jeff, Maddie never made any decisions without first checking with Jeff. She never had to face the consequences of a bad decision or feel the sense of accomplishment at making a good one. Now she's doing that. Right or wrong, she's making decisions that will affect the rest of her life, and she's willing to live with the consequences."

"You sound like a recording of what I told her a few months ago."

"Exactly. What she needs from us is encouragement and support. She needs to know she's not alone, and even if the choices she makes aren't all good ones, we still support her."

Silence.

Maddie could picture Carolyn giving Alex the sweet look she saved just for him. The two had something she had never seen in another couple. Maybe they clung to each other because they were never able to have children. There was always a twinge of regret that Maddie had never been able to look at Jeff like that. *I need to go, for them and for me.*

The sound of a soft kiss broke into her thoughts. "I love you, Carolyn."

She hoped Carolyn didn't have any doubts. They were too hard to live with. Alex loved Carolyn. And Maddie would never do anything to hurt her. Maddie smiled, thankful for such wonderful friends. She resolved to spend the day looking for a rental. There had to be *something* out there. A long sigh passed her lips as she slipped into her robe. If nothing else, it was time she got to know the people of Jacob's Bend better.

After breakfast Maddie excused herself, telling Carolyn she wanted to walk around town. Carolyn offered a couple of suggestions but didn't volunteer to go along. Maddie loved that about her. She knew when to push and when to leave her friend to her thoughts.

The fresh air soothed Maddie's soul. The fragrant scent of impatiens and day lilies invaded her senses. Her stroll downtown took her past the old buildings she had seen when she first arrived.

It was time to learn more about them and the people inside.

*   *   *

Katie Lou, whose name tag identified her as "Head Librarian," stood behind the counter staring at a computer screen. The woman, who appeared to be of American Indian ancestry and had piercing brown eyes, and short jet-black hair parted to fall over her left eye, admitted she loved giving library tours. She introduced Maddie to every square foot of the two-story, stately building. From research to fiction, the well-stocked Jacob's Bend Library encouraged one of Maddie's favorite pastimes—reading.

"Katie, do you happen to know of any property for sale or for rent in the immediate vicinity of Jacob's Bend?"

"No, I can't think of anything, but I'll be sure to keep my eyes and ears open." Katie tapped her fingers on the counter. "I can check area real estate on the computer during my lunch hour."

"That would be great. Thanks."

"I really love research. Besides, it's one way I can welcome you to Jacob's Bend."

Maddie returned her open smile and gestured to the stack of titles she'd collected during the tour. "Between you and my friends who live here, I feel very welcome."

After gathering up her stack of books, Maddie headed to the Pine Needle quilt shop. She'd been saving it for her last stop of the morning.

A woman in her late fifties sat behind a weathered BERNINA sewing machine connecting patches of cloth.

"Hi. Welcome."

"Hi. I'm Madison Crane. Most people call me Maddie. I'm new in town and love to quilt."

The woman stayed seated and grinned at her patron. "Well, you came to the right place. I'm Helen Steinberg, I own the Pine Needle. Have a look around, and if there is anything I can help you with, let me know."

Maddie set her books on the cutting table so she could browse more freely. She was glad she had brought her machine with her instead of storing it. This would help fill the long hours until she found a house.

Grazing through row after row, bolt after bolt of colors and textures, Maddie gently touched those that caught her eye. "You have some beautiful fabric."

Helen mumbled something.

Maddie peeked around the corner at the older woman, pins caught between her lips. Maddie laughed. "I agree completely."

Helen's eyes smiled. She removed the pins. "Thanks. I get it from all over the country. Flannel, watercolor, thirties. I try to find eclectic designs to fill in the gaps."

"You've got a great selection."

"You said you were new in town. Where are you staying?"

"Actually, I'm staying with friends at the moment, but I'm planning to make Jacob's Bend home."

"Where are you from?"

"Chicago area."

"That's quite a move. What brought you to Jacob's Bend?"

"My best friend and her husband live here. Maybe you know them? Alex and Carolyn Moreno?"

"I do know Alex and Carolyn. Nice couple. It's hard *not* to know everyone—and their business—in a small town like Jacob's Bend."

Maddie smiled. "I'm actually looking for a place to buy. Doesn't have to be much."

Helen shook her head. "Hard to find in Jacob's Bend. People seldom move."

Maddie gave a one-sided grin and sighed. "I know."

"But I'll keep my ears open for anything that might come up."

"Thanks, Helen. I appreciate that. Think I'll just take my books home and have a little lunch."

"It was good to meet you, Maddie. I'm sure we'll see a lot more of each other."

"I'm sure we will. I'll be back. Soon."

THIRTY-EIGHT

On her way back to Carolyn's house, one particular store caught Maddie's eye. O'Donnell's Brier had a window display of colorful flowers, a worn bench, cobblestones, and old birdhouses. It made her want to pack a picnic lunch, take off her shoes, and lounge in the beautiful atrium garden.

This is what she envisioned England might look like. What was this place? Gift shop? Deli? Coffee house?

Wrong on all three counts. A woman's vintage clothing store, O'Donnell's Brier also carried a variety of unique gifts. A pretty woman with curly auburn hair falling gently down her back, sides held in place by blingy barrettes, stood in the corner steaming a colorful summer dress. She welcomed Maddie into the quaint shop.

Maddie had the sense of standing in the middle of an English garden, snuggled behind an old-world cottage. It was exquisite. The clothing racks were designed to look like trees, with metal branches doubling as clothes hangers. A fountain in the middle of the shop added peaceful ambiance. Two antique chairs encouraged a seat next to the fountain, while fresh flowers in a stunning crystal vase sat atop a black cast-iron bistro table with a plate of scones that beckoned her.

"I'm Madison Crane." She extended her hand. "My friends call me Maddie. What an enchanting place."

"Hello, Maddie. I'm Gael O'Donnell, the proprietor. I thank ya for the compliment."

"I detect an accent. Are you from England?"

"No, no. Ireland." The woman chuckled.

Embarrassed, Maddie admitted she never could tell one accent from another. She should have guessed by her name.

Gael grinned as her eyes rested on Maddie's own auburn hair. "You look like you might have a touch o' the Irish yourself."

"I've never been there, that's for sure." Maddie looked around with interest. "Is your shop representative of some special place in Ireland?"

"Why, yes, sort of. It's a jumble of some of me favorite places."

"You sure do have a knack for decorating. I feel as if I'm in an Irish garden, enjoying teatime."

"Super. That's exactly the feelin' I wanted this time."

"This time? Do you change the decor often?"

"When I begin to feel homesick for Ireland I redo the place. Of course durin' the holidays everythin' changes. Over time I had to buy a place to house all me paraphernalia. Me little apartment upstairs no longer sufficed."

Maddie caught that. Little apartment upstairs?

"I haven't seen ya round Jacob's Bend before. Are ya here on holiday?"

"Actually, I just moved here. My friends, the Morenos, have lived in Jacob's Bend for three years. They finally talked me into moving."

"Ah yes, Carolyn. Such a dear lady. She comes in often."

"Have you lived in Jacob's Bend long?"

"I'd say goin' on ten years now. Me husband, Shane, and I came here on business. That is, he came on business. His company asked him to open a division of the parent company in the states, preferably in the Pacific Northwest. They were very generous. Bought our home in Ireland, gave him a large raise and relocation package. We settled in a lovely home just up the street. I opened this store 'bout a year after we moved here. I needed somethin' to do. I was bored to the rafters. Shane died three years after we arrived."

Maddie caught her breath, and the woman paused to look at her. A sense of sympathy drifted across the room, even though Gael turned her attention back to the dress she was working with. "Still miss him terribly, even after seven years."

It seemed strange that she had met so many widows. She never would have given widowhood a thought until Jeff's death. Or even how drastically it changed someone's life.

Maddie cleared her throat and gathered herself. "That must have been, um, difficult," she offered. "What did you do?"

"Our house was really too large for one person. So many memories. I sold it and moved into the small apartment upstairs. Missin' Shane and all the lovely places we visited, I decided to decorate the shop more elaborately, mimickin' their special charm. It's a lot a fun."

"Well, it's delightful. You must draw a lot of people into the area."

"I do a pretty good business. Ya wouldn't think in a small town like Jacob's Bend a business like mine could survive. Word of mouth brings people from all over. Fortunately, with the sale of the house and me husband's life insurance, it's not a struggle to make ends meet. It don't take a whole lot to support a widow.

"Anyway, I soon begun to run out of storage space, decided to buy a house smaller than the original, but larger than the apartment. The house I live in now has a huge shop out back where I keep everythin' cataloged and ready to go."

She expertly flipped the dress she was steaming. "What about you, Maddie, have ya found a place ta live yet?"

"Actually, no, not yet. Elias over at the county says there aren't any homes for sale. Carolyn and I looked at a few Elias said *might* come up for sale, but they were . . . not quite what I had in mind. I'm staying with Alex and Carolyn for the time being. However, I am looking for a place to rent while I look for a house to buy. Your apartment upstairs wouldn't happen to be for rent, would it?"

Gael gave Maddie an odd look.

Maddie pursed her lips. "What?" Had she said something wrong?

"Are you sure you don't have a touch o' the Irish? I was just thinkin' yesterday I should do somethin' with that apartment. It's just sittin' there gatherin' dust. Would ya like to see it?"

"Oh yes, please."

"It's only got one bedroom and a bath. The rest of the place is one big room. Kitchen, dinin', livin', all in one. There's a separate entrance in the back."

"One bedroom and a bath sounds great."

Excitement filled Maddie's heart when she saw the modest, furnished apartment, decorated just as lovely as the shop. "It's perfect, Gael. Perfect."

"I don't quite know what to charge for rent. I own the buildin' so it costs me nothin' much extra. How does five hundred dollars a month sound?"

"That sounds very generous."

"Then it's a deal. When would ya like to be movin' in?"

"Is tomorrow too soon?"

Gael laughed out loud. "Ya really mean business, don't ya?"

"I do. Alex and Carolyn's home is wonderful, but it's really only big enough for the two of them. Besides, they need their space as much as I need mine. Do you want a cleaning deposit or first and last month's rent?"

"Not to worry, dear, not to worry. I'm a trustin' soul. Me intuition hasn't failed me yet. Ya just bring your things over first thing in the mornin' and make yourself at home."

"You don't know how much I appreciate this. My friends have been great letting me stay with them, but I don't want to impose on their friendship any longer than need-be. Is nine o'clock too early?"

"Nine works fine."

"Thanks for the tea and scones, Gael. I'll reciprocate when I get settled." Maddie smiled over her shoulder at her new landlady on her way out the door.

Having very little to move, it took Maddie no time to settle in. It took longer to explain the sudden departure to Carolyn, but in the end she and Alex helped transport her few boxes up the stairs to her new, if temporary, home.

Maddie placed Jewell's painting on the long narrow table along the left wall near the front door. In that spot she could admire it from anywhere in the small apartment. Unpacking the few boxes she brought with her would have to wait until after her walk to River's Edge Market down the street.

By two o'clock everything rested in place. Three bags of groceries filled the cupboards and refrigerator. She brewed a cup of tea and sat in the chair next to the window taking in the sights and sounds of downtown Jacob's Bend. Sipping her tea, she pulled the lace curtain back.

A couple strolled hand in hand along Main Street. The woman looked up at her young man with an admiring smile that clearly revealed her tender feelings for him. There it was again, that something that had died in her own marriage.

What had happened? She shook her head.

They had been so much in love. Jeff's crazy sense of humor made it fun to work together to achieve their goals. She could still see the grin on his face and twinkle in his eye when she would catch him watching her at a party. She felt so special then.

Maddie looked up at the clear blue sky. "Did you know I watched you too?" She had watched him do odd jobs around the house, work in the yard. She loved watching him do the things he enjoyed, taking on a challenge.

And then it all seemed to fall apart. He worked harder, got angrier, started keeping secrets.

Let it go, Maddie.

But where to? It was something Maddie hadn't really asked before, and her question hung in the quiet apartment.

If I'm supposed to let it go, where to?

Maddie looked around the room. Her eyes landed on Gael's antique secretary. Pen in hand, hesitant at first, she stared into the distance, and gathering her courage, penned her heart's dictation.

Did You See?

Did you see me when I watched you walk the path alone?
Sometimes I watched with a heavy heart,
Mostly with a smile.

Did you see me when I thought of you throughout the busy day?
Sometimes with concern or anxiety,
Mostly with thankfulness.

Did you see me when I cried over your aching heart?
Sometimes with guilt,
Mostly with anticipation of healing.

Did you see me when I wondered what was in your mind?
Sometimes with fear,
Mostly with great anticipation to hear.

Did you see me when my heart ached to share?
Sometimes sorrow and hurt,
Mostly excitement and hope.

Did you see my love enfold you in the hundred tiny things?
Sometimes with a look,
Mostly with a touch.

Did you see my admiration for you?
Sometimes with the helping,
Mostly with grateful words.

Did you know how much I loved you, as I knew from you?
Sometimes with silence,
Mostly with acts of appreciation.

Do you see me now missing you and longing for your smile?
Sometimes tears and anguish,
Mostly grateful for the time we shared.

I love you,
Maddie

Maddie put her head down on the desk and wept.

THIRTY-NINE

Week after week, the residents of Jacob's Bend became more endearing.

Still, the frustration of not finding a home played heavy on Maddie's mind. What if she never found a permanent place to live? This tiny apartment was comfy, but it wasn't where she wanted to stay. She felt as though the walls were closing in on her. She scanned the small room. *Give it time, Maddie.*

A walk about town took her to an area she had not visited before. Three blocks from her apartment the homes were run-down, some with boarded windows and graffiti on the now-abandoned ruins. The landscape up and down the street was less than manicured. A ramshackled house with bed-sheets hanging off-kilter in the front window spoke of this being the poor side of town.

Farther up the block, half a dozen boys shouted obscenities and threw rocks at an old shack. When a withered old woman hobbled out flailing a broom at the young juveniles, they took off running in Maddie's direction.

Maddie caught one wide-eyed delinquent by the arm. "Hey, what are you guys doing throwing rocks at that lady's house?"

"She's no lady. That's Witch Hazel."

"Witch Hazel?"

"Yeah, she's meaner and uglier than Sappy Lange."

Maddie squinted at the boy who looked to be around ten years old. "Who is Sappy Lange?"

He looked over his shoulder, fear etched in his eyes. "Listen, lady, I can't hang around here and wait for Witch Hazel to cast a spell on me." He pulled his arm free and ran with all his might after the other boys.

Maddie cautiously walked up the block and stopped in front of Witch Hazel's house. So tiny, the place couldn't have more than two rooms. The heavy growth of bushes, trees, and vines left little room to walk the path to the chipped and faded yellow shack. A dim light shone through a grimy front window.

An old sink, a toilet, several car engines, bricks, rocks, and trash littered the property. A faded, handwritten sign that read "Night Crawlers—$2" lay propped against a tree trunk.

Maddie considered walking up to the door and introducing herself to the elderly woman to offer some kind of assistance. She thought better of it, and instead asked a few questions around town. Carolyn and Gael both confessed to knowing nothing about the old woman. They were seldom in that part of town.

"Why are you so curious about her, Maddie?" Carolyn asked over a shared muffin the next morning.

"Why isn't somebody helping her?" Maddie thought again about the boys throwing rocks at the house. She would have been terrified if she had been the one inside. Maddie sat up abruptly, an idea awakening in her mind. "I wonder if Angela's church could take her on as a project. I promised Angela I'd go to church with her this Sunday. Maybe I'll just have a talk with the pastor over there."

Carolyn grinned. "You do that."

*   *   *

Maddie did talk to the pastor that day. And she also found herself coming every Sunday after that. She had overheard a group of people talking out on the front lawn as she passed by. They were sharing with a man who had just started attending the church what a wonderful pastor Ben Farrington was. The man wanted some background on their pastor before he committed.

Ben Farrington had been pastor of North Hills Chapel just shy of five years, gaining the congregation's trust by working through a mountain of unresolved problems left by the previous pastor who had moved east to care for his wife's ailing parents.

Ever so slowly the folks at North Hills saw Pastor Ben as an honest man. His compassionate heart had captured the members, as it had Maddie.

Pastor Ben stressed the needs of their small community and those living nearby, reminding everyone of what Jesus said, "Go into all the world" and "You shall be my witnesses both in Jerusalem, and in all Judea and Samaria, and even to the remotest part of the earth."

Over the past year and a half, because of Pastor Ben's influence, many people had taken on uncomfortable challenges they never would have in the past. Like volunteering at the homeless shelters in Carterville or collecting and distributing clothing and food to the poor right in Jacob's Bend.

Jacob's Bend had the look of a perfect little village, but there were those who had major needs just like anywhere else. Just like Witch Hazel. Maddie hated calling her that, but no one seemed to know her real name.

Maddie jumped right in to help the others at North Hills with the projects Pastor Ben brought before them. This was what she was made for. Even Carolyn said so.

Of course Carolyn said so. She thought just like Gram.

Longtime member Madelyn Simpson took it upon herself however, to make sure North Hills also had plenty of fun diversions. After all, church shouldn't be all solemn and serious.

Each week Maddie received a little more insight into the man behind the pastor when Pastor Ben applied his sermon to events in his own life. Never embarrassed to share his mistakes and faults, he attributed his changed life to his relationship with Jesus. The more intimately he became acquainted with his Savior the more he saw life as an opportunity to serve and give. From that passion came a servant's heart. Maddie could see that many in the congregation, and the community, were changing as a result of Pastor Ben's example.

FORTY

From the outside, Weatherby's Bookstore looked like a place where men would go to smoke their pipes and talk about the stock market. But Maddie quickly discovered the large area in the back of the store was the heart of the owners.

Peter Weatherby, an only child, was raised in Jacob's Bend after his parents happened upon the town on their trip headed west to make their fortune. They fell in love with the lush beauty and made it their home. Peter and his wife, Vickie, childhood friends, married right out of high school.

After twenty-five years at the hospital in Carterville as an ER nurse, Vickie's seniority meant she could limit her schedule to only two ten-hour shifts a week. On off days she helped Peter in the bookstore. Having lost their only son to leukemia when he was three, the two doted on every child who came into the shop.

Every Saturday dozens of children and adults, Maddie included, gathered at Weatherby's among the miniature tables and chairs to sit on colorful wall-to-wall Winnie the Pooh carpet for Tall Tales Storytime with Vickie. Peter often joined her, acting out the scenes and the characters of a variety of animals and people. Whether an itty-bitty spider or a hulking lumberjack, Peter improvised with each character, changing his tone, inflection, and facial expressions. A history buff and storyteller himself, Peter threw in fun facts along with flights of fancy.

Maddie loved Saturday-morning Tall Tales. The stories told amid the stacks of children's books and games quickly became her favorite activity of the week.

One Friday afternoon, while Vickie stocked shelves with new arrivals, Maddie tracked Peter down in the young adult fiction section of the store.

"Peter, I've wondered about this since the first day I came to Jacob's Bend. Would you tell me the story of the horn?"

Peter grinned. "Got time for coffee?"

"Always."

Vickie poured three cups and joined them. "I love to hear this story."

Peter sipped his coffee recalling the details. "A few years before the town of Jacob's Bend was established, it wasn't much more than a general store, saloon, and church that doubled as a school. The Donation Land Act gave 320 acres to every unmarried white male citizen if they were eighteen or older. Every married couple arriving in the Oregon Territory before December 1, 1850, got 640 acres. Applicants had to live on the land and make use of it for four years and then they could own it outright.

"Some miles south of town a foreigner and his family squatted, as the townspeople called it, on fifty acres of unsurveyed land. The family farmed and raised a few head of cattle.

"People called Jacob Hertzog aloof because he and his family spoke a strange language. The townspeople ostracized Jacob's family, not understanding their ways. The Hertzogs were friendly enough when in town, but they never joined in church gatherings or any town festivities.

"The story goes that Jacob had this funny-looking horn he blew for various occasions. Looked like an animal horn of some sort. Called it a shofar. Some said he used it to call his children in from the fields. A different blast warned against wildfires or danger. Although Jacob and his family didn't mix much with the rest of the town, the people always listened up when they heard Jacob's horn ring out a disaster call.

"Every Friday just before sundown, Jacob blew the horn with another distinct sound to announce their church service. They called it Shabbat. The Hertzogs were Jewish. When Jacob learned enough English to explain his religion to the townsfolk, they were awestruck by how much he knew about the goings-on in their own Bibles, especially the Old Testament. Not knowing exactly what a Jewish reverend might be called, they nicknamed him Rev.

"Once, Jacob shared how the prophet Isaiah spoke of how the Spirit of the Lord told of good tidings for the poor, healing for the brokenhearted, liberty for the captives, comfort for all who mourn, giving them beauty for ashes and the oil of joy for mourning. Most churchgoers knew the story, but Jacob's telling made it come to life.

"After recounting the story, Jacob took out his horn and blew the saddest wailing sound anyone had ever heard. It sounded like the ache in Jacob's own heart for broken people came right through the horn.

"He knew about broken people. There was an old, weathered home situated along the river where the feeble, blind and lame, misfits and out-casts—so the townspeople called them—lived with an old missionary, Sister Langley. Come to find out, Jacob and his family visited twice a month, taking food, wood, blankets, and making repairs to the old place. Few knew the Hertzogs were helping the poor and downtrodden."

Maddie and Vickie wiped tears from their cheeks.

"As the story goes, one particularly bitter winter it rained for twenty-five days straight. The river near town looked like it couldn't take another drop. When the townspeople heard the wailing disaster call of Jacob's horn, word spread fast that help was needed at Sister Langley's. The whole town turned out in their buckboards. When they arrived, the river had risen to the top step of the old place, lapping the porch. A continual deluge of rain kept Sister Langley and her people huddled together just inside the front door of the house, some crying, others shivering, wide-eyed.

"Jacob tied a rope from his buckboard to the front door. Plodding through the chest-high water, he helped every single person wade across the water to safety. Good thing the whole town turned out to help, because about the time the last person, Sister Langley, climbed into the buckboard and Jacob slapped the backside of his horses with the reins, the raging river ripped through the town."

Peter stopped to take a sip of coffee as Maddie gasped.

"What happened?"

"Jacob shouted for everyone to follow him to higher ground. You see, Jacob had built his home high on a hill above the river's ravaging effects.

"The Hertzog family welcomed everyone, using every square inch of floor space for sleeping. Many, after warming themselves and enjoying the good food provided by the Hertzogs found comfort boarding in the barn.

Quilts, soft hay, and plenty of body heat kept them warm through the night. The townspeople slept peacefully and thanked God for such caring, giving neighbors.

"That's why many of the businesses in town have the man blowing the horn etched on their buildings, to honor Jacob Hertzog for saving the people of Jacob's Bend. They wanted to name the river after him, but being a humble man, he wouldn't hear of it. So they named it Rev's River, with fondness, of course.

"When it came time to name the town, it was unanimous that it should be Jacob's Bend. The bend, signifying the sharp turn in the river that caused the water to rise quickly and overflow onto Sister Langley's property, was a reminder of the kind, courageous efforts of Jacob and his family.

"Most signed a petition asking the US government to allow Jacob to legally claim the fifty acres he and his family farmed. After hearing the story, the government sent an accommodation to recognize the Hertzog family's heroic efforts. About a year later, while the town was still rebuilding after the flood, a government official arrived and with great fanfare presented Jacob with the land deed to his property, free and clear." Peter smiled at the two women.

"Isn't that a great story?" Vickie looked over at Maddie.

"That is an amazing story."

Maddie sat back in her chair, a half-formed idea springing up in her mind. Carolyn had always said Maddie had this insatiable need to help people. She wondered if there was some way she might take up Sister Langley and Jacob Hertzog's mantle. She would love to leave a worthwhile legacy like Jacob and his family.

Maddie, you are such a dreamer. Maddie glanced behind her, expecting to see Jeff smirking.

FORTY-ONE

One particularly dark, rainy morning, Maddie slipped into her sweats and sat in the chair by the window sipping fresh brewed coffee. Her mood matched the weather outside, and she found herself wrestling with the circle of doubts that had plagued her during the worst years of her marriage.

Why was this so hard?

Elias had called the previous morning with another possible lead for her, but Maddie couldn't muster up the energy to go check it out. The parade of wet fields, broken-down barns, and dismal roads seemed like too much to face today.

You're almost that dismal inside. Are you avoiding that too?

A dream from two nights before came back to her. In the dream she stood, arms crossed, in a room with a man she was to marry the next day. He slouched on the couch, sneered at her, and suggested they not wait for the wedding night to consummate their relationship.

"I don't do that," Maddie said, disgusted.

"We can make it quick," he said.

"I don't do that either. As a matter of fact, I don't know what I was thinking marrying you. This wedding is off. For good."

The obnoxious man shrugged. "Whatever."

"I will not give up my freedom that easy."

She turned from the man, walked out of the room, and found herself on the phone with Jeff. He was somewhere far away. But he sounded happy, ecstatic actually, to hear her voice.

"Jeff, I want to see you. No matter where you are, I need to be with you. I'll meet you wherever you say."

"Sure, Maddie, that sounds great. But I thought you wanted your freedom."

"I want you."

"But I'm not there."

"You never were. You were never here," Maddie found herself yelling into the telephone. "You weren't there until it was too late."

"I know." His voice whispered sadness.

"You abandoned me. For your work. Your trysts. All those company parties, wondering, *Is she the one?* And now you've abandoned me again. This time forever."

"I'm sorry, Maddie. We did try, right? We tried to make it better . . ." Jeff's voice faded.

She felt a small ray of peace inside as she let go of the dream. Freedom did not come easy for Maddie. Yet releasing the anger and bitterness felt like a dove taking flight.

"Jeff, what am I doing? I can't stay angry with you any longer. Enough."

Later that day, with a rain-washed landscape before her and an unleashed sense of purpose, Maddie decided to take a drive and have a look at the only piece of property available in or around Jacob's Bend. The Riley farm.

Why was she doing this? There was no way she needed 427 acres of land. Good grief, she was all alone. Those words still cut deep.

Located six miles south of Jacob's Bend, the lush countryside made the drive to the Riley farm pure pleasure. According to Elias's directions, she was to turn left off Highway 25 at the old Coca-Cola sign. That would put her onto Kendall Lane. Her instructions were to follow Kendall Lane, a bumpy dirt road, for about a half mile, give or take a tree, until she came to Paddy's Pond. Just past Paddy's Pond, on the left, she'd see the Riley place. Elias said she would have to get out and open the large wooden gate to the driveway.

He also made a point of telling her to remember to close the gate. Strangers or homeless people might try to find shelter there. People might even use the property for target practice. The gate really didn't do much but give a mental stop sign. For some reason Elias felt that was enough.

When Maddie saw the pond and the gate next to a faded red mailbox the size of a miniature covered wagon that read, "Riley, 727 Kendall Lane," an unsettling feeling started gnawing in the pit of her stomach. Pushing the gate open, she looked around to see if someone might be hiding behind a tree or in the bushes. *No movement. Good.*

She drove slowly through the opening. A few yards up the driveway she got out of her car to shut the gate. This place was out in the middle of nowhere. Who would ever come through that gate? Her obedience came from hearing that slow drawl in the back of her mind, "Don't fergit to—"

"Okay, okay, Elias. It's done."

The dirt driveway, overgrown with dead grass and weeds, took her past a collection of shattered bottles and rusty cans scattered on the ground near a large rock.

Target practice.

Driving farther up the long driveway, the gnawing in her stomach intensified. *What did I eat for lunch? Did I even eat lunch?*

About two hundred yards from the gate, a small knoll promised a glimpse of the property. By the time she reached the top of the knoll her heart was pounding. The gnawing in her stomach grew into flutters of . . . excitement?

What was going on?

Taking a deep breath to steady herself, Maddie stepped out of the car. The setting sun shone directly in her face. Squinting to get a glimpse of the farm, Maddie shaded her eyes with her hand. She pressed a hand to her mouth and gasped as the absolute calm of the old farm enveloped her.

The landscape stretched across endless miles with the Riley farm encompassing acres of farmland, two houses, a barn, and a few small out-buildings. To Maddie, it felt like . . . home.

Maddie became conscious of a slide show streaming through her mind. *Jeff's death. Funeral. Provision. Protection. Decisions. Sale of the house. Drive from Chicago. Rescue by the Walterses'. Their kindness. Beautiful guest room. Georgia. Billy. Café. Jewell's Tomes. Sam's Bar. Jacob's Bend. O'Donnell apartment.*

And through them all ran her grandmother's convincing voice. *"You can do this, Mads."*

Maddie wiped the tears from her eyes so she could take in the beauty of the farm. To the right of the driveway, the stately main house sat on a knoll surrounded by a cluster of trees, overlooking a large courtyard with a pathway that led past an outbuilding down a gently sloping hill to several acres of fallow fields awaiting spring planting.

Circling past a tree-filled orchard, the driveway split off toward the barn. A rocky dirt path flowed into the orderly fields below. The driveway veered around to the left, leading to a smaller house surrounded by ancient oaks, also resting on a knoll.

Who wouldn't love to feast on that view every day?

She scanned the farmland below. How would she ever take care of all this? Her hand swept the breadth of the farm. Maddie found herself fighting a losing battle with the growing certainty that this was it—this was the right place for her. But why on earth would she want to live on this huge piece of property all alone? It was so run-down. It would take months, maybe years to repair everything. No. This was not right.

Jeff would hate it. The gnawing in her stomach began again. *But he's not here.*

Glancing at the old buildings and overgrown plants, Maddie shook her head. "No. This is ridiculous. I'm dreaming." She turned to leave but gave in to the urge for one last look. When she turned back around, the sky displayed the most magnificent sunset she had ever seen.

You're kidding me.

Back behind the steering wheel of her car, she wondered, *Maybe I should come back to see it again more closely. If for no other reason than to put this ridiculous idea to rest. A gorgeous sky doesn't fix bad plumbing, Maddie. Be real.*

She decided she would come back on Saturday, bring Alex and Carolyn. If they thought she should buy this farm, then maybe she'd consider it. That felt safe, because they would never agree to that.

She looked back over her shoulder when she closed the gate. Why would she want to live out here on this broken-down old farm?

*   *   *

Maddie was starving by the time she reached her apartment. It was after seven when she dialed Carolyn's number.

"Hi, Carolyn."

"Hey, Maddie, how was your day?"

"Different."

"Huh?"

"Well, since I haven't been able to find a single home I'd consider buying in a radius of fifty miles, I took a trip out to see the Riley place."

"Really?"

"Just needed something to do."

"Well, I'm sure glad you finally invested in a cell phone since you're traveling out in the country all alone."

"Yeah, me too. What would you think about you, Alex, and me taking a drive out to the Riley farm on Saturday to look around? Just for fun."

"Sure, why not? I hear it's beautiful out there."

By Saturday, after several sleepless nights of wrestling with her uncertainty, fear and doubt consumed Maddie. A dozen excuses came to her why she should *not* buy the farm. Only one why she should: Gram's voice.

She decided that stomach-gnawing thing was probably hunger. Besides, Alex and Carolyn would think it was just a silly emotional impulse. She had no doubt the three of them would agree that farm could not possibly be the home she was looking for.

*   *   *

Nine o'clock Saturday morning Alex opened the gate to the Riley farm. The quiet stillness of the country calmed Maddie's nerves until they drove through the gate. Then the odd gnawing started, lasting until Alex crested the hill. Maddie heard Carolyn suck in air and whisper, "Oh my."

Maddie's heart beat harder. *I'm in big trouble.*

Alex drove the car up to the big house and parked. The trio could not take their eyes off the stately white house as they walked up the steps to the front porch. With the doors locked and the windows boarded up, there was little they could see inside. The massive structure had two, maybe three stories. A dormer sat atop the house and quite possibly embodied an attic or maybe even a secret room.

Shifting their attention to the rest of the property, they saw weed-infested rosebushes on both sides of the path that led from the big house to the apple orchard, which ran to the smaller residence. The orchard itself resembled a magical forest, dark and foreboding. Trees interlocked one another from years of neglect. Eerie. Most of the bushes looked dead. Still, rosebushes just the same. Maddie hadn't noticed on her last visit the path leading through the orchard connecting the two dwellings.

Heavy with rotting apples, the branches hung low. Dead fruit lay on the ground. The foul, putrid scent of fermented apples filled the air. Broken branches laden with fruit sprawled across the path, making the short walk difficult. Trudging up to the smaller house, persistent gnawing in Maddie's stomach caused her to stop and take a deep breath. *Not again.*

The closer they got, the stronger her heart pulsed, until she thought it might pound out of her chest.

They tried the front door of the cottage. Locked. Maddie led the troupe around the building. The windows here were also boarded. She took a mental inventory: dead flowers, dead shrubs, damaged trees. Coming from the back of the cottage around to the front, she stopped so abruptly that Alex and Carolyn ran into her.

There, sprawled before them, sat not only acres of neatly plowed fields ready for spring planting and acres of grazing cattle, but to the west, magnificent pine-covered mountains stretching for miles. The scene took Maddie's breath away.

Carolyn and Alex stood on either side of her, mouths wide open.

Alex broke the silence, "Wow. What a view."

Maddie turned to the couple, arms crossed over her chest. "Okay, go ahead, tell me you think I should buy this place. Watching your responses, it's evident you think this is pretty amazing. Actually, I kinda thought you would tell me I'm crazy for even considering buying it."

Carolyn's raised eyebrows said something different. "What are you talking about?"

Maddie described her experience the last time she came to the farm and how her stomach was about to erupt at that moment.

Carolyn laughed. "Maddie, you're either in love or have a stomach bug. And I know you haven't met anyone."

Maddie uncrossed her arms. "Carolyn, I'm serious. There is something about this place."

Alex's brow creased. "Maddie, you can't be serious. There is no way you could handle this place by yourself. I'm sorry, but I would *never* advise you to buy this farm."

Maddie looked out over the farm again.

"You'd be all alone out here. Not to mention you know absolutely nothing about farming. No way. You're dreaming."

"Then please explain to me what all this stomach gnawing and heart pounding is about?"

Alex glanced over at Carolyn.

Confused, Maddie looked at the two. "Okay, so, I was right the first time I thought about showing you the place. You're telling me *not* to buy the Riley farm."

Carolyn agreed. "That's right, it's unanimous. *Do not* buy this farm."

Carolyn put her arm around Maddie's shoulder and gave her a squeeze. "I know you are a little anxious over not being able to find a house." Carolyn scrunched up her nose. "But that doesn't mean you buy the first thing that comes along."

"Yeah, I guess."

By the time they got back to town, Maddie talked herself into accepting Alex and Carolyn's advice. Before they dropped her off at the apartment, she told Carolyn, "Well, at least now I'll be able to get some sleep. I am going to put the Riley farm out of my mind for good."

By eleven o'clock she knew that wasn't going to happen. She woke up with a start, sat straight up in bed, and whispered, "Broken acres."

What was a broken acre? Running her fingers through her hair, she pulled the strands away from her face.

Looking up, she argued her point with her grandmother. She usually only did that when she was desperate. "Gram, I thought we agreed I would take whatever Alex and Carolyn recommended?"

Nothing.

"427 acres for one person?"

Nothing.

"Okay, okay. I'll go out there one more time." This was ridiculous. "But I need a definite sign. You know how my mind runs off with my own plans. If I get some kind of sign, I'll buy the property. If not, I'll chalk this up to silly dreaming. Okay?"

Nothing.

*   *   *

Before sunup Maddie found herself opening the gate to the Riley farm. Once again, the same gnawing in her stomach began when she closed the gate behind her. Topping the hill, she parked the car. Slowly walking the entire yard, she stopped in front of the cottage, hands on her hips. She walked around the back and turned the doorknob.

It opened.

She jumped back and looked around. No one there. Walking slowly through the door, her heart palpitations intensified.

Maddie found herself in a kitchen obviously left to time but with gracious proportions that connected with the living room. Pulling back the heavy dust-encrusted living room drapes, Maddie coughed and blinked to clear her eyes. Two picture windows, darkened by outside boards, promised a view of the big house. It took no time to walk through the entire cottage. Every room had at least two windows. Even the bathroom had a large window and a smaller one above the shower.

Back where she started, Maddie slipped out the back door and made sure it was secure. She walked around to the front porch. The rising sun shot brilliant rays of light directly at the boarded-up picture windows. The big house stood tall and proud beyond the orchard. Out past the barn, fields glistened from morning frost. *What an incredible sight this would be to wake up to every morning.*

Canvassing the orchard, something caught her eye. She squinted as if to get a better look. What was that red thing under that clump of buckbrush? Probably some old beer can. She took a step forward to get a better look . . . when something skittered across the porch.

Eyes wide, Maddie screamed. Her heart threatened to explode. She ran as fast as she could down the path to the orchard to get as far away from the cottage as she could. Stopping to catch her breath, she bent over, hands on her knees. The buckbrush she had seen from the porch sat a couple of feet to her left.

There among the weeds and brush was one lone flower. Her *favorite* flower.

No, this couldn't be. She was seeing things. This flower only bloomed in late spring, early summer. It was the end of November.

Maddie moved the thick overgrowth to reveal a beautiful long-stemmed red poppy. Somewhat stunted from the thicket of weeds, but a red poppy nonetheless.

Her face upward, she asked, "Gram, is this the sign?" A shiver traveled down her back as the poppy nodded gently in the breeze. "Okay, okay, it's a sign. So I am supposed to buy this big ole broken-down farm? And why?"

Nothing.

Frustrated, Maddie threw up her hands.

"Okay, but I hope you know what you're doing."

Caressing the poppy, she probed her doubts. Maybe she should ask for another sign.

This is where you are meant to be, Mads.

Alex and Carolyn were going think she was crazy.

Maddie rolled her eyes. *Good grief, I think I'm crazy.*

FORTY-TWO

The next day Maddie hurried to the county offices to uncover every bit of information available on the land auction process.

"Elias, I've been out to the Riley farm and I need some information on how to go about making a bid at the county auction. The land is beautiful, but the buildings look like they might need a lot of work."

"That's true enough, although it coulda been a lot worse. You see, when the property taxes weren't paid in November some years back, the county found that Edgar had died in August, and since there were no heirs to his estate, someone had the idea to go out and shore up the place to keep vandalism at bay, much as possible."

"Oh, so that's why the windows are all boarded up."

Elias nodded. "As far as the county auction goes, when property is owned outright, there are no heirs, and the taxes haven't been paid for four consecutive years, the property goes inta foreclosure. A delinquent notice is posted announcing a two-year redemption period. After two years, if the back taxes, along with fees and interest of course, ain't paid, the property is deeded over to the county. They decide if'n it can be used for county business. If not, it goes to auction, which takes place on the courthouse steps once a year. Real market value of the property is posted before the auction. Minimum bid begins at seventy-five percent of the real market value. If'n the property ain't sold at auction, anyone can purchase it at the minimum bid price."

Elias paused in his explanation and gave her a quizzical look. "But are ya sure ya want it?"

Everyone seemed to have an opinion about Maddie's decision to buy the farm. Mostly negative.

*   *   *

"What on earth are you going to do with a 427-acre farm, Maddie?"

"Honestly, Carolyn, I don't have a clue. But I still think it's the right thing to do."

Alex's crossed arms gave a clear message of his concern. "You mean to tell me you are buying a huge farm and you don't have any idea what you're going to do with it?"

"Well, not exactly. I do know I'll continue to rent out parcels of land to those farmers who have a need."

Carolyn stretched out her hands to show the vastness of the place. "What are you going to do with two houses, a barn, and the other buildings?"

"Well, I'm not sure. But it will become clear as time goes by." *I hope.*

"Maddie, for one person?" Alex clearly wasn't ready to give in.

"Couldn't you start with some smaller decisions?"

Carolyn studied her for some time. "Maddie, you are definitely a different woman from the one I left behind when we moved here. That woman had absolutely no confidence in herself. Look at you. You're healthy. You're self-confident. And brave. I've always considered you very pretty. But this . . . this woman standing in front of me has become flat-out beautiful, inside and out. When did this metamorphosis take place?"

Maddie looked down at the floor and shrugged. "I couldn't tell you when it happened, but I can tell you I feel like a different woman than I was even a few months ago."

Carolyn scrunched up her nose. "But I have to wonder if you're taking this responsibility thing to extremes. Are you sure this is a wise thing to do?"

Maddie paced. Defensive, but sure of her decision, she went about convincing Alex and Carolyn. "I . . . ah, I'm not sure wise is the right word. I do know this is definitely where I am meant to be. You of all people should understand."

"But, Maddie—"

"It's not like I'm hearing the voice of God or anything. It's Gram."

Carolyn raised an eyebrow. "And that's supposed to make me feel better?"

FORTY-THREE

Maddie had spent a fun white Christmas with Bracy at Wheaton. January and February flew by with Gael needing her help in the shop. She packed up the Christmas decorations and took inventory. She even helped decorate for Valentine's Day.

Gael had introduced her to the most amazing woman. It seemed the Harper family had lived in the area, farming, for generations. Granny Harper, a strong, very encouraging woman who had been widowed twice, invited Maddie to the farm to help with canning come summer. It was as if they had been kindred spirits for years on their first meeting. Excitement ran through Maddie's thoughts knowing she had a new friend and possibly a mentor.

Now, with nothing to do but make plans, she waited impatiently for the county land auction.

Set for March thirteenth, the county land auction was held on the steps of the old courthouse in Carterville. The real market value for the Riley farm was set at $500,000 with a minimum bid of $375,000. People said she should consider anything less than $1,000 an acre, even with auction property, a steal. Funny how no one else wanted to steal the property at that price.

Elias, in all his glory, thoroughly enjoyed the power his gavel wielded every time he hit the podium with the finality of a sale.

Maddie purchased the farm for the minimum bid plus $10,000 in back taxes and fees. After paying the taxes, she put $300,000 into the mortgage, figuring she could manage the monthly payment on a $75,000 loan with the money she received from those who rented parcels. That still left her plenty of money from the sale of the Chicago house and her investments to make repairs and transform the run-down farm into a comfortable home and whatever else it would be used for.

That is, until she found out the farmers and cattle owners hadn't made a rental payment since Edgar died. It looked like Maddie would have to renegotiate with each of them. Could Alex help her with that? She had no idea what fair rent might be.

Lunch with Alex and Carolyn proved interesting. They could not believe Maddie had attended the auction and bought the property. All by herself.

Alex actually seemed proud of her, although he had a question or two. "Maddie, what are you going to do with two houses?"

"Good question. I can't see myself rambling around in that big house, way too much space. That's one of the reasons I sold my other house. Good grief, now I have *two*." The three laughed out loud.

"With some elbow grease and a little help from my friends"—she smiled big at Alex and Carolyn—"I think I can make that little place very comfortable. Now that the property is mine, or at least after I sign the papers, I'll tackle the small projects first. Paint and refurbish the cottage. Actually, first thing is to call out pest control to fumigate and remove all those nasty, beady-eyed—" Maddie shivered at the thought. "I am not stepping foot in that place until I'm sure *all* the mice, and every other kind of horrible critter, are dead and gone."

Carolyn gave a shiver herself, nodding her agreement.

"Prune the orchard; weed the garden; restore the rose-lined path. Whew, there is a lot to do. The cottage is first priority, though. I need to get it ready to live in. I'll tackle the big house when I have some idea what to do with it."

Carolyn grinned at her friend. "You're really excited about this, aren't you?"

"I am."

"Okay, then. We're in. Ready and willing to help with any and all projects you have planned for the cottage."

Alex agreed. "You bet. But, Maddie, the big house? I think you're gonna have to hire a professional contractor for that one."

"I know." Sigh.

"Maddie, have you talked to Isaac Birnbaum about your plans?" Alex looked concerned.

"Not exactly, but I will."

*   *   *

While waiting for the wheels of county bureaucracy to swing into motion, Maddie continued planning. Sometime in June would mark the close of escrow—quick, according to Elias—and she wanted to be ready to move forward with the cottage renovation.

Like a kid in a candy shop unable to decide which barrel to choose from first, she decided the exterior of the cottage needed a coat of white paint. It would not only look great with the dark green shingles she planned for the roof, but also a new roof would alleviate any concerns she had about leaks from the present patched roof come winter.

Her mental list grew as she thought about the inside of the house. *Rip up disgusting olive green shag carpet. Clear out cobwebs. Pull down ugly brown drapes. Wash walls and cupboards. A fresh coat of paint.* The bathroom definitely required a complete gutting and redesign.

Soon she would be the proud owner of—*Hmm, this place needs a name.* She didn't want to call it the old Riley farm. Admiring the beautiful landscape, she smiled. This was going to be her home.

She glanced across the orchard. She would need an awful lot of furniture to fill that big house. A deep sigh whistled past her lips.

"Not goin' there. Cross that bridge when I come to it. First, the cottage."

Just before sundown Maddie stood at the top of the hill scanning her farm. This was going to be a huge job. A lot of hard work. She could do this. She *could* do this.

She looked up. "I can do this, right, Gram?"

FORTY-FOUR

Ben Farrington had captured Maddie's attention the first time she heard him speak. He had a commanding presence and his voice held her captive. Actually, he looked and sounded an awful lot like the cowboy who gave them directions to the Plainsview property. She couldn't tell for sure, with the sunglasses he had been wearing.

Maddie had started going to church to support Angela, but eventually she had to admit that wasn't the only reason she went. She wanted to meet the people who were going to be her neighbors as well as the business owners in town, and some of them attended North Hills Chapel.

Pastor Ben had a way of drawing people in; talking about historical background, clothing, and customs and showing pictures and maps placed his congregants right in the setting of the stories he took from the Bible.

The man was easy to look at too. Handsome actually. His six-foot-three frame carried his broad shoulders well. He had amazingly strong arms for a man who only lifted a Bible. At least that's what she thought a pastor did. Maybe he also helped out on some of the ranches? Who knew what pastors did in their spare time?

Maddie had seen Pastor Ben take a bale of hay from his Jeep and toss it into the bed of a pickup like it was a bag of cotton. His intense brown eyes and short-cropped brown hair, usually hidden under a large black cowboy hat, could be called attractive. His normal attire included hat, jeans, white shirt, sleeves rolled up to the elbows, and cowboy boots. Sunday mornings he left the hat on the rack.

Madelyn Simpson, the bustling fifty-something vivid redhead who dressed, oddly enough, in 1940s thrift store chic garb, made a point of telling Maddie she considered Pastor Ben the most eligible bachelor in the county. Madelyn suspected he had been jilted some time in the past. "That's why he rarely dates."

The woman's tendency to gossip roused some latent antagonism within Maddie. "So, you say Pastor Ben *rarely* dates. Have you met any of the women he's dated?"

"Well, no, I haven't, but I'm pretty sure he's dating right now. He's been going to Carterville two, three times a week for the past several months."

Maddie raised her eyebrows. "Maybe he's taking classes at the junior college or visiting relatives."

"Oh no, Pastor Ben doesn't have any relatives here. His aunt and uncle who raised him live in Idaho. His parents died when he was young. Ten or twelve, I think. They were missionaries in Africa. Caught some terrible jungle disease and died one summer when he was staying at his aunt and uncle's horse ranch. He's an only child, raised with his cousins."

"I'm sorry to hear about his parents."

"I know, it's sad. Still, he turned out real good, don't you think?"

Maddie smiled.

Maddie told herself the reason she kept going back to North Hills was to help Angela and Brian through the grieving process. And of course, to get better acquainted with the people of Jacob's Bend. Still, there was something about Ben Farrington that drew her week after week. But the reasons that might be true didn't bear looking at. Not at all.

FORTY-FIVE

Ben glanced over at the woman sitting in the passenger seat of the church van. Madison Crane was quietly watching the landscape flow by. On their way to deliver baby quilts to Carterville General Hospital, other members of the Jacob's Bend Quilter's Guild chattered in the seats behind them.

"How are you finding life in Jacob's Bend?" Ben found himself startled again by the clear green depth of the gaze she turned on him.

"It's wonderful." Maddie's voice held a ripple of laughter. "Trips like this remind me of where I came from."

A small shadow appeared between her eyes, and Ben wondered what caused it. He didn't know much about this woman and was curious to learn more. His sources, even against his advice not to gossip, had informed him she was a widow from Chicago but she hadn't been willing to share much more. He had to admire someone who could keep her own counsel that well. On his part, he knew her to be friendly, giving, and, he had to admit, quite beautiful.

"It's a nice drive."

Maddie raised an eyebrow. "Madelyn Simpson thinks you have a girl-friend in Carterville, Pastor Ben, since you go there so often."

Ben swung his head in Maddie's direction. "She what?" He shook his head. "Madelyn, Madelyn. I go to Carterville to help at the shelters, visit shut-ins, and pray with other pastors."

"Oh-h-h, I see." Maddie grinned and turned to take in the landscape rolling by.

Why is that funny? Ben found himself wondering.

Ben also found himself wondering if Maddie liked riding horses. He boarded a couple of horses outside of town, and it was always easier to exercise them with a friend along.

Friend. Just a friendly ride.

*　　*　　*

Thursday night while serving dinner to the homeless, to his surprise, Ben popped the question.

"Maddie, would you like to go riding with me this Saturday? I board two horses at Sunset Stables just west of town."

He asked as if it were the most natural thing in the world to invite a woman to go riding with him. Inside, however, his heart felt like a time bomb ready to explode. *Why do I get so nervous around her?*

Maddie's eyes grew big. "Ah, sure. That sounds like fun. I'm not a very experienced rider. I've only ridden a few times."

"No problem. Teri is very gentle. That's why I named her after my mom. Tomas, on the other hand, is full of spirit, like my dad." He smiled.

"Was that your dad's name? Tomas?"

"Actually, it was Tom, but I thought Tomas fit the horse better."

Maddie gave Pastor Ben a mischievous grin. "I'll start with Teri, but I'd really like to try riding Tomas sometime."

Ben looked into Maddie's eyes. *Is this woman brave or just foolish?*

*　　*　　*

Saturday turned out as close to perfect as a day could be.

Ben took the back stairs up to Maddie's apartment, two at a time. When he knocked on the door, Maddie came out in hiking boots, jeans, and a lightweight lavender sweater.

Her smile caused his heart rate to pick up speed and threatened to buckle his knees. Ben steadied himself by holding tight to the railing. He cleared his throat. "Ready to go?"

"You bet, but remember, I'm not an experienced rider. I've only been on a horse twice in my whole life."

"You'll be fine."

While traveling the ten miles to Sunset Stables, Maddie asked him a slew of questions about his Jeep. "I probably ought to have a work vehicle since I just purchased a 427-acre farm."

"I'm curious. What are you going to do with all that land?"

Maddie looked out the side window. "Actually, I don't quite know except that I'll continue renting some of it to farmers and cattle owners."

Ben cocked his head and looked at the spunky woman over the top of his sunglasses.

"I know. I know. I get that same look from most people. I'm not sure what I'm supposed to do with it. I just know it's where I'm supposed to be, Pastor Ben."

"God knows," he said.

"If you say so."

*   *   *

Small but well kept, Sunset Stables housed horses in fenced pastures as well as sheltered corrals in the stable. Ben grabbed a picnic basket and blanket out of the back of the Jeep and handed them to Maddie. One of the stable hands helped him saddle the horses.

"Maddie, this is Teri and this guy is Tomas." He stroked the tall, muscular black stallion's short mane.

Maddie smiled. "I recognize this horse. I knew you were the cowboy who gave us directions."

Ben gave a half grin. "Yeah, I recognized you the first time you came to North Hills, but I didn't want to make you feel uncomfortable by mentioning it."

Maddie walked over to where Teri stood. She ran her hand over the horse's smooth face. "She's beautiful."

Ben grinned, looking into Maddie's sea-green eyes. A breeze caused soft auburn curls to dance on her shoulders. "Yes, she is."

The flush that rose on her cheeks brought Ben back to his senses. *Easy, Ben,* he told himself.

"Need help climbing up?"

"No, I think I've"—she grunted and swung her right leg over the saddle—"got it." Maddie pushed the hair out of her eyes, sat up straight, and smiled at him.

This woman was something else. Very independent. Or was that stubborn? Ben shook his head and chuckled.

Teri and Tomas sauntered side by side until they came to a narrow trail. Ben took the lead.

Maddie seemed enthralled with the landscape as the horses carried them over rolling foothills. "Is this where you normally ride?"

"Sometimes. I like to get out and as far away as I can when I ride."

"I can understand that. You've got people who need your time and attention constantly."

"Most of the time I'm good with it. But there are days." Ben took a deep breath.

When they stopped, Maddie explored the meadow where wildflowers bloomed everywhere. "This is absolutely beautiful."

Ben dismounted near a large oak. Helping Maddie down from Teri, he was aware his hands lingered on her waist a little longer than necessary when she glanced up at him and moved away nervously.

"I'm starved. What's for lunch?"

Ben realized the color in her cheeks was not just from the wind.

"Oh yeah, lunch." Ben grinned.

With their picnic spread on the blanket, Maddie kept the conversation casual and Ben gladly followed her lead.

"So, Pastor Ben, tell me about the ranch you grew up on."

"Do you think you could drop the pastor thing and just call me Ben?"

"Okay, Ben."

Hoisted up on his elbows, legs stretched the length of the blanket, Ben looked out at the blue sky beyond Maddie. "It's in Idaho. Beautiful. Rugged. Been in my uncle's family for generations. They raise horses, board some. Mainly for cattle ranchers."

"They still ride horseback to herd cows?"

"Oh yeah. Real cowboys don't use trucks out on the range. Trucks are for hauling and for town."

"Oh." Maddie took a bite of her sandwich.

"I had planned to live out my life on that ranch."

"What happened?"

Ben set his cowboy hat on the blanket near the picnic basket and ran his fingers through his hair. "God."

"Huh?"

Ben shrugged. "Long story short, I was out on the range herding strays and had set up camp to stay overnight. I settled in near the fire, laid my head against my saddle, and marveled at the stars. I had been a Christian since I was a kid, eight or nine. My parents were missionaries."

Maddie nodded. Her grin suggested he would know who her source was.

"Anyway, I thought about the host of stars, knowing this earth was just a speck in the billions of galaxies God created. I thought about how insignificant my life was, how I was just a puff, a breath." Ben looked up at the sky.

"I remembered God telling Abraham He would multiply Abraham's descendants as the stars of the heavens."

Maddie scanned the afternoon sky.

Ben glanced at her. "I know this is going to sound strange."

Maddie smiled, chewing a slice of apple she had taken from the basket.

"I heard God say—not in an audible voice, but it sure sounded like it in my spirit—God said to me, *"Tend my sheep. Abraham's seed. My Son's Beloved. Shepherd my sheep."*

Maddie sat, mouth ajar, eyes wide.

Ben laughed. "Of course, then I had to figure out what all that meant. Was I to be a missionary like my folks? Go to Abraham's people, the Jews and Arabs? When I read what Jesus said to Peter at the end of the book of John, I knew deep inside God meant for me to become a shepherd, a pastor, and tend His sheep. So I went to college and seminary. A little later in life than most, I graduated six years ago at the ripe old age of thirty-five. A year later I became the pastor at North Hills Chapel."

Ben gave Maddie a one-sided grin. "I love being a shepherd. And I love God's sheep."

"It shows. I admire your courage, Ben, doing what you think God wants you to do when you don't even know what the end result will be."

"Aren't you doing the same thing? You bought that farm not knowing what you are going to do with it."

"But that's different. I'm not shepherding people or helping anyone."

"Yet," Ben said with conviction.

"Unless you know something I don't, I can't see how that farm is going to do anything like that."

"You are helping people. The farmers and ranchers who rent your land. And Angela. You've been a great help to her."

Maddie stared past Ben. "I guess you're right."

A cool breeze whipped around them. Maddie shivered. Ben wasn't sure if it was the breeze or a thought that prompted it.

Ben looked at the sky. "We'd better head back. It's starting to cool down."

FORTY-SIX

Maddie looked up at the pulpit from the back pew. She had a hard time understanding Ben's logic. How could a relationship with a dead man do everything this Paul guy said it could? Gram had said the same thing. She didn't get it then, and she didn't get it now. She eyed Pastor Ben. *But I'd like to.*

"The apostle Paul wrote, 'Be kind to one another, tenderhearted, forgiving one other, even as God in Christ forgave you.'" Pastor Ben looked out over the congregation.

"Forgiveness is not so much for the other person's benefit as it brings healing to our own souls." He scanned several of the people before him. Admonishing eyes pierced Maddie's soul.

"We have all sinned against God. All. And those who have received the gift of salvation through Jesus Christ know what this forgiveness is. Yet, are we kind, tenderhearted, forgiving to those who have hurt us? Unforgiveness keeps us from living fully alive because we are weighted down with bitterness, anger, resentment. Forgiveness is the salve that heals a tortured heart."

Maddie whispered to Angela when everyone stood to sing the last song, "Will you excuse me, Angela, I need to leave a little early." She rushed to her car, nostrils flaring. Fumbling to open the car door, she dropped her keys. What did he know? There were some things you just couldn't forgive.

Back in her apartment, Maddie sat in the chair by the window, fuming. How could she forgive all he'd done, all the pain he'd caused? She could never forgive Jeff or forget his violent attacks, his control, his . . . She hung her head. Yet, their last few months together had been wonderful. She closed her eyes and rubbed her temples.

When she opened her eyes, she caught sight of Gram's old Bible sitting under several other books on the small bookshelf. It was the only thing left to her after Gram died. She closed her eyes again and took a deep breath.

"Okay, Gram, let's see what you have to say about those words in the Bible that Pastor Ben read."

Maddie thumbed through the table of contents to find where Ephesians was located in the book. The church bulletin said Pastor Ben was speaking from chapter four. Her finger traveled down to verse thirty-two. In the margin, Gram's handwriting: *Give grace, forgive others—forgiveness does deep healing.*

Maddie held her head in her hands. "I can't, Gram. I can't forgive him." The Bible fell from her lap to the floor. Several pieces of paper fluttered about the room.

Maddie smiled. "Gram, you stuffed everything from recipes to crayon love notes from the kids in Sunday school in your Bible."

Holding the Bible in one hand, she retrieved faded notes and old bulletins with the other. Her eyes lit on a piece of paper with familiar handwriting.

And it wasn't Gram's.

FORTY-SEVEN

Maddie's heart hammered against the wall of her chest. She looked around expecting to see that Jeff had entered the room. Which he had—in the form of the letter she held in her trembling hands.

Maddie,

If you are reading this letter two things have taken place. One, I've run out of time to muster up enough courage to share face-to-face what I'm about to tell you. God knows I've tried.

Maddie shook her head and crumbled up the letter into a tight ball. She couldn't take another confession. The last one almost killed her. She clenched her teeth together, fighting hard to resist the urge to hurl the paper as far as she could. But the urge to hear Jeff's voice was stronger, and she slowly opened the wrinkled pages, smoothing them out.

And two, you've finally realized what a treasure you hold in your hands. Not just because it belonged to your sweet Gram, more because the words in this book are alive and have the power to change even the most disgraceful sinner—me.

I know you've seen a change in me, you have said it more than once, but you never asked how that change came about. I could not live with the tremendous guilt I felt over my affair and the disrespectful way I treated you for so many years. Prestige, money, fancy cars, property, none of it relieved the anguishing pain of betraying you and disappointing the kids, should they ever find out.

One night, not too long ago, while you and Bracy were at the movies, I held a bottle of prescribed sleeping pills in one hand and a bottle of wine in the other.

I figured if I drank half the wine, I'd have enough guts to take the pills. Then I realized it was only right that I leave a note for you and the kids, so I rummaged through the junk drawer for a pen and some paper. Lots of pens, no paper. When I looked up, there among your cookbooks, I saw some papers sticking out of one of the books. I pulled one out and it had a Bible verse on it. When I looked back at the book it came from, I realized it was your Gram's Bible. The verse on the paper was Jeremiah 31:3, 'The LORD appeared to him from afar, saying, "I have loved you with an everlasting love; therefore I have drawn you with loving kindness."' I thought, yeah, right.

I couldn't write my suicide note on that paper. It seemed too sacred. I opened the Bible to look for another piece of paper and there before me was Jeremiah 31:3. Your Gram had written in the margin Romans 6:23 and Romans 10:9–10. I couldn't help myself. When I found and read those verses, I knew deep inside me I had found the one thing, Person, rather, who could take away my guilt. I cried like a baby and told God every sin I could remember and desperately asked him to forgive me. Now here is the unbelievable part, within a few minutes the guilt was completely gone and I felt loved, truly loved, for the first time in my life.

Maddie, I can only hope you have found this incredible love too, and that you can find it in your heart to forgive me.

I love you,
Jeff

Maddie frowned and shook her head, trying to comprehend Jeff's words. No, there had to be another explanation. This couldn't be true. Not Jeff. She looked at the book that had fallen to the floor. Shoving Gram's papers into her Bible, Maddie put the book back on the shelf. She pitched Jeff's letter in the bedside table drawer beneath two books and a calendar.

All those years of abuse and pain and all it took was a couple of Bible verses to change him? Disgust and resentment resounded in her heart.

Maddie slumped to the floor into a heap of uncertainty and shock, unable to believe what she had just read. So was this why?

FORTY-EIGHT

Three months had passed quickly since the March auction. On June eighteenth Maddie sat at the bank escrow officer's desk, signing her name to loan documents. A whole brood of butterflies fluttered wildly inside her stomach.

Out of nowhere the words *broken acres* popped into her head again, as they had in her dream. In the middle of the signing process she stopped abruptly. "What's a broken acre?"

The loan officer gave her a questioning look. He glanced down at the papers on his desk, then back up. "A what?"

Maddie shook her head. "Never mind, it doesn't matter."

With more than a little apprehension, Maddie signed each document. She couldn't believe she was really buying property on her own, without Jeff. Her heart raced. She closed her eyes. *Breathe in, breathe out. Breathe in, breathe out.*

Maddie looked at the papers on the desk in front of her and took another deep breath. After placing her signature on what looked like an entire ream of paper, it was final. The farm belonged to her. The bank employee collected the papers, smiled, and handed her the keys to her new home.

"Congratulations, Mrs. Crane."

Maddie took the keys in one hand and shook the man's outstretched hand with the other. "Thank you."

She could not believe it was actually true. Okay, so, an underlying sense of impending panic was threatening to spoil the moment, but she was going to focus on the excitement she felt.

In a matter of moments Maddie experienced happiness and misery. Her days had been so consumed with helping the homeless through the church outreach and the anticipation of buying and renovating the farm, she had completely lost track of time. Imagining the day the movers would deliver her belongings, she caught a glimpse of a large Norman Rockwell calendar behind the escrow officer's desk.

She'd need at least a month to get the cottage livable. So, one month from today was—July eighteenth. The date hit her like a runaway boulder at top speed. Two years ago, Jeff had suffered a fatal heart attack and her life had changed forever. On that very night, her metamorphosis from a distraught, frightened woman had begun. She couldn't help but think how different her life was today. How different *she* was today. Staring out the bank window, her thoughts drifted to the trials and adventures she had experienced.

Why aren't I crying? I should be crying.

Emptiness, sometimes extreme pain, still swelled in her heart. Although not as excruciating and haunting as it had been in the beginning. Her whispers told her one thing would never change. "I will always love you, Jeff."

FORTY-NINE

Renovation. Another thing she had never done. And time was running out. They had a little less than a month to refurbish the cottage before she moved in.

When Maddie shared her to-do list, Alex just laughed. "Maddie, do you really think you can replace the roof, clean and paint the inside and outside, and redo the entire bathroom in the time we have?"

"Sure, why not?"

"Have you taken a close look at the bathroom? The sink and tub are covered in rust and ought to be replaced. Who knows how old the plumbing is or what's under that old linoleum. And you'd better pray that dark spot in the ceiling is only rain damage and not mold or you've got major problems."

"I thought all that was approved by the inspector before I bought it?"

"Did you read the inspector's report?"

"Um, well, not completely. But they wouldn't let me buy it if it wasn't okay, would they?"

Alex shook his head. "Maddie, now that you don't have Jeff to check things over, you are going to have to do that yourself or ask someone who is knowledgeable about that kind of stuff."

Maddie's forlorn look changed his tone. The deed was already done. "You may have to work on the painting after you've moved in. How about if we just cross those bridges when we come to them?"

"That sounds like a good plan. Thank you."

While Alex pulled out the sink and tub in the bathroom, Carolyn and Maddie tore out the old carpet in the living room and bedroom. Years of caked mud, dead moths, and critter droppings came out right along with it. But the beautiful hardwood hiding underneath made the job worth the effort.

"Maddie, you might want to come in here," Alex called from the bathroom.

She looked at Carolyn and rolled her eyes.

Alex had poked a pretty good-size hole in the ceiling and was standing over the partially removed linoleum looking at the floor.

Maddie looked up. "Did you find mold in the ceiling?"

Alex shook his head. "No, thankfully it must be an old leak they never painted over because they did patch the roof and it looks like it's been holding solid for a long time."

They all looked down at the floor.

"Now, the floor, that's a different story. The toilet must have leaked for some time before the water was turned off. You can see the subflooring is warped and pretty flimsy. I can do the flooring part, but I'm afraid you're gonna need to hire a plumber to plumb the new shower, tub, and sink. You'll need a new toilet too."

Maddie took a deep breath. "I wonder how long that will take."

Alex shrugged.

Carolyn encouraged the two. "One of the ladies in my exercise class is married to a plumber. I'll call her when we get home."

"Thanks, Carolyn."

*   *   *

"Mrs. Crane, this is Dennis Smith, the plumber."

"Oh yes, Dennis, thank you for calling so quickly. I was afraid Carolyn might not reach you tonight. I'm wondering if you could come out tomorrow and take a look at the bathroom? I'll need you to order a new sink, shower, and toilet. I'd really like to get this completed before I move in."

"And when would that be?"

"About two and a half weeks." Maddie smiled at the phone.

"Sorry, that's impossible."

"Why?"

"I've got four jobs me and my guys are working on right now. Couldn't get to it for another month at least."

"Really?" Maddie held the tears at bay. The disappointment in her voice was evident.

"My wife is standing here with her hands on her hips shaking her head. I guess I could come out early tomorrow morning before I meet the guys on the jobsite to at least see what you've got going on."

"Thank you so much, Dennis. I really appreciate it. I'll be there at seven o'clock. Is that early enough?"

*   *   *

After some bantering, Dennis finally agreed to do the work on Sundays, although it would cost more. He would do it as a favor to Carolyn. Dennis held a high opinion of Carolyn since she had helped his wife out of her depression and into a size ten after delivering their third child. Her exercise class had saved his marriage.

Maddie was willing to agree to just about anything to have her bathroom in working order when she moved in. Maybe she ought to ask David to move out here and help. He knew a lot about construction. She shook her head. *There is so much you don't know, Maddie. This is only a single dose of reality.*

*   *   *

Even though her muscles throbbed and ached, extending deeper into Maddie's body with each new project she tackled, a sense of accomplishment pulsed through her. She and Carolyn were able to give the kitchen cupboards a fresh coat of white paint. Dennis said he would have the bathroom finished within the next two weeks. The roofers were scheduled for Monday. Everything was coming together.

A wellspring of comfort rose within her when the movers placed familiar possessions throughout the cottage. An hour later, the few antiques and family heirlooms she had not sold rested comfortably in their chosen spots. Even so, the house looked pretty bare. Furniture shopping would come after she finished the painting. *Maddie, you are such a dreamer, just like Jeff used to say.* What made her think she could finish all the things on that list in a month?

While still in Chicago, after days of debating what furniture to let go, their bed was the one piece Maddie could not part with. Even though she sometimes had fits of anger remembering his actions, memories of intimate moments in Jeff's embrace made her smile. Why had it taken her so long to see that her love was a lot deeper than she realized? Maddie placed a quilt across the foot of the bed and gently traced the wedding ring design. "It wasn't all bad, was it?"

Sitting on the floor next to a box marked *family room pics/misc*, Maddie hesitated opening the lid. Knowing what she would find wrapped inside, she wasn't sure she was ready. She pulled out several pieces and removed the wrappings. Memories of people she had known over the years and places she and Jeff had frequented flooded her mind. When she found a picture of her and Jeff poised in front of a house, tears filled her eyes. Jeff stood behind her, his arms encircling her waist, his cheek next to hers. Both grinned at the new adventure they were about to take. Their first—and only—home.

Life seemed so simple then. Still newlyweds after a year, they were ready to take on whatever the world tossed at them. That was another time, before the anger, the betrayal, the abandonment. *Enough, Maddie.*

This was a new season. She was not going to dwell on the past. There was a bright future ahead.

Placing the picture back in the box, she caught sight of the diamond wedding ring on her left hand. She turned the ring on her finger. *It's been two years.* She slowly removed the ring and tucked it in a hidden compartment in an old jewelry box that sat on the floor next to the open box.

Jeff is gone. It's time.

She put the jewelry box along with the other items inside the shipping box, closed the lid, and sealed it. This belonged in the attic, out of sight.

The first night alone in the cottage gave way to some serious trepidation. Heavy winds whistled through cracks in the old house, moaning like a lonely ghost lost in time. Haunting cricket noises and croaking tree frogs caused her imagination to run wild, raising the temperature of an already hot night.

What if someone tried to break in? What if one of those target shooters got drunk and—*Stop it, Maddie.* Snuggling under the bedsheet, she pulled it up to her eyes and looked around the room. *I can't help it.*

She wondered if she should have taken Alex and Carolyn up on their offer to spend the night with her. No. She would have to be alone sooner or later. She might just as well start off that way.

She rethought her bravery. "Maddie, you are a fool. It wouldn't have hurt to have had them stay the first night."

An owl, perched on a limb of the huge oak that sheltered her home, hooted at the moon. She pictured drunks invading and hordes of critters roaming the woods. Thoughts of wild animals scratching at her front door sent shivers and a cold sweat over her body.

Pulling the sheet over her head, she spoke into the stifling darkness. "If this continues, I'll be useless tomorrow."

FIFTY

Sunrays streamed through the bedroom window.

Maddie pried open sleepy eyes. As she stretched, the fuzziness in her head cleared. Startled, she sat up and considered her surroundings. *Where am I?*

The sight of scattered, half-empty boxes gave way to a happy reminder. *I am in my new home.* "My home."

Stillness. No cricket. No owl. Only quiet. She had made it through the entire night. By herself. Pumping her fist, she congratulated herself. "Yes."

A stagnant silence hung over the house. This was nice, but every day? She wondered how long it would take to get used to this nothingness. A little noise would be good. Music. Yeah, she needed music. And *coffee.*

Her body screamed at her when she pulled herself out of bed. Back, arms, and thighs were not happy for the years of random, intermittent exercise. Tiny limping steps took her to the kitchen. Ouch. She thought the pain from demolition and renovation was supposed get better with time. Ooh. Ouch. Maddie stood up straight and rubbed her lower back.

Dodging boxes, she stopped to gaze out the picture windows that framed the two adjoining walls in the front of the cottage, giving a panoramic view of her farm. Her farm.

Big smile.

Maddie watched farmers acres away on their tractors working the fields. She was glad to be able to help those farmers make a living. Another thought moved in. Hmm, she really needed to talk to them about rent so they cold help *her.*

She hit the power button on the CD player sitting on the kitchen counter. Kenny G's mellow saxophone vanquished the silence.

"Coffee. I need coffee."

Frantically rummaging through boxes, she found the coffeemaker on the bottom of a box that had been wedged between the wall and a tall clothing box.

Waiting for her morning brew, Maddie scanned the open room. The empty beige wall above the heavy wood mantel brought back her promise to make Jewell's painting the first priority after moving in. Before she unpacked another box, the painting would find its place of honor. She was itching to get some color on the dreary beige walls that covered the entire house. She'd had her fill of beige in Chicago.

Maddie breathed deep the bold scent of fresh brewed coffee. Mug in hand, she stepped onto the timeworn porch and glanced over her shoulder when the squeaky screen door slammed behind her.

Find WD-40.

While scanning the fields, she imagined the life of each farmer. Soon she would meet them and add names and faces. And renegotiate their rental agreements. She shook her head. So many new things she had never done before.

Sipping her coffee, she was once again awed by the beauty of the land and the fact she wasn't scared out of her wits. No, she had come to terms with her insecurities and knew she could handle the job before her. She looked up. "Right, Gram?"

Maddie sat on the top step and took another sip of hot coffee. Something stirred near the barn, moving in the direction of the house. Whatever it was walked haltingly slow.

What if that was one of those wild animals she was worried about last night? What if it was a coyote or a mountain lion?

Buy a gun.

A baseball bat, good for all types of sport, was one of the first things Maddie had unpacked and placed inside the front door. Moving slowly, she reached in, pulling the bat to her side.

The closer the creature came, the more cautiously it walked. Limping heavily, favoring the right front leg, it looked to be nothing more than a dog. Filthy, matted hair, boney legs, and thin body, the poor animal looked like it was starving. He struggled to breathe; his tongue hung loose while panting hard.

The poor creature was on his last leg. Literally. He looked like he was in terrible pain.

Back in the house, Maddie filled a pie tin with pieces of bread and cheese she'd snacked on the night before. A large salad bowl made for a good water dish. Carrying both outside, she slowly approached the pitiful animal. The dog's legs shook with each unsteady step. He stopped about six feet from where she stood and gave a low, menacing growl at her approach.

With careful movements, Maddie placed the food and water on the ground and backed up the stairs. She sat perfectly still on the top step, watching.

The starving animal stood on shaky legs looking from Maddie to the food.

"Come on. Come on, I won't hurt you. You know you're hungry. Come on," she said in a soothing voice.

One last glance at Maddie, and the dog limped as fast as the poor animal could to the tin of food.

He gobbled the food and looked up at Maddie, eyes pleading for more. When he bowed his head to drink, Maddie took slow steps back inside the house and came back out bringing the rest of the cheese and bread with her. When she cautiously moved toward the dog, he stepped back several steps.

Standing over the now full tin, Maddie waited to see if he would trust her enough to eat with her standing there. The dog edged his way toward the tin. When he growled, Maddie stepped back.

Content with a full stomach, the dog made an awkward attempt to lie down. Collapsing to the ground, he sighed and passed out.

Maddie ran inside, threw on some jeans and an oversized T-shirt, and grabbed her purse and keys. She headed for town to find a veterinarian and buy food for herself and the half-dead dog.

The sight of the starving, abused, misfit of a dog kept running through her mind. He looked like he'd been on the road a long time, caked with all that mud and grime. That dog needed someone to love and care for him. That dog needed a name. Not that he'd stay around long enough to learn his name. Once his stomach was full, his wounds healed, he'll probably be back on the road again. *Hmm. Rusty. That might fit.*

After a quick trip to the mini-mart, Maddie searched for the vet's office. She vaguely remembered seeing a sign on a red brick building a half mile or so outside of town. *Ah, there it is.*

A lovely young woman with American Indian features looked up from behind the counter.

"I'm looking for the doctor, ah, veterinarian." Maddie scanned the office.

The woman smiled, extending her hand. "I'm Dr. Adams. Our receptionist just ran to the post office, so I'm the official greeter while she's gone."

Dr. Adams's thick ebony hair lay twisted up in a clip on the back of her head. Her casual dress code of work boots, blue jeans, and cotton shirt, sleeves rolled to the elbow under a sterile white jacket, reminded Maddie this doctor worked in the trenches with sick animals. Her gentle brown eyes and calm demeanor gave testimony to her choice of professions.

Maddie shook her hand. "Hi. Madison Crane. Everybody calls me Maddie."

"I'm Jenny." She gave Maddie a knowing look. "I know exactly who you are."

"You do?"

"Sure, everybody in town and probably two counties over knows who you are."

"W-why would everybody know me? I haven't lived here very long. I don't know that many people."

Jenny chuckled. "Well, according to our local, self-proclaimed dispatcher of pertinent information, Abigail Jones, you're the crazy lady who bought the Riley farm. Abigail says crazy because you're a single woman from the big city with absolutely no background in, or knowledge of, farming."

Maddie frowned. "How does someone I don't even know come up with all that information?"

"Abigail is married to Elias Jones."

"Oh."

"Can I help you with something, Maddie?"

A dark cloud fell over Maddie's face. "I had a visit this morning from a stray dog. He looks like he might not last through the day without some medical care."

Jenny's eyes showed concern. "What's wrong with him?"

"Well, I can't really tell the extent of his injuries. It's difficult to get close enough to check. I think he might have a broken leg. His coat is so matted and filthy, it's tough to know whether he has any scrapes or cuts."

Jenny darted into a back office and returned with a larger-than-normal doctor's bag, without the white coat. Her small stature, all of five feet two, meant nothing when you considered her slightly stocky frame and firm muscles. She smiled when the receptionist walked in with the mail.

"Let's go see what's goin' on with this guy."

"I hope he's still there when we get back."

"How did you leave him?"

"I'd say I left him content. I fed him a little bread and cheese. That's all I had. Gave him some water. After his meal, he plopped down on the ground and passed out."

Jenny offered a comfortable smile. "That was a very brave thing to do. If it's true he hasn't eaten for some time, the introduction of food more than likely caused his body to completely relax. Not to mention he probably hasn't had much sleep if his leg is broken."

Maddie's heart raced. "Brave? Jenny, you said brave."

"Yes, brave. When an animal has been injured and is starving, sometimes they'll attack anything that moves, hoping it's something to eat."

"Really? I never gave it a second thought once I saw he was hurt and hungry. He didn't seem vicious."

"No, many don't until they turn on you."

"I hope he doesn't attack you. Do you think he'll let you examine him?"

"Oh, I don't think we'll have any trouble. I'm going to give him a sedative to put him in a deep sleep. He won't even know what hit him."

Maddie took the lead up the long driveway. Cresting the hill, she could see the dog still sound asleep.

Jenny pulled her mobile veterinary unit within twenty yards of where the dog rested. He woke up when he heard Maddie's car. As he struggled to get to his feet, a small dart hit his left hindquarter. He slumped back to the ground.

Jenny rushed forward, laying her rifle on the ground near the dog. She squatted down and gently stroked his neck and back.

Maddie's eyes grew wide. "Whoa, now I see what you meant when you said he wouldn't know what hit him. You're a pretty good shot with that thing."

"Yeah, well, my dad was a cop. He wanted all his women to feel comfortable with a gun. My older sister, Katie Lou, is a better shot than I am. We were trained in the art of killing beer cans and soda bottles. Spent many a Saturday morning at the shooting range honing our skills. Today, in my business, I'm glad for the experience."

Maddie nodded, trying to find some resemblance between the two sisters. Katie Lou, quiet, reserved librarian researcher extraordinaire and Jenny, outgoing, compassionate veterinarian. What did they share in common?

Jenny checked the dog from head to tail, finding his leg wasn't broken, he just had a swollen, sprained muscle. Dried blood covered welts on his back from what could have been a beating. Jenny applied disinfectant to the welts and cuts on his body and advised Maddie to keep him down and quiet if possible. She left additional medication to add to his food.

Maddie's heart nearly burst with hope. "Do you think he'll stay?"

"It's hard to tell. If he feels safe, he may adopt you."

"And if he doesn't feel safe?"

"One day you'll look for him and he'll be gone."

Maddie's eyes turned sad. "Oh."

"Why do you ask?"

"My late husband never wanted pets. I would love to have a dog for companionship out here."

Jenny's dark chocolate eyes shone genuine sympathy. "You're a widow?"

"Yes. Two years."

Jenny looked from the unconscious dog to Maddie. "A dog is a good idea. It's not safe for a woman to live alone way out here. You never know. He might just stay. You know the old saying, 'Never bite the hand that feeds you.' Most dogs are loyal and protective of the person who feeds and cares for them."

Maddie smiled at Jenny. *I like this woman.*

Jenny smiled and offered her hand. "I'll say goodbye for now."

FIFTY-ONE

Georgia's text message tore at Maddie's heart. Previous communication mentioning Billy had been optimistic and encouraging. Now the news was not good.

Seemed they'd had a silly quarrel. Billy's temper had flared, and he'd taken off, swearing she'd be sorry.

Why would a silly quarrel cause such a huge error in judgment? Billy was being held in the hospital sector of the county jail, recuperating from injuries that happened during a robbery at a local mini-mart.

How could he let himself get mixed up in such a mess?

Rocking the porch swing and petting Rusty's soft coat, Maddie breathed a long sigh. "Poor Billy." She wished there was something she could do to help him. Rusty lifted his head at the sound of her voice.

It had taken Rusty only a few days to warm to Maddie, his trust growing each time she fed him. Her gentle care brought an appreciative wag of the tail, lick on the hand, and finally an all-out cleaning of her face. Before long they were good friends.

After Maddie bathed him twice in the old watering trough near the barn, keeping his wrapped leg out of the water as best she could, Rusty turned out to be an extremely handsome golden retriever. Now her hand rested on Rusty's silky coat as the two lounged on the swing, room to spare. Maddie smiled at her companion. Who would have guessed that filthy frightened animal that showed up a month ago was the same dog?

Maddie watched Rusty sigh and close his eyes. "Are you here to stay, buddy?" *Don't cling to that hope, Maddie.*

Gram's old saying encouraged her, *"If you love someone, set them free. They will run back to love you."*

Maddie relaxed her head against the back of the swing, thinking again about Billy. What would it take to set him free?

*   *   *

Maddie startled awake when Rusty's head came up from between his paws, ears alert, eyeing something that moved stealthily across the porch toward his food dish. Rusty jumped from the swing and tore after a screaming cat. Maddie grabbed the baseball bat from inside the door and ran after the two into the orchard.

Rusty paced near an apple tree, limping slightly from his sprain. He stopped and rested his front paws on the trunk of the tree while his fierce bark caused the cat to shiver.

She tiptoed to where Rusty howled at the foot of the tree. Her eyes focused up as she cautiously moved closer. From one of the branches a scrawny black cat screeched, causing Rusty to bark louder. The mangy feline favored its left front paw. There appeared to be dried blood on its side, with several patches of fur missing. She patted Rusty. "Calm down, boy."

Rusty sat quietly at the base of the tree looking up. "Well, Rusty, how are we gonna get it down?"

Coaxing the cat down from the tree proved futile.

They didn't have long to consider a solution. The cat stretched its right paw up to reach a branch, missed, and fell to the ground. It tried, unsuccessfully, to rise up, laid its head down, and grew silent. Rusty walked over and sniffed the fallen cat.

Maddie panicked. "Oh no." Was the cat dead? She knelt down, placing her hand on its side. It was still breathing. She needed to call Jenny.

She walked back across the orchard as fast as her feet would take her, grabbed a towel, and ran back to the apple tree. Gently wrapping the towel around the fallen cat, she carried it to the porch.

Within twenty minutes Jenny hovered over the motionless animal. "What happened to him?"

While Maddie explained, Jenny checked the cat for injuries. "It looks like he's been in a fight or two. His back is ripped to shreds. His paw has a deep cut."

"He looks like he hasn't eaten in days."

"He must really be starving. You say he was reaching for an apple when he fell?"

"That's what it looked like. How can I help him?"

Jenny grinned. "You're collecting a regular menagerie out here, Maddie. He'll need liquids only for a few days. Introduce solid foods a little each day after that. When his wounds are healed and he's fattened up a little, he should be good as new."

"Okay, thanks. We'll take good care of him."

Jenny looked beyond Maddie into the cottage. "We?"

"Yeah. Me and Rusty."

"Oh." Jenny patted Rusty's head.

Maddie glanced over at Jenny's mobile unit. A little boy slept in a car seat in the back.

"Who's your passenger?" Maddie nodded her head toward the van.

Jenny smiled big. "Oh, that's my son, Michael."

"I didn't know you were married." Maddie looked at Jenny's left ring finger.

Jenny glanced at her hand. "I'm not."

"Oh."

I'd love to hear that story, Maddie thought.

"How old is Michael?"

"Two, going on twelve. When people talk about terrible twos, they aren't kidding. He has got an independent spirit like you wouldn't believe."

"Sounds like my David at that age. I'd love to meet Michael sometime."

"He would love to come to the farm and play with Rusty and this guy." Jenny pointed to the fallen cat.

"Great. Why don't we plan a playday?"

"Sounds good. Better get him back home." Jenny motioned her head toward the van. "We'll see you later."

*   *   *

Maddie carefully washed the cat with warm soapy water. "I better do this now, Rusty. After he wakes up he probably won't have anything to do with a bath."

Rusty sniffed the air.

"I know. He smells pretty bad."

It took a few days before the cat was able to hobble around the house. He slurped up the liquids set out for him then laid back down on a bed Maddie had fashioned from a cushion. He refused to acknowledge her or Rusty.

One night the cat jumped up on the couch and plopped down next to Maddie. Rusty, on the other side, lifted his head, ears perked. When the cat placed his front paws on Maddie's lap, Rusty settled his head back down between his paws.

Maddie laughed. "Well, aren't we the trio?"

"So, Rusty, what do you think we should call this tough guy?"

Admiring the cat's black body and white markings, she traced a white stripe that covered the entire length of his tail. "Tough guy with a stripe. How about Sarg?"

Rusty lifted his head and cocked it to one side as if to say, "Yep, that fits." Then laid his head down and gave a contented sigh.

FIFTY-TWO

The little cottage was starting to feel like home.

Determined to finish painting the inside walls the cool sage green she had chosen so she could rest from all the renovating and moving chaos, Maddie worked long hours. The white ceiling and trim gave the cottage a friendly, comfortable feel. After painting the railing that separated the upper loft white, she glowed, realizing that her choices fit the cottage perfectly. She had always thought those colors would compliment each other. She glanced at the rooms around her. Who would have thought she could renovate and decorate an entire house by herself? Maddie shook her head.

Barely able to bend over from lethargic, sore muscles, she stood upright to roll more paint on the wall and rubbed the middle of her aching back. She really did need to sign up for one of Carolyn's exercise classes. Maddie blew out a puff of air.

Maddie talked to the guys like they would join in the conversation. "Just imagine how beautiful it will be when I'm finished. We've been here six weeks and I'm still in awe. I can't wait for the farmers to begin planting."

With Rusty and Sarg curled up together by the idle fireplace on the braided multicolor rug in the living room, Maddie went into the kitchen to brew some coffee. Her pals woke up when they heard the screen door creak. Rusty, ingenious canine that he was, had figured out how to push the slightly warped door open with his paw, releasing the two friends from the confines of the house.

"Rusty, Sarg, look. Isn't that the most beautiful sight you've ever laid eyes on?" Maddie sipped her coffee while scanning the horizon. The two looked up at her. Rusty lay down on the top step while Sarg curled up on the swing.

"Fall is in the air."

September cool breezes. Sweater weather. A few farmers harvested the last of the summer hay crop while other fields waited spring planting.

The telephone's sharp peal interrupted the one-sided conversation. The screen door groaned when it slapped against the doorpost behind her. Maddie looked over her shoulder and shook her head.

"Hello. Hi, Carolyn. How's your week going?"

"What are you doing, Maddie? Did I catch you in the middle of something?"

"The boys and I are out on the porch, chatting."

"That sounds relaxing. Are you available to come over for dinner tonight?"

"Sure, I'd love to come to dinner. I just finished painting the living room, and I need a break. What time do you want me? Is this a black-tie affair?" Maddie grinned.

"Oh, I should have dinner on the table by six thirty."

"Okay, six thirty. Casual, gotcha. Can I bring anything?"

Maddie smiled at Carolyn's response. "I always bring that. Okay. See you in a little while."

Rusty joined Sarg and Maddie on the swing. "Why would Carolyn ask me to bring along a sense of humor? That's a funny thing to say. She sounded a little anxious. I hope nothing is wrong with Alex."

Two hours later Maddie found herself at the Morenos' front door. When she walked in, the aromas of lasagna, baked bread, and apple pie instantly stirred her senses. All her favorites. She closed her eyes and breathed deep.

"Hey, where are you guys?"

Carolyn stuck her head around the corner, silverware in hand. "We're in the kitchen."

Alex came to meet Maddie on her way to the kitchen, giving her a bear hug. Carolyn wiped wet hands on her apron and joined them.

"How are you and the guys doin' out there in the wilderness?"

"Come on, Carolyn, it's not *that* far out of town. You make it sound like I'm stuck out on the tundra of Alaska. I love my farm. Although I'm still not quite sure *why* I'm out there."

Alex smiled. "You know, at first we thought you were crazy buying that big old place. But now we're starting to think God really does have a plan for you and those 427 acres."

"God? Hmm. Thanks for the vote of confidence, but I'm getting a little anxious with this waiting and wondering. What am I going to do when I finish the cottage?"

"Start on the big house," Carolyn encouraged.

Alex crossed his arms over his chest. "That project is going to take a lot of time, energy, *and* money. Not to mention a good contractor."

"Yeah. I've been thinking about that. Do you think I'll have enough money to renovate and furnish that big place?"

"Only Isaac can answer that." Alex lifted his eyebrows.

"Have you given any thought to renting out the big house?"

"Sure. But, Carolyn, who on earth would need a house that big?"

Alex and Carolyn looked at each other and laughed.

"What?"

Alex shook his head. "That's exactly what we thought when you bought the farm."

That brought a chuckle from Maddie.

Alex looked at Maddie with a sideways glance. "God knows what He's doing, Maddie."

"Yeah, yeah. I hear you. You both sound just like Gram. 'I need to wait patiently,' she used to say. But do you know how hard that is for me?"

Her two friends responded in unison, "Uh-huh." Then Carolyn added, "But it didn't stop you from waiting to buy the place, did it?"

Did I have a choice?

Reminiscing over dinner, the fun times they had shared, the three laughed until their sides ached remembering the time Jeff tried to create a gourmet dinner out of corned beef hash, eggs, and spices.

Maddie smiled. "It tasted like Chinese, Italian, Mexican, something. Remember none of us could gag it down no matter how hard we tried? Jeff had many talents. Cooking was not one of them."

Carolyn patted Maddie's hand. "How's your heart these days, friend? Do you still miss him?"

Maddie stared past Carolyn, her eyes misting. "There are times I miss him so much. His smile, his touch, his kisses. This horrible grief comes in waves.

"One thing's for sure, I've learned an awful lot about myself over the last two years. Things I probably never would have realized if Jeff were still alive."

Carolyn nodded. "I've seen a lot of changes in you."

Maddie gave a lopsided grin and shook her head.

"No, really. I remember a time when you were so entrenched in Jeff and the kids' lives, you didn't know who Madison Crane was or what she wanted out of life."

Maddie looked deep into Carolyn's eyes.

"In a strange kind of way, you made Jeff your god. Whatever he wanted, you desperately tried to give him. I'll bet this *has* been eye-opening for you."

"I never did get it right with Jeff." Maddie sighed. "This has been a huge learning curve for me. And you know what? I think I'm beginning to get a glimpse of just who Madison Crane really is. I actually kinda like her. That hasn't always been true." Maddie gave a half smile. "You'll be happy to hear I'm learning not to lean on Jeff, or anyone else."

Alex hung his head, then looked over at Carolyn. "There's no time like the present to tell her."

"Tell me what? Alex, are you okay? Are you sick?" She looked from one to the other. "Carolyn, is there something wrong with you? What's going on?"

Tears formed in Carolyn's eyes. "Well——"

Looking from Alex to Carolyn, her breathing labored, Maddie was frantic. "What's wrong?"

Alex broke in, "Maddie, my company is transferring me back to the East Coast. They are giving me a promotion. Regional insurance sales manager, supervising the eastern regional managers. Can you believe it?"

Maddie stared, wide-eyed, and flopped back in her chair.

"When?" She looked in Carolyn's direction.

"We're putting the house up for sale right away. Alex will commute, fly home on weekends, until we sell the house."

Alex looked into his coffee cup. "We shouldn't have any trouble selling since it's rare for a house to go on the market here, as you well know."

Maddie stared at Carolyn, tears falling on her lap. "What am I going to do without you? I only came here because you were here. Now what?"

Carolyn attempted a smile. "Maddie, you just told us this has been good for you. A growing experience that has caused you not to depend on others. Did you mean that?"

"Yes. Yes, I meant it. But I never expected to be *completely* alone here."

I can't do this, live here without Alex and Carolyn. I cannot do this.

"Do you *have* to go? Alex, can't you tell your company you don't want to move? Tell them you're settled, satisfied right where you are."

"I'm sorry, Maddie. We already tried that. They made it clear if I want to keep my job, I have to take this transfer."

Carolyn took Maddie's hand. "I'm so sorry. I never would have asked you to move if I'd known this was going to happen."

Maddie's head dropped. Tears fell on her plate. "What am I going to do? I just bought that huge farm. I was counting on you to help me with, well, with . . ."

She walked to the window, covered her eyes with her hands, and sobbed. "With whatever I'm supposed to be doing with that place."

Carolyn went to her friend and placed her hands firmly on Maddie's shoulders. She looked her straight in the eyes, voice tender, yet firm. "Maddie, you are never alone. I've told you that a thousand times.

"Besides, Alex and I know, and so do you, even though you won't admit it, God has plans for that property. Big plans. Would you really want to be anywhere else?"

Maddie wiped her tears. "I'm really getting tired of everyone telling me God is going to handle everything." She took a deep breath. "I was so certain Jacob's Bend is where I am meant to be. I've grown fond of this little town and its people in the short time I've lived here."

Maddie envisioned her property. "I don't think I could live in the city again. I feel such peace when I'm on the farm. And awe every time I drive up the hill and catch sight of the beauty. I really do think this is where I'm supposed to be."

Carolyn questioned the look of surprise in Maddie's eyes and the grin on her face. "Maddie? What's so funny?"

Her grin turned to a chuckle. "I'm not just sure this is where I am supposed to be. I can't picture myself living anywhere else. That farm is home." Maddie hugged Carolyn. "I'm sorry for being so selfish. You have to do what is best for you and Alex, not me."

Carolyn gave her a warm smile. "You've made a lot of friends since you moved here. You'll be fine. And you can always get *Pastor Ben* to help." Her grin turned mischievous.

"Stop it."

Alex cut in, "Maddie, are you okay?"

"It's like you said, Alex, I'm growing up through all the losses and the suffering." Maddie looked past Alex. "Maybe there is some kind of plan for me."

Carolyn smiled. "You bet there is. Besides, you are going to be so busy with that big place of yours, you won't have time to miss us."

"Are you kidding? I am definitely going to miss you. A lot."

*   *   *

Leaving Alex and Carolyn's house, Maddie drove slowly along Highway 25. A full moon guided her toward home as she dreamed of the future. She smiled into the illuminated sky. "Just what are those plans? What exactly is going to consume my time?"

She listened, hoping to sense something within her.

Nothing.

That night she had an odd dream. Walking through the big house, every room she entered, a broken, discarded piece of furniture lay on the floor. Settled next to the piece sat a person, crying. When they saw her enter the room, each one quickly grabbed the broken piece that sat next to them, held it tight to their chest, and rocked. Maddie gently placed her arm around each man and each woman, encouraging them to come with her.

One by one she escorted them into the living room, where a blazing fire warmed the comfortable chamber. A lavishly adorned, oversized table sat against the back wall, bountifully arrayed with food and drink. Before long, people filled the room. Each sat on the floor rocking, clutching a broken piece of furniture.

No longer crying, they talked with one another. However, they would not release the broken furniture they clenched tightly over their hearts. Attempting to pry a broken piece from one young man proved impossible. No matter how hard Maddie coaxed them to release their chattel, none would relent. There was no way to get those people to part with their broken possessions.

The next morning Maddie clearly remembered the dream. Slipping into an oversized sweatshirt and pair of jeans, mug in hand to warm her, she headed to the porch. She couldn't help but wonder what the dream meant. The cushioned swing created a quiet spot for reflection. Maddie pulled her legs up under her, sipped her coffee, wondering. Summoning the dream, she remembered a whispering voice. *"Love one another, even as I have loved you."*

Perusing the big white house across the orchard sent a chill up her neck. She slipped from the swing, pulled the bat from inside the door, and walked from one end of the porch to the other. She quickly turned, bat ready, to see if someone stood behind her.

No one.

Within seconds of shaking off the unsettling feeling, another whisper from the dream caused her to catch her breath. *"Gather the outcasts, heal the brokenhearted, bind up their wounds."*

Exasperated, she paced.

Her hands flew wildly, the bat whipping through the air like a swashbuckler's sword. Rusty and Sarg startled awake, eyes and ears alert. "What does that mean? Is that you, Gram?"

Nothing.

Who was she supposed to love that she was not loving? She was trying to love others, just like Pastor Ben told her to.

Her dream came back vividly. All those hurting people grasping their broken pieces of furniture, hanging on as if their lives depended on it. Each had been alone in a room until she brought them all together in front of a warm fire to eat, drink, and talk. They even laughed.

Chills ran up her arms. Shivers went through her body.

Was that it? Was that her purpose for being there? For doing the absolutely ridiculous and buying this property?

Could this big house be a home for hurt and broken people? But, why her? Why here? Why now?

The two commands once again whispered to her as if a gentle breeze stroked her face.

Love one another, even as I have loved you.

Gather the outcasts, heal the brokenhearted, bind up their wounds.

FIFTY-THREE

Maddie went through the big house, taking inventory of the work to be done. This project was going to be monumental.

The house had not been occupied for over eight years. When Edgar Riley's wife died, he'd moved into the cottage, living there until he joined her.

Chipped, peeling paint, stairs needed reinforcing, a new water heater was a must, as well as total replacement of all the plumbing and electrical.

Sure that rodents, spiders, roaches, and other critters had set up home in the walls of the old abandoned house, she added *pest control, plaster removed, and new walls constructed* to her list.

A sigh slipped past her lips. More doubts.

Was this project really worth all the time and money it was going to take? She strummed her fingers on the clipboard.

Yes. Absolutely. If she had her way, this would be a home where lonely, broken people could become whole again. And why couldn't she have it her way? She could do whatever she wanted. With seven large bedrooms, each guest could have their own private bath. This was definitely doable.

Gather the outcasts kept reverberating in her mind.

Well, if she was going to do this, she was going to do it right. The discarded, broken outcasts who lived here would get plenty of love and respect. Their surroundings would be lovely and peaceful and comfortable. This would not be some sterile institution.

With Rusty by her side, Maddie checked the entire house while attentively listening for uninvited varmints. She sat on the steps of the spacious front porch, scanning her inventory. This was going to be expensive.

Maddie glanced at the dilapidated orchard and weed-infested garden at the foot of the small knoll between the two houses. A sudden sense of defeat pulsed through her veins.

The vegetable section now covered with pokeweeds, tansy ragwort, and thistles rather than the customary peppers, onions, corn, squash, and herbs broke her heart. Most of the tomato trellises lay on the ground mangled and twisted. Overgrown with weeds, the roses along the path leading up to the big house needed a lot more than just tender loving care. Dead flowers hung by a thread on most of the broken brambles. Branches torn from fruit trees after years of brutal weather left gaping holes throughout the orchard. Several were broken beyond hope of restoration.

Broken. Just about everything on these 427 acres was broken. Maddie let out a deep sigh.

"Broken, broken . . . Broken acres."

Wide-eyed, Maddie put her hand to her heart. "Oh my gosh." This farm was Broken Acres. She could see it clearly now. Her wild heart beat a cadence to the whispering commands:

"Love one another, even as I have loved you."

"Gather the outcasts, heal the brokenhearted, bind up their wounds."

She thought of Rusty and Sarg. They had been abused, broken, discarded. *And now look at them.*

A slew of emotions rushed through her. Excitement, apprehension, trepidation. She was looking forward to this challenge, but she desperately needed help. She didn't have the skills or resources for this kind of thing.

"Love one another, even as I have loved you," rang in her head.

Then she thought, *I can do that. I've had a lot of practice loving my family.*

Her eyes grew even wider. She put her hand to her mouth.

Madison Crane, you do have the training for this kind of thing. Jeff, the children, Southside Manor. You've been preparing for this for years. A huge grin spread across her face.

Even Carolyn had said helping people was who she was. She pumped her fist. Yes. She could do this.

Maddie strolled through the orchard toward the cottage. She would call Elias first thing in the morning and get a list of local contractors. Get a few quotes, choose the best man for the job, and go for it. Imagine the possibilities.

Glancing back at the big house, she looked down at Rusty at her side. "I *can* do this, right?"

FIFTY-FOUR

Elias, it seemed, was slow at doing just about everything. His easygoing drawl only added to the tedium. "I suppose I could check for y'all 'n see iffen I can come up with a couple of names. Might not be till next week or the week after."

"Elias, why on earth would it take so long?"

"Now, now, young lady. Don't get your corset tied in knots. Next week is tha last week a' trout season. Everybody works half a day so's we can go on out to our favorite fishin' hole 'fore winter hits."

Maddie rolled her eyes. "For an entire week?"

"Yep. Been doin' that since I was just a youngin'. My daddy and his daddy 'fore him. We come here from Kentucky to visit relatives every year Just for the fishin'. I loved this part of the country so much, moved here when I was eighteen.

"The whole town joins in the fishin' competition to see who can catch the first, the biggest, and the most fish. Why, Charley Taylor done won last year with a thirty-five pound bull trout. Everybody told ole Charley he shouldn't eat that beauty. They said he ought to make it into one of them plaque things for the wall. Sure 'nuff he mounted it on one of them plaques, but didn't have a wall big enough to hold it in his little place. So Glenn Harper took it for his hardware store. Hung it right there above the fishin' gear. Draws in lotsa lookers. It's a beauty, all right."

Maddie pictured Elias's eyes glazing over admiring the trophy that hung above live worms and dead bugs.

"Charley said he done caught that there baby usin' peanut butter pretzels. I don't believe a word he says. He just made that up so's nobody'd figure out what his secret bait is. You cain't put a pretzel on a hook."

Maddie let out a long, slow sigh, looked at her watch and the calendar on the wall. "Okay, Elias. Can I get those names as soon as fishing season is officially over? Say, week after next?"

"Well now, let's see. I'll need to check my calendar, see if'n anything's goin' on that week. I'm a busy man, ya know."

Her patience was waning. If the merchants back in Chicago ran their businesses like this town, they'd go bankrupt. She chuckled to herself. If these merchants were just like the ones in Chicago it wouldn't be peaceful, laid-back, Jacob's Bend.

Maddie took off her watch and tossed it in the junk drawer. If she wanted to be a part of this town, she needed to learn to slow down. This was going to be her home now. There was plenty of time to get those names and get the work done.

Elias came back on the phone. "Ah, well, looks like I might just have a little time next Monday. Gotta come in the office anyways. That sound okay?"

Maddie smiled. "Thanks, Elias. I really appreciate any help you can give me."

*   *   *

Maddie finished the painting projects in the cottage as well as sketching plans and a list of changes to be implemented on the big house for the contractor.

With a call in for Isaac Birnbaum, she, Rusty, and Sarg curled up on the porch swing under a heavy quilt, the boys content to sleep. Savoring her coffee, Maddie gazed out over the land. Fall was definitely upon them.

A red sky on the horizon framed her farmland. "Look, Rusty, Sarg. Isn't it magnificent?" Neither stirred.

She couldn't believe all this belonged to her. *Me, Madison Crane. That frightened, self-conscious woman who didn't have a clue what she wanted from life.* She never would have guessed how much her life would change after becoming a widow.

Widow. She hated that word. It described so much, yet said nothing. Starring into the vast sky, she couldn't help but feel lonely. She loved her new friends, but when Carolyn and Alex were gone, who would be left that she was really close to?

Is there another someone out there for me to love?

She shook her head. What was she thinking? It had only been two years. Why would she want to fall in love again? It was too hard a road to walk. Wasn't it?

Sarg stretched and climbed into Maddie's lap. She stroked his soft fur, his contented purr sweet comfort in the twilight that surrounded them.

*   *   *

Monday afternoon Elias called with the promised list. It seemed only one contractor lived close by, but Elias said he was a little questionable.

"Questionable?"

"Oh, it's probably nothin' to worry 'bout. I heard rumors that 'fore he moved here, he was the best gall darn contractor in the surroundin' six counties."

"Was? What do you mean, was?"

"Well, 'bout a year ago the man moved over here and people been sayin' his work has been gettin' a little sloppy. Not the top-notch buildin' he did before. They say his past is catchin' up with him."

"What does that mean? What happened a year ago?"

"Don't rightly know. He don't talk much. Lives over off Highway 47. Rents tha ole Thompson place. He's a strange one. Not real friendly. Kinda secretive. Only time I see him is when he comes in for plan approval. Not sure people know that much 'bout him really. It's just talk."

Elias's remarks made her uneasy. "Are you sure there isn't someone else I can call? Anyone else?"

"Nope, he's it."

Maddie hesitated. "Okay, let me have his phone number."

While the phone rang she whispered under her breath, "Please let this man be nice."

A gruff, raspy voice answered, "Yeah, this is Carter. What?"

He sounded angry. "I—I'm looking for Nathan Carter."

"Yeah, that's me. What do you want?"

"I have a house that needs some renovating. I was told you are a contractor who does that kind of work."

The man responded in a slightly calmer, friendlier manner, "Yes, I do."

Maddie rubbed the tingling from her left arm.

"Where do you live, ma'am?" Still sharp, edgy.

"I live in Jacob's Bend. Well, actually about six miles outside of Jacob's Bend, off Highway 25. I bought the old Riley farm. Do you know it?"

"No, can't say I do. I don't spend much time out that way."

"Would you be interested in looking at my house, give me an estimate for the project?"

"Ah, yeah, sure. When can we meet?"

"How about Wednesday morning, say around nine o'clock?"

"That sounds good. Can you give me a little better idea where your farm is located?"

It sounded like the man frantically tossed things around in a drawer. He dropped something. Then swore.

Maddie winced.

"Okay, ma'am. Now where did you say you are?"

Uneasiness settled in her chest, but she gave him directions. Maybe she should call someone from another county. No, that would cost a fortune. *Stop being so suspicious. Relax.*

FIFTY-FIVE

At precisely nine o'clock Wednesday morning, a newer model black dual-cab truck came over the hill and parked in front of the big house.

Maddie had half expected a beat-up old pickup with a crusty old man inside. To her delight, a man about her age got out to inspect the house. She made her way to the edge of the porch, her left hand shading her eyes from the sun. *Nice looking truck. Clean.*

She took a deep breath and walked toward the big house to meet Mr. Carter. Approaching the man, an uneasy queasiness rumbled in the pit of her stomach. Though Maddie slowed her pace to take it in, the man's tall muscular frame did nothing to jolt her memory, but something seemed familiar about him.

But how could she know him? She had never even heard of him until three days ago.

Carter had his back to her, arms crossed, appraising the old house. Maddie took small steps, focusing on the business at hand while examining his stance and the taut muscles in his back.

Her skin crawled.

Dried branches crackled under her feet. Carter started, and turned around.

Maddie shaded her eyes and cautiously walked toward him. She stopped abruptly. Her eyes went wide. Her heart pounded in her ears.

"You!"

Carter pulled back. "Have we met?"

"Oh, we've never been formally introduced, but we have definitely met. Don't tell me you've forgotten those tender moments we shared."

Nathan looked into her eyes. "No, I'm afraid I don't have any idea what you're talking about."

He studied her body, a sly smirk on his face. "Trust me, I would definitely remember if we had met."

Maddie's face burned. Her fury took on short breaths. How dare he look at her like that. Who did he think he was? Why, she ought to—

She slapped his face.

Turning on her heels, she marched to the cottage, stomped up the steps, threw open the screen, and slammed the heavy wooden door behind her.

Carter hollered after her, "Who are you?"

Maddie paced like a caged tigress. "Who am I? Who am I?" Well, she wouldn't give him the satisfaction of finding out. If he were the last contractor on the planet she would *never* hire him.

Within minutes, she heard pounding on the cottage door.

Maddie yelled at the man on the other side, "Go away."

He yelled back, his own anger apparent, "Listen, lady, I don't know who you think I am, but I have never laid eyes on you before."

Maddie continued pacing, her anger rising.

"Open the door and at least let me introduce myself. Then if you still think you know me and hate me as much as you seem to, I'll leave."

Maddie opened the wood door with such force it caught Mr. Carter off guard causing him to stumble backwards barely maintaining his balance.

Even through her rage, the man's rugged physical appearance stunned Maddie. *He is handsome.*

Once again his eyes perused her body with that cocky smirk.

Her temper flared, remembering the last time they met.

Maddie pointed toward his truck and through clenched teeth spit her words at him, "Get. Off. My. Property."

Carter yelled back, "What is it you think I did to you to make you hate me so much? I don't even know you."

Shaking with rage, she tried unsuccessfully to control herself while spewing forth another command, "If you are not off my property in three minutes, I am going to call Sheriff Harper and have you physically removed." Rusty growled, baring his teeth at the man on the other side of the screen door.

Carter glanced down at Rusty, then looked at Maddie, the question clear in his eyes. *Who are you?*

He stomped down the steps and over to his truck, slammed the door, and punched the accelerator, taking the loop around the driveway with such speed he left a cloud of dust in his wake.

Maddie's whole body shook. She had never confronted anyone like that before.

Sinking into the couch, her hands trembled. Where did all that anger come from?

The simple reason behind her response was, of course, his behavior the first time they met. But she wondered, *Could this be twenty-five years of pent-up anger I was afraid to unleash on Jeff?*

Her surge of anger gave way to a flood of tears. *What am I doing out here in the middle of nowhere? How could I have been so foolish to buy this run-down, dilapidated place? I can't even take care of myself out here, let alone this huge farm and the broken people who are going to live here.*

Like the light from a match struck in a dark cave, the memory of her conversation with Georgia came to her. *My Gram always said I can do more than I think I can.* The tension in her body faded.

Washing her angry tears with a washcloth, she saw something in the bathroom mirror that both startled and pleased her. The woman gazing back appeared strong, confident. And just that. A mature *woman*. No longer a frightened, fragile caterpillar. The beauty of a butterfly shone in her eyes.

Broken Acres was her home now. This was where she was staying, no matter how difficult it got. He couldn't be the only contractor who could do the job.

The vision of the man who had so infuriated her flashed through her mind. His shaggy, dark-brown hair, strong, solid physique, and handsome bronze face caused her heart to flutter, even over the draining anger. When he had removed his sunglasses, she'd noticed his striking blue eyes, although she didn't like what she saw in those eyes when he scanned her body.

No. No way. Not this guy. Not now. Not ever.

FIFTY-SIX

Friday at three o'clock Elias Jones finally returned her calls after she had left five messages. "Hey, Maddie. What can I do for ya?"

"Hello, Elias. Are you sure there isn't another contractor I can call? Maybe one from another county close by?"

"Couldn't get ahold of that Carter fella?"

"No, Elias. I talked to him. Can't you think of another name? Anyone?"

"Well now, there's Sam Taylor."

Smiling, expectant, pen in hand. "Great. How can I get in touch with him?"

"He's kinda semiretired, ya might say. He's probly up at his cabin right now, fishin'. He works when the inklin' hits him. Ya might be able to get ahold of him, say in 'bout two, three months, that's if he wants to put the time in. He's pretty happy just fishin' and relaxin'. Ya probly won't be able to get him away from his rockin' chair." Elias cackled at his own joke.

Frustrated, Maddie tried again. "Is there no one else anywhere around here?"

"Not unless you wanna have someone come all the way from Portsmouth."

Maddie blasted back, "That's a hundred and eighty-five miles away."

"Yup, sure is. Whatever happened with that Carter fella? I heard he's a perty good builder."

"I don't care how good he is. I don't want that man on my property."

"Well, Maddie, all's I can tell ya is, it's either Carter or Sam Taylor."

FIFTY-SEVEN

A self-made man, Nathan Carter co-owned the multimillion-dollar company NT Construction, building large commercial structures. Nathan had built his company from the ground up. Originally responsible for all the work, over time he grew the business into a megacompany with several hundred employees.

With the county seat named after his great-great-grandfather, Nathan felt pressure to succeed. Especially since his father had brought shame and poverty to the family.

Even though Nathan was the owner of a prestigious company, he often dressed in work boots and jeans and joined his men in the trenches. He missed getting his hands dirty with good hard physical labor. Meetings in the boardroom and working in his spacious office at the gigantic cherry-wood desk his partner had insisted he buy made him feel claustrophobic.

Nathan hated the city, but he never intended to plant himself out in the boondocks. After driving aimlessly for days, running from his pain, he had ended up exhausted at the Haystack Motel on the edge of a hick town called Jacob's Bend. He'd woken up the next afternoon not sure where he was.

Nathan had asked Ken and Lettie Sands to put the word out that he knew construction and was looking for odd jobs, remodeling, renovations. His reputation grew throughout the county in a short time as an honest, hard worker who knew his stuff. Still, his work lacked creativity. Nathan had lost that the day he left the city.

Sitting on the porch of the Thompson place, Nathan recalled the scene at the Riley farm. Who did that woman think she was, ordering him off her property? That farm probably belonged to her husband, anyway.

Racking his memory, he could not remember ever meeting the woman. And her sarcasm.

If she wanted renovation done in this county, she'd have to come to him. When she did, he would demand an apology.

The vision of her shocked look when he turned around and her furious demeanor puzzled him. It also invoked the memory of her slender body. The jeans she wore fit her shapely form just snug enough to give a man something to think about. He had to admit she was beautiful, even in her anger. No, especially in her anger.

I always was attracted to redheads.

Her thick hair, soft and inviting, begged some man to passionately run his hands through it. Red hair, flashing green eyes, with a temper to match, what a challenge she would be. His blood warmed at the thought.

Oh, no. He was not getting involved with women ever again. Too painful. And especially not *that* woman. Whoever she was.

FIFTY-EIGHT

Maddie hung up the phone, disgusted with Elias's response. Even if Nathan Carter was the only contractor in the surrounding five counties, she would never hire him.

Angry and frustrated, Maddie stepped out to the porch and let the screen door slam behind her. Sarg lay quietly on the top step. He looked up at her and purred. When she walked over to pet him, which always had a calming effect on her, she noticed he had something between his paws. He stood and walked over to curl himself around her legs, leaving his treasure at her feet. Wide-eyed, Maddie opened her mouth to scream.

Click, click, click. Squealing. She pulled the covers up over her head. Don't scream. Mom won't like it. Dad, come rescue me.

Maddie's trembling hands covered her tear-lined face. Paralyzed, her lungs pleaded for air, her heart threatened to explode, she let loose a piercing shriek. Sarg took off on a stealthy run toward the orchard.

Rusty barked from inside the house, pushing the screen door open. He ran back and forth across the porch, barking loud and fierce, looking for the culprit that had caused Maddie to scream.

When she pointed to her feet, Rusty looked at the dead mouse, then back at Maddie. He started barking again, looking around the yard as if telling Sarg to get back here and dispose of the critter. Sarg was nowhere to be found.

Maddie closed her eyes, took a deep breath, and told herself to stop shaking. She felt the warmth of Rusty's body touch hers. When she opened her eyes, Rusty had picked up the disgusting vermin in his mouth and was shaking it with all his might. Maddie screamed louder. He dropped the mouse and looked up at Maddie, distressed.

"Rusty, if you can understand me, please pick that thing up and take it off to the back forty." She waved her hand to show Rusty what she wanted him to do. He must have understood because he picked up the lifeless rodent and trotted off toward the barn.

Weak in the knees, Maddie collapsed onto the porch swing. *Am I ever going to get over this terrible fear?* Gram had told Maddie when her cat laid a dead mouse or bird at her feet he was bringing a gift. *That kind of gift I can do without.*

Rusty's fierce bark from the other side of the barn sent Sarg screeching, running for the big house, Rusty in hot pursuit. Maddie wanted to believe Rusty's bark was a warning that said, "Don't ever do that again, you idiot."

*   *   *

Sam Taylor's phone rang seven times before his answering machine picked up. "I'm up at the cabin. Don't know how long I'll be gone. I check my machine once or twice a month, so leave a message and I'll get back to you sometime."

When she heard the beep, Maddie made her plea for help with the house. The second beep came about thirty seconds after the first. She looked at the phone in her hand and gave an aggravated sigh. Dialing the number again, she continued her message. Another beep. The third time she just pleaded for Sam to call her.

Now what am I supposed to do, wait till next Christmas for Sam Taylor to return my calls?

Maddie checked her calendar. Knowing the winter rain and occasional snowstorm would halt the exterior work on the project, she glanced at Nathan Carter's phone number next to the phone. Grabbing the piece of paper, she crushed it into a little ball and tossed it in the trash.

"I definitely won't need that number."

A week later Sam Taylor called.

"Mrs. Crane?"

"Yes."

"This here's Sam Taylor. I—"

A huge grin spread across her face. She eagerly interrupted Sam mid-sentence. "Mr. Taylor, I am so glad you returned my call. When can you come out here and look at my house?"

"Well now"—Sam cleared his throat—"don't think that's gonna be happenin' anytime too soon, Mrs. Crane."

"Why not?"

"Well, you see, when I was out on my boat the other day I hooked a fifteen-pound rainbow. Got so excited I stood up and the boat capsized. Hit my head on a big rock. Passed clean out. Somehow ended up breaking my ankle too."

Maddie's heart sank. "I'm sorry you had such a terrible accident, Mr. Taylor."

"Call me Sam. Don't worry yourself. I'm doin' fine. Fortunately for me, Elias Jones was in his boat a few yards away fishin' with his grandson. They saw the whole thing. His grandson is a pretty good-sized boy. He dove in and saved my life."

"Oh my. You sure were lucky."

"You betcha. So you see, my leg is in a cast and my eyes still aren't seeing too clear. Probably couldn't even think about looking at your place until next spring when the snow melts."

Maddie let out a long sigh. "I understand. Could you possibly recommend another contractor?"

"Sure. I hear he's pretty good. Maybe even better than me. Well, that's only because I'm not as spry as I once was."

Maddie chuckled. "Of course. What's the name of this super-duper-faster-than-a-speeding-bullet-able-to-leap-tall-buildings-in-a-single-bound contractor?"

Sam laughed on the other end. "That's a good one. Can I use it?"

"Absolutely. If you'll give me the name and phone number of this super hero."

"Well, his name is, ah, now let me see, what was his name? My memory must have got shook up from the concussion. Let me get my book out, see if I can find it." Sam dropped the phone.

Maddie pulled the handset away from her ear when the phone hit something hard. "Ah, let's see. Oh yeah, here it is. You got a pencil and paper?"

"Sure do, right here in my hand."

"His name is, ah, Carter. Nathan Carter."

Maddie's shoulders drooped. "Yes, I know Mr. Carter. Are you sure there isn't another contractor I can call?"

"Nope, there isn't anybody else unless you want to go clear to Portsmouth. Most of the locals are working on the new hospital there. That's a two to three year project. What's wrong with Carter?"

Maddie took a deep breath. "Mr. Carter and I have already met. He is definitely not the man for the job."

"Well, Mrs. Crane, he's the *only* one you're gonna find to do the work around here."

"Thank you for your help, Mr. Taylor. I'll give it some thought." She slammed the phone down. There was no way she was going to hire that man.

Maddie paced. Suddenly Pastor Ben's Sunday message rang in her mind. *"Love your enemies—if you love those who love you, what reward have you?"*

"Seriously? No way."

Pray for those who persecute you.

But he didn't really persecute her. More like harassment. He was a dangerous man.

Do not be overcome with evil, but overcome evil with good.

"Really?" She ground her teeth. "I really do not want to do this." She crossed her arms over her chest and shook her head.

Never take your own revenge.

Heavy sigh.

Maddie looked at the number Sam Taylor had given her. She rolled her eyes.

"This is Carter. Leave a message after the beep."

Relieved she didn't have to talk to the man, she left a somewhat civil message on his machine.

FIFTY-NINE

It was well after nine thirty when Nathan got home from his renovation job at Harper's Hardware. He flipped on the light, hit the play button on the answering machine, and leaned back on the couch to pull his boots off.

He listened, uninterested. A message from his partner with an update on the Portsmouth hospital project, a telemarketer, a dial tone, a woman's voice. He shot straight up in his seat.

No, it couldn't be.

He played the message again. Listening to the rigid voice, a sly, satisfied expression moved across his face.

"Mr. Carter, this is Madison Crane. You, ah, you came to my farm the other day to give me an estimate on some renovation work. Please call me back at your convenience." *Click.*

"So, it's Madison Crane, is it?" Speaking her name sent a chill down his arms. What was that all about? He played the message again.

He'd known she would eventually call. There was no way she would have been able to find anyone within a hundred miles who had time to do that job. Should he make her wait or call back right away?

He checked the clock. Almost ten.

He might wake her up if he called now. But what did he care if he woke her up? The phone rang twice.

"Hello."

"Mrs. Crane?"

"Yes. Who is this?"

She knows darn well who this is.

"You called this afternoon about giving you an estimate on your renovation project."

"Mr. Carter. I'd like to get this project started as soon as possible, before the weather gets bad."

"Well now, let me check my calendar and see if I can fit you in." He knew he had nothing to do except finish enlarging the bathroom at Harper's.

"Yes, I think I might be able to fit you in. Say, four weeks from now."

"Four weeks? I can't wait four weeks," she snapped back.

"Well, Mrs. Crane, I really can't see how I can make it over there much sooner than that. There is another option."

Her response came back cautious, suspicious, "Yes?"

"You could bring your ideas and meet me here at my house."

Seething silence.

"You can't be serious. What do you think I am?"

"Ah, excuse me, lady. But you called me."

"Yes, but I expected you to come here, check out the house, and give me your estimate. What can we possibly accomplish there? The house is *here*."

"I got a good look at the outside of the house when I was there the other day. You *do* remember that day, don't you?"

"What if we meet at Lettie's Café?"

"They probably won't be open. I don't get home until late from the job I'm working on and after cleaning up—"

Her rage came spitting through the phone, "Where exactly do you live, Mr. Carter, and when can we meet?"

A satisfied grin. "I live out on Highway 47, the old Thompson place."

"I'll find it."

"How about day after tomorrow? Say, around nine o'clock? I should be home from work by then. Would that work for you?" Nathan tried not to laugh out loud, imagining those flashing green eyes.

Maddie's reply came in a subdued tone, "The day after tomorrow will be fine."

"Okay then, Wednesday, nine o'clock, my house. Ah, will your husband be coming with you?"

She spat back, "I don't have a husband."

"What?"

"I'm a widow."

"Oh."

"I'll see you Wednesday, Mr. Carter."

*   *   *

Maddie paced from the kitchen to the living room, back to the kitchen.

Why did she tell him she was a widow? What was she thinking? She couldn't go over to that man's house. Maybe she should take a gun with her. She needed to buy one to defend herself against wild animals anyway. But Alex said she had to take a class and get a permit. That wouldn't help her now. But she couldn't go over there all alone.

Her pacing ceased. A smile of satisfaction. "I won't go alone."

SIXTY

Wednesday night Maddie drove to the address she had been given. Nathan Carter's truck was parked in the driveway. She stepped out of the new truck she had bought just the week before to use as a work truck around the property. She took a deep breath and walked up the path to the front porch.

"Okay, let's get this over with."

Marching up the steps, she knocked on the door. It opened at her touch. A far-off voice hollered, "Come on in, door's open."

Maddie gave the unlocked door a slight push and walked into a comfortable room that definitely had a man's touch. A hunter green leather couch, matching chair, and ottoman sat facing the fireplace where a welcome fire burned.

A man's voice yelled from another part of the house, "Have a seat, I'll be right out."

Maddie tentatively sat on the edge of the chair. Warmed by the fire, she looked around the room.

What was he doing back there? He knew she would be there at nine.

A deep voice to her left caught her off guard. Startled, she turned to see Nathan Carter standing a few feet from her chair with nothing but a towel wrapped around his lower torso, drying his hair with another towel. Wide-eyed, she turned her head back to the fire.

"Sorry, Mrs. Crane, but I didn't want to meet with you all grubby from a hard day's work." His grin stretched across his face like the Cheshire cat.

Nathan moved toward her until a loud growl caused him to step back. He looked down at Maddie's feet. Rusty bared his teeth.

"I didn't think it was wise to come alone," Maddie informed him as she attempted to regain her composure.

Nathan frowned. "Excuse me," he spat at her and walked toward the back of the house.

Maddie's heart beat so fast she couldn't catch her breath. She pet Rusty's silky coat and railed inside for putting herself in this position in the first place.

Not more than five minutes later Nathan Carter walked back into the living room dressed casually in jeans and a blue cotton shirt, sleeves rolled to the elbows.

Maddie thought his disheveled hair rugged and appealing. He didn't smell of aftershave, but carried the fresh scent of soap. *Stop that. Madison Crane, what are you thinking? What are you doing here?*

Nathan carefully walked around Rusty, who kept his eyes glued to the man. He sat on the couch to the right of Maddie's chair. "Let's get this over with."

"Fine with me."

Nathan looked Maddie square in the face. "I will ask you one more time. Do we know each other? You said we met before."

Maddie eyed him suspiciously.

"Oh yes, we've met. A little over a year ago, to be specific. On my drive out here from Chicago. It was getting late one night and my stomach kept growling, reminding me I hadn't eaten. The only place open on the highway was a bar and grill. *Sam's* Bar and Grill." She paused for any sign of recognition. His eyes revealed absolutely no recollection.

Maddie's voice was tense and grew louder as she spoke. "You were drunk. You caged me in my seat at the bar, harassing and groping me while I ate. *Now* do you remember?"

Nathan ran his hands through his damp hair and closed his eyes. "Oh. That was you?" His blue eyes opened again to look at her. "I don't really remember much about that night. Honestly, Mrs. Crane, that is the only time—"

Maddie held up her hand.

"I really don't want to think about that night." She pointed to the pages on the coffee table. "Here are a few hand drawings and a list of what I'd like done to the house."

Nathan sighed, shook his head, and thumbed through the papers. "This is a big project."

"So what do you think? Can we get on this right away? I would need an estimate first, of course."

Maddie kept her eyes set on the papers, the dog's leash rested on her thigh. She was all too aware of his scrutiny of her.

He rubbed the stubble on his chin. "Mrs. Crane, I don't believe I have time to take on this project."

"What? Then why did you have me come all the way over here?"

Nathan looked her in the eyes, his voice stern, authoritative, "To tell *you* to get off *my* property."

Tears pooled at the back of Maddie's eyes. Rusty growled and jumped to his feet when the man raised his voice.

The fire in her eyes, her clenched teeth dismissed Nathan Carter with a look of pure hatred. Gathering up her papers, Maddie walked out the front door, her trusty protector at her side.

*   *   *

Nathan watched her drive off.

Carter, what is your problem? You just lost a job that would keep you busy for months. He was bored stiff. Not to mention he brutally wounded a woman who had every right to hate him. *You jerk.* From her description of that night, he had practically mauled her. And tonight. Ugh. She was almost in tears. He hung his head and ran his hands through his hair.

Now he'd really done it.

*   *   *

Tears welled up in Maddie's eyes as she slammed the truck into gear and drove away. No. She was not going to cry because some arrogant jerk offended her.

Still, tears spotted her cheeks. Rusty's sorrowful, compassionate eyes looked her way from the passenger seat. When she reached over to pet his soft nose, he licked the salty tears from her cheek.

Maddie ruffled the hair on his neck. "Thank you, Rusty. Now what am I going to do?"

All the way home she thought about the man she'd met in the bar and the man she'd seen tonight. *Seen*, that was the key word. She had to admit he was an extremely handsome man. But a real jerk. Why was she even giving him a second thought? When he came out dressed in nothing but a towel, something definitely stirred inside.

"No way. Not this guy. Not ever."

When she arrived home, Maddie hung her keys on the hook just inside the door. The light flashing on the answering machine caught her eye. Rusty jumped up on the couch alongside Sarg.

"Mrs. Crane? This is Nathan Carter." She gritted her teeth.

"I called to apologize for my behavior. I was being spiteful because of the way you treated me when I came to your farm the other day. You have every right to be upset, no, let's make that furious with me after what I did at the bar. If you are still interested in considering my services, I would very much like to bid on your project. Should you decide against my doing the work, I'll understand."

SIXTY-ONE

Maddie phoned Nathan Carter and called a truce.

Plans for the renovation were drawn up by one of Nathan's business associates in record time, but the ideas Maddie had for the big house needed alteration. Nathan suggested she build only three additional bathrooms, reminding her the cost would be exorbitant to add six more bathrooms to the already existing bath.

"But I want each guest to have their own private bath."

"Mrs. Crane, that would overload the septic system. The county would probably demand you redo the entire system, not to mention anything else they see that might need updating."

"Oh."

"The bedrooms in this old house are big enough to add a bath between them. Easy access from both rooms."

Maddie had grandiose ideas about redoing the dining room and parlor. Nathan shot those down too. She stood her ground on the kitchen, however. She had big plans for the kitchen.

Nathan felt certain he could finish much of the exterior work and begin interior demolition before the snow started to fall.

Even with renovation underway, the emotional wall between Maddie and Nathan stood tall and strong. They were cordial, but each had volatile tempers. The majority of their communication was accomplished through the written word.

Maddie wanted to help with the renovation but thought better of it. Besides, she had plenty to do with the cottage, orchard, garden, and land rentals. An old barn on the property also needed renovation. That would have to wait for another year.

Things progressed slowly, much too slowly for Maddie. One day she left Nathan a note asking him if he could speed it up a little.

He returned a less than cordial response.

Mrs. Crane,

You know nothing about construction. It is a slow process, especially with only one man doing all the work. Leave the building to me. You just play in your orchard and garden.

That hit a nerve.

Mr. Carter,

You know absolutely nothing about me. I intend to be involved in every decision that affects Broken Acres. Including the construction.

Mrs. Crane,

If you want this job done faster, then hire me a helper.

Mr. Carter,

I have the perfect person in mind.

*   *   *

When Billy received Maddie's letter he had just been released from jail, having been held for almost two months awaiting a hearing before a judge. The clerk at the 7-Eleven couldn't absolutely testify to Billy's involvement in the robbery since he came in after the other two, so he was released. Sammy and Alfred would never break the guys' no-snitching code to testify against Billy. The judge told Billy if he ever saw him in his court again he would not be lenient with his sentencing.

Billy read Maddie's letter again before making his decision. What did he have to lose? Besides, he'd be helping Maddie out, doing her a favor. Who knew, maybe he'd even start his own construction company someday. There was nothing keeping him there except bad memories.

Billy called and left a message that he would take the bus and be there within a week.

*   *   *

Nathan was less than pleased with Maddie's choice of helpers. He should have hired one of his own men. He never thought she would actually take the bait and hire someone.

Sunday afternoon he was about to write her a note but decided to speak with her face-to-face. Walking up the steps to the cottage, he felt a strange uncertainty tug at him. He shrugged. It was only business, and it was his business to do it right.

A pleasant fall day, the front door stood open with only the screen door between Nathan and the inside of the cozy little house. He reached up to knock on the screen but held back.

Maddie was humming a light tune. Nathan leaned against the support post of the porch, his arms crossed, right ankle resting on his left, captivated by the melodious sound coming from the woman's lips.

Singing now. What was that song? He couldn't make out the words.

"Falling in love, yeah, yeah, falling in love with you." Humming again.

Without warning, Chelsea's face sprang into Nathan's mind. He stepped forward and pounded on the door.

"Mrs. Crane, I need to talk to you."

*   *   *

Maddie's heart raced at the sound of Nathan—Mr. Carter's, voice. It was getting to be a habit. *Don't be ridiculous. It was just the surprise of hearing him bang on the door.*

Dish towel in hand, she walked to the door, determined to love him as her neighbor, just as Pastor Ben had charged his congregation on Sunday, even if it killed her. She chose to be cordial. "Good afternoon, Mr. Carter. How are you this beautiful day?"

Gruff skepticism filled his voice. "Who is this guy you hired to help me with the renovation job?"

Who did he think he was? No, she was not going to let him get under her skin.

"He's a young man I met on my trip out here. He has had some . . . disappointments. He's coming here to make a new life for himself."

"Oh, great. I know what that means. He's a juvenile delinquent, probably an ex-con. How old is this guy anyway?"

"I don't know. I'd guess nineteen or twenty."

"No way. I am not gonna take on some snot-nose kid. He probably doesn't know a hammer from a chisel or have a clue how hard construction work is. I don't want some kid his parents threw away."

"He does know construction. From what I understand he spent the last three summers working construction. And doing a great job."

"Listen, lady, I need a helper, not a hindrance. If you want the exterior of this job finished before winter, you better find a mature man who knows his stuff."

Once again he succeeded in provoking her temper. "Mr. Carter, Broken Acres will one day be a refuge for people exactly like Billy Chambers. People no one wants. Throwaways, as you put it. Misfits, as society sees them."

"So you're gonna take in strays, huh?"

"If that's what you want to call them. Two of these discarded misfits are already settled and comfortable here." She pointed to the pair. "With a little bit of loving care, Rusty and Sarg have turned out to be wonderful companions."

"Those are animals, not people."

"Yes, well, like it or not, Billy Chambers is coming here to help you with the renovation of *my* house." With that she closed the inside door in his face.

Maddie heard Nathan stomp off the porch, mumbling.

Her heart pounded. Once again she felt drained by another argument. She had never been comfortable confronting people, but here she was standing up to this brute of a man.

She turned back to the baking she had begun before Nathan's interruption. A church potluck and pie auction on Saturday had her making two of her family's favorite dishes: chili relleno casserole and enchiladas. Not to mention six of her favorite pies: two apple, two cherry, and two peanut butter chocolate chip.

The next morning when Maddie went out to the porch with her coffee, a note rested on the swing. Nathan's handwriting. She rolled her eyes.

Now what? Maybe he was apologizing for being so rude. Yeah, right.

Mrs. Crane,

We need to come to an understanding. As long as I am the foreman on this job I expect to be involved in decisions with regard to personnel and, of course, any improvements you can't seem to make a final decision on. I know it is difficult for women, sorry, people, to make up their minds on such large projects. If we cannot come to some kind of agreement you will have to find yourself another contractor.

Nathan Carter

"Why that arrogant, egotistical—" Rusty raised his head from the comfort of the swing at Maddie's angry voice. "No, I am not going to let him get to me again." She turned the sheet of paper over and scribbled a note in the most syrupy language she could conjure up.

Dear Mr. Carter,

I would be more than happy to discuss the decisions regarding my renovation project.

Madison Crane

She knew Nathan would catch the exaggeration in the words *discuss* and *my*.

She didn't have to get angry. She would simply *discuss* her ideas and then make whatever decision she wanted. She knew how to kill him with kindness. After all, hadn't she done that with Jeff for years? The only difference was she didn't have the final word with Jeff. With this man, she did.

SIXTY-TWO

Maddie ran like a scared rabbit across the orchard, tears streaming down her cheeks, screaming, "Mr. Carter. Nathan. Nathan."

Nathan had been hard at work for over an hour. Uncharacteristically warm for this time of year, he worked bare-chested, his shirt hanging on the side mirror of his truck. At the sound of his employer using his first name, he looked up. Wiping the sweat from his forehead with his forearm, he squinted and shaded his eyes with his hand. The alarmed woman ran full force toward him.

"Nathan, help. Please help me."

"Maddie, what's wrong? Are you all right?" Nathan's manly instincts kicked into full gear. He grabbed her shoulders to get her attention. When he saw tears, it was all he could do to keep from pulling her into a protective embrace.

Maddie pointed toward the cottage. Her words came haltingly, "He's— I don't—He's inside."

Nathan looked past the distraught woman to the cottage. His clenched jaw made the tense veins in his neck stand out. "Who's inside?"

Nathan could tell Maddie was fighting to gain her composure, but she couldn't talk.

Nathan walked to the truck and pulled out his shotgun.

The terrified woman shook her head, eyes wide with fear.

"No, no." She gasped for air.

"You stay here." Nathan walked toward the cottage.

"Nathan, no. It-it's a bat."

"A bat? For Pete's sake. I thought——"

"I know. I-I'm sorry. Could you please come up to th-the cottage and help m-me get it out of the house?"

Nathan hung the shotgun back on its rack in the truck and grabbed a fishing net from behind the seat. He shook his head at her. "Let's go."

The two walked quickly across the orchard and up the steps to the porch. Nathan stopped. Maddie ran into his back. He could feel her warm breath on his neck. He closed his eyes and took a deep breath.

Focus. She's only trouble.

He carefully opened the screen door.

"He's over there, on the wall." She pointed over his shoulder, pressing in closer.

Nathan wasn't too sure what to do with the sensations pulsing through his body. He wanted to take the frightened woman in his arms and make her forget her fear.

Maddie whispered in his ear, "I think he might be asleep."

He took another deep breath, concentrating on the bat. "Do you have something we can trap him with? How about something like a tennis racket?"

"Yeah, there's one in the closet under the stairs."

Nathan tiptoed to the closet and found the tennis racket. He snuck up on the furry rodent and slapped the racket over him, pinning him to the wall. The bat didn't even twitch.

"Hold this racket while I move to the other side and scoop him up with the fishing net."

"Are you sure it's safe? He reminds me of a hideous black mouse with wings." She shivered. "I don't think I can."

Nathan looked sideways at her, grinning. "He's sound asleep."

"O-okay."

Taking the racket from Nathan, Maddie stood as far away from the beast as possible, arms outstretched, on her tiptoes, eyes closed tight. Nathan moved behind her to grab the fishing net.

When he turned around, his heart rate doubled. Taking in the beauty standing before him, his blood warmed and he promptly forgot about the bat.

Hair clipped up, fine wisps lay loose on Maddie's neck and her knit top hugged her slender body. With her hands above her head, the tiniest bit of skin showed at her waist. Nathan's eyes followed the contour of her body down the length of her form-fitting jeans.

He leaned over and kissed the back of her neck.

Maddie tensed. Her eyes flew open.

His hands came to her waist. She dropped the tennis racket. Nathan slowly turned her to him and kissed her lips.

She kissed him back. Nathan felt soft hands run over his tan arms and defined shoulder muscles.

Moments later, Maddie drew back, out of breath. "Nathan."

He pulled her close again, kissed her face, her neck, whispered in her ear, "Maddie, let me take you to a place you haven't been in a long time."

"Nathan, I wish—"

He lifted her, drew her in his strong arms against his chest, and passionately kissed her lips. When he backed her against the wall, he suddenly felt her tense and she shoved at him. "No. *No.*"

Stunned, Nathan looked at her. Confusion and the sudden change in her reaction jolted him out of his mood and he realized she was terrified. And not of the bat this time. Of him.

Her rejection was like a slap in the face. He set her feet back on the floor. "Listen, Maddie—"

Maddie scrambled away to the opposite side of the room. She stood against the door gasping, her disheveled hair escaping the clip and falling around her shoulders. "Nathan, I-I can't."

"Don't give me that crap. I know you want me as much as I want you. Why don't you just tell the truth?"

*   *   *

Maddie stood, reeling from the memories that had knifed their way through the moment. *Jeff, in a rage, springing across the room, grabbing her forcefully by the shoulders, picking her up and pinning her against the wall. With his face inches from hers, he had told her if she ever did that again she would be sorry.*

A shiver ran through her body. She closed her eyes tight.

*   *   *

Nathan watched Maddie wrap her arms around herself, shivering. In fear?

He took a step forward, reaching his arms out to pull her in.

Maddie put her hands up in front of her. "No. Please try to understand. I can't."

Nathan's nostrils flared. He shook his head and stepped back.

"I didn't know what I was doing. I mean, I was terrified of that, that thing on the wall." Her voice softened. "Would you please just take it out of my house?"

Nathan turned his gaze back to the bat. How could it sleep through the frantic chaos of the last few minutes? Tempted to tell her to do it herself, his protective instincts kept him from lashing out. He grabbed the tennis racket and fishing net and maneuvered the bat into the net and outdoors. It flew off screeching like a barn owl.

*   *   *

Maddie gently clicked the door shut behind him and fell against it, breathing hard, weak as a starving kitten. "I can't believe I let that happen."

She touched her lips.

*   *   *

Nathan stared at the closed door behind him.

What just happened?

SIXTY-THREE

Maddie saw Jenny at River's Edge Market pushing a cart overflowing with forty-pound bags of dog food. Her son, Michael, rambled in a language only two-year-olds and moms could understand.

"Hi, Maddie. How are the guys doing?"

"Really well. Rusty keeps packing on the weight. His leg is good as new. Chases squirrels and just about catches them. Sarg's fur has grown back, he's eating well. He's still skittish around most people. How are you and Michael doing?" She ruffled the little boy's hair. He grinned and rubbed his eyes with balled fists.

"It's past his naptime. My sister had him this morning. I was late picking him up, calf born out at the Kelly farm." She looked at her son. "He's getting a little crabby."

"Are you going to be in my neck of the woods any time soon? I'd love to have you both out to the farm. Michael can play with the guys, well, Rusty anyway. Sarg will probably ignore him."

"Actually, I take Fridays and Mondays off. So many of the farmers need my services over the weekend. We are so busy these days, Jeremy, the other vet, and I have been talking about adding another vet to our practice." She stared into the distance. "Someday."

Jenny smiled at Maddie. "Is tomorrow too soon for a visit?"

"Not at all. Why don't you come for lunch? I'll make chicken salad. What would Michael like?" She smiled at the little man now asleep in the cart. "PB&J?"

"His favorite."

"My son's too."

"How many children do you have?"

"Three. Boy, girl, girl." A cloud passed across Maddie's face. "David always wanted to be a veterinarian. He started his studies but ended up quitting school. I'm not really sure why."

"Really?"

Maddie smiled at the lovely young woman. "Yeah. But we can share stories tomorrow. Looks like you need to get this guy home."

"Sounds good. See you around eleven thirty?"

"Perfect."

*   *   *

Michael sat on Rusty's side, encouraging the tranquil dog to get up and trot across the floor. He yanked his ears and pulled his collar with no success.

"We have a yellow Lab at home. He rides Bridgette all over the place."

"Sorry, Michael, I don't think Rusty knows how to play horsey."

He shot her a grin.

Maddie cocked her head. *What a cute little guy.*

Michael rubbed his eyes and crawled into his mother's lap. Jenny rocked him until he fell asleep.

Maddie shared her adventures of the trip to Jacob's Bend and a bit of her kids' growing-up years. "If it hadn't been for Carolyn and Alex, not to mention the caring people in Jacob's Bend, I don't know where I'd be right now. Probably still rambling around in that modern mausoleum back in Chicago on prescription drugs for depression.

"I am especially fond of Granny Harper. What an incredible woman. She only lives a couple of miles up the road. She has been so helpful. Checks on me at least every other week. She's determined to teach me everything I need to know about being a farmer woman."

"Granny is amazing. Outlived two husbands."

"I know. Both being widows, we often ride to church together on Sundays."

Jenny gave Maddie a quizzical look. "We didn't attend church much. We lived in California and my dad had odd hours as a cop; my mom worked in real estate. I did meet a guy in vet school who kept inviting me to church." She looked over at Michael asleep on the couch.

"Is he Michael's father?"

"Yes. He doesn't know about Michael."

"Really?"

Jenny shook her head. "I don't even know where he is or his name."

Maddie raised her eyebrows.

Jenny chewed the inside of her mouth and let out a heavy sigh.

"Let me start from the beginning. I was in my final year at veterinary school. We met when he delivered pizza to my friend's house. He was funny, cute, smart, had a job. What more could a girl want, right?"

Maddie smiled and gave Jenny an understanding nod.

"Anyway, I saw him in the school lounge the next week and said, 'Hey, you're the pizza guy.' He asked my name but I just told him Jay R., short for Jennifer Ruth. We started dating and thought it would be fun and mysterious if we didn't know each other's real names or share any details of our lives. We actually made up stories and played off each other, topping each unbelievable event. Always meeting at some clandestine location to add to the mystery. Looking back, I see how silly that was. I went to church with him once, a big church, overwhelming. He kept asking me to go back, but I always had other plans."

Maddie nodded.

"The thing is, we were only together once. It was a huge mistake." She looked at her son. "But Michael is not a mistake. I love him to pieces. He makes my life worthwhile. Neither of us had ever been with anyone before. I know in this day that sounds strange." Jenny blushed.

"Not at all. Refreshing, actually."

"I was always too busy with school to have time for guys. We just got carried away in the passion of the moment."

Maddie closed her eyes, remembering Nathan's kisses.

"The funny thing is, I fell in love with the pizza guy. Even though I didn't know his name or anything about him. You can tell a lot about a person the way they react to the everyday frustrations of life.

"I felt so ashamed of what we had done. With finals and graduation just a few weeks away, I never saw him again. I really don't know what happened to him." A distant sadness clouded her eyes.

"I'm sorry, Jenny."

Jenny shrugged. "I came here to live with my older sister, Katie Lou. You know, the librarian?"

Maddie nodded. "I really like your sister. She's so smart and full of helpful information."

"That's Katie Lou. She absolutely loves doing any kind of research. You need to find out information on *anything*, she's your girl. Anyway, about two months before I graduated, she called to tell me one of the vets in Jacob's Bend was about to retire. Perfect, right? Then, when I got here, I found out I was pregnant."

"Did you try to find Michael's father to let him know?"

"At first, no, because I didn't want him to feel obligated. My sister said it wasn't fair to him. So I called the pizza place, described him, and asked for his phone number. They said nobody fitting that description had ever worked there." Jenny shook her head. "I thought of going to look for him. But I had Doc Sawyer's practice to learn and—so it's just me and Michael."

"Well, you are doing a wonderful job raising him, Jenny. He's a cutie. Hey, since I don't have any grandchildren yet, do you think Michael would let me adopt him?"

Michael opened his eyes, stretched, and grinned at Maddie. He walked over, sat on her lap, and laid his head against her chest.

Jenny laughed. "I guess the answer is yes."

SIXTY-FOUR

When Ben called, inviting Maddie to take another horseback ride to see the fall colors, she sounded pleased he had called.

Now on her doorstep, he knocked on her door, and she yelled down through the upstairs window, "Come on in. I'll be down in a minute."

Ben stepped inside and took in all the improvements Maddie had made to the house. He had visited Edgar Riley the last few months before he died. The place had been dark and depressing, heavy curtains drawn. Amazing what a little paint could do. Maddie had brought new life to the place.

The warm sun shone through the large picture windows caressing the rustic wood floor.

Wood floor? Ben did a double take. He remembered a dingy, green shag carpet. Had this beautiful floor been under that ugly carpet all these years?

"Hey, Ben."

He breathed deep taking in the beauty before him. Her thick auburn hair rested on her shoulders, with a wisp she pushed behind her ear drawing attention to her beautiful green eyes. "Ready to go?"

On their way to the Jeep, Ben asked to see the work being done on the big house.

"Oh, Ben, it's all torn apart. Why not wait until it's completed?" Maddie smiled, fidgeting with her hands.

"Why not a before and after?"

Maddie sighed. "Okay."

Ben noticed Maddie shy away nervously as a tall man came around the corner of the cottage. She stopped to introduce them.

"Ben, this is Nathan Carter. He's the contractor I've hired to do the renovation work for me."

"Hi, Nathan. Ben Farrington."

The two men shook hands.

"Ben is the pastor at North Hills Chapel in Jacob's Bend."

"Hmm." Nathan didn't look impressed, Ben noticed with an internal smile. He also saw the contractor look at Maddie with a concerned expression on his face. Maddie smiled weakly and turned to Ben.

Maddie showed Ben around the big house and on their way to the Jeep, Ben stopped to shake Nathan's hand again.

"It was nice to meet you, Nathan. I hope to see you again."

Ben watched Nathan's eyes linger on Maddie. What was it with this guy?

Maddie seemed nervous and clutched her hands together. "Ready to go, Ben?"

"Yeah, sure."

As before, Ben had brought along a picnic lunch. Sitting under the same oak tree, the two marveled at variegated greens melding together with gold and red leaves. The gentle wind caused the rustling leaves to glide through the air and rest among a splattering of fall colors.

"Beautiful." Maddie stretched her legs and laid back on her elbows, head back, eyes closed.

"Yes." Ben stood, walked a few paces, turned to look at her, and walked back. He had to admit that his lecture to himself about respect and friendship was failing fast. He finally sat and propped his back against the oak.

"Ben, did I tell you Peter Weatherby told me the story of the horn?"

"It's quite a story, isn't it? This little town has a lot of history."

He watched her ruminate, wondering about her thoughts. "Jacob Hertzog would be proud of what you're doing out there at Broken Acres, Maddie. You might want to learn how to blow the shofar." He chuckled at his own joke, but Maddie seemed lost in thought.

"Beauty for ashes. My Gram would say that to me when I'd ask her why God let my dad die. He gives beauty for ashes."

"Yes, He does." Ben looked at her delicate profile. "Tell me about your family, Maddie."

She looked past the large oak where Ben sat, closed her eyes, and shrugged. "Well, my family lived on my grandparents' farm until I was about eight. I met my best friend, Carolyn Moreno, there when I was five. She lived on the next farm over. Our family moved around a lot. She stayed there. My dad worked construction, and like I said, we moved around a lot. After my dad died—"

"Maddie, I'm so sorry. I'm sure that was very difficult for your family."

Maddie shrugged. "After my dad died, I spent summers with my Gram and Gramps. They were very religious. Church every Sunday, Bible reading. Carolyn was just like them. I went to summer camp once with her, but never really understood what they were talking about.

"Growing up, my grandparents' lives showed me what it meant to be a good Christian. Their pastor talked about the Bible and Christianity in different terms, with excitement. A lot like you, Ben."

Ben lounged against a sturdy oak, a slight frown between his eyes. He nodded.

"As an adult, I tried to copy their example, not very well, I'm afraid. One Sunday night I needed a break." Ben noticed Maddie looked down at her left hand.

"From life. Jeff watched the kids while I went for a walk. I saw a bunch of cars parked outside this little church near our home and not knowing what was going on inside, I decided to go in and just sit.

"Never in my life had I heard anyone with so much enthusiasm as the man speaking. He said, 'In my home the Bible was just a book that was always around. Oh, believe me, I knew all the stories backward and forward, but that's all they were, stories. Until one night I decided I was sick of living such a phony life. I held the Bible in my hands, stretched out my arms as high as I could above my head, looked up, and shouted to God, "If You are real, then I need to know it, right now. Because if You're not, I'm going to throw this book in the trash, give up this stupid hoax called Christianity, and live my life the way I want." Lightning didn't strike or anything, but when I lowered my arms and looked at the page open in front of me, I couldn't believe my eyes. "And you will seek Me and find Me, when you search for Me with all your heart. And I will be found by you,' declares the Lord." It was as if God spoke directly to me. I couldn't put the book down.'

"At that moment I whispered, 'I want what this man has.' But I wouldn't have been surprised if God had ignored me. I had closed Him out of my life for so long.

"On my way home I sat on a bench in the park. I said, 'God, I am begging You, I need to know if You are real, like that man said. My life is one big mess. Show me, somehow, if You are real.'"

"And did He?"

"No. I opened my eyes, fully expecting something to infuse me with the excitement I saw in the speaker, but I didn't feel a thing. I thought, *I guess that experience is only for a few special people.* I knew right then and there that God was only a figment of my Gram's imagination."

Ben's heart broke for this woman. If she didn't know God's love how would she ever truly love anyone else? How could she possibly make it through life being all alone?

"You seem to have relied on your grandmother a lot."

"Yeah." Maddie smiled. "I still hear her sometimes."

She needs to be listening to God. Lord, make a way for her to know You. "Did you ever stop to think that maybe the things your Gram was saying were the same things God might be trying to say to you?"

Maddie looked at the ground, then back at him. "Why would you say that?"

"Well," Ben answered, "think about it. Someone who knows you well, loves you without any expectations, and wants what's best for you. Does that sound like your Gram?"

"Yes, of course."

"Well, it sounds like God too." Ben let that sink in for a minute, then prompted her. "What happened after that?"

"After that experience, any spiritual passion I had waned. Jeff spent more and more time growing his career, traveling to meet with corporate clients in other states. That left me to be mother and father, carrying the responsibility to raise the kids, mostly on my own. Our sporadic church attendance and my poor example became evident in the lives of my children. With the exception of Bracy. She's the strong, committed one in the family."

"She's at Wheaton College, isn't she?"

"Yes, she is. I hope you get to meet my kids, Ben."

"I would like that very much." He smiled when he saw Maddie light up talking about her children.

"You've come a long way, Maddie."

"Have I?"

Ben reached over and took her hand.

"Yes, you have."

SIXTY-FIVE

Wednesday evening Maddie drove the sixty miles to Carterville, arriving at the bus station at six o'clock. When she saw a thin, scruffy Billy Chambers get off the bus, she wrapped the broken boy in a tender hug.

"Billy, it's so good to see you. I'm glad you decided to come help with the renovation." Maddie's concern mounted when she saw his dark sunken eyes, the scar across his forehead, and the frailty of his once well-built body. He must have lost at least twenty pounds. His eyes looked a little glassy. Georgia hadn't said anything about drugs.

Billy returned a genuine smile and hug. "Hey, Maddie. Man, I didn't realize you lived clear across the country. But then, I really didn't give it a second thought where I'd end up. I just wanted out."

"I'm so happy you decided to accept my invitation, Billy. You are going to love it here. Fresh air, beautiful surroundings, less hectic pace, and my home cooking." She was going to fatten this boy up.

His engaging smile told her he was happy to be there.

"Sounds great. When do I meet the super on the job?"

"Oh, Nathan? I mean, Mr. Carter. He'll be at the farm first thing in the morning. His one redeeming quality. He's punctual."

Billy cocked his head. "Ah, does he know I'll be working with him?"

"Oh yes, it was his idea to hire a helper." Not wanting to do anything to discourage him, she left out the rest of the story. Maddie wanted to encourage Billy from the moment he stepped off the bus that he had made the right decision coming to Jacob's Bend.

"Let's pick up your luggage and get on the road. It's about a forty-five minute drive from here. Dinner is waiting at home."

Billy pointed to the backpack he had slung over his shoulder. "This is it."

"That's all you brought with you?"

"Yep, there wasn't much else I wanted or needed."

On the ride home Billy caught Maddie up on the happenings in the Walterses' household. Grant and Georgia would graduate in June. Grant received a scholarship from some college out west and Georgia was still undecided about her future. Maddie saw disappointment in Billy's eyes when he mentioned Georgia.

"Are you and Georgia still seeing each other?"

Billy looked at his hands in his lap. "We don't talk much anymore."

Maddie knew from talking with Georgia that she and Billy were having trouble but decided to change the subject. "So, have you ever lived on a farm before?"

"Nope, been a city boy all my life. I'm not sure there's going to be enough action out here for me. This doesn't look like much of a town."

Good grief, if he thinks Carterville is small, wait until he sees Jacob's Bend.

Maddie frowned. "You'll get some action, all right. Mr. Carter will no doubt see to that."

Billy looked up with a grin. "Why would you say that? Sounds like maybe you've had a run-in with him."

Maddie's thoughts ran to Nathan's passionate kisses. Her face burned red. "He-he's a local contractor. Actually, he's the only contractor within miles of Jacob's Bend who has time to do the work. I don't really know much about him other than he seems to know his business. He's punctual, efficient, and very assertive."

Billy raised his eyebrows and ran a finger across the scar on his forehead. "So, what's this work you're having done?"

"Wait till you see the farm, Billy. You will think you died and went to heaven. I want to hold off until you see it to explain the project, okay?"

"Sure. Are we almost there?"

"Only a few more miles. We'll drive through Jacob's Bend before we get to Broken Acres."

"Huh? What's a broken acre?"

Maddie laughed. "Broken Acres is the name of my farm."

Billy nodded, then stared out the passenger-side window.

Silence held the rest of the way to Jacob's Bend.

Maddie slowed to the twenty-five-miles-per-hour speed limit. "This is Jacob's Bend, Billy. It's small, but the people are friendly and its home to me."

Billy nodded.

Driving down Main Street, Maddie gave Billy the little bit of history she knew about the town.

Heading out of town toward Broken Acres, Maddie breathed in the beauty. She smiled over at Billy. "Isn't it beautiful?"

Once again, no comment, simply a shrug. More silence.

Maddie proudly announced their arrival when they pulled up to the gate. "Here we are."

The faded red mailbox now read "Broken Acres" in bold black letters. She put the truck in park and jumped out to open the gate. When she returned to the driver's seat, Billy seemed a little more coherent.

"You need a solar-operated gate. That would save you a lot of time and steps."

"That's a good idea, Billy. I'll have to look into that." In fact she had already asked the neighbors if they knew where she could buy one. Not a single neighbor had a solar gate. They all wanted to know, "What's the hurry? We like gettin' out and openin' our gates."

As they crested the little hill overlooking Broken Acres, Billy sat up on the edge of his seat. Maddie paused their journey to take in the panorama before them. She never tired of seeing her farm from this vantage point. "Isn't it magnificent?"

"Wow."

"I fell in love with it the first time I saw it, but couldn't for the life of me figure out why I would want to buy a huge farm like this." Maddie looked over at Billy. There was delight in his smiling eyes.

"So what do you think? Could you feel at home here?"

"Yeah," Billy said in a whisper, "it's amazing. I feel . . . how can I describe it?"

"Peace?"

"Yeah, that's it, peaceful."

Maddie drove toward the big house to give Billy a look at the project he would be working on.

"Man, that's a big house. You live there all by yourself?"

"No, no. I live over there in the small cottage." Maddie pointed in the opposite direction. "Speaking of which, I'll bet you're starving. Let's head to the house and have dinner. What do you say?"

"That sounds great. I'm really hungry. Haven't eaten since this morning."

"What?" Maddie stared at Billy. "Well, I made enough for an army."

Maddie watched Billy eat dinner, amazed at all he consumed. Two helpings of spaghetti and meatballs, four rolls with butter, and two helpings of peach cobbler and vanilla ice cream. He reminded her of Rusty and Sarg when they first showed up.

"That was delicious, Maddie." Billy sighed, patting his full stomach.

"Thank you."

Maddie smiled when the Fearsome Twosome took to Billy right away. Animals always seemed to know when a person had a kind heart. Billy lay on the floor playing with both animals until all three were worn out.

They would sleep well tonight.

"You're probably ready for some sleep in a comfortable bed after riding on that bus for three nights. I've made up a bed for you in the loft. My room is downstairs, down the hall."

"No way, Maddie."

His remark caught her off guard.

"I'll sleep in the barn or on the porch. It wouldn't look right if I slept here in your house with you."

Touched by his thoughtfulness, she smiled at the young man the courts and his family had given up on. "Billy, it's okay, really. We know everything is on the up-and-up."

"Yeah, but your neighbors and the people in this little town don't know that, not to mention Mr. Carter. I don't want him driving up in the morning and see me coming out of your house after sleeping here all night. No, I'll sleep on the swing outside, if you don't mind, and tomorrow we'll decide where I'm going to stay. That okay with you?"

Maddie shrugged. "It gets pretty cold at night, but if that's what you want. I appreciate your concern for my reputation, but it's really not necessary. Maybe we can set up something in one of the outbuildings."

"Settled. Good." Billy ran his finger over his scar. "Maddie, I hate to be a party pooper, but I'm really tired. Could we pick up this conversation tomorrow?"

"Of course. Let me get the down sleeping bag and some quilts. You might have some company tonight. Sarg has taken a liking to you. You're only the second person he has come near, other than me. For some unexplainable reason, he adores Nath—Mr. Carter. Sarg normally makes his evening resting place on the swing. If that bothers you, I'll keep him inside."

"No, he's welcome to sleep with me. After all, I'm taking his bed from him. He sure is a beautiful cat, and Rusty, what a great dog."

Rusty lifted his head from between his paws, looking from Billy to Maddie, his head tilted.

"Both were a mess when they first wandered in here. They had obviously been brutally mistreated."

"Did they show up together?"

"No, Rusty limped in first, then Sarg a few weeks later. I'll tell you their stories sometime. You'd better get to bed. Mr. Carter will be here early in the morning. Like I said, his one good trait it that he's punctual."

Maddie slipped up to the loft and brought down the sleeping bag, a couple of quilts, and a pillow.

"You know, it's gonna be cold out there tonight. Are you sure you'll be okay?"

Billy yawned. "Yeah, I'll be fine." He grinned. "Thanks, Maddie. I promise I won't let you down."

Maddie put her arm in the crook of his elbow and gave him a squeeze. "It never once crossed my mind that you would."

Sixty-Six

Early the next morning Nathan Carter drove up to the big house. He dragged himself out of his truck, stumbled over his feet, catching his balance before he fell. He took the thermos out of the front seat with the hope the coffee would wake him up and clear his head.

As with most mornings, his exhaustion came from having stayed up most of the night rehashing the past and wondering about the future. Not to mention, though he loved working with his hands, his body wasn't accustomed to this much heavy labor every day. Just about every muscle felt as if it intimately knew the thrust of a sledgehammer. Hopefully, within the next half hour the extra shots of caffeine would take effect. Then he could get busy with the job he was hired to do.

As was his habit, Nathan glanced up at the cottage to see if Maddie sat on the swing with her morning coffee. No Maddie. Just a mass of blankets heaped on the swing.

Did she sleep outside last night? She was crazy, a woman out here all alone, sleeping outside where anyone or anything could attack. What was she thinking? Oh yeah, she didn't think. She just did what she darn well pleased. Nathan shook his head, his protective instincts frustrated.

Through bits of gossip he had overheard at Lettie's Café, he gathered Maddie had a less than perfect marriage. Although he sometimes heard her give glowing praises about her husband, he pieced together that for years she had been the submissive little housewife. Time now for her to spread her wings and make her own decisions. No matter how ridiculous or unsafe.

A slight smile shone in Nathan's eyes. Actually, he liked her strength. She had a mind of her own. He really liked that she didn't play games like other women. A heavy frown replaced his smile. *Enough of this.*

Nathan took another swig of coffee and walked into the big house, ready to tackle the tasks ahead of him. When he came around the corner into the kitchen, he almost smashed into what looked like a vagrant. Panic hit. Nathan looked at the man before him and back toward the cottage.

He knew she shouldn't have slept outside. Was she okay?

The stranger offered his hand. "You must be Mr. Carter."

Nathan looked down and reluctantly shook the young man's hand. "Yeah. And who might you be?"

"Billy Chambers. Didn't Maddie tell you about me?"

Nathan sized up Billy. He was too skinny to even lift a hammer, let alone two-by-fours and siding. So, he was on a first-name basis with her. For some reason Nathan didn't like that. "Yeah, she told me about you. She said you've got some construction background. What kind?"

"Large office buildings mostly. A few houses. I'm good with a hammer. I'm stronger than I look and I learn fast."

"That's good, because we don't have much time before the snow falls. We have to get the outside work completed before then. You better hold your own kid, 'cause I'm not here to babysit."

Billy hung his tool belt on his hips. He stared Nathan in the eyes. "What are we waiting for? Let's get started."

SIXTY-SEVEN

Coffee in hand, Maddie tiptoed past the swing and sat down on the top step of the porch, soaking in the quiet. There was nothing like the first cup of coffee in the morning.

She didn't want to disturb Billy, but she *did* want to see Nathan Carter. It intrigued her watching him get ready for the day. Doing all the manly things construction guys do. Strap on a tool belt, unload tools from his truck, slurp down coffee.

Glancing over at the swing, the blankets sat neatly folded. No Billy. She looked toward the big house and saw movement. Two men at work.

Nathan must have arrived earlier than usual.

She went into the kitchen to fix Billy some breakfast. Once inside she put together four eggs, three pieces of toast, and a thermos of hot coffee. That would keep him going for a while.

Much later that day, Maddie leaned against the support post of the porch gazing over her property. The sun had just started to set. *I wonder if this sense of awe will ever fade. It never looks the same twice.* The resident blue sky had transitioned into dramatic wisps of red enclosed in subtle shades of yellow. The porch view took her as far as the eye could see.

Scanning the horizon, her eyes fell on the big house. Nathan and Billy were still hard at work. Stretched for time, she knew Nathan wanted to get as much done as possible before the light of day slipped away.

Determined to put some meat on Billy's bones, Maddie had given him two turkey sandwiches, chips, an apple, and a piece of pie for lunch. After the morning of hard work she knew Nathan expected of him, she felt a hearty lunch would see Billy through until dinner.

A slight pang of guilt at not having considered Nathan's needs had caused her to put an extra sandwich and piece of pie in the basket. His appreciative smile caught Maddie off guard. She had expected a sarcastic, "No thanks, I can take care of myself" remark.

Hours later the aroma of chili and corn bread drifted from the kitchen. She wondered if they could smell dinner over at the big house. Maybe she should see if Billy was about finished for the day. And it would be impolite not to include Nathan. Maybe she'd invite him to dinner.

Approaching the big house, she heard uproarious laughter. Eavesdropping normally made her uncomfortable. It was, after all, unethical. But curiosity got the best of her.

"Yeah, she is really something. Needs attention all the time, and when she doesn't get it, she squawks something awful."

Billy laughed so hard at Nathan's description tears ran down his face. "You say she started it as soon as you began this project?"

"Yep, and hasn't stopped shrieking yet. I'm not quite sure how to handle it. At first I got angry. I really wanted to see if I could find a muzzle. I knew that wouldn't go over very well. Then I ignored her. That was a waste of time."

"What did you do?" Billy asked through his laughter.

"I decided I'm gonna dump her as soon as this job is over. What do I want with an, I-want-it-my-way female in my life anyway? Her squawking grates on my nerves."

Maddie's eyes grew wider with every insult. Her stomach churned. He had some nerve, talking about her like that. And Billy thought it was so funny.

One of her Gram's favorite sayings bounced around in her mind. *"Pride will bring one low but a humble spirit will obtain honor."*

Frowning, she looked up. This wasn't pride. It . . . it was self-defense. *"Pride goes before destruction and a haughty spirit before stumbling."*

Exhaling, she breathed a heavy sigh. What was she supposed to do, just let it go without saying a word?

Put on a happy face, Maddie. She pasted on a fake smile and walked to Nathan's truck. The two men still cackled.

"Hello, Billy. Mr. Carter."

Billy's sheepish grin caused her to grind her teeth. "Oh hi, Maddie."

"What's so funny?" Maddie asked coyly, silently kicking herself for asking. She didn't really want to hear the response, suspecting her anger would once again get the better of her.

She glanced in Nathan's direction to see if he was gloating. He gave her a warm smile that made her go weak in the knees. Remembering his caustic remarks, she hardened her expression.

Billy glanced at Nathan. "Oh, it's nothing, really."

Maddie inhaled deep trying desperately to hold back her anger. "No, really, I'd like to join in on the joke."

Billy looked over at Nathan. Nathan shrugged.

"Well, Nathan was telling me—"

Incensed by Nathan's response, she retorted sharply. "Never mind, I really don't care."

"No, Maddie, it's funny. You'll get a kick out of it."

Maddie's eyes burned ebony. "I said I don't want to hear about it."

The two men looked at each other. Their grinning faces turned to surprise. Nathan shook his head. He gathered up his tools and put them in the toolbox in the back of his truck. Billy shot Maddie a *what's your problem* look.

She snapped at Billy, "Dinner is ready."

"Ah, okay. Let me help Nathan and I'll be up in a few minutes."

Maddie turned on her heels, fists clenched, and stomped off toward the cottage, mumbling under her breath.

*   *   *

Billy walked over to help Nathan. "What was that all about?"

"You got me, kid. She does that. One minute she's the most tender, compassionate woman you've ever met and the next, snake venom oozes from every pore. I never know if I'm gonna get a sweet smile or a slap in the face."

"She's slapped you?"

Nathan revisited his initial visit to the farm and her revulsion at his presence. Suddenly the bat incident entered his thoughts. He groaned. "Well, I guess you could say those dirty looks and sarcastic remarks sure feel like a slap in the face."

"Whoa, this is a new side to Maddie I haven't seen before. Actually, I don't know her all that well. We've only been writing for a few months.

I thought I knew her pretty well from her letters. Guess you don't really know someone until you live with them. Ah, what I mean is—"

"It's okay, I know what you mean."

Nathan shook his head. "I tell you what, she won't let her defenses down long enough for me to even get a glimpse of who the real Madison Crane is. It's probably better this way.

"I'll see you in the morning, kid. By the way, you're a hard worker. I'm glad Mad—Mrs. Crane asked you to come out to help with this project. Sleep tight, seven a.m. comes awful early."

"See ya tomorrow, Nathan. Thanks for giving me a chance to prove myself."

"You don't have to prove anything to me." He looked over at the cottage.

Billy washed up in the kitchen of the big house and mounted the cottage steps. The spicy aroma of chili and hot corn bread floated through the air, reminding him just how hungry he was. He liked putting in a hard day's work and actually feeling hunger again.

He knocked lightly on the screen door. "Maddie, it's me, Billy. Can I come in?"

"Sure, come in."

Maddie stood at the stove, her back to him. "Sit down. I'm dishing up your dinner."

He obeyed, offering a hopeful smile when she brought the food to the table. Maddie took a seat across from him.

Billy looked over at Maddie and frowned.

They ate in silence until he couldn't stand it any longer. "Maddie, have I done something to offend you?"

"Offend me? Why would you ask that, Billy? Do you have a guilty conscience?"

"Guilty for what?"

*   *   *

Maddie considered whether to admit to eavesdropping.

"I had planned on inviting Mr. Carter to join us for dinner. I heard the two of you howling and decided to listen to hear what all the laughter was about. After all, it might have been something I should hear."

Okay, okay, that's not completely true.

Maddie studied Billy to see if his demeanor changed. He sat there watching as if waiting for the punch line.

Lips pursed, she crossed her arms. "I heard what Mr. Carter said about the squawking woman needing attention all the time. He said he wanted to put a muzzle on her." She gave Billy a searing look. "I know he was talking about me."

Billy broke into hysterical laughter.

Maddie snatched the dishes from the table and tossed them in the sink. "What's so funny? I don't think it's funny at all. I think he's the most inconsiderate, rude, arrogant, egotistical, overbearing man I have ever had the misfortune of knowing. If he weren't the only contractor around I'd fire him right now."

Maddie watched as Billy contained himself. "Maddie, he wasn't talking about you."

"He wasn't?" She sank into her chair.

"No. He was talking about his pet parrot. He bought her about six weeks ago and has regretted it ever since."

Maddie held her head in her hands. *I am such a fool.* Now it was her turn to apologize to Nathan Carter.

"Excuse me, Billy. I need to make a call."

Nathan's answering machine picked up. "This is Carter, leave a message after the beep."

"Mr. Carter, Nathan, this is Madison Crane. I owe you an apology. I overheard your conversation with Billy about your, ah, parrot and I—I misunderstood."

You can't get away with that. Tell him the whole thing.

"I, um, thought you were making fun of *me.* It sounded like you were referring to me when you mentioned the squawking woman. I apologize for my reaction. Will you please forgive me?" She cleared her throat. "I'll . . . I'll see you tomorrow morning."

Maddie carefully replaced the receiver before turning around.

"Billy, I owe you an apology too. I'm sorry for jumping to conclusions and thinking the worst. That was pretty self-centered, wasn't it, thinking your conversation revolved around me? I think I've learned my lesson not to eavesdrop and to get the facts before assuming the worst."

*   *   *

Nathan stepped out of the shower and heard someone talking. The sound of a human voice instantly put him on guard. He listened carefully to get a bearing where the sound was coming from. A woman's voice. From his answering machine.

He wrapped a towel around his waist, walked into the living room, and pressed the button on the machine. Nathan stood silently, wondering who the voice belonged to. The minute he heard Maddie's voice his heart jumped. The shock of her calling him Nathan, instead of Mr. Carter, caused him to collapse on the couch.

Her voice was so engaging and her attitude so conciliatory, he couldn't help but feel compassion. He thought there might even be a trace of vulnerability in her confession. At one point in her message he found himself once again feeling protective. More than that, he felt a sense of awe that she would actually call to apologize.

Nathan played the message over and over, turning up the volume so he could hear it in the bedroom while he dressed. Each time he played it, his heart became more entwined with the intoxicating voice. *It's not the voice, you idiot. It's the woman.*

In his mind Nathan could see Maddie's lovely freckled face breaking out in animated laughter. A few weeks before, he happened upon her in the orchard. He had taken a break from his work, curious to see what kind of trees were planted there.

Maddie stood on a ladder trimming dead branches from one of the apple trees. He startled her when he stepped on some dried twigs. She turned to face him and with a gloved hand brushed a strand of hair from her eyes. Her smile seemed to say she was actually relieved it was him standing there.

At that very moment an apple fell from the tree and hit Nathan on the head. Her laughter put a smile on his face. His body warmed at the way the sun embraced her auburn hair, causing it to shine with the softest touch of gold.

What a beautiful woman.

Their hands lingered when he handed the fallen apple to her. For a brief moment they entered into an unspoken heart conversation.

Uncomfortable, Nathan had pulled back, smiled, and returned to his work. He was an emotional mess the rest of the afternoon, his heart racing every time he thought of Maddie standing on the ladder.

Again he listened to her message. Should he call her back? No. What would he say? His tender feelings for Madison Crane troubled him.

Once again he hit the Play button. An hour later he fell asleep on the couch listening to Maddie's apology.

*   *   *

Maddie hummed one of her favorite songs while preparing a pan of home-made cinnamon rolls. The finishing touches included a thin layer of vanilla icing and a sprinkling of chopped walnuts. When she heard Nathan's truck drive up to the big house, she quickly walked to the window. Surely after she had left him that message he would show her a little more consideration and respect.

Her dreams had included Nathan most of the night. These new dreams confused and troubled her. Oh, she had dreamt of him before, but the two of them were always doing battle. This was different. It was as if he was a new, no, different man. In the dream excitement ran through her each time she saw him. They never spoke, but the unspoken message was clear.

Billy poked his head around the corner of the house when he heard Nathan drive up. Billy had set up a cot in the studio apartment in the big house, located just off the kitchen. It had a bedroom, sitting area, and a full bath. Built, no doubt, with a live-in cook or housekeeper in mind. Perfect for his needs. Sparse furnishings, but comfortable. A space heater kept the small bedroom warm and cozy.

Nathan lifted his left hand to cover his eyes from the blinding sun. He reached, unsuccessfully, with his right hand to secure his thermos. Maddie could tell from his body language that he was probably cussing up a storm.

Maddie placed the cinnamon rolls in a cloth-lined basket and covered them with a matching napkin. Grabbing a carafe of hot coffee and two mugs, she headed for the big house. She smiled at the pounding of two hammers, at first in sync, then individually. She set the basket, coffee, and mugs on the front porch where Nathan and Billy were sure to see them when they came around the front for more supplies. Having watched the two men work together, she knew every few minutes one or the other would walk around from the side of the house to pick up siding from the stack that lay at the foot of the porch steps.

After gently placing a card atop the cinnamon rolls she walked back to the cottage.

*   *   *

Billy, the first to see the gift, called Nathan to come take a look. When Nathan walked to the porch and saw the offering, he smiled and shook his head. Billy handed him the card. "Open it."

Nathan closed his eyes and bathed his senses in Maddie's perfume that lingered on the envelope. He carefully slipped his pocketknife through the back fold, removed the card, and read aloud.

Nathan and Billy,

Please accept this humble offering as a symbol of my appreciation for all your hard work on this project. Also, please consider this a peace offering to accompany my sincere apology for my ungracious response yesterday. Enjoy.

Maddie

SIXTY-EIGHT

For weeks Maddie had been looking forward to attending the fall festival at North Hills Chapel, with old-fashioned games, bobbing for apples, and a dunk tank with Pastor Ben in the hot seat. Or, in this case, the very cold seat. There would even be a three-legged race. She longed for a gathering like this. The festivals she attended with the kids and their friends in the city were more like carnivals, attended by hundreds of people. The games consisted of rented rides and huge jump houses. It was never a comfortable activity for her, especially since she always went alone.

Thrilled with the success of the previous pie auction, Madelyn Simpson, the festival coordinator, expressed with great fanfare her appreciation for Maddie's contribution. After all, the woman had baked *six* pies. When Maddie explained how much she loved to bake, Madelyn promised to make a mental note for future reference to ask for more than the two pies she had originally requested Maddie bring.

Pastor Ben approached the group of women at the dessert table. "Anyone want to take my place in the dunk tank?" No takers.

Ben smiled and turned to Maddie. "Could I speak with you privately, Maddie?"

"Sure." Maddie noticed that Pastor Ben's use of her given name raised eyebrows and smirks from the rest of the group.

"I'm sorry to take you from the ladies."

"No problem. We were just sharing pie recipes."

Ben glanced at the crowd staring in their direction and shook his head. "How's it going out at the farm?"

"Good. Really good."

A troubled sadness crept into his eyes.

"Is everything okay, Ben?"

"Maddie, I know of a young woman who could use a home like Broken Acres right about now."

This was what Maddie had been waiting for, wasn't it? Someone who needed Broken Acres as much as she did.

A woman called Ben's name and they both looked over to see Madelyn Simpson, wearing a bright floral dress, orange high heels, and a large sunflower clip holding one side of her flamboyant red hair, headed straight for them, hollering over the noise, "It's time for the dunk tank, Pastor Ben. Come on now."

He shivered looking at the tank. "Maddie, can we discuss this situation another time?"

"Of course, whenever you like. Just give me a call."

Madelyn took Ben by the arm and steered him straight for the dunk tank.

Chills ran down Maddie's spine at the thought of being immersed in that freezing water, time after time, at the mercy of a little white ball. Surely the committee had shown compassion for their pastor and filled the tank with warm water.

*   *   *

The renovation project moved along swiftly now that Nathan had Billy's help. Costing a lot more than Maddie anticipated, Isaac Birnbaum counseled her to slow down with the spending or she would run out of money. "Come on, Isaac, the money won't run out. There's plenty."

Still, the caution in his voice caused her to question. *This is the first time in my life I've had control of my finances. Have I already blown it?* Maddie asked Isaac for an accounting so she could be sure to make wise decisions in the future.

*   *   *

Monday morning Ben called to see if they could meet at Lettie's to finish their conversation. He didn't sound good. "Are you all right?"

"I've just got a little cold."

"From the freezing water in the dunk tank, no doubt."

Ben sniffed and blew his nose. His nasal reply left little doubt. "Yeah, probably. How about tomorrow afternoon, about three?"

"Sure. That works for me."

The next day, upstairs in the loft, Maddie passed the freestanding full-length mirror. Her hair was disheveled, her clothes covered with white dust. Earlier she had taken breakfast to Billy at the big house. He and Nathan were putting up drywall and needed a third hand. They asked her to lean her body up against the drywall while the two men pounded nails as fast as they could.

After four sheets of drywall, standing under Nathan's ladder, Maddie looked up to question if he still needed her help. He stared down at her. When their eyes met, he gave her that knee-buckling smile. Maddie's stomach turned summersaults, but she managed to return his friendly gesture with a smile of her own.

Billy interrupted the momentary exchange, "Hey, you two. Can you stop ogling each other long enough to get this last piece of drywall up?"

It unnerved Maddie that every time Nathan smiled at her she had the same unsettling response.

Standing in front of the mirror, she fluffed her hair. "I'm a mess." She checked the clock on the dresser. She needed to head for town in fifteen minutes. Good grief.

There had to be something she could change into. Browsing through the clothes, she found a snug pair of blue jeans and a pale green sweater. After applying lipstick, she ran a brush through her hair and spritzed her favorite perfume. Giving one last glance at her image, she smiled with satisfaction and galloped down the stairs.

*   *   *

Maddie opened the door to Lettie's and waved at Ken standing at the grill. He was becoming a regular back there.

Ken smiled. "Hey, Maddie."

Ben took in Maddie's appearance from head to toe. He couldn't help but think what a beautiful woman she was. He wondered if she would go on a date with him. Not just horseback riding, but a real date.

Ben stood and cleared his throat. "Hi, Maddie. Thanks for meeting with me."

Maddie smiled, her eyes sparkling.

Ben's knees threatened to fold. He pointed to the seat in the booth across from him.

A voice hollered from behind the counter, "Coffee, Maddie?"

"Yes, thanks, Kelly."

Keep your cool, Ben. Talk about the subject you came here to discuss. Oh brother, what was that subject?

"Ben, you mentioned something about a young woman who needed a place to stay?"

He glanced up. *Thank You, Lord.*

"Her name is Shauna Flanagan. She's a seventeen-year-old who came to Carterville to live with her aunt and uncle. When her mother died she had no other relatives to care for her. Her aunt and uncle attended our church."

Maddie tilted her head. "They came all the way from Carterville every Sunday? What do you mean they attended? Are they going to church somewhere else now?"

"They planned to move to a little piece of property they owned outside of Jacob's Bend and build a home there. Their home in Carterville sold a few months ago." Ben looked into Maddie's questioning eyes.

"Shauna's aunt and uncle were killed in a head-on collision two months ago. They were in the process of getting ready to move when the accident occurred. They were what many would consider quite wealthy, although they never flaunted their wealth. However, they were very generous people.

"As their only living relative, Shauna stands to receive a large inheritance when she turns twenty-one. Shauna has no idea of the fortune she will inherit. Her aunt and uncle set up a trust for Shauna in case something happened to them, but never told her. Shauna believes her small monthly allowance is from the sale of their house."

Ben's eyes pleaded. "Maddie, the truth is, Shauna has nowhere to go."

"Her father?" Maddie asked.

"Ran off with another woman and they don't know where he is."

"Poor thing. She must be scared to death." Maddie's heart ached for the girl.

"One more thing you need to know. Shauna has not spoken a word in two months. The doctors believe the death of her aunt and uncle was more than she could handle emotionally."

"If she doesn't talk, how does she communicate?"

"Oh, she's cognizant, just silent. Shauna seems to be reflecting much of the time, lost in her own world. When you talk to her she understands and responds. I think more than anything she needs someone to care about her."

Maddie sat for several minutes, obviously giving thought to Ben's idea. "I'm really not ready for anyone to move into the big house, but I suppose she could live with me in the cottage until we finish the renovation."

Ben's vibrant smile revealed his relief. "I hoped you would say that. Shauna is a nice girl. She'll be a big help to you around the farm."

"What about school?"

"She's a senior. The doctors felt it would be better if she went on independent study. However, she will need to be enrolled in a high school a little closer to Jacob's Bend to take advantage of the independent study program here."

"Would I be her legal guardian?"

"That's what the lawyers suggested. They left it in my hands to find someone appropriate. Their words, not mine. I thought of you right away. Shauna will be good company too. Except she's quiet."

Ben watched as Maddie closed her eyes. "If you want some time to think about it, you can let me know next week."

Maddie shook her head and gently touched Ben's hand.

Something like an electric shock pulsed through his body.

"Shauna is welcome. This is what Broken Acres is all about."

Ben took Maddie's two hands in his. *Come on, Ben, spit it out.* What he wanted to do was kiss her. But they were nowhere near that point in their relationship. *Relationship? What relationship?*

"Thank you, Maddie. I really appreciate your help."

Maddie gave him a knowing smile. "Where is Shauna staying now?"

Ben drew his hands back. "She's staying at the Simpsons'. They have plenty of room since their kids are off to college. But that arrangement would never be a long-term match. Shauna is too quiet for Madelyn. If it's okay with you, I'll bring Shauna to the farm on Saturday." Ben could not take his eyes off Maddie's perfectly shaped lips and sensitive green eyes.

"I'll be ready for her."

*   *   *

After Ben walked Maddie to her truck, she watched him drop his keys twice on the way to his Jeep. She grinned. *A man's man who loves people. Now wouldn't that be a change?*

What am I thinking? I do not need nor want to get involved with any man at this point in my life. Maybe never. She shook her head as a picture of Nathan drifted through her thoughts.

Her dreamy thoughts came back to Ben. If there ever was a time to consider dating, Ben Farrington would be at the top of her list. What list? *Do you think men are lined up to fall in love with you, especially a man like Ben Farrington? Get a grip, girl.*

SIXTY-NINE

"Well, I have my first resident," Maddie told Rusty, plopping down on the couch that faced the picture windows. She fluffed her hair when she saw her reflection.

Third resident. Those two words raced across her mind.

"Huh?" She glanced sideways at Rusty, who let out a sigh.

Maddie thought and thought. "Hmm, Rusty and Sarg? No . . ."

Then it hit her. Billy. She thought she had brought him here to lend her a hand, when all along he was here so she could help him.

"Okay, Billy, Shauna. Who is the third?"

Maddie smiled big at her reflection in the window. Her eyes grew wide. Oh. It was her. She was the third resident. Broken misfit, not willing to let go of her security, to let go of Jeff.

Maddie smoothed Rusty's coat, his head resting on her lap. "But I have now, haven't I?"

*   *   *

When Billy first met Shauna, he was less than cordial. He followed Maddie to the sink with his dinner dishes. Intolerance permeated his voice. "What's her problem? She won't answer anything I ask her."

Maddie took him aside. "Billy, remember I told you Shauna has had a lot of tragedy in her life. Three family deaths, all in a pretty short period of time. We need to be patient with her."

Maddie was thankful when Billy's responses to the girl softened. She had to admit it was nice to have another woman on the farm to talk to. Well, talk *at.*

Shauna's tiny five-foot frame and bouncy blonde hair that hung to the middle of her back were a stark contrast to her hollow hazel eyes. Try as she might, Maddie could not coax a smile out of her and of course, just as Ben had said, she never uttered a word.

Maddie drew Shauna into her world, hoping she would feel like family. An incredible cook and neater than a marine in boot camp, Shauna only got excited about one thing: gardening. At least they had that in common.

It tore at Maddie's heart when Shauna curled up on the couch searching her scrapbooks for memories of her mother, aunt, and uncle. Sometimes she studied them for hours. Probably remembering the faces and events, tears would trickle down her cheeks.

*   *   *

The renovation project will be finished in a few months and I'll be on my way. Billy looked up, startled as the thought crossed his mind. He rubbed the scar on his forehead.

"On my way? Where? Da——" He stopped short, remembering the last time he swore and Maddie leveled him with one of her not-in-this-house looks.

He liked it here. He couldn't find a better place to live. The countryside was spectacular, the people friendly, and the food great. He hadn't had a drink or a joint since he'd gotten there, and it was gonna stay that way.

Billy's weight had returned to normal, and with daily manual labor his strength and muscle tone looked good. He had no time to think of past heartaches, not when his future looked so promising.

His future. Maybe he could work with Nathan after they finished this project. He said he'd been doing odd construction jobs in the area. He really liked Nathan. He had been a good mentor.

Why not stay and make a new life for himself right here in Jacob's Bend? Things were good here. Very good.

Billy had decided to take Shauna on as a project. One way or another he would get her to talk again. He often sat with her on the porch, helping with her schoolwork. When it got too cold to sit outside any longer, Maddie insisted they study inside.

*   *   *

Maddie grinned, watching the two.

The telephone rang into her thoughts.

"Hi, Maddie."

"Hey, Ben. What's up?"

"Would you, Billy, and Shauna like to go to a movie in Carterville on Friday night?"

"Let me ask."

Two heads bobbed up and down at the offer. "They are excited to go."

"Great. I'll pick you up at five thirty. Will that work?"

"Five thirty?" She looked over at the pair. "They are both nodding yes."

"Okay, see you then."

*   *   *

The construction project dragged on due to difficulty receiving materials, or so Nathan said. Maddie wasn't so sure. Nathan often came to the cottage and asked her opinion on the most menial things. What caused concern were the emotions that stirred inside every time the tan, muscular construction foreman came near. *There is no way this man is worming his way into my affections.*

When she felt that overwhelming physical attraction toward him, she conjured up the scene from the bar. That fanned an angry flame that released her from the unwelcome tender emotions.

With the exterior of the big house pretty much finished, painting would have to wait for warm weather. Although they had a good start on the interior demolition and had dry-walled Billy's rooms, she knew the inside work would take longer than the exterior. Still Maddie badgered Nathan for a completion date, reminding him she was not made of money.

Defensive, Nathan would tell her to finish the job herself if she thought she could. She had half a mind to do just that.

It was no use wrangling with the man. Maddie finally threw her hands up and quit asking for a date.

SEVENTY

Thursday evenings the Jacob's Bend library remained open until nine o'clock. Billy often took Shauna there to work on school projects. They drove Maddie's truck, and she enjoyed a quiet evening alone.

This Thursday would be different. Maddie had an ingenious plan. Wanting to find out once and for all where she and Ben stood, she planned an intimate candlelight dinner at the cottage.

A brief twinge of guilt played in Maddie's mind, remembering the gossip about some woman who, as Madelyn Simpson suggested, *enticed* Pastor Ben to drive her all the way to Portsmouth on the pretense of needing to see a doctor just so she could get him alone for dinner.

What was the big deal? It was only an hour or two. They had spent more time than that alone when they went horseback riding. Besides, Billy and Shauna would be home just about the time they finished dinner. No impropriety there.

Excited, yet a little uneasy about having dinner alone with a man, Maddie remembered when she and Jeff occasionally enjoyed candlelight dinners. Unfortunately, Jeff would drink half a bottle of wine, giving him license to let his temper erupt.

Maddie sighed. Nothing to worry about with Ben in that area.

The plan set and the invitation accepted, Maddie was beside herself with anticipation to find out if Ben had feelings for her, as she believed she might have for him. Billy and Shauna left early, choosing to grab a hamburger in town. Perfect.

The delicate lace tablecloth Gael O'Donnell brought back from her most recent shopping excursion to Ireland graced the dining room table.

Crystal water goblets added elegance to the blue and yellow French table settings. Crystal candlesticks with sapphire blue tapers complemented the yellow rose centerpiece.

Chicken cordon bleu made up the main course. Caesar salad, home-made bread, fresh green beans, and peach cobbler rounded out the menu. Energized, Maddie couldn't wait to see Ben.

All the dinner preparations complete, Maddie turned her attention to her appearance. It had to be perfect. *Yeah right, like that's gonna happen.*

Dressed in her favorite cobalt blue silk top and black slacks, she carefully applied her makeup and set the final touches to her hair. She fussed with it up, then down, then up again. The final outcome was a soft wave of auburn curls that rested on her shoulders. Spritzing a touch of her favorite perfume, she took one last look in the mirror. Her reflection startled her. Not at all what she'd expected. She actually looked—pretty. A glow of satisfaction spread across her face, then a frown.

"Are you sure you want to go through with this, Maddie?" Not so long ago she had decided she didn't want another man in her life. But this man was different. He seemed to like her. Maybe it was just her imagination. She fluffed her hair. Tonight would tell one way or the other.

Banishing Rusty and Sarg to the loft would allow them to keep watch over the dinner party below without getting in the way.

Maddie walked to the window. The first snowfall of the year. What a perfect backdrop for the evening. Earlier in the day she had heard radio warnings for the local population to prepare for a blizzard.

A blizzard. That was ridiculous. The snow wasn't even sticking. There wouldn't be any blizzard tonight.

Her confidence grew when she saw a handful of clouds whispering past the full moon. Not to mention the weatherman on the radio had said it would be highly unlikely, since they hadn't had a blizzard in the valley for over thirty years.

Maddie surveyed her surroundings. Gael O'Donnell had helped transform her cottage into the lovely, comfortable home she saw around her now. Maddie's friendship with Gael had blossomed. When Carolyn moved back East, loneliness once again engulfed Maddie. She needed a good friend and Gael stepped in.

A sensation of utter contentment swept over her. A warm fire, soft silk against her body, juicy chicken and homemade bread in the oven, melodic guitar in the background, snowflakes gently touching the ground. Did it get any better than this?

Heavy sigh. Yes. If she had someone to share it with.

*   *   *

With dinner warming in the oven, sparkling cider on ice, at precisely seven o'clock Ben's Jeep pulled up in front of the cottage. Maddie took one more look in the mirror. Ben knocked twice. Taking a deep breath, she opened the door.

A satisfied sparkle came to her eyes when she saw the surprised look on Ben's face. He surveyed Maddie, head to toe, then quickly looked beyond her into the living room, up the stairs. "Where are Shauna and Billy?"

Maddie frowned slightly. "They're at the library. They'll be home later. Here, let me take your hat and coat." Ben clung to his coat as if it were a life jacket.

Looking Maddie in the eyes, Ben cleared his dry throat. "I, ah, don't know what to say."

Maddie smiled. "Don't say anything. Just give me your hat and coat, then come in and sit down."

Ben took in the table setting. "Maddie, I'm not so sure this is a good idea."

Maddie crossed her arms, tapped her foot and frowned at the man standing before her. "What are you talking about? We're just having dinner together. Relax, Ben. *You* are not on the menu."

He gave her a nervous grin.

*   *   *

Ben relinquished his leather jacket and black cowboy hat with some misgiving and told himself to calm down.

He chose the chair nearest the fire while Maddie hung his hat and coat on the rack. Ben carefully scrutinized the ambience Maddie had created. Was she trying to seduce him? It wouldn't take much for that to happen. *Come on, Ben. You're a forty-two-year-old adult man. Quit acting like a nervous teenager. It's not like you've never been alone with a woman before.* Ben hung his head and ran his fingers through his hair. *That's what I'm afraid of.*

His thoughts ran wild. *Get a grip, Ben.*

True, he enjoyed Maddie's company. He found himself missing her when he was home alone and disappointed when she wasn't at church on Sunday morning. But this was more than that.

Without realizing it, Madison Crane had become an integral part of his life. The simplest thought of her caused a warm desire that threatened to turn hot until he captured it and put the thought out of his mind.

Analyzing the cozy surroundings, he could see the huge amount of effort she had put into the evening. *Why didn't you bring flowers, you idiot?* There was no doubt about the mood she was trying to create, the music, fire, candlelight, and that mouthwatering smell coming from the kitchen. What was she cooking?

*   *   *

Maddie wondered if she had done the right thing. Ben was obviously uncomfortable. But why would he be? This was a simple dinner together, nothing more. Maybe she had been reading him wrong. She glanced his way while hanging his hat and coat on the rack. A striking man, his profile strong set against the fire. Ben fit nicely in his black jeans, jade green sweater, and black cowboy boots. The emotions she felt for Ben were different from what she felt when she and Jeff first dated. She couldn't quite put her finger on it.

*   *   *

When Maddie walked to the kitchen, the scent of her perfume drew Ben's eyes from the fire to her shapely body. *God, keep me strong.*

Maddie spoke over her shoulder as she tied an apron around her waist. "I'm glad you were able to join me for dinner. I hope you like chicken cordon bleu."

Ben found himself watching her every move. Graceful fingers tied the apron around her small waist, accentuating her slender body. His body warmed, the palms of his hands growing clammy as he studied her from the back. Her soft auburn hair swayed when she moved. Small shoulders joined her sleek back, which took his eyes to her tiny waist and on down to her hips. He barely heard her speak.

"Ben, are you all right?"

"Wh-what did you say?"

"I said, I hope you like chicken cordon bleu."

Get it together, Ben. "Oh yeah, sure, absolutely. Of course I do." He didn't even know what chicken cordon bleu was, and he had definitely lost his appetite. For food, anyway.

Her naïve look made him wonder if she had any idea what she was doing to him.

Maddie carried a bottle of sparkling cider over to him. The slight brush of her leg against his arm when she handed him the bottle sent a sensation equal to a lightning bolt through his body. *I need to leave. Now.*

"Would you mind doing the honors?"

Her quiet, alluring voice caused Ben to suck in as much air as his lungs could hold. He forced a smile up at her and nodded. *Talk, you imbecile. Talk.*

"Do you have a corkscrew?"

Maddie stared down at him, a curious look on her face. "Ben, it's cider. There is no cork."

"Oh, yeah. Of course."

The room was getting hotter by the second. Couldn't she at least open a window somewhere?

He determined not to look at her again. He would stare at his food, the floor, the wall, anywhere but in her direction. His eyes once again came upon her. *God, is this a test? Because if it is, I think I am about to fail.*

Ben looked back to the bottle in his hand. He finally managed to get the cap off. Walking to the table, he poured the cider into crystal wine glasses.

Maddie drew close to where he stood and smiled up at him. She took the bottle and set it on the table. "Shall we have a toast?"

Receiving the glass of cider, Ben knew he'd better distance himself from such close proximity to temptation. He walked to the other side of the table, where he hung on to the back of a chair to steady himself.

Feeling less vulnerable, he posed a question, "What should we toast to?"

Maddie cocked her head. "Oh, you think of something."

He caught the sly look. She knew exactly what she was doing. What had happened to the innocent widow? His composure returned with the distance between them, and he looked into her eyes. *Let's just see what she has on her mind.*

"Okay. Here's to our . . . our friendship." He lifted his glass in the air to meet hers, all the while watching her response.

Uncertain if she had planned the entire evening to tempt him, he would know for sure if her reaction showed he had insulted her. He was not ready for her reply.

Maddie smiled. Her eyes bore into his. "I like that. To our friendship." But was that a disappointed sigh that escaped under her breath?

"Ready for dinner?" She placed her glass on the table and walked into the kitchen.

"That sounds great."

Dinner went well. The two laughed over stories Ben told about the people in his congregation.

"You shepherd some very colorful people, Ben."

"I guess you could call them that. What I really love about them is they're real. Good old-fashioned, down-home folks who don't put on airs. They would be the first to tell the same stories about themselves."

"Would you like some coffee with dessert? We could have it in front of the fire."

Once again Ben went on the defensive. *Relax, Ben. You can do this.* She'd only asked if he wanted coffee and dessert.

He stood to clear the table. "Sure."

"Oh, no you don't. Go have a seat on the couch and I'll bring the coffee and cobbler over."

"Are you sure? I'm happy to help clean up."

"No, the dishes can wait. As Granny Harper says, we'll just put 'em under the sink."

Her captivating smile caused his heart to pound. "I'll put another log on the fire." Ben stoked the fire a couple of times, adding another log. Without thinking he sat on the couch.

Maddie slightly brushed his knee when she handed him his dessert. Electric shock.

Think friend, Ben. Friend. No good, that didn't help. *Think of her as a member of your flock.* Still no good. He could feel his body temperature rising.

Maddie set the tray with coffee and fixings on the coffee table and sat down next to Ben on the couch. He jumped up.

"What's wrong?" Maddie asked, alarm on her face.

Ben rubbed the back of his neck. "Ah, nothing. Would you mind if I cracked that window over there?"

"Of course. Is it too hot in here? Should I open the one over the sink?"
He crossed the room in seconds. "No, no, this should do it."
Keep your cool, Ben.

He strolled back to the couch, allowing himself time to regain his composure. He sat down, picked up his cobbler, and consumed a third of it with one bite.

"So, Ben, tell me, why have you never married?"

He choked on the cobbler.

"Are you all right? Here, let me get you some water."

"N-no, I'm fine. Just let me clear my throat. Must have gone down the wrong pipe," he confessed in a hoarse whisper.

Ben collected himself after gulping an entire glass of water. Choosing not to answer her question, he gobbled down the rest of the cobbler as if he hadn't eaten in days.

"Oh my goodness. Would you like some more?"

"No. No, thank you, it was delicious."

While Maddie sipped her coffee, Ben struggled to get his mind onto something other than her nearness.

He really did want to know more about her life. Maybe if he could get the focus on something else.

Ben asked about her husband and his untimely death. Their dialogue grew serious, yet honest. He watched the pain in her eyes grow as she remembered days gone by.

His heart ached for her. At one point he felt the urge to hold her in his arms, to comfort and protect her. Instead, he leaned over and kissed her gently on the lips.

Maddie kissed him back.

SEVENTY-ONE

Nathan sat on the couch, head in his hands, thoughts of Maddie consuming him.

"Why are you just sitting here, Carter? Get yourself cleaned up and go see the woman. Sitting here thinking about her won't get you anywhere but frustrated."

Every time Nathan thought of Maddie, an unfamiliar tenderness enveloped his heart. He wanted to protect her from the world. Although he knew she would never allow that.

That woman had a way of getting under his skin, in more ways than one.

Desperate to see her and tell her how much he appreciated her and cared about her, he ran his hands through his hair. He looked at the answering machine.

What he really wanted to tell her was that he was in love with her.

He paced. Why not tell her right now? He was driving himself crazy with this thing. *Just do it, Carter.* She was probably just playing board games with Shauna and Billy, anyway.

Nathan jumped in the shower and dressed in a pair of black jeans and a tan shirt. He remembered her response the last time he wore the outfit. She looked at him with an expression that seemed to say, "Whoa, who is this guy?" He enjoyed the fact he caught her off guard and that she obviously liked what she saw.

On his way out to the truck, a thought struck him. He turned, ran back inside, and grabbed the bottle of wine Glenn Harper had given him when he finished the bathroom renovation at the hardware store. Just in case a toast was in order. A slight twinge of guilt pushed its way past his conscience. He dismissed it just as quickly. *This is different. It's a celebration.*

The snowdrifts were heavier now. What did he care if a blizzard hit. He had his four-by-four and could make it through anything. Moving slowly, the other drivers were too cautious. It was taking forever to reach her farm.

Just before he crested the hill overlooking Broken Acres, he remembered it was Thursday. Billy and Shauna would be at the library.

He continued up the knoll. Would she be surprised? His thoughts ran ahead with anticipation. Maybe tonight they could be honest with each other.

At the top of the hill, he stopped to survey the property. One of the most exceptional pieces of land he had ever seen, it always took his breath away when he crested the hill. His eyes scanned the view, traveling from the big house to the outbuildings, over the fields, white with snow, to the orchard, on up to the cottage. His surveillance made an abrupt halt. Whose car was that? Maybe it was that vet, Dr. Adams. She'd been out here before.

Inching his truck down the driveway, he parked several feet from the cottage so not to make much noise.

Nathan crept to the side window to peek in. What he saw sent his temperature skyrocketing and his anger flaring. There they were, just the two of them, on the couch. Pastor Ben with her chin in his hand gently kissing her, and she enjoying every minute of it.

What was he doing here? When she'd introduced him they didn't seem that cozy.

Seething, and tempted to smash his fist through the window and into the other man's face, Nathan remembered the bottle of wine in his truck. Stomping through the deepening snow, he found his way back to the truck. Once inside he seized the bottle of wine and rummaged through the glove compartment to find the corkscrew his partner, Tim, had thrown in there a long time ago.

What about your dad? Nathan looked around. "Who said that?" *What about your promise?* "I don't care about my promise. I've already broken it once."

With added force the corkscrew tore pieces of cork out of the bottle. Nathan guzzled down the soothing liquid with fierce determination. He started the engine and floored the accelerator. The truck skidded dangerously through the deep snow as he sped up the driveway, bottle to his mouth.

*   *   *

The squeal of tires brought Ben and Maddie's tender moment to an end.

"What was that?" Ben asked.

They both went to the window just in time to see the back end of Nathan's truck spin out over the hill.

"Isn't that Nathan Carter's truck?"

"Yes, it is."

"Were you expecting him?"

Maddie furrowed her brow. "No, I wasn't expecting him. I hope nothing is wrong. I wonder why he would be out here so late at night."

"I was wondering the same thing."

A shrill peal moved Maddie's attention to her cell phone sitting on the counter. It was Billy. The roads were really bad. He and Shauna met Angela and Brian Metzger at the library. Angela had asked if they wanted to stay at her place tonight.

"That's fine, Billy. I'd rather have you safe at Angela's house than on the road in this storm. Give me Angela's phone number. I know I have it around here somewhere, but just let me have it so I can set it right by the phone."

"Um, she already left the library to stop by the market and stock up on some things. She said she would meet us at her house."

Red flags went up all over the place. Should she trust Billy with Shauna or risk his anger and the possibility of him doing something stupid?

Ben broke in, "Are they all right? Do they need me to pick them up?"

"No, they're going to stay at Angela Metzger's tonight.

"Billy, call me when you get to Angela's."

"Okay. Are you all right out there all alone?"

"I'm fine. You two be careful."

Ben touched Maddie's arm. "I guess I'd better get going before I get stuck in this." They both looked out the window, watching the snow grow deeper.

*   *   *

"I can't remember it ever snowing this hard since I've lived here." Ben looked down at Maddie's beautiful face and felt his blood warm again. *I need to do something about this, and quick.*

He lowered his head and kissed her lips with as much tenderness as before. He pulled away and looked into her eyes, his voice hoarse with emotion. "Thank you for a wonderful evening."

Maddie cleared her throat. "It *has* been a wonderful evening. Be careful on your way home. And, Ben, will you call me when you get there? So I won't be awake all night wondering if you made it safely or not."

"Sure, I'll give you a call as soon as I get home."

Maddie handed Ben his hat and held his coat up for him to slip his arms in. Their eyes met. Maddie turned to open the door.

"Good night, Ben."

"See you on Sunday."

"Okay. But you *are* going to call me tonight, right?"

"Yes." He smiled.

Ben made a quick dash for his Jeep.

*   *   *

Maddie leaned against the inside of the door. What an amazing man. Handsome, great sense of humor, tender yet manly, kind, thoughtful. He had it all. She couldn't have ordered a better man. A contented sigh. *It was just dinner, Maddie. He didn't propose.*

Cleaning up, Maddie listened to the news on the radio. "The weather service is reporting record snowfall and it doesn't look like it's going to let up anytime soon."

Maddie sat on the couch, mesmerized by the flames in the fireplace. The clock showed nine forty-five. Ben should be home by ten fifteen. She would give him until ten thirty to call, just in case the roads were as bad as Billy said. Maddie sipped a cup of hot tea, breathing in the beauty of Jewell's painting above the fireplace.

What was Nathan doing out here? If it was something important, surely he would have come to the door. Maybe he would call when he got home.

The minutes ticked by in slow motion. Ten fifteen came and went. Ten thirty. At eleven, Maddie dialed Ben's number. She got his voice mail and left a message.

Where was he? Maybe she should call the sheriff to see if any accidents had been reported. She decided to give him until eleven twenty and then she'd call the sheriff.

Maddie paced, fear penetrating her heart as each minute passed. At eleven fifteen, her phone rang.

"Ben, are you all right?"

Ben's voice was subdued. "Yes, Maddie, I'm fine."

"Why did it take you so long to get home?"

"I'm not at home. I'm at the hospital in Carterville."

Fear gripped her heart. "What? You just said you were fine."

"I am, I am. It's . . . well—"

"What, Ben? What is going on?"

"It's Nathan Carter. He's been in an accident. He's in critical condition. They don't expect him to live."

Maddie gasped for air. Her body shook. She screamed into the phone, but no sound came from her lips. Her heart caught in her throat, choking off the air she needed to breathe.

"I know Nathan has been working for you. The sheriff is looking for information so they can contact his family. Maddie, are you there? Maddie?"

Tears cascaded down her cheeks, her efforts to slow the frantic pounding of her heart failing. "I-I'm here, Ben." She choked out the words, her voice barely audible as she struggled to speak. "I want to c-come to the h-hospital."

"No, Maddie, that's not necessary. It's too dangerous for you to be out in this blizzard."

She spoke sternly and made her demands clear. "Ben, either you get one of those officers with their huge four-wheel drive vans to come out here and get me or I'll find another way to get there. Do you hear me?"

*　　*　　*

Ben looked at the phone in his hand. Who was this woman? Certainly not the sweet, tender woman he'd been with earlier that night. Why was she so concerned about a contractor she'd only met a few months ago? And where had this temper come from?

He liked a woman with spunk, and this spunky woman was doing some drastic things to his mind and body. One more thing to love. *Love?*

"Ben, are you going to tell them to come get me or—"

"Okay, okay. I'll have the sheriff send one of his men out to pick you up. Just stay calm, okay?

"Oh, and Maddie—"

"Yes?"

"Pray."

SEVENTY-TWO

Beep—beep—beep

Maddie's heart kept pace with the steady rhythm.

A trash truck backed into the driveway. Cars sped by on the busy highway. *What's a trash truck doing out here? We burn our weeds and trash. Wait. The city. What am I doing back in the city? No, I need to be at Broken Acres, getting it ready for the guests.*

Beep—beep—beep.

The driver is waving at me? Who is that? Ben? Her heart fluttered. She smiled. Images of her in a wedding dress. Ben standing at the altar, rapidly turning pages of a Bible.

Wh-what is Ben doing in the city? "You're still here?"

Someone rang an old dinner bell. "Time for breakfast. Come and get it, orange scones, your favorite." George turned and disappeared into the big house. Maddie shook her head. *No, this is all wrong.*

A man's voice whispered, "Maddie."

Beep—beeeeeeeeeeep

Maddie awoke to voices. Lots of voices. Lifting her head from her position at the foot of the hospital bed, her eyes flew to the heart monitor. She'd seen that line before.

Maddie screamed for the nurse.

A team of doctors and nurses were already running into the room with a crash cart. Someone took Maddie by the arm and moved her to the other side of the room.

She watched in horror while the attendants pushed, prodded, and counted. When they brought out the shock paddles, flashbacks of Jeff lying on the floor shot terror through her.

"No-o-o-o."

Her heart pounded fiercely in her chest, her body shook violently. Breathing shallow. Burying her face in her hands, she screamed. "This can't be happening. This *is not* happening. Not him. Not now."

The doctor's words, "He's stable," called her back.

Nathan was stable.

Wide-eyed, Maddie watched him breathe. The monitor was a steady blip. A nurse asked if she would like to move in closer to her husband.

She moved to the head of the bed. The color had returned to his face.

Husband? Maddie remembered the vision of Ben in her dream standing at the altar. She reached her hand out to the nurse leaving the room. "He's not my hus—"

No matter. She didn't care who they thought she was as long as she could stay in this room by Nathan's side so she could tell him what she had to say when he woke up.

Maddie pulled up a chair and sat as close as she could to this man she barely knew, her mind jumbled contradictions.

Plaster casts swallowed Nathan's right arm and his left leg, held up in a leg sling. Bruises covered most of his face. Bandages shrouded the top of his head down across his forehead. He had multiple cuts and stitches from crashing through the windshield, his seatbelt unfastened. The sight of tubes and wires and the steady clunk of a ventilator gave way to a wave of grief Maddie hadn't felt in months. *God, please don't let him die. I need to tell him I'm sorry. Tell him that I love him.* She gasped, her hand over her mouth.

No, she loved Ben. Didn't she? She closed her eyes and rubbed her forehead.

"Maddie? You're still here?"

She turned at the sound of Ben's voice.

"Is he all right?" Ben glanced at the patient, then rested his gaze back on Maddie's startled eyes.

"Yes, thanks to the quick response of the hospital staff."

"Have you been here all night?"

Sheepishly she answered Ben's curious look, "Yeah. Sleeping off and on."

"Ben, tell me. Shauna, Rusty, Sarg?" Anxious for answers, her hurried questions came without taking a breath.

"They're all fine, Maddie. Shauna is with the Haines family from church. Angela offered to have her to stay with her and Brian, but Shauna decided to go with the Haineses. Seems they remind her of her aunt and uncle. The guys are with Billy, comfortably settled in his room in the big house. He's still working on the house. He wanted me to ask if that was okay."

She closed her eyes and released a deep breath. "Sure, I can't see why not. Besides, it will give him something to do, to keep busy."

Ben looked from Maddie to the unconscious man in the bed. "Maddie, I'm a little confused. Last night—"

Maddie looked up into the most compassionate brown eyes she'd ever encountered. "Yes, last night." Her mind and her heart bolted back and forth through fits of confusion. *What am I doing here waiting for Nathan to wake up when it's Ben I love? Isn't it? Really, Maddie, just because of two kisses?*

Ben walked over and squatted down on one knee next to Maddie's chair, gazing into her eyes. "Maddie, last night while waiting to hear if Nathan would live or die, I realized once again how fragile life is. It can be lost in a moment. I was awake most of the night thinking about how we waste so much time because of caution or pride or insecurity. I can't tell you exactly when it all came together, but I do know—"

Maddie put her fingers on Ben's lips. "Ben, I'm not sure this is the best time to talk about this."

Ben looked over at Nathan. "You're probably right."

Maddie thought back to her dream. "Ben, I've got so many things going through my mind right now that I need to sort out. Things are jumbled and confused." She smiled into the kind eyes of her pastor.

"You are a wonderful man, Ben Farrington."

He pressed in to kiss her lips—

A loud gasp came from the open door. The nurse who'd assumed Maddie was Nathan's wife stood wide-eyed, shaking her head.

SEVENTY-THREE

Even though his eyes were blurry thanks to the five beers he had downed in the last couple of hours, Nathan still recognized the petite redhead who walked through the door. *Now, what is her name? Think I'll mosey on over and talk to this sweet thing.*

He stumbled up behind the barstool, almost falling face-first into her. With slurred words he asked her to dance.

Beep—beep—beep

Nathan searched the bar to see where the beeping came from. The TV monitor? The Emergency Broadcast System?

Beep—beep—beep

He couldn't take his eyes off the lovely creature he had encased between his two arms. His hands rested on the bar.

Darkness.

Beep—beep—beep

Nathan stood in front of an old three-story house in desperate need of repair. Who in their right mind would want to spend the money to renovate that place? What would you use it for? Maybe a couple of families were going to share it. No matter, the lady just wanted an estimate. This job would be quite a challenge. Let's see, roof, siding, paint . . .

Beep—beep—beep

Is my cell phone battery running low? The crackle of leaves. A woman shaded her eyes from the sun.

"You!"

Who is this woman? She seems to know me, but I can't place her. Redhead. Fiery temper.

"Nathan. Nathan, can you hear me?"

The gentle words coming from the woman's mouth didn't match what he saw in her eyes.

"Get off my property."

"Nathan, please don't leave me. Please wake up. I have something to tell you."

The same voice. Who is this woman?

Beep—beep—beep

Where is that stupid beeping coming from?

Beep—beep—beep

Crying. *Who is that?* A woman. *Why is she crying?*

Darkness.

This storm is turning into a blizzard. I can hardly see the road. Why don't the cars either pull over or move faster.

Smiling. *I can see the look on her face when she sees me at her door. Tonight will be different. I'll tell her I love her and hope her reaction is the same. Of course, it will be the same. Won't it?*

Finally. There's the driveway. Why doesn't she get an automatic gate for this place? It would give her more security. It's freezing out here.

What's that car doing here this late at night? Maybe she's in trouble.

Beep—beep—beep

He checked his cell phone. *Where is that sound coming from?*

I need a weapon. Rummaging around in his truck, he found a fishing net.

Who is that guy? He's . . . he's kissing her. She's kissing him back.

He grabbed the wine on the seat of the truck and chugged the warm liquid.

Carter, what are you doing? You swore you would never do this again. What are you doing?

He floored the accelerator. The truck skidded in the snow.

Who needs her, anyway?

Another swig of wine. Pastor Ben?

Another gulp. Who cares? *You do, you dummy.*

Lights. Glaring lights. Squealing tires. Metal crunching. Breaking glass.

One word escaped his lips.

"Maddie."

Darkness.

Beep—beeeeeeeeeeep

*   *   *

Ben was surprised when he walked into Nathan Carter's hospital room. "Maddie, you've been here for two days and three nights. What are you doing?"

Maddie looked up. Embarrassment shone on her face. "Ben, I have to be here when he wakes up. I need to talk to him, to explain."

"Explain what?"

The disheveled woman looked from Ben to Nathan. Pushing the unkempt hair out of her eyes, she bit her bottom lip. "Well, I need to explain that I need him out there on the farm to finish up the project he started. I need to tell him how I feel."

Ben frowned.

"I mean, that I'm not mad at him."

"Maddie, I don't understand. Why are you so concerned about a man you hardly know and have a hard time working with?"

"Well, he's the only contractor who can do the work. Besides, aren't we supposed to love our fellow man, even if we can't stand him?"

Ben gave an exasperated sigh. He gently lifted her chin. "Maddie, the roads are clear. Why don't you take my Jeep? Go home, grab a shower, and catch a few hours of sleep. I'll wait right here. If he stirs, I'll call you. Okay?"

Tilting her head, she smiled. "You're right, Ben. Thanks." She took his keys and headed for the car.

Ben took a wrapped package out of his backpack. Standing over Nathan's bed, he looked down at the unconscious man.

"Nathan, I don't really know you, only met you once, but God does. Nothing is by chance, even your being here in this hospital bed. I just want you to know I'm praying for you." Ben slipped the package in the drawer of the bedside stand.

SEVENTY-FOUR

After not being able to reach Nathan for more than three days, Tim O'Leary, Nathan's business partner, was shocked when he read the account of Nathan's accident in the newspaper. He called the hospital for details. They declined any information. They did, however, ask for details regarding Nathan's family. With Nathan still in critical condition, they needed any information Tim could offer.

"Nathan's father lives in Washington. He hasn't seen him in years. They're not on good terms."

However he did have an ex-fiancée who, Tim suspected, would love to get back with him.

"He's been on a leave of absence from our company for the past year. I'm his partner, his best friend. The closest thing to family he has. Can I see him?"

"I'm a little confused, Mr. O'Leary. There's a woman who has been at his bedside night and day since he was brought in three days ago. She isn't his wife?"

"Wife? Are you kidding? Nathan does not have a wife."

"This is very disturbing. Then who is she?"

"I'd like to ask the same question. I'm driving down this afternoon. I'll be at the hospital around seven. Nurse Henderson, will you be there so I won't have to explain the situation to someone else?"

"We change shifts at seven, but I'll let the night nurse know who you are. You won't have any trouble."

"Thank you."

*　　*　　*

Chelsea had read the newspaper account of Nathan's accident. She wasn't so sure he would be happy to see her. But if he was unconscious . . .

"Tim, Chelsea Hodges."

"Hello, Chelsea. What can I do for you?"

"I just read about Nathan's accident. I have to see him."

"But I thought—"

"You've probably heard some terrible things about me from Nathan. I can tell you they are definitely exaggerated."

"I really don't know the intimate details of what happened with you and Nathan. He is in critical condition at a hospital in Carterville. I'm headed there in about an hour. You want to ride along?"

"Yes, yes, that would be great. I'll be packed and ready to go."

*   *   *

Maddie had hurried to pick up takeout at a favorite Chinese restaurant.

Snoring lightly in the corner chair, Ben looked so peaceful. And handsome. Maddie sighed.

Nathan lay just as she had left him. Breathing on his own now, with a regular pattern, no longer raspy. His eyelids fluttered. Was he dreaming? Maddie gently brushed his hair back from his forehead. "You *are* going to get better, Nathan. You are."

Ben stretched in his chair. "You're back. Something smells good."

Maddie jumped. "Good grief, Ben, you scared the pajiggers out of me."

Ben grinned. "Granny Harper's lingo is starting to come natural to you. Sorry."

Maddie chuckled. "I know. I love that woman. Did I tell you she's determined to make a farmer out of me?"

"Really? Doesn't surprise me. She is pretty independent. Had to be, married to a traveling salesman and then a farmer. Salt of the earth. I don't know what we'd do without her at North Hills. Granny is a pillar of faith." He glanced at the bag in her hand.

"I brought dinner. Stopped by Choy Lin's. I hope you like kung pao chicken."

"A woman after my own heart. I'm starving. Thanks. Are you going to join me?"

"Sure, I'll have a taste."

"Did you get some rest?"

"Yeah."

Maddie was aware of Ben looking intensely at her and she blushed.

"Has he opened his eyes or said anything?"

"Nothing. But nurse Henderson *did* want to know where his *wife* was."

Maddie scrunched up her nose. "Well, they just assumed. I tried to tell one of the nurses that I wasn't his wife, but she didn't hear me. I think when the sheriff himself ushered me into the emergency room the other night, they just assumed I was Nathan's wife." Those words sent a chill up her back.

Maddie sat at the table facing Nathan's bed, watching for signs of him coming back into this world.

Whispering while they ate, Ben gave Maddie an update on what had been going on in the outside world over the last several days.

Quick steps in the hallway brought loud voices into Nathan's room. A loud gasp from a woman's mouth. Tears streamed down a man's face.

Nurse Henderson interrupted, "Pastor Ben, Maddie, this is Mr. Carter's friend, Tim O'Leary." Turning to the woman. "And this is Mr. Carter's fiancée, Chelsea Hodges." The nurse gave Maddie a frown.

Ben looked at Maddie, eyes wide, clearly questioning who the people were standing there.

She shrugged.

He turned to the new arrivals. "Hello. I'm Ben Farrington and this is Madison Crane, Nathan's boss."

Maddie's heart raced. She frowned. "Well, I'm not actually his boss. He's been doing some renovation work at my farm." She extended her hand to Tim, then Chelsea.

Tim wiped the tears from his face. "So you're the redhead."

Ben frowned at Tim.

"Ah, sorry. I mean Nathan has told me a lot about the project he's been working on. It's been a real lifesaver for him." He glanced in Chelsea's direction.

"Well, Ms. Crane."

"Miss Hodges."

One needed an icepick to chip the air.

Tim turned his attention to Nathan's still body. "How is he doing?"

Nurse Henderson picked up Nathan's chart and glanced through several pages. "In all honesty, he's extremely lucky to be alive. We almost lost him twice. He seems to be improving more every day. The good news is we were able to take him off the ventilator. He's breathing on his own now."

Ben agreed, "A major answer to prayer. Thank God."

Tim turned to Nathan's bed. "Has he been awake at all? Has he said anything?"

The nurse bristled. "I've only heard him whisper one word." She glared in Maddie's direction.

Everyone waited.

"Maddie."

Maddie sucked in air.

Ben's furrowed brow asked the question everyone else probably wanted an answer for. He looked from Nurse Henderson to Nathan to Maddie.

Chelsea cleared her throat. "Well, I'm sure Nathan will be very appreciative for your concern. I'll tell him you were here when he wakes up." She extended her hand. "Thank you for coming."

Maddie looked at Ben. She opened her mouth to speak.

Ben spoke first, "Miss Hodges, Mr. O'Leary, here's my card. Please don't hesitate to call if we can do anything else to help." Ben grabbed his cowboy hat and backpack and took Maddie by the elbow, ushering her out of the room.

"But, Ben, I have something to say to that woman."

"Yes, I'm sure you do. But, Maddie, she is his fiancée. Don't you think we ought to leave them alone?"

Maddie looked over her shoulder at the door to Nathan's room.

Her shoulders went limp. "You're right. Let's go. Suddenly I feel very tired."

*   *   *

Ten days later the doctor transferred Nathan to a rehab center in Portsmouth. Tim drilled him about the accident. "They said you'd been drinking. What were you thinking? I thought you swore never to drink because your dad was a drunk who lost the family fortune and good name?"

Nathan ran his free hand through his hair. "Yeah, well. He lost more than that."

"Exactly my point. What got into you?"

"I don't know. But I can tell you it won't *ever* happen again."

Tim shook his head and gave a long sigh.

Chelsea visited daily. She told him how frightened she was that he would die and she wouldn't have a chance to apologize, to tell him she realized months ago how much she loved him.

"Chelsea, I kind of remember or maybe I was dreaming. There was a woman asleep at the foot of my bed. Was that you?"

"Of course, sweetheart. Who else could it have been?"

"Well, I thought maybe it was——"

She smiled, and Nathan noticed that it didn't quite reach her eyes. "I couldn't leave you there alone, not knowing if you would live or die."

Nathan searched the woman, unsure of his feelings. After all, she had hurt him deeply. Could he trust her?

As if reading his mind, tears dropped onto Nathan's hand. Chelsea took a hankie from her purse. "Nathan, I was such a fool. Can you ever forgive me? I was blind. You are the only man for me. Can't we just pick up where we left off?"

"What about what's-his-name?"

"Oh, that was over before it even began. He's a loser."

His words dripped with sarcasm, "Uh-huh. A loser, huh? You didn't think so last year. Back then, he was the greatest real estate baron in the Northwest."

Chelsea frowned and stood tall, shoulders back. "Nathan, *you* are all that matters to me. I won't let anything get in the way of our happiness. Why don't we set a date? What do you say?"

Nathan wanted to believe her.

"Come on, Nathan. I'm here now, aren't I? Taking care of you?"

"That's true."

"And I was there for you at the hospital."

"Yes."

"Can't we just let the past stay in the past? I love you."

Nathan looked into the sapphire eyes of the shapely model standing before him. *I did love her once, didn't I? Maybe I should give her another chance.*

Chelsea flashed her most engaging smile.

Nathan closed his eyes. A feisty redhead immediately appeared. He whispered, "Maddie."

"What, dear? You're mad at me for what?"

Let her go, Nathan. She loves someone else.

Even though he had this beautiful woman begging him to set a wedding date, he felt as if he had left his heart miles away on a farm called Broken Acres.

"Okay. How about May?"

Chelsea squealed and hugged Nathan's neck. "We are going to be so happy."

He gave his bride-to-be a reluctant smile.

Nathan shook his shoulders to ward off the chill moving down his back.

*   *   *

Maddie sat in her living room in front of a warm fire admiring the beauty of the watercolor her friend, Jewell, had given her, which was tipped against the wall on the mantel. Rusty and Sarg sat beside her on the couch.

Lost love. That's what that painting represented.

"Well, guys, lost love." That was the story of Jewell's life, and hers. Jeff gone. Nathan engaged. Ben out of reach. What had made her think she could ever fall in love again? A pastor, of all people. Best to leave things as they were. Friendship was less painful.

Maddie grabbed her cell phone from the coffee table when she heard it ringing. "Hi, son. What's up?"

"Hi, Mom. Hey, what do you know about the veterinary college there?"

"Veterinary college? David. Are you going back to school?"

"Yeah, I'm ready for a fresh start. And the last time we talked you said you could use my help there on the farm."

"Yes, I could definitely use your help." Maddie grinned over at Rusty, his ears perked up listening.

"I'll check into the college and let you know. When are you planning on making the move?"

"As soon as this construction job I'm on is finished."

"David, I'm so excited. This will be a fresh start for both of us."

MYRIAD THANKS

The word *myriad* tends to draw our minds to an immense number. Honestly, there are not myriad people to acknowledge and thank, rather I have innumerable words of appreciation for help, input, suggestions, ideas, thoughts, encouragement.

First and certainly most important, deepest, heartfelt thanksgiving to Jesus Christ, my Lord, for being everything I need to live through the reality of mourning, perseverance to finish, and hope for the future. He is enough.

Who would have thought that years ago, while my husband tested his ability to fly-fish, I would complete the first draft of this novel in seven days? With sincere gratitude, I offer thanks to my husband, Bruce, for consistently encouraging me to publish *Broken Acres*. Who would have thought it would be eight years after his death that Bruce's encouragement would come to fruition?

Smiling appreciation and affection to Jewell Swertfeger, my first editor and purveyor of encouraging words regarding the art of writing, whose challenge years ago took me to Jacob's Bend.

To Val Coulman, multitalented author, artist, creative wonder, and gracious editor with the ever-helpful red pen, thank you for every insightful suggestion and inspired idea.

The cover photos, taken through the lens of the artistic eye of Janis Rubus, tell a story themselves. Her art has a way of doing that. Thank you more than anything for your treasured friendship and listening ear.

To my gifted beta readers, Alisha Geyer, Jessica Sperbeck, and Janis Rubus, thanks to each of you for your unique look at the story, precision in finding those areas that needed tweaking, and bravery for telling me exactly what would make *Broken Acres* a better read. How you have blessed me.

Special thanks to techie extraordinaire Benton Coulman, for your untiring determination to smooth out every technical bump in the road. This book is a reality in great part to your diligence and perseverance.

Watch for Book 2 in the Jacob's Bend series, Splintered Lives, coming soon.